James Domenighini's *Chaos Company* is a gripping, character-driven military science fiction novel that delivers both relentless action and deep emotional resonance. As a seasoned author of multiple science fiction and historical novels, Domenighini expertly crafts a tale that is as much about the bonds of brotherhood as it is about the brutality of war. With its cinematic storytelling, compelling characters, and high-stakes conflict, *Chaos Company* is a prime candidate for adaptation into film or television, making it an enticing prospect for publishers, literary agents, and producers.

At its core, *Chaos Company* follows Lion Biyela, a Marine officer who abandons a prestigious career path to fight on the front lines as an enlisted soldier. Now a battle-hardened sergeant, Lion leads a close-knit fire team on the war-torn colonial world of Eos, where humanity faces an existential threat from alien invaders. But the true test of survival extends beyond the battlefield—Lion and his team must also navigate the treacherous internal politics of their own military, contending with ruthless officers, cold-hearted comrades, and the ever-present fear of losing one another.

Domenighini's storytelling stands out for its realism and authenticity, drawing inspiration from real-world military history and the personal sacrifices of soldiers. His ability to balance pulse-pounding combat with introspective character development places *Chaos Company* in the tradition of legendary military sci-fi works like *Starship Troopers*, *The Forever War*, and *Halo: The Fall of Reach*. The novel's gritty realism, combined with its heart-wrenching moments of camaraderie and sacrifice, ensures that readers are fully immersed in the chaos of war.

With a universe rich in lore and a protagonist whose journey is as inspiring as it is harrowing, *Chaos Company* is a standout entry in modern military science fiction. It is not just a story of war—it is a testament to the resilience, loyalty, and humanity of those who fight. Publishers looking for the next breakout sci-fi hit, literary agents seeking a compelling and marketable series, and movie producers hunting for a high-stakes, action-packed adaptation will find *Chaos Company* to be an exceptional opportunity.

James Domenighini has already established himself as a skilled storyteller, and *Chaos Company* marks a bold new chapter in his writing career—one that is destined to make a lasting impact on the genre.

Chaos Company

James Domenighini

978-1-965552-22-3 (Paperback)

BOOKWRIGHTS
HOUSE

admin@bookwrightshouse.com
☎ (213) 286 6700

ONE

D EATH WAITED FOR ME around the corner. An alien, a killer, a
nightmare out of the darkest of all nightmares, desired
my death. It knew where I waited just as I knew where it
waited. The sensors on our armored suits revealed where
we were to each other, because we both had our defensive
energy screens powered up. We knew each other's location.
We even knew how dedicated we were to killing each other.
We just didn't know what the other was going to do next.

The alien probably had a name, just as I did. But it
didn't know my name nor did I know its name. Whatever a
human was in its language was what it knew me as. I knew
it as a Gorgon, named after the ancient Greek monster its
race resembled.

We each sought the other's destruction. I hated it
because of the way its race slaughtered the human colonists
on the planet Eos by the thousands every day, as well as
their butchering of my fellow Marines. And it hated me
because humanity's very existence drove its race insane.

"Hey, Lion, you gonna do something about that
wormhead around the corner, or are you just waiting for it
to die of boredom?"

The call over my suit's comm system came from Sergeant Charles "Chip" Saunders, the leader of Team C. His team, and my Team B, both belonged to First Squad, Second Platoon. We had been pulling back after a five-hour patrol into the ruined city of Belden when the Gorgon around the corner had fried one of my Marines with its plasma rifle.

Private First Class Ella Jenkins had just joined my team this morning. She had survived the patrol, including an hour-long firefight with the Gorgons, only to be roasted in her suit by this alien sniper. Now I had to kill it before it killed anyone else, including and especially me.

Jenkins had seemed a sweet and kind person, hardly what you'd expect in a Marine. But she had fought well, holding her position even when cut off from the rest of us and surrounded by the enemy. She had killed five Gorgons and held our flank for the hour it took us to reach her. Now she was gone and none of us would ever really get to know her.

It was a terrible waste.

"Well, Lion?" Chip demanded.

"Hush!" I replied. I checked my sensors. The Gorgon hadn't moved. It still stood three meters around the corner, probably behind a pile of rubble from the ruined building that concealed us from each other.

I stepped off of my grav disc. It could propel me quickly at velocities up to one hundred kilometers per hour and at altitudes up to several thousand meters. But by flying around the corner I'd be out in the open, a perfect target for the alien sniper. Besides, on foot, I moved much slower. When hunting a sniper, stealth is more important than speed.

Crouching low, I crept forward. It was half a meter to the corner. Seconds stood between life and death.

My sensors revealed movement to my right. Chip crept forward with me. He moved down the far side of the rubble-strewn street, just a bit behind. He had my back, just as I always had his.

My suit detected movement ahead. The Gorgon was changing position.

Though my suit maintained a comfortable atmosphere for me, I was soaked in nervous sweat. I bit my lower lip. I had to move now, while the alien also moved.

Jumping around the corner, I fired wildly. From my rifle streamed a white-hot bright burst of metallic gas superheated to three thousand degrees Celsius. The plasma stream caught the Gorgon dead center and it flew backwards.

But most of my burst cascaded from the alien's energy screen. Before it could fire at me, I fired again. This time, though, I aimed at the crystal-clear helmet surrounding its head, where its screen was the weakest. I caught a brief glimpse of the wildly waving sensory tentacles covering its head, and of the two orifices forming its face: a thin horizontal slit occupying the location where the nose on a human would have been. Beneath it stretched its wide-open mouth, as if screaming. But the Gorgon possessed no vocal cords. Then its head and helmet exploded in a cloud of transparent metal and vaporized flesh.

As I watched its headless corpse tumble into the rubble, several brilliant-white plasma streams flashed past my head. Ten meters down the street two more headless Gorgons collapsed to the ground. Behind them dozens of other Gorgons ran forward.

"Let's get out of here!" Chip exclaimed.

I darted back around the corner as part of the wall behind me exploded. I hopped onto my grav disk. My boots clicked into place. The organic microchip within my brain gave me full interface with my disk and armored suit. I thought of flying up over the rubble and down the street. My disk complied. I was airborne and away.

I zipped over the debris-strewn street at eighty kilometers an hour. My team carried Jenkins's suit, her body just a burnt mass of flesh and bone. We also carried the burnt bodies of Chip's three Marines. This patrol had cost me a promising Marine, while it had cost Chip's fire team half its strength. Though we had killed twenty Gorgons today, it wasn't enough. They out-numbered us fifty-to-one. At this rate we'd all be dead and gone before we could stop them from taking the colonial planet Eos away from us. Both the Gorgons and humanity claimed it. They wanted it and we wanted it and they were willing to kill every human for it.

There's no victory in death. The only victory is survival. And we had survived today.

Eight of us had survived, at least. For the others the penalty had been far too severe.

TWO

W E ZIGZAGGED DOWN THE city's ruined streets for several kilometers until, near the city's edge, we darted down into the remnants of Belden's subway system, switching off our energy screens.

This was where Chaos Company maintained its base. A rifle company, it was part of the First Battalion, Twenty-fourth Marine Brigade. The battalion's other three rifle companies, along with its Headquarters and Support Company, occupied an underground base a kilometer further back, outside of the city's perimeter. Situated on either side of us, a kilometer away in each direction, were the forward companies of Third and Fourth battalions. Robot plasma cannons guarded all approaches to each company's location. They knew friend from foe.

We flew down a long, dark tunnel. Our sensors revealed the tunnel to us as if it were filled with bright light. We saw maintenance and repair robots moving throughout the subway. We also saw the suited Marines of Third platoon, some standing guard with the robots, while others prepared for another patrol.

Captain Vang, our company commander, wanted to keep pressure on the enemy in the portion of the ruined city that we owned. Except we didn't own the city, the Gorgons did. They had blasted it to ruins months ago, murdering any civilians who had failed to evacuate.

Like all of the human cities on the northern hemisphere of Eos, it had once been quite beautiful. But the Gorgons hated all things human and they had torn this city apart. Now it was a battleground for the First, Third and Fourth battalions of the Twenty-fourth Marine Brigade. The brigade's other two battalions had been transferred to hotter sectors. But for the four Marines who had died on our patrol today, no sector was hotter than this one.

We veered to the left and flew down a side passage. Ahead were two thick blast doors, similar to the bulkhead doors found on any starship in the Interstellar Navy. Combat engineers and robots had installed the doors months before, when the company moved into this location.

Chip had led the way back. He'd been a sergeant a year more than me. More experienced in practically everything, he always led the way.

He was my closest friend.

The doors opened. A landing dock filled with light and activity appeared before us. We drifted inside.

As we settled to the deck, medical robots came forward to relieve us of the corpse-filled suits we carried. I watched as two robots gently removed Jenkins's burnt body from its ruined suit and carried it away.

"You gonna stay in there all day?" Chip asked. He was already out of his suit and stood beside mine. His voice had been picked up by my exterior microphones and whispered into my ears.

My suit expanded. The nanotube armor created an opening behind me and I stepped out. The air in my suit had smelled fresh but not as fresh as the air in the tunnel. Air from outside the base had been carefully filtered for toxins and then pumped into the tunnels. It smelled better and fresher than anything inside my suit.

"We need to write our after action reports," I said.

"Yeah," Chip said. "And then we can get drunk."

"I'd rather eat and sleep."

"Always the pragmatist."

I stared at him. He grinned back.

I glanced over at where the robots began removing the remains of the other dead Marines from their suits. "I hate watching all these young people die."

"Is that why you resigned your commission so you could become a grunt, Biyela?" a voice growled at me. It belonged to a big, muscular man, Gunnery Sergeant Mokoto Kano, our platoon sergeant.

"You know better than that, Mo," Chip said, grinning. "He didn't like the food they served at the Naval Academy. Lion knows grunts eat better than officers."

"You keep saying that," Mo replied. "But the food never tastes any better."

I put my arm around Chip's neck and pulled him into a headlock. "He's just an optimistic eater."

Chip easily escaped my hold. I had him tight, but he understood judo escapes better than me.

"Why did you resign?" Mo asked.

"You keep asking me," I replied, "and I keep explaining it. After graduation, I realized I didn't really want to be an officer. I just wanted to be a Marine."

"That you are." Mo looked around at the rest of our patrol. They had dismounted from their suits and were now exiting the landing dock. "But I suspect that someday that decision is going to bite you in the ass."

"Why?" Chip questioned. "We have a shortage of officers?"

"You never know. Get those reports written, will you? The lieutenant wants them right away."

"Aye, aye, admiral," Chip quipped.

Mo grunted and walked away.

"He's lucky he left," Chip said, his eyes twinkling.

"You're lucky he walked away," I replied.

"I could take him."

"With your mouth, maybe."

"Listen," Chip said. "I'm pretty good at judo."

"That you are, but he's still the brigade's judo champion," I reminded him.

"Judo, smudo."

"Smudo?" I asked.

Chip sighed. "Listen, I'm tired of this conversation. Let's find something to eat."

I jabbed my finger at him. "Now that's a good idea."

THREE

ONE SIDE CORRIDOR TOOK us to another side corridor, which led to another side corridor, which eventually emptied out into the mess hall. It seemed like half of Chaos Company was eating. So we got into the line.

"Lion, we're sitting over here," one of my Marines, Private First Class Ruby Johnson, called to me. I looked her way and saw the rest of my team, and what was left of Chip's team, sitting at a long table. They occupied six of the table's fourteen seats. The other seats were empty.

The line moved forward. Chip shoved me. I stumbled and glared at him. "What did you do that for?"

"Everyone knows better than to get between me and my food."

I grunted.

We moved forward again, coming abreast of the buffet. Chip clapped his hands together and rubbed them. He had a pleased expression on his face. "Look at that! Tofu beef, tofu chicken, tofu pork. Enough gas to power me across the universe and back again!"

"And they even have tofu fish, tofu lettuce, and tofu chocolate cake," I remarked, a devilish grin on my face.

"No," Chip corrected me, "I think the chocolate cake is real. They can stuff all of the bean shit they want down us but I think they have to give us real chocolate cake. If they don't, what's to keep us from tearing this place apart? A Marine can only take so much before he explodes."

"Maybe," I replied, laughing. "But I think the Navy only has to make sure the cake is chocolate-flavored. It's still tofu."

Chip's head fell. He shook it. Then he looked up at me. "This world's an agricultural paradise. Even with all the fighting, its farmers still produce enough food for seven worlds. Why can't the Navy just buy something from them? Why does all our food have to be hundred-year-old tofu? Why? Tell me that!"

"At least it's injected with vitamins and protein," I said. "Besides, it can't be a hundred years old."

"Tastes like it."

The Interstellar Marine Corps received all its food and other supplies courtesy of the Interstellar Navy. Even cooks and medical personnel came from the Navy, though all of the cooks and medics were robots. However, for units as far forward as our battalion was, the Navy depended upon the Eosian Army to get our supplies to us, which it was having trouble doing.

"You guys gonna bitch or eat?"

We turned around. Behind us stood Staff Sergeant Dana Sinclair. A tall and powerfully built woman, she led Second Squad. Her face looked tired. Her eyes appeared red and angry.

"Well?" she demanded.

"Eat, of course," Chip said.

"Then be quick about it."

"Aye, aye, ma'am," we said.

Chip picked up a plate. He presented it to the robot server and said, "My good machine, I'd like the chicken and beef on top of the stuffing, with lots of gravy. And a slice of that magnificent chocolate cake, if you would, good sir."

"Affirmative," the server replied. "Anything else, sir?"

"No, thank you," Chip said. "And by the way, I'm not a 'sir'. I'm a sergeant, I work for a living!"

"Very good, sir," the robot pleasantly replied. Chip glared at the server but kept quiet.

While the robot expertly scooped the tofu onto Chip's plate, I leaned over and whispered into his ear, "When did you learn to talk like a man?"

"Shaddup, or I'll stuff that tofu into you where the sun don't shine."

"The sun doesn't shine into a lot of your places," I said.

"Be quiet, you freak Zulu giant!" he snapped at me, but I knew he was just kidding.

I laughed. So did Chip. But not Sinclair.

"Put something on your plate, Biyela, or get out of my way," she snarled.

"Aye, ma'am," I replied. I got the tofu pork chops, the tofu asparagus, the tofu stuffing, and the tofu gravy. Then I followed Chip to our table. We sat beside our Marines.

"Is there any salt? Any spices? Any catsup or mustard?"

"Now why would there be anything like that?" Ruby replied.

"He's just being hopeful," Corporal Khalid Kamal, my assistant team leader, said.

"We could all use a little hope right now," said Corporal Samantha "Sami" Souza, Chip's assistant team leader.

"There ain't no hope for nobody," Staff Sergeant Sinclair hissed, sitting down across from Chip and myself.

I looked at her. "What happened?" I asked.

"I lost a whole fire team today, that's what!" she growled. She glanced away. I saw tears filling her eyes.

We were all under so much stress out here, all of the time. No one, not even the coldest-hearted Marine, thought less of anyone who wept over lost friends and fellow Marines. Cursing, complaining, laughter, even crying, was an acceptable means of relieving stress.

I started to reach across the table to touch her hand, but she glared at me and I pulled my hand back. Female Marines tried to be the toughest, the strongest, the meanest Marines around. They didn't just want to deny their femininity; they wanted to crush their humanity.

After centuries of fighting alongside men throughout the stars, many women still wanted to prove their emotional superiority over men. I felt a deep sadness for Sinclair's defiance.

I couldn't think of anything to say so I ate my food instead. It tasted like pork chops, asparagus, bread stuffing and brown gravy, but the consistency was wrong. A good cook can fake a lot of things, and the Navy has plenty of good cooks, but when your customer knows the food is faked, you can't hide that. My food looked like and tasted like the real thing yet in my mouth it felt like tofu. Which it was.

"I don't know how long since I've eaten real food," PFC Raymond Carlyle, said. Carlyle was one of my best Marines; you could count on him in a fight. Everyone called him RC.

"Join the crowd, RC," Corporal Kamal said. He spat a small bit of food at an empty seat across the table from him. We all watched as the tofu bounced off the tabletop and disappeared from view.

RC put his utensils down. Placing his elbows on the table, he balled his hands into fists and rested his head on them. "I'm getting tired of this place."

"Who isn't?" Ruby said.

"I really thought Jenkins had a chance," RC said. "She fought good, held her own, and seemed to know what she was doing. I thought she might make it. I was sure she'd be one of us."

"No one knows when they're going to get it," Chip said.

"Yeah," RC agreed. "Trouble was, I liked her."

"That was your big mistake," Sinclair snarled. "You can't get close to anyone out here. You do that, you get soft. You get soft, you make mistakes. You make mistakes, you die. Or someone else does. You gotta be a stone cold killer to survive out here. There's no other way."

"Is that why your team's dead?" Chip asked. "Because they weren't cold enough?"

Sinclair reached across the table and slapped Chip across the face. She left a bright red mark on his unshaven cheek. "You talk too much!"

"So do you," Corporal Souza said.

The two women stood. They glared down the table at each other. Sinclair picked up her fork, as did Souza.

Then gobs of tofu dressing splattered across their faces. They turned, enraged, to find out who had thrown the food at them. But then the entire table erupted with flying food. Even I threw my food at them.

The corporal and the staff sergeant picked up their plates and heaved every remaining bit of food at me. Chip ducked out of the way. I was slower.

Covered head to toe in tofu, I grabbed a handful of food to fling at my attackers. However, they had dived beneath the table, laughing like children.

Then all hell broke loose as everyone else in the mess hall began throwing food my way. I crawled under the table, where my teammates, and Chip, and his team, hid. We watched, while the mess hall truly became a mess. Food even hung from the serving robots.

Marines laughed and hooted and cheered in delight. They were kids again. They were human. They lived the moment. They were free.

"What the hell's going on in here!" bellowed First Sergeant Jonah Jones, our company sergeant.

"Oops," Chip said. "Busted."

Laughing, wheezing, giggling, gasping for breath, the other hundred or so Marines in the mess hall struggled to attention.

We crawled out from under our table. We were covered in varying amounts of tofu. I was the filthiest. We came to attention.

Jones looked us over first. He stared at me, then at Sinclair and Chip. Amusement failed to fill his face. His lips were tight. He frowned. He shook his head in disgust.

A giggle behind him caught his attention. He twisted around and then back again. He addressed the other Marines. "Clean this place up!" he bellowed, his voice so loud it hurt my ears. "And I mean right now!"

He turned back to us. "You sorry excuses for sergeants got five minutes to get cleaned up and report to the skipper at the CP. Dismissed!"

I started wiping tofu off of me as he marched out. I carried a huge gob of the greasy goo over to a waste disposal unit near the hatch. Out in the corridor I heard someone let loose with a loud belly laugh. Glancing through the hatch, I saw the first sergeant laughing and shaking his head as he walked away.

FOUR

AFTER JONES LEFT, I walked to my team's quarters where I washed up and then changed into a clean field uniform. Finished, I deposited my tofu-soiled fatigues into a reclamation bin and then proceeded to sprint to the company's command post.

The command post, the CP, was located halfway between the landing dock, where my armored suit waited for me, and the mess hall. Holographic images originating within tiny hidden projectors floated like walls of light around the CP. Robot and human technicians observed the floating images and otherwise tended to various devices. A bluish-gray light illuminated the room.

In the center of the CP stood our company commander, Captain Vang Trang, otherwise known as 'the skipper'. Beside her stood First Sergeant Jones and First Lieutenant Gino Magliano, our executive officer. Across from these three stood my platoon leader, Second Lieutenant Kwung Neeyo, Gunnery Sergeant Kano, and the rest of Second Platoon's sergeants, minus me. With long strides, I quickly crossed the room.

First Sergeant Jones frowned at me, then turned to Captain Vang. "Everyone's here, ma'am," he said.

Of course, he was wrong. And right at the same time. Only one sergeant was missing, Sergeant April Bond, leader of Second Squad's B team. The team wiped out earlier today. The team Sinclair mourned.

"Excellent," the captain replied. She turned to us. Smaller than most other captains, she was smaller even than most of the Marines in her company, including some of her sergeants like Sinclair. She didn't even come up to my chest. But then again, I was the tallest Marine in our company, if not the entire battalion or maybe even the brigade.

Short of stature though Captain Vang was, she had proven her strength and courage many times since we had deployed to Eos. We were all willing to follow her into hell, as we had many times since arriving on this world.

"Hello, everyone," Vang said. Her voice was soft and musical, much like my mother's voice was. "We've had a challenging time this year. Yet that's when we Marines thrive, during the challenges. There's an ancient saying in the Corps: 'When going gets tough, the tough get going.' Well, that's who we are, the tough.

"You can guess there's another challenge coming, one that will test us yet again." She stopped and smiled at us, a wan and tired smile.

"I'll give you a little background," she continued. "Since the Gorgons ran into the Auster Line to our immediate east and the Asopus Line to our far west, they've been stymied. They've pulled out most of their forces here in the center of the continent to concentrate on the Asopus Line to the west and on a new fortified line far over on the eastern coast, the McKittridge Line. Only light forces oppose the Auster Line, of which we here in Belden form the western-most frontier.

"For that reason, our generals and admirals have decided to move our brigade's Third and Fourth Battalions west, along with the brigade's headquarters and support units. That leaves First Battalion, us, here."

"Alone," chimed in our X.O., First Lieutenant Magliano.

"Alone?" asked my squad leader, Staff Sergeant Jim Thur.

"Very much so," the skipper continued. "Brigadier General Clarke, our new brigade commander..."

"What happened to Brigadier Niehues?" asked Lieutenant Kwung.

"He's been promoted and given command of a brigade group along the Asopus Line," the exec explained.

"Good for him," I said.

"Indeed, Biyela," the skipper said. "It's good to know that hard work can pay out."

"So, what's going to happen, skipper?" Gunnery Sergeant Kano asked.

"Always to the point, aren't ya, Mo?" Jones said.

"It's one of my endearing traits, J.J.," Mo replied.

"And a very good one, too," the skipper said. She took a deep breath and sighed. "What will happen is this: Apex and Binary companies will move up along our flanks as Third and Fourth Battalions pull out. Our battalion will keep all the robots and support forces already present. The battalion will also keep the combat engineer platoon assigned to it from Brigade.

"Furthermore, Deny Company and the Headquarters Company and all the rest of the support units will remain at the Battalion's base, just outside of Belden.

"Finally, while Brigadier Clarke reforms the brigade with Fifth Battalion, Second Battalion will dig in thirty kilometers to our rear."

"Skipper, that's a good thing, right?" Sinclair asked. "I mean, they'll be there to back us up, right?"

"Not exactly," the exec explained. "Second Battalion has experienced more than sixty percent casualties in the last few months. Nominally, it's there to support us. But actually, it'll be there to rest, refit and reform."

"We won't be able to ask them for help for quite a while," the skipper explained.

"Now, for all this to work, we'll have to set up a forward base. We have to make the enemy think that we're bigger and badder than we really are. That's where Second Platoon comes in. You'll be moving six kilometers forward, into the center of the city."

"Smack dab in wormhead country," Chip quipped.

The captain laughed, a big guffaw that was surprising from such a small person. "Yes! That's where you'll be. We'll give you all the support and firepower we can."

"And replacements?" Sinclair asked.

"I have one replacement for the platoon. And I'm giving him to Biyela's team. You'll understand later. That's all, everyone."

"Tennshun!" the First Sergeant snapped. We straightened up and saluted. Then Kano ushered everyone but Lieutenant Kwung out.

FIVE

WE HAD THE NIGHT to rest. Chip looked for some alcohol. I retired to my team's quarters. I spent some time writing my after action report and a little letter to PFC Jenkins's family. I hadn't known her well and neither had the lieutenant, who would write the more formal letter to her family. But I'd known Jenkins for almost a day, which was much more than the two minutes Kwung had spent with her.

I told her family how well she had performed in combat. How she held off the enemy. And how everyone liked her, especially RC. I told them how he regretted her loss.

When I was done with those projects, I blogged to my family back on our colonial world of El Diablo Verde. I'd received a vid letter from my father more than a week back but hadn't had time to answer it before now.

I didn't know what to say. When you spend most of your time fighting, you don't have much to say otherwise.

I realized how depressing my life, the war, and this world was, so I didn't mention any of that. Instead, I told about today's food fight and how it washed away the tension of combat from all of us. I told of how the first sergeant had caught us and cussed us out. And how he had laughed long and hard after he left the mess hall. The blog wasn't long, but it was good.

When I finished writing it, I forwarded it to the battalion's out-going mail tag.

Afterwards, I stared at the ceiling. It was blank and barren. No images appeared on it. Our quarters had all the basics: light, fresh air, access to lavatory facilities, bunks, lockers for uniforms and personal effects, even hookups for personal electronic devices. But the special touches, such as the imaging equipment found on starships and bases on civilized worlds, was missing.

When this forward base was carved out of these subway tunnels six months back, it was assumed the base would only be temporary, perhaps a few weeks. That hundreds of Marines would occupy it for six months and maybe much more, had escaped the imaginations of the engineers and the brigade's staff. It just seemed improbable.

But here we were, waiting, fighting, and waiting even longer. And what were we waiting for? Was it success, victory, a good meal, maybe a pat on the back with a "Well done, Marines," whispered in our ears?

No, what we were waiting for was an opportunity to go home, to leave this world, to escape from all the death and destruction that everyone on Eos, the Dawn World, faced. The only success, the only victory in combat, was survival. And survival meant going home whole, alive, and well.

SIX

THE NEXT MORNING, WE bustled and hustled. The lieutenant had assigned Third Squad to load and protect the supply sleds that would carry everything we needed, including food, medical supplies, ordnance and quartermaster supplies, and whatever the team of combat engineers needed, to our new location, wherever that might be. Second Squad would provide flanking protection for the move and First Squad would scout ahead.

As with any patrol, there were many things to do. First and foremost was to make certain our armored suits were in good working order. We did this by entering our suits and interfacing with them. First we checked whether our micro-fusion power plants, located behind our buttocks, once our suits had closed, were fueled and fully functional.

Then we made sure we had plenty of ammunition for our plasma rifles. This ammunition consisted of small iron pellets kept in an ammunition hopper within our suits. Each slug was a single centimeter in diameter. When we fired our rifles, our suits' power plants would superheat these slugs to three thousand degrees Celsius, turning them into white-hot plasma streams ejected from our rifles by an antigrav field at a velocity of fifteen hundred kilometers per second that vaporized just about everything in their paths.

Our hoppers could carry a maximum of two hundred pellets, though a normal combat load averaged around one hundred and fifty slugs.

We also checked to make certain that each suit had plenty of fresh air, with a small emergency supply in case the suit's environmental system failed. We made sure we had plenty of water and food, too, and that our septic systems worked. We couldn't eject solid waste from our suits but liquid waste was not a problem. It was recycled into a usable product once more.

We also checked that we had daily rations for when we were outside of our suits. We made certain all our eating and sleeping materials, and any other materials, were where we could access them. And then we made certain each suit had emergency survival gear, including water, medical supplies, and a good combat knife, in case our suits were damaged and we had to exit them. These last items were unneeded because in this war, if your suit was damaged it meant you were dead. Dead Marines don't need survival gear. But we still carried it, as per regulations.

Finally, we inspected our sensors, our nano-processors, and our communications systems. Then we tested our defensive energy screens, making sure they worked. Finally, we made certain our gravitic discs and their systems were fully functional and that all interfaces worked.

When everything checked out we closed our suits and contacted the CP. Then we floated up, rotated around, and left the landing dock.

We didn't leave our base the way we entered it yesterday. Instead, we turned left and traversed down a side passage, along which a maglev train had once glided. We traveled a few kilometers and stopped.

Team A, led by our squad leader, Staff Sergeant Thur, waited for us. "Everyone here, Lion?" he asked.

I checked my sensors and looked around. It was a good habit not to rely too much on your suit's sensors. "We're all here, Jim." I had yet to receive my replacement for Jenkins.

Thur pointed toward the side of the tunnel. A big black hole gaped before me. "We're going down that?" I asked.

"We are," he replied. "The lieutenant's up ahead with Chip and what's left of his team. In case you're wondering where this leads, it's into the city's old sewer system."

"I suspected so."

Thur laughed. "I'll lead the way. You wait for Sinclair's squad. When it gets here, let them know where we're going and to wait for Third Squad and the supplies. Then follow us. Got it?"

"Got it," I replied.

"Good. See ya." With that, he dived into the darkness, followed, one at a time, by his five teammates.

We waited in silence. Because of the small size of Chip's team, the lieutenant had assigned it to be the platoon's security. Chip and I weren't going to be patrolling together while on outpost duty.

I missed him already.

We waited maybe five minutes and then Sinclair's squad arrived. She led the way, which was how we Marines always moved. Officers and NCOs in front, while everyone else followed. The only exception was when a scouting patrol preceded the main body and even then the patrol leader led.

We couldn't claim that "Lead the Way" as one of our mottos. That belonged to the Colonial Rangers. But "First to Fight" was ours, though we borrowed it from the long gone United States Marine Corps of old Earth.

I passed the word to Sinclair of the platoon's formation.

"Typical," she groused. "We're always second place."

I was grateful that Chip wasn't here. He would've baited her with a comeback such as: "That's why you're second squad," implying that they were indeed second place. While Chip's great to have around most of the time, sometimes he can be a real ass.

I didn't reply to Sinclair's complaint. I signaled my team via my suit's comm system, said goodbye to Sinclair, and dropped into the hole.

The moment I entered the hole all of my passive sensors came online. They revealed little information to me. The tunnel was deep, cold, and very dark. I fell one hundred meters before reaching the sewer tunnels. Then I switched on my active sensors. They immediately presented a virtual visual representation of the sewer in front of me. It displayed in front of my face, on the inside of my suit, on what we derisively called our "faceplate."

I led my team down the tunnel. After one hundred meters, we reached a crosscut passageway. Glancing down both sides of the lateral tube, my sensors didn't locate any threats.

As my team caught up to me, I guided them across the intersection. The last Marine in my team was Lance Corporal Berk. He paused beside me and glanced down the side tunnels.

"See anything?" he asked.

"Negative," I replied.

"Got it."

"Everything alright back there, Lion?" Corporal Kamal inquired from up ahead.

"Everything's good," I said. "Wait one while I come up."

"You got it, Lion."

I eased up the sewer to the right of my Marines. Pausing by Kamal, I asked him: "Where are we in relation to the surface?"

"We're about four kilometers to the right of Chaos Company and about a kilometer in front of Third Battalion. When are they supposed to start pulling out?" he asked.

"Sometime today, I think. The fact that we haven't met any of their patrols down here suggests they might already be gone."

"When is Apex Company supposed to move in?"

I shook my head, but of course he couldn't see it move. Our suits looked like a big sack covered our heads and entire torsos, ending where our hips began, with our legs dangling down from there. Our arms poked out partway down. Any head or facial motion failed to translate outside our suits.

"Sometime today, I think."

"Think we'll come across one of their patrols?"

"I doubt it."

"You think we'll encounter any Gorgons down here?"

"It's possible. But they don't usually come underground."

"Aren't they supposed to be tunnel dwellers?" asked RC over the comm system.

"Where did you get an idea like that?"

"It's common knowledge," Berk replied.

I glanced around. My Marines had bunched together, not a good tactical situation.

"Spread out," I said. "You know better than to bunch up."

"Aye, aye, Lion," they replied, moving away from each other.

"We know little about them," I reminded my team. "However, as far as I do know, no one's ever seen them underground, let alone down in the sewers."

"Why's that?" RC asked.

"Because it stinks like human down here," Ruby Johnson explained. "They can't stand anything human so why would they want to come down here?"

"Good point," Kamal said.

"Even so," I said, "keep alert. They might be willing to come down here so they can get the jump on us. Be ready for anything."

"Lion's right," Berk agreed.

"Let's move out." I continued down the sewer. "Second Squad will be coming up at any moment."

SEVEN

TWO KILOMETERS FURTHER DOWN the tunnel, we reached a dead end. It wasn't man-made but rather Gorgon-made. Sometime many months back Gorgon gunboats had attacked a building towering above the streets of Belden. They had fired upon the building with their plasma cannons until the structure, probably a sky scraping apartment building, had collapsed through the streets, through the subways, down, down, down into the sewers. Ten thousand tons, maybe a million tons, of concrete, metal, plastic and glass had compressed before us. Even our combat engineers couldn't cut through that.

But all was not lost. Where the wreckage obstructed our way stood Corporal Sami Sousa, Chip's assistant team leader.

"Where to now?" Kamal asked her as he came up beside me.

She pointed straight up. We followed her gesture and saw a wide black hole above us.

"What's up there?" I asked.

"Our new home," Sousa replied.

I thanked her and floated up. Darkness engulfed me, but only for a moment. As I drifted up, I noticed the hole was quite wide. It was wide enough, in fact, to accommodate the supply sleds accompanying Third Squad. A few moments later, I found myself in the ruins of another building, smaller, but uncompressed, littered with rubble from the crushed building beside it. Some of the rubble had come from this building's caved-in roof, the rest from the nearby collapsed tower.

The first suit I saw belonged to Chip. "Welcome to Paradise!"

"Hilarious," I replied, unamused.

"No, seriously." He spread his arms out, his plasma rifle holstered down his back. "This was a very popular restaurant located beside what's left of an even more popular hotel, now ruined. It was called 'Paradise'. You're floating in what's left of its middle."

"Really?"

"Really."

"Lion, you're blocking everyone's way," Ruby said, from beneath me.

"Sorry." I floated over to Chip. "You another guide?"

"You bet."

"Where's the lieutenant?"

"About half a kilometer down the street, in our new digs. She's got Thur's team and a couple of the combat engineers with her. She's waiting for you. Some guy from the brigade's Headquarters and Service Battalion is with her. Probably your new Marine."

"How do we get there?"

"Carefully," he said. "Stay on the street, keep down, the usual stuff."

I moved away from Chip and over to what once was a wide window, now just a glassless hole. The sky was overcast, the clouds light rather than dark. It was summer in this region, the rainy season. My suit said the outside temperature was moderately hot, with a high humidity. Belden sat in the southern middle of the continent. It occupied a region dry most of the year, but the summer brought rain from the west coast thousands of kilometers away.

"The way clear?" I inquired.

"Far as I know. But you never know."

"Got it."

"Good. She wants you there right away," Chip said, referring to Lieutenant Kwung.

"Got it." Turning back, I saw that my team had arrived. "Let's go," I said to them. 'Ruby, you stay close to me. RC and Berk follow. Kamal, bring up the rear."

"Got it, Lion," they confirmed.

"Kurmanski's just inside what used to be some sort of government building. He's keeping on the lookout for you. He'll guide you to where everyone else is," Chip said.

"Got it."

"Good. Get goin'." Chip unslung his plasma rifle and stepped over to the window. He pointed to a jagged gap in the wall that led to the street. The wrecked masonry looked cooked.

I unslung my rifle and powered it up. I checked my sensors, saw Ruby a meter behind me, and then I zipped out onto the street, as hunched down as I could be in my huge, bulky suit.

A light rain fell as we cruised carefully down the street, dodging rubble, checking our sensors and moving along at twenty kilometers an hour. Too much movement might draw an enemy's attention as much as anything else might.

A few minutes passed and we reached the building. Just inside, PFC Kurmanski, the last surviving member of Chip's team, waved at me. I darted in, followed by Ruby. Moments later the rest of my team arrived.

"Lion, that just seem weird to you?" Ruby asked me.

"No more than usual," I replied.

"Well, it did to me!" she exclaimed. "I felt like somebody or something had me in its sights."

"You're letting the world get to you, Ruby," Berk said.

"Probably not," Kurmanski said.

"How so?" Kamal asked.

"That new guy, he probably had his sights on Ruby. He probably had them on all of you," Kurmanski replied.

"Why would he do that?" I asked.

"Go find out. Chip's just told me that Sinclair's arrived. She'll be here in a few moments."

"Where's the lieutenant?" I asked.

Kurmanski pointed toward a blackened wall. "There's a lift shaft over there. The car's gone and the doors are shattered. It goes up to the top floor, sixteen levels. The lieutenant's got her CP up there."

"Got it."

I moved to the lift. Darkness filled it. I switched on my exterior lights and started up. Ruby waited until I had climbed two levels before following. The rest of my team kept the same interval.

At the top, I met Corporal Rita Peres, assistant leader for Team A. "Welcome to Outpost Shithole," she said.

"That's its name?" I asked.

"Might as well be," she replied. "We're at the top of this building where we can see everything and everything can see us. What better name is there for such a bad location?"

"None that I can think of."

EIGHT

STARED AT PERES FOR a moment. All I saw was a blank suit, just like mine. "Where's the lieutenant at?"

She pointed down the dark hallway. "Go down to the end. You'll find an intersection. Turn left. A little bit down from there you'll see a wide opening. Go in and you're there."

"Got it." I floated down the hallway, my grav disc just a centimeter above the floor. Tall though I was, my suit increased my height by several centimeters. Added to that was the thickness of the disc I rode. The hallway had been designed for normal people walking in normal clothes along the way, not for Marines in huge, bulky armor. I practically filled the corridor. Two armored Marines couldn't drift side by side down this hallway.

I kept my suit lights on as I traversed the dark corridor to the intersection. As I neared the turn, my suit detected faint light coming from either side of the intersecting hallway. I turned my lights off. My sensors revealed Ruby close behind me.

"You and the others wait here," I told her.

"Must we?"

"Yes."

I went left around the corner. Ruby followed me.

"What part about waiting didn't you understand?" I asked.

"It'll be too crowded back there. It won't hurt for us to spread out a little. You said not to bunch up."

"You got me. Just wait here."

"Got it."

Proceeding toward the light, I entered a large room that appeared to cover one entire side of the building. Square pillars, located every ten meters, supported the ceiling. To my left, just past the entrance, stood dozens of chairs shoved together. Each chair possessed a small holographic imager.

Ahead and to my right, large windows filtered the light from outside. Unlike most of the other windows I'd seen in Belden, these seemed intact. The glass had not been vaporized or blown out. The walls supporting the windows appeared undamaged.

Thirty meters away from me stood Lieutenant Kwung. She was in her field utility uniform and out of her armor. In fact, only I wore armor. Staff Sergeant Thur was unarmored, as were Gunnery Sergeant Kano, two combat engineers, and another Marine I didn't recognize.

"Biyela." I heard her voice over my exterior microphones. "Park your armor over to your left and join us over here."

"Aye, aye, ma'am." I glided to the left. Several suits stood open and empty. I found a space, settled to the floor, and as my suit opened behind me, I backed out.

Straightening my uniform, I strode over to the lieutenant. She smiled at me and motioned toward the window. "Beautiful, isn't it?" she said.

I leaned forward and glanced at the broken and blasted buildings that constituted the general remnants of Belden. Turning to her, I shrugged.

"Not the destruction, you idiot," Sergeant Thur said. "She means the window."

"It is amazing that it survived all this time," I said.

Thur sighed. "It hasn't survived all this time! It was only emplaced a few hours ago."

"I don't understand."

Kwung laughed, a gentle laugh for such a tough woman. "The engineers and their robots put it in this morning. The robots have finished fitting the windows on this level and the next one below and are currently working on the third level down. The windows are solid and are strengthened by a tiny energy field, which should protect them from enemy fire while remaining undetectable to Gorgon sensors."

"Oh."

"This will be our base of operations," the lieutenant continued explaining. "We have a shielded micro fusion power plant. We will have two robot twin plasma cannons for defensive support. On the level just below us we have individual and team quarters, as well as latrine facilities and a small mess hall. On the third level, we'll keep our suits and repair facilities."

"And here," Mo explained, "is our operations center, observation location, and otherwise command post."

"Impressive," I replied. "How long are we supposed to stay here?"

"If everything works out, three weeks" Mo said. "Maybe even a month."

I stared at my gunnery sergeant. "A month?"

"Affirmative. After that, Third Platoon will rotate here. And after that, it will be First Platoon's turn. Then we'll see what happens next."

"And what will happen next?" I asked.

"You see, Lion," the lieutenant began, "now that we're down to only one battalion defending Belden we have to appear larger that we really are. To do that, we have to aggressively patrol as far in front of the battalion as we can. We have to appear as big as a full company.

"Battalion headquarters hopes this outpost will be the answer to all our needs. It may not be, and if it isn't, then we boost out of here as fast as we can."

"Battalion and the skipper both hope our outpost will answer the strategic situation," Mo added.

Glancing from Mo to the lieutenant and back again, I asked, "Does that make us decoys or prey?"

"The first but not the last," Mo said.

"I don't follow."

"What Mo's trying to say," the lieutenant explained, "is that we are decoys, yes. But we'll also be hunters. We're going to aggressively patrol a two-kilometer radius around this structure. We will scout the streets, we will hunt the enemy, and we will be careful to succeed without casualties."

"Which means what, ma'am?" I asked.

"That we kill as many of the enemy as we can without getting ourselves killed," the lieutenant replied.

"That might be a bit difficult."

"It might, indeed," she agreed. "Square your team away. Mo will brief you again when you're finished. Oh, and by the way, this is Lance Corporal Hunter. He's your newest replacement. Try to keep him alive."

Frowning, I turned to meet my newest team member.

A tall Marine with brown hair and cheeks that dimpled as he smiled, stuck his hand out at me. His smile was wide and friendly.

"Lance Corporal Hunter?" I inquired.

"Mah friends call me Virgil."

"Virgil, then. New?"

"Jist ta yew guys. Ah came planetside with the brigade eight months ago. But Ah heah First Battalion's been heah a might longer."

"We arrived a month before the rest of the brigade did."

"Sheee-it, yew guys musta seen a lotta combat then!"

I glanced at Mo. He shrugged and walked away. I glanced back at Hunter. "A bit."

Hunter laughed. Then he noticed Mo moving off. "Gunnery Sahgant, thanks fo' watchin' out fo' me."

Mo turned around. "Anytime, Marine. Anytime." Then Mo left the room.

Hunter turned back to me. "That gunny's a real nice guy."

"He is. Where's your suit at?"

"Ovah theah, 'bout third from the end."

I waved him to follow me and walked toward my suit. "Where are you from?"

"Any outlyin' colony. Yew?"

"The same."

"Ah heah yer a Zulu? Dint yer people come from Earth?"

"They did."

"Then that makes yew from Al Diabla Verde?"

"El Diablo Verde," I corrected him. I was having trouble understanding his thick accent.

"That's what Ah said. It means The Green Devil, don't it?"

"It does."

"Well, everyone has a hell ta live thru sometimes."

I nodded. "Some do. Suit up. I'll introduce you to the team."

"Good!"

NINE

SUITED UP, I SPUN around. The suit and the grav disc negated the sensation of motion. Only my sensors and the view before me revealed my change of perspective.

One of the many great things about our armored suits was the fact that while our exterior appeared opaque to outside viewers we could see through every centimeter of our suits. It was as if we didn't wear any suit at all, but stood on our grav discs in our everyday uniforms. Yet we were inside our suits and if we wanted to only see through where a faceplate might be, with the interior as opaque as the exterior, we told the suit through our biochips just that, and it did so.

I preferred the faux faceplate view, while many others, including Chip, preferred the full view. So, as I rotated around, I saw just what was in front of me, even though my sensors made me aware of the world around me.

Hunter and I both moved out at the same time, though he moved a little smoother and faster than me. As we moved toward the exit, I contacted Kamal on my team's frequency.

"Take everyone two levels down," I told him. "It's where the flight deck and armory will be. If the engineers give you the go-ahead, unsuit and wait for me there."

"Got it, Lion," Kamal replied.

Lance Corporal Hunter preceded me into the hallway. As I followed, I noticed that Hunter's rifle, slung down his back, appeared different from my plasma rifle. Though a thin power cable connected his rifle to his suit, just as a similar cable connected my rifle to my suit, his weapon plainly was different.

"Hunter."

"Virgil, sahgent."

"Just call me Lion, Virgil. What kind of weapon do you carry?"

"Sahgeant, Ah mean, Lyin', how 'bout Ah tell ya when Ah tell yer team?"

"Fair enough. And its Lion, not lying," I said. Hunter turned right at the corner. When I switched my lights on, so did he.

As we approached the lift shaft, Corporal Peres snarled at us, "Move your asses, Marines. Staff Sergeant Sinclair is down below and she's pissed as hell that she has to wait for you!"

"Got it," I replied. "Virgil, hop in and drop two levels."

"Aye, aye, Lye-un."

I rolled my eyes, a gesture untranslated by my suit. Body language was wasted when wearing armor.

Hunter disappeared into the lift shaft. A moment later, I dropped over the edge. Hunter slid into the landing two levels down. As I waited for him to clear away, bright light flooded the shaft from beneath me.

"Get the hell out of my way! Now!"

There was no mistaking Dana Sinclair's voice.

Hunter evaporated from view. I followed him. Sinclair continued cursing at us as she cruised by.

Brilliant light filled the landing bay. Four engineering robots stood to one side, motionless. No windows revealed the outer world, nor did any windows expose the secrets of this floor. The walls appeared solid and thick.

To my left, four armored suits stood open and empty. Above them glowed a sign reading: *First Squad, Team C*. There were two slots left, one on either side of the suits. I drifted to the far right side while Hunter scooted over to the far left.

It took less than a minute for me to power down and step from my suit.

"Hey, Lion!" Berk called out, his arms spread wide, indicating the vast expanse of the hidden landing bay. "Would you look at this place? Wow."

"Yeah," RC agreed. "Looks like an army could hide here."

"Or at least Second Platoon," Ruby said.

"Yeah," RC concurred. "Yeah."

"Is that our new Marine over there," Kamal asked, pointing to Hunter as he exited from his suit.

"It is," I said. "He's Lance Corporal..."

"Virge, is that you? RC, it's Virge!" Berk exclaimed.

RC spun around. "Virgil!"

Like two little kids, Berk and RC ran over to Hunter and bear-hugged him.

"Guess they got a new boyfriend," Ruby said, smirking.

Kamal looked at me. I shrugged. The happy trio came to us.

"Lion!" Berk said. "You won't find a better Marine than this guy. This here's Sergeant Virgil Hunter. He's...hey, Virge, where's your insignia? What's going on?"

"Bet he got busted again," RC said. "He's always doing that, Lion. He doesn't like rank."

"Is that so?" Berk inquired. "What'd you do this time?"

"I bet it has something to do with some officer's wife," RC explained. "He's a ladies' man, Lion. Women love him and he loves them. They can't keep their eyes off of him. Or their hands."

Berk guffawed at RC's comments.

"More likely it's the other way around," Ruby said.

"Ruby!" RC exclaimed. "Virgil's a good guy. It's not his fault he's so adorable."

"Yeah, Ruby," Berk warned. "You're a woman. You might find it hard to keep your hands off of him some night."

"What did you say?" Ruby growled. RC and Berk backed away, raising their open hands in front of them.

"Ah never thought of myself as bein' adorable, RC," Hunter said. "Ah'm just a regular guy and Ah got my weaknesses, like any other guy."

"Sure," Ruby spat.

Before I could respond to any of this conversation, Berk tried consoling Ruby. "Don't worry, Rube, we got your ass."

"You've got my what!" she exclaimed.

I shook my head. Some guys never know when to keep quiet.

Kamal stepped between Ruby and Berk. "Back off," he said to both of them.

"Hey, Ruby, he didn't mean nothing by that," RC explained. "He means we're watching out for you."

Ruby shoved Kamal out of the way. She marched over to RC and jabbed him in the chest with one of her fingers. "Mind your own goddamned business."

"You know me better than that, Ruby," RC said, stepping back from her and rubbing his chest where she had jabbed him.

"So, you're not going to mind your own business?" Ruby growled at him.

"No, no, no, that's not what I meant," he said, squirming.

"Then what do you mean?" Ruby glared at him, making the room feel cold.

I watched as Berk's eyes darted from Ruby to RC and back again. Just as I decided to interfere, Berk changed the subject. "Hey, Virge, what kind of rifle's this? It doesn't look like any kind of plasma weapon I've seen before. What the hell is it?"

TEN

TOOK A DEEP BREATH and let it out forcefully. I noticed Kamal and Hunter relaxing, too, as the conversation veered away from the dangerous ground it had travelled.

Hunter walked over to his suit, where Berk stood looking at the strange weapon I had earlier noticed. "This heah's a lasuh rifle. An X-ray lasuh. It's fo' snipin'."

"What's he talking about?" Ruby asked me.

"What are you talking about?" I asked Hunter.

"Snipin'. Pickin' the enemy off without him knowin' it."

"You mean snipering," I said.

"That's what Ah said, Lye-un. Snipin'."

"Got it."

"Well, I don't get it!" Ruby growled. She steamed. I'd never before seen her so angry. It worried me.

"Ah'll explain. There's a tradition of snipin' goin' way back ta when Marines fought on ol' Earth. General Gallant pioneered it in the modern Marine Corps back durin' the Great Interstellar War. But we haven't used it fo' fifty years. Until now."

"So, you're saying that you're going to be picking off the wormheads without them knowing it?" Kamal asked. "How's that going to help us when we're out patrolling?"

"I think I understand," I said. "We're not going to be patrolling. We're going to watch out for him while he picks off the Gorgons."

"Yew got it, Lye-un."

"But how're you gonna do that with this tiny thing?" RC wondered.

"Yes," Kamal agreed. "The wormheads have energy screens just as good as ours. And their body armor's almost as good as ours. Their helmets are their only real weakness."

"Jist as our asses are ours," Hunter said, grinning. "Shoot a Marine in his or her ass an' jist as soon as not the power plant fries him."

"So how are you going to do it?" Ruby asked.

"Well, first thin', this is an X-ray lasuh, the most powerful lasuh we got, 'cept maybe fo' maybe a gamma lasuh an' them things are too dangerous ta use on a modern battlefield."

"You're still not saying anything of value," Ruby chided.

"Ah'm getting ta it, little lady," Hunter snapped at her.

"You're taking too long!" she snapped back.

"When Ah shoot at a Gorgon, mah lasuh's gonna fire three shots instead o' one, but all at once. The first two shots will penetrate the Gorgon's defensive screen and armor. The next kills it. Even if it's a glancin' shot, the X-rays'll fry its ass.

"Ah can fire ten triple shots in the time it takes yew ta shoot two, maybe three times. What Ah'll do is find me a nice little hidey-hole, where Ah can see them but they can't see me. Then Ah'll pick 'em off slicker'n snot!

"An what yew'll be doin' while Ah'm shootin' is watchin' mah ass an' keepin' 'em offa me."

"I don't think so," Kamal said.

"I think so. In fact, I know so," a voice behind us said.

We turned around as Mo came in. "What he's describing is exactly your team's mission. You're going to take care of him and protect him while he kills the enemy. His rifle has better range than your weapons do. He's going to hunt the Gorgons and you're going make certain the Gorgons don't hunt him.

"If you get the chance to do a little hunting on the side, great. But first and foremost he's the shooter and you're the guards. Got it?"

My team started to protest. I cut them off. "We got it, Mo."

"Good. Your first mission is tomorrow. Get settled in, get some food, and get some rest. I'll brief you at Oh Four Hundred. See you then." Without another word, he left us.

ELEVEN

WE ZIPPED AMONG THE crumbled rooftops of the city. We traveled tighter than usual. Instead of ten-meter intervals, we flew just three meters apart. Kamal and Ruby led. Berk and RC followed. And Hunter and I brought up the rear. There was something about Lance Corporal Hunter that worried me so I intended on keeping him close whenever possible.

A normal patrol keeps to the ground, never climbing higher than necessary. An enemy can spot Marines flying high more easily than when they creep through cover such as the massive amounts of rubble littering the streets below. But our sniper needed high ground to hunt his prey. So we darted and dodged about the shattered towers and rooftops of the ruined city.

Lieutenant Kwung had established a two-kilometer search radius around our outpost. But my team's orders were to hunt beyond that radius. So here we were a kilometer further out, deep inside the heart of the city.

"Lion," Kamal called. "How much farther should we go?"

"I don't know," I replied. "Everyone hold your current position. Be alert and be careful."

Rotating my disc ninety degrees to my right, I faced Hunter. He couldn't see my face but he saw my suit turn toward him.

"Found what you want yet?" I asked him.

"Long ago, Lye-un. Ah jest wanted ta see what yew were up ta. There's lots o' nice hidey-holes all around us."

"Pick one."

"Yew got it, Lye-un." Hunter spun around and scooted two hundred meters back, then dodged to his left. I followed him. My team followed me.

Our defensive energy screens were down, our power plants at minimum. We operated on passive sensors only, with communications encrypted and at minimum power and range. All this left us vulnerable but virtually invisible as well. If the Gorgons didn't see us, they wouldn't find us. We wouldn't show up on their sensors.

At least, I hoped not.

Hunter stopped at the top of a towering structure covering an entire city block. The top seven floors had suffered some sort of catastrophic failure, half of one side had collapsed, its debris having fallen to the streets far below. However, the other half still stood. Now the top stories formed an L-shape, with what had been an interior floor before now forming an exterior ledge. A debris-covered ledge, half a block wide.

"Is this what you want?" I stared in amazement at the building. What still stood was a testament to its builders.

"Does it look like anyone'd be in heah, Lye-un? If it don't look like it ta yew, it sure as hell won't look like it ta any wormheads either," Hunter said.

"You got a point."

"But what if it comes down on us?" Ruby asked.

"Then it comes down on us!" Hunter snapped. "Yer job's not ta complain but ta pertect me. Yew got it, Marine?"

"I got it!" She switched to my private channel. "Lion, he's going to get us killed."

"I hope not."

"I just hope he'll do some good with that light stick of his."

"Me, too," I said.

"I'm sorry, Lion, but he just pisses me off."

"I know, Ruby, but he's on our side."

"Are you certain?" she asked.

"I hope so. Let's do our mission and keep him safe."

She grunted.

We'd all been hiding near the building, bunched up again. Bunching up made an excellent target for the enemy. Even with years of training and experience, many Marines made that mistake, sometimes with fatal consequences. When you were afraid or nervous, you bunched up. It was an emotional thing.

Hunter drifted down onto the floor that was now the new roof. The still remaining floors towered above and behind him. I followed him down.

Kamal led the rest of the team inside, searching within the still-intact portion of the structure.

When I reached Hunter he had already unlimbered his rifle. He had discarded his grav disc and shoved it out of the way.

Inspecting his weapon while he walked, he glanced around the rubble-covered rooftop. After a few moments, he holstered his weapon and began shoving chunks of rubble together, forming a barricade. One piece he pushed too far and it tumbled to the street below. It fell a hundred stories before slamming into a pile of broken masonry. Rocks and bricks and dust scattered every which way when it hit. It rolled down the pile before settling on the street below.

"Oooo-whee! That was beautiful! Too bad theah weren't any Gorgons down theah, eh, Lye-un?"

"We could've had a hundred Gorgons coming up here just now!"

"There ain't none around heah. If theah was, they'd be scramblin' up heah right now, tryin' ta get at us an' Ah'd be pickin' 'em off faster than they could fall. Only a quarter o' them would get up heah an' yew an' yer team coulda taken care o' them."

"How do you know there aren't any Gorgons around?" I asked.

"Cause mah sensors haven't shown any, jist as yers haven't. Yew been lookin', an' Ah been lookin'. One o' us woulda seen them if they were around."

"True."

"Besides, every now an' again Ah been sendin' out a single radar pulse. I haven't hit anythin' movin' but us."

"You did what? I ordered silent running. That means no active sensors, Marine!" I shouted. My voice was louder in my suit than what came out of the speakers in his suit. But I needed to yell, to release my anger at him.

"Don't worry, Lye-un. They didn't detect it. And if they did, they still have ta find us."

I watched as he turned back to his makeshift barricade, moving some larger blocks over near the edge.

All the masonry looked the same. The brutal beams from the plasma cannons on Gorgon gunboats had battered, split, and blown it apart. Here and there the melted remnants of steel and titanium rods stuck out of the shattered masonry. Electrical conduits and fiber optic cords lay splayed among the debris, as did sewage and water pipes, and ventilation tubes. Sometimes, bits of furniture and porcelain lay among the rubble.

I glanced at the sky. We had left the outpost two hours before sunrise. Now the sun was at a thirty-degree angle in the sky. Brilliant morning sunbeams revealed details, while the ever-receding shadows revealed hiding places.

"Lye-un, have somebody guard this hide fer me. I'm gonna search fer another one."

"Ruby," I called.

"What is it, Lion?"

"Come keep an eye on Hunter's first hide. But keep out of sight. I don't want any Gorgons spotting one of us up here."

"Got it, Lion."

"Kamal," I said.

"Lion?" Kamal answered.

"Where are you at?"

"We're floating in the shadow of the tower's still standing upper floors."

"Get down here. Hunter's on the move again," I explained. "I got a feeling he's going to want guards for his hides."

"Got it. On the way."

I made my way to the slab. Peering up to the top, I wondered what kept it standing. It seemed about to crumble at any moment, yet it hadn't done so.

"Lye-un."

My sensors told me Hunter was directly under the center of the slab. I floated inside, finding him on a level with the slab and the new rooftop. He drifted beside a huge hole in the floor.

"Dont this look great?" he said. "Ah radar pulsed it. Goes clear down into the basements and even the sewer line. It'll be perfect fer scootin' between my hidey-holes."

"How many do you think you'll need?" I asked, peering over the edge. It was dark as death all the way down.

"Four or five more will do jist fine," he said. "How 'bout we take a look-see?"

"We'll wait for Kamal."

"Why bother?" he said. Slipping around behind me, he shoved me into the shaft.

I tumbled down, end over end, unable to get my grav disc beneath me. I couldn't use it if it wasn't under me. I fell several floors out of control, arms and shoulders bouncing off of metal bars and pipes sticking out from the side. My armor absorbed most of the impacts but even so I felt the blows. My arms and shoulders ached as I struggled to gain a proper flight attitude.

Finally managing to tuck my knees against my chest, I rolled back a bit and my grav disc came under me. It stopped my fall. I straightened my legs and ran a suit diagnostic. At the same time, I checked my medical readouts. The millions of tiny nanites in my body, made from my own DNA, worked hard repairing the damage to my limbs. The microchip in my brain, also made from my DNA, governed the nanites. The chip's seamless interface with them worked the same as it did with my suit.

"Yew okay there, Lye-un?" Hunter inquired as he drifted down beside me. "It took me a mite longer than yew ta git down heah."

Spinning around, I shoved him away from me with both hands. "What'd you do that for? You trying to kill me?" I bellowed. Adrenalin made me angrier than I wanted to be. It took an effort to calm myself down.

"Ah meant nothin' by it, Lion. I jist wanted ta get us down heah. Waitin' fer everybody ta get where their goin' wastes a lotta time."

"We don't waste time, Marine! Care and caution keeps us alive." I still didn't have my emotions under control.

"Caution can also get yew killed."

"That's a matter of opinion. Don't do that again." Taking a few deeps breaths, I managed to calm myself down. It helped that my suit had noticed my increased heart rate and had released a little more oxygen into my air supply. As I calmed down, my suit restored my normal air mixture.

"All right, all right! Can we look around now? We're wastin' time. Ah need a few more hides before Ah'm gonna feel good about this buildin'."

"Get with it," I said. He dropped to a lower level and scooted into it. I followed him. I knew it would take more than a few hiding places for me to trust him.

TWELVE

WE SPENT THE REST of the first day in the building we now called The Slab finding more hides for our sniper. While Berk and RC enjoyed Hunter's company, Ruby, Kamal, and I did not.

Ever since Hunter had shoved me down The Hole, as we now called it, I kept my eyes on him. When I couldn't watch him my suit watched him. If he did anything peculiar or threatening, it would inform me.

No Marine, not even Hunter, liked spending every minute of every day secured in his or her armor. However, my suit was sophisticated enough to contact me, even when I was outside of it, through my chip. If sleeping, it would awaken me the instant Hunter, armored or not, moved near me.

Six Marines cannot cover an entire building the size of The Slab. Knowing that this might occur we had brought microprobes with us. Each probe, the size of a small ball, possessed its own engine, with enough fuel to fly several dozen kilometers. An antigravity unit helped with its flight. And a wide variety of passive and active sensors performed its missions.

We each brought two microprobes. Two flew down into the sewers, while three others scattered about The Slab's interior. We directed the other seven to patrol outside the building and find good hiding places from which to observe any possible enemy movement. All of the probes sought the enemy while observing from safe locations.

As we settled into The Slab, I set day and night watches. Whoever was on duty remained suited up while the rest of us exited our suits. We rested, ate, slept and talked near our armor. For latrines, we used whatever surviving lavatories we could find. While The Slab still possessed potable drinking water, none of the toilets worked. Fortunately, the building contained hundreds of clean, usable toilets.

Three days passed without enemy activity. We grew bored.

We were in constant communication with Lieutenant Kwung at the outpost three kilometers away. She informed us that other patrols from the platoon hadn't made any contact with the enemy, either. This lack of contact made her jittery.

Captain Vang, back at the company base, seemed as troubled as Kwung was. Since our battalion first began fighting the Gorgons almost a year before, not a day passed when we didn't make some sort of contact with the enemy. Not to see the enemy for three days worried everyone.

What were the Gorgons up to anyways? Had they pulled back to the city's perimeter? Were they transferring troops to other fronts? Were they maneuvering to get behind the battalion? Were they setting a trap, maybe waiting for a larger patrol or even a platoon, to probe forward and then become surrounded and wiped out? What was going on?

"Maybe we should move somewhere else," Ruby suggested.

We sat around a little table Kamal had located the second day. Most of The Slab's remaining furniture had been fried or blasted to pieces, tossed about with the rest of the vast debris scattered across each floor. But Kamal, searching various rooms with Ruby and Berk, had found a large black wooden table in a mostly undamaged conference room seven floors down from the broken area. A large, still intact window dominated one wall. Since outside power was unavailable, we were restricted to using the room only during daylight hours for meetings.

When not using the conference room we stayed in a cleared area near The Hole, a few floors up. When using the conference room, we parked our suits outside in the foyer beyond, near The Hole.

"I don't know what good that would do," Kamal said, responding to Ruby's comment.

"Patience is one o' the best tools when snipin'," Hunter explained. "Sometimes ya gotta wait fer days before a target comes along."

"But we've been waiting three days. Even Battalion doesn't know where the Gorgons are," Ruby protested. She squinted out the window. Though it was a cloudy day, a bright beam of light poked through near the horizon as Thea, Eos's sun, rose beneath the cloud cover. "Wherever they are, they aren't near us."

Kamal nodded. Hunter rolled his eyes in contempt. And I sighed. Ruby was right. But Hunter knew his job better than any of us did.

At the moment, Berk was on watch. And RC, who'd just finished a four-hour stint, slept.

"It ain't like patrollin', is it?" Hunter said.

"It isn't," I agreed. "When you're on patrol, you seek the enemy out. Sometimes you set up an ambush and wait awhile."

"But you don't wait for three days!" Ruby snarled.

"That's the difference between patrollin' an' snipin'," Hunter said. "Ah'm waitin' fer targets, Ah'm not seekin' them out."

"It's strange, isn't it?" Kamal said.

"What is?" I asked.

"Patrolling and snipering, ambushes and how we're fighting this war."

"Ah don't follow yew," Hunter said.

"Wow, an admission of stupidity by the killer himself," Ruby exclaimed, smirking.

"Close yer hole!" Hunter growled.

"Is that any way to talk to a lady?" Ruby replied, a twinkle in her eyes.

"Who said yer a lady?"

"Keep it civil," I commanded.

Both looked away, Ruby out the window again and Hunter at the tabletop. "Ah still don't understand what yer sayin'."

"We weren't trained for this kind of combat," Kamal explained, spreading his arms. "We're Fleet Marines."

"I get it," I said. "You're right. Our job is to provide security aboard naval vessels. And to board errant vessels." Which didn't happen very often. Spatial warfare most often resulted in the complete destruction of targeted vessels, whether they belonged to an enemy or were just smugglers.

"And to provide planetside security at Naval installations, not to mention Association administrative buildings," Kamal reminded.

"That, too," I agreed. "Our suits are designed for spatial combat, not ground combat. Grav discs were never part of our original mission or equipment."

"Lucky for us someone saw the value in a piece of sports equipment," Ruby added.

Some years back the Interstellar Marines' engineering department noticed our need for quick transport over long planetary distances. So the engineers found an elegant and simple solution: grav discs.

The discs were used in a sport where the players carried a ball over a long playing field, with goals set at various angles and heights. Opposing players on discs defended these goals while others sought to steal the ball from their attackers. Played over a safety net, the greatest danger came from collisions rather than tumbles to the net below, often thirty meters down. It was said the game known as Grav Disc mimicked a game described in a series of fantasy stories written centuries before where the players rode broomsticks rather than antigravity platforms.

I didn't how true that assertion was, nor did I care. I only knew that lumbering through the streets of Belden limited to two-dimensional movement would have resulted in a higher casualty rate fighting the Gorgons, with a less successful outcome.

"We are lucky," Kamal agreed. "But what I don't understand is the need for a sniper."

"Or how we designed such a program so quickly," I added.

"It's been in the makin' fer years," Hunter explained. "An' it ain't new. General Gallant, back when he was a lewtenant, came up with it durin' the Great Interstellah

War. He took the idea fer it from the ol' American Marine Corps, along with some o' the tactics we use taday ta fight the Gorgons, includin' waitin' fer the enemy rather than seekin' him out. The general was a smart man."

"He was," I agreed. "Well, I guess we wait then."

"Good," Hunter said, grinning. "Heah that, little lady?"

Ruby glared at him, but turned back to the window. After a moment, she said, "Lion, what's that?"

"What's what?" I asked.

"That." She pointed out the window at a small dot coming our way.

THIRTEEN

"**S**UIT UP!" I ORDERED.

Kamal, sitting beside the door, jumped up, yanked the door open, and ran out. Our suits stood just a meter beyond the entrance.

Ruby followed Kamal.

Hunter stood and went to the window. "That's not one little dot, that's three little dots," he said.

I hurried around the table. Pressing against the window, I stared out. "You're right." I grabbed Hunter and pulled him away from the window. "Let's go."

"Quit yer pullin'! Ah can move mahself."

"Then do so, because those dots aren't ours."

I made certain I was the last one out. Glancing back through the window once more, I realized the dots were Gorgon gunboats escorting a larger sky vehicle, of a class unknown to us. I wondered whether it was a lifeboat or a supply boat. Whatever it was, it was much bigger than the very large enemy gunboats.

I secured the door behind me and turned around. Kamal and Ruby stood encased in their suits. Hunter vanished into his suit. I hurried toward mine.

"Getting telemetry from three of the probes," Kamal informed me as my suit swallowed me up. Instantly, without any instructions, the power was on, my suit and its systems operational, and I was connected to my suit.

"Two probes just disappeared," Ruby said.

I connected to one of the probes down on the street. It revealed large and small bits of broken rubble, some as big as boulders, scattered in front of The Slab and down the street. A large shadow undulated across the rubble and toward a distant intersection. A moment later a brilliant bluish-white light engulfed the probe. I lost all contact with it.

Kamal called to me. "Lion, the gunboats are hosing the streets. They must be vaporizing our probes."

"Apparently so," I replied. "Berk, you there?"

"Here, Lion," Berk said. "Those gunboats are sanitizing the streets and buildings. They swept some of the floors at the bottom of The Slab and the street in front of it."

"Got it. Where's RC?"

"Right here, Lion," RC said. "My suit just woke me. I need to pee and then I'll climb aboard."

"Pee in yer suit," Hunter said. "That's what that tube's fer."

"Right, Virge. Guess I'm not awake enough yet."

"City livin's makin' yew soft."

"Guess so."

"Cut the chatter," Kamal growled. "What do we do, Lion?"

"What's happening outside?" I asked.

"The big boat's settling down two blocks east of us, in the direction of the platoon's outpost," Ruby said.

"Got it." I checked my sensors. RC was in The Hole and ascending toward Berk. And Berk was one floor down from The Ledge, just beneath the monolith we named The Slab.

"RC," I commanded, "stay where you are. Berk, join RC."

"Got it," they echoed.

"Lion, the gunboats are hovering over the big boat. It's almost on the street," Ruby said.

"I see it," I said. "Hunter, do you have a hide where you can see that boat?"

"Mah first one."

"Too exposed," I said. "Do you have another one?"

Silence reigned for a moment. Golden silence. Then he replied, "Yeah. Got one two floors down from heah. View ain't as good, though."

"It'll have to do."

"It'll do," Hunter confirmed.

"Let's go," I said.

"Got it, Lye-un." He drifted forward on his grav disc. I followed him.

"Kamal, you and Ruby set up as far right of our position as you can. Don't go either too far high up or down. If we need to leave quickly, I don't want us scattered all over the place."

"Got it," he replied.

"Want us to do the same on the left, Lion?" RC asked.

"Yes."

"We'll keep from getting' too far away," Berk added.

"Good. And don't let any wormheads see you," Kamal added. "We can't afford losing even you guys."

"Thanks," Berk grunted derisively.

"Let's move," Kamal said.

Moments later, we reached Hunter's hide. A large hole gaped from the building's side. It stretched ten meters across and included part of the floors above and below.

To the left of the tear, obscured by the building's intact wall, drifted Hunter. Stepping away from his grav disc, he stood still, his suit supporting him like a piece of tall furniture.

I left my grav disc and approached Hunter. "Anything?"

"Lots."

I peered toward the distant Gorgon boat, now settled among the street's rubble. My suit adjusted my view, telescoping toward the scene. I watched as dozens of Gorgons exited through small hatches from the boat's sides.

"Lion, it's a troop transport," Ruby suggested.

"Yew got it, little lady," Hunter sarcastically agreed.

"Shut up!" she snapped back.

Hunter chuckled.

"Give her a little slack," I said to Hunter on a channel opened just between the two of us.

"Why would Ah do that?"

"Some day you might need her to watch your back," I said.

"Ah'd rather not. Ah'd rather none o' yew did."

"Then why are we here?"

"Beats the hell outta me."

I wondered myself.

"I count fifty Gorgons so far, Lion," Kamal reported.

"Lion," Berk called. "There's a platoon-sized force of Gorgons coming down a side street from the left. It intersects a block back from that big boat's location."

Unable to locate the forces from the left, I accessed Berk's suit and watched through its viewing system. Beyond this new force the street appeared clear far into the distance.

Turning back to the troop boat, my suit seamlessly changed my viewing perspective. "Keep me apprised."

"You got it, Lion," Berk said.

"What are we going to do, Lion?" Ruby asked.

"Nothing."

"Nothing?" my teammates said at once.

"It's Hunter's show," I said. "We're just here to observe and keep him safe."

"What Ah want is ta do mah job an' nothin' else."

"Then do it," I said.

We continued watching as the force below increased by fifty more Gorgons from the troop boat. At least a hundred milled about, while more continued coming out.

"It can't be that big, can it?" Ruby asked.

"If they pack 'em tight enough they could hold a small army in there," RC commented.

"Let's hope not," I said.

"Company," Kamal said.

I looked up. One of the gunboats drifted our way. I stepped back from the opening. Hunter pancaked against the wall, his weapon and suit hidden from view.

"Everyone keep quiet and hidden," I said. My sensors showed my Marines retreating into the building's interior.

With my passive sensors, I followed the gunboat's movements. It travelled around The Slab, scanning for movement and life. With active sensors it probed the interior. If it saw just one of us, it would open fire.

And it would probably call for reinforcements.

Several minutes passed while it scanned the building. Then it pulled away. Once certain it was gone, I directed everyone back to their positions.

"Lye-un, yew think that Gorgon might be an officer?"

I glanced down at the troop boat. Dozens of Gorgons surrounded a central figure. I noticed that the back of its suit glittered.

For almost a year we'd been fighting the Gorgons and no one, not the Marines, not the Eosian military forces, not even the Colonial Guards, had been able to pick out the leaders from the grunts.

Until now.

Maybe.

"Might be," I said. "Does that make a good target?"

"A sweet one," Hunter gleefully replied.

I changed channels and contacted the outpost.

"Whatcha got, Lion?" Gunnery Sergeant Kano asked.

"Is the lieutenant available?"

"She's a bit busy. Why?"

"Well, we got a lot of enemy activity, including a troop boat that's off-loaded at least a hundred Gorgons and more are coming out every minute. We also have two gunboats cruising about."

"Sounds interesting," Mo said. "I'll let her know."

"Thanks. Oh, and we might have an officer."

"You certain?" he asked, his voice excited.

"Very much."

There was a pause, during which time I transmitted a visual feed of the view below.

"I'm here, Lion," Lieutenant Kwung replied. "Where's the officer?"

I concentrated on the glittering Gorgon.

"Mo," I heard the lieutenant say, "forward this to the captain."

"Already on the way, ma'am," Mo said.

As I watched, the glittering Gorgon collapsed. The other Gorgons closed in around it. When another fell, they scattered.

"Lion, what just happened?" the lieutenant asked.

"I don't know, but I'll find out."

"Do that!" Mo growled.

I switched channels, deadening my contact with the outpost. "Hunter, did you do that?"

"Yew bet. Nice shot, too. Even got a second one."

I switched back to the outpost. "Lance Corporal Hunter shot them."

After a long pause, the lieutenant came back. "Very well. Keep me apprised of the situation."

"Ticked 'em off a bit, huh?" Hunter said.

"The Gorgons or the lieutenant?" I asked.

"Both. Officers don't know what ta do with me. Been that way since Ah joined the Twenty-fourth Brigade. They want me, but they don't. What a bunch of screwed up piss heads!"

"That'll be enough," I snapped.

"It sure will. Things are changin' down there."

I glanced back at the street. The gunboats and Gorgons fired on all the buildings to their front and sides. They ignored everything behind them.

The platoon coming down the side street joined them. It leaped into action beside the others, attacking the empty buildings.

"Got me another officer," Hunter said.

"Where?"

"He came up with that platoon. See him? His back's not so glittery, though."

"Don't shoot yet."

"Why not? It's a good shot."

"Just wait." I recorded the scene while I contacted my team. "See that Gorgon's glittering back?"

Everyone replied in the affirmative.

"That's an officer. Hunter has already taken one down. It might have been the leader of the enemy's expedition. See if you can spot any others."

"Got it, Lion," four excited voices replied.

"You can shoot now," I said to Hunter.

"Can't," Hunter said, exasperation in his voice. "He's dropped behind some rubble."

"What can you do?"

"This!" I saw one of the Gorgons out in front drop. Then another. And another. Suddenly, the frontal assault stopped and the Gorgons took cover.

"Lion, I got one. No, two. Three!" Ruby exclaimed.

I thought she'd shot three Gorgons. "Where'd they go down?" I demanded.

"They didn't drop. They're standing over by the side of that big boat. On the starboard side. They're squatting up near the front, consulting some sort of flat screen."

"Good spotting job, Ruby," I said.

"Thanks, Lion."

"Hunter?" I called.

"Can't get 'em. The boat's blockin' 'em from mah view."

"What can you do?" I asked.

"Nothin' much while they're hidin' ovah theah."

"Lion?" Berk called. "We got something for you."

"What is it?"

"There's something glittering in an open doorway down there," RC said. "On the left of the street just fifty meters down from the boat. Looks like its directing traffic."

I accessed Berk's view. I sent the visual to Hunter. "Got it?" I asked him.

"Nope. Can't see nothin', Lye-un."

I switched to RC's image, then I transmitted it to Hunter.

"Don't see it," Hunter said. "Wait. Got it. Kiss yer ass goodbye, yew ugly alien!"

As I watched through RC's suit the glittering officer collapsed. One of the Gorgons ran over to it, dropping along the way. Another Gorgon tried to help the rescuer and died, too. Two more hopped up and ran for the doorway. One fell meters away. The other died in the doorway.

In the scene below, all movement stopped. The Gorgons remained under cover. The gunboats darted back and forth over the ground forces, sometimes firing at shadows among the buildings.

Nothing came our way.

"Lion, the glittering officers on the starboard side have entered the big boat," Ruby said.

"Got it."

I transferred back from RC's suit. "Nice shooting, Hunter."

"Yeah, Virge, you done good! We coulda used you a few days back," Berk exclaimed. "Man, with a sniper, there's no muss nor fuss. Man oh man, what fine shooting!"

"How many did you get, Virge?" RC asked. "I lost count."

"Eight, by mah reckonin'," Hunter replied.

"Eight!" Berk exclaimed. "We couldn't get that many without somebody gettin' killed. I sure like this snipering business. Maybe I should try it."

"Nah," Hunter replied. "Yer good at what yew do, Berk. Just keep doin' it."

"Well, I'm glad you're with us," Berk replied.

"Thanks," Hunter said.

"It embarrasses me, Lion," Ruby said on one of my secured channels. "But I'm glad he's with us, too."

"So am I, Ruby," I said. "So am I."

FOURTEEN

WE WAITED ALL MORNING for the Gorgons to move but they stayed hidden. Morning shifted to afternoon. The hours drifted slowly along. The day had started overcast and by mid-afternoon rain arrived.

Darker clouds preceded the rain. Visibility decreased. However, as the sky darkened our suits' visual sensors automatically shifted into the infrared and ultraviolet spectrums and for us, visibility increased.

Then flashing lightning decreased our new visual acuity. Every bolt and blast, every flash, overwhelmed our sensors. And our suits adjusted to that, too.

Our suits were not run by a computer brain but by thousands of sub-processors and micro units organized into a central neural network, a sort of electronic nervous system. This system adjusted our suits and sensors much as the human body's central nervous system operated a variety of systems, including the heart, the lungs, the muscles, the flow of blood, and a legion of organs and other bodily functions. Our suits were not separate from us but rather connected, forming a second skin and additional muscle power. All of this operated through the microchips in our brains forming the seamless interface with our suits, so necessary for control and operation.

"How long are we going to keep this up, Lion?" Ruby asked.

"Good question," I replied. "Hunter, see any targets?"

"What? Oh, sorry Lye-un, Ah was sleepin'."

"Sleeping!" Ruby exclaimed.

"That's right, little darlin', sleepin'. Mah suit will let me know if somethin's going on down theah. An' if it didn't, yew guys would, because it's part o' yer job."

"Lion, tell him to quit calling me 'little lady' or 'little darling' or anything like that. If he doesn't, I swear I'm going to shove my rifle up his ass and burn him where the sun will never shine," Ruby growled.

"Ah'm so scared!" Hunter mocked her.

"Play nice, you two," I said. I knew they were just burning up the tension they felt. And yet, I needed them sharp and focused.

"But Ah don't want ta, Lye-un!" he said, laughing.

"Lion!" Ruby cried out. I heard the anger in her voice. Ruby was one of my best Marines: sharp, clear-headed, focused. She was a dependable fighter, there when you needed her. However, I had my doubts about Hunter's dependability.

"Calm down, Ruby," Kamal said. "You're letting him do exactly what he wants to you."

"And what do you think that is?" she demanded. I heard the anger in her voice. Everyone in the team did.

"He's annoying you so he can feel superior to you," Kamal explained. "So let go of it."

"You think it's that easy?" she complained.

"It is if you're willing for it to be," Kamal replied.

"Hey, Virge, let up on Rube," Berk interrupted. "She's okay and we need her."

Hunter grunted. "Okay, if yew says so, Berk. But a man's gotta do what he can ta stay awake an' sharp out heah."

"I know," Berk replied. "But don't do it to your friends and neighbors, okay?"

I heard Hunter yawn. "Whatever. Sorry, little lady, don't mean nothin' by it."

Ruby didn't reply.

Afternoon turned to evening. The rain let up and the sky cleared. The sky became a deep blue as the sun, Thea, settled beyond the horizon. Darkness came. The stars appeared. Eos had yet to evolve any intelligent life forms to name the alien constellations filling the night sky.

The troop carrier and gunboats departed. A few minutes later, a pair of Sky Command fighters raced across the sky.

"Haven't seen them for a while," RC remarked.

"They've been busy fighting over the coasts," Berk said.

"Well, it's nice they flew by for a visit."

"Yeah. They sure chased those gunboats away."

"It is," I agreed. I wondered if the lieutenant or the skipper had requested them. "Anyone see anything on the street below?"

"If yew mean them wormheads, they're still there. They're still movin' 'bout but I ain't got any good shots," Hunter explained.

"Anyone else see anything?" I asked.

Berk and RC replied in the negative.

"I've seen movement," Kamal said.

"Me, too, Lion," Ruby added. "However, if I had fart mouth's rifle I'd have had a few good shots. They're squirming down about the rubble like bugs and snakes."

"Thanks for that vivid imagery, Ruby."

"Lion," Kamal said, "now that it's dark do you want our partnerships to remain the same?"

"What do you have in mind?" I asked.

"Well, if we form groups of three rather than two, then one member can keep guard while the other two eat or sleep."

"That's a good idea, Kamal. How about you join Berk and RC. Ruby can join Hunter and me."

"D'you think that's a good idea?" he wondered.

"I do. Ruby will help me keep a close watch on our sniper and maybe I'll get some sleep."

"Aren't you worried about what those two might do to each other?"

"Less than I am about not getting any sleep tonight. I don't function well without sleep."

"Your suit has plenty of stimulants."

"No thanks. Sleep will do fine."

"Got it. Want me to report in?"

"No," I said. "I've sent telemetry to the lieutenant."

"Good. I'll round up the boys and send Ruby your way."

"Don't forget to duck when Ruby finds out," I said.

"I won't forget."

FIFTEEN

RUBY WAS NOT PLEASED. Her voice sounded flat and cold as she approached Hunter's and my position. "You don't think I can play nice with the two morons?" she demanded.

"They can hear you, you know," I reminded her. She referred to Berk and RC.

"I don't care. Ever since the love of their lives joined the team they think everything he says or does is golden. They let him walk all over me because they're hard for him."

"Ruby!" Kamal exclaimed. "Such language."

"You know it's true," she said to Kamal. "After all, you protested, not them."

"All right," I said. I switched communications for Kamal, Ruby, and myself to a secure channel only I could activate. "So you're not happy. But you understand why I picked you. Kamal is second-in-command and I need his experience watching over those two. Just as I need your help in keeping an eye on Hunter."

"I get it, but I don't like it. I'd rather back shoot him than keep an eye on him."

"Marines don't do that to each other," Kamal said.

"It happens," Ruby said.

"It does," I said, "but not in my team."

Neither of them said anything.

"Ruby, you take the first watch. I'll set my suit to keep me informed if Hunter does anything he shouldn't. But you keep an eye on him and on the street below. Wake me in three hours."

"Got it," she replied, her voice still cold.

I retreated to The Hole. I kicked debris away from the opening and exited my suit. Linked to me, my suit kept me informed of everything I needed to know from everyone's suits, plus from the remaining microprobes guarding The Slab. I instructed it to awaken me in an emergency and for no other reason.

I had something to eat and relieved myself in one of the unused lavatories. Then I curled up on the hard floor beside my suit to sleep. Before my eyes closed, I was out.

My suit didn't awaken me, but did record when Hunter came over and parked his suit a meter from mine. He exited his suit and stretched out on the floor a short distance away.

I don't know how long I slept before Ruby awakened me.

"Get up, sleepy head," Ruby said, her hands grasping me. "My turn to eat and sleep."

I struggled awake. Then I sat up, rubbed my eyes, and said: "I just went to sleep. What's up?"

"You're up, that's what's up. And by the way, I let you sleep a whole extra hour."

"Why?"

"Why, he asks?" She shook her head, her dark brown hair bouncing around on her shoulders. "Because you needed the sleep, that's why, stupid."

I stared at her.

"Why are you staring at me?" she demanded.

"I just realized you're out of your suit."

"Is that a problem?"

"No."

"Then why are you still staring at me?" she demanded.

"It's been such a long time since I saw you with your hair down. Since I've seen any woman with her hair down."

"Shut up!" she snarled. Ruby reached behind her head with her hands, gathering her hair together, twisting it into a braid, and then fashioning it into a Marine-grade bun. "Get up. I want to sleep and it's your turn to keep watch."

I nodded. I noticed Hunter's nearby suit. Ruby's suit was parked on the other side of mine. I inquired of my suit and it informed me of when Hunter had arrived and what he did, which wasn't of any consequence.

"Do you feel okay sleeping this near him?" I asked her.

"I'd feel better if we just dumped him down The Hole."

"I wouldn't feel better." I stood, stretched, and walked around for a few minutes. From a pocket inside my suit I retrieved a bottle of cold water and drank from it. "I'll have your suit inform me if anything's going on with Hunter."

"Just freaking great, you'll be back right after he dumps me down The Hole!"

"At least I'll know where to look for you," I replied, smiling. She didn't smile back.

Ruby lay down and went to sleep.

I sighed. I climbed into my suit. After it sealed behind me, I switched to the team channel. "Who's on duty?"

"I am, Lion," RC responded.

"See anything?"

"Negative. The wormheads are still hunkered down in the rubble. I've seen a little movement, but nothing much."

"What kind of movement?"

"Squirming around in position, trying to get comfortable, that sort of thing. Nothing out of the ordinary."

"What's ordinary for the Gorgons?" I wondered.

"Good point, Lion," RC said.

"How long have you been on watch?"

"About an hour. I replaced Berk. I'll wake Kamal in two more hours."

"Got it. I'm going to look around a bit."

"Got it, Lion."

I wandered around the building. Everything was as before: full of rubble, destruction and darkness. From a couple of different locations, I glanced down at the Gorgons under cover in the street below and two blocks away. Nothing moved, though I could see bits of their bodies and heads.

What were they waiting for, a rescue party? Or were they waiting for us to do something foolish such as going out and checking on them? Maybe they thought we'd grow tired or bored or would just leave.

Maybe. Maybe. Maybe.

They were as alien as alien came in relation to humanity. Communications with them proved almost impossible. During the brief border war with the Gorgons almost a century back they only responded to a truce after the fighting became too costly for them. And whether that cost was economical or casualty-wise remained a mystery to mankind. We only knew that after three years of peace attempts they finally responded to suggestions, through three-dimensional co-ordinates, of a halt to the fighting and a division of the planet Eos. And now, after decades of peace, they sought humanity's extermination once more.

After my brief recon, I checked with the microprobes. Almost every probe reported the same thing: either everything was all clear or else they couldn't see the Gorgons' location.

The only exception was one of the two probes sent into the sewers below. One reported an all clear in its location. The other probe reported nothing. Even the most tried and true technology had its weaknesses.

So, the final result of my inspection: we were safe and the Gorgons hadn't moved. But what were they waiting for, a rescue or a counter-attack? And who would provide it?

I returned to Hunter's sniper hide and waited. The minutes ground slowly along.

After about two hours, Hunter, suited up, drifted over on his grav disc. He peered out the wound in the wall. I looked out, too. Nothing moved. All seemed still.

"So," he said after several minutes of silence, "are yew goin' ta let me stand watch or are yew goin' ta keep on distrustin' me?"

"Distrust seems reasonable," I responded.

"Why?"

"You shoved me down The Hole. That's why!" I snapped at him.

"Ah was only funnin' with yew. Yer suit would protect yew. There was no danger. I knew yew'd be fine and so yew were. Why so much anger an' distrust?"

I said nothing. I just kept looking out at the peaceful view. My suit's infrared and ultraviolet sensors revealed the bones of a once beautiful city, now dead. The sky was clear. An abundance of beautiful stars filled the night sky.

Somewhere up above us in the night sky, tens of thousands of kilometers away, orbited the hundreds of starships making up our fleet. Thousands of men and women crewed those ships. Sky Command pilots flew their fighters from their carriers among those ships. Marines and Colonial Guardsmen arrived every other day aboard transports, protected by warships from our fleet. For all the power we possessed and all the troops we deployed, we barely checked the enemy's advance. We out-gunned and out-fought them, but they out-numbered us. How were we going to win?

"Talk ta me!" Hunter growled at me. "Ah'm right heah. Ah deserve courtesy."

I turned to him. "You do."

"Then why don't yew trust me? Why don't yew let me stand mah watch?"

"I don't trust you, that's why. You've proven to me that I shouldn't trust you."

"Yew're still upset about me pushin' yew down that hole? It was a joke! Jist a joke. Sometimes mah sense o' humor gets the better o' me. It's why Ah was busted from sahgeant ta private. It's been a slow climb back up. It's taken me a couple o' years ta get ta lance corporal again. Give me a chance, Lye-un. Give me a chance."

I wished I could see his face, his eyes. Maybe if I could, I might be able to tell whether he was lying or not. His words seemed convincing. But words were cheap.

However, my grandfather had always said words were powerful. And if a man or woman gave his or her word, then it was your responsibility to respect it. At least, until he or she proved you wrong.

Yet Hunter hadn't given me his word. There was no contract, no bond. I was under no obligation to trust or believe him.

"I can't," I said.

"Yew sumbitch, why can't yew trust me? Ah'm a man an' a Marine. Ah deserve as much respect as anyone. Ah made a mistake an' Ah'm sorry. But Ah'm part o' this team. Ah have the right to respect an' trust. Give it ta me!"

I wanted to trust him. I did. But I couldn't. I just couldn't. "No."

He was angry and upset and even though I couldn't see his face, I imagined it was quite red.

"Ah deserve ta be part o' this team! Please, Sahgeant Biyela. Please! Ah give yew mah word. Ah'll do right by yew. Yew'll see. Ah will."

There it was. Grandfather had said to respect a man's word. Now, if I said no, I'd dishonor my grandfather and myself, not to mention Hunter as well.

I sighed. "All right. You can stand this next watch."

"Thanks, Lye-un. Thank yew! Yew can trust me. Yew'll see. Ah won't let yew down."

"I hope not."

"Yew'll see, Lye-un."

I drifted back toward The Hole. As I left him behind, I heard him mutter, "Yew sumbitch, yew."

I spun around. "What did you just say?"

"What?" he asked, sounding surprised.

"You said something!" I growled at him.

"Oh. Oh. Ah'm sorry, Lye-un. Ah didn't mean nothin' by it. Ah wasn't cursin' yew, I was cursin' mahself. Ah was jist lettin' off steam. Ah don't want ta mess up again."

"I see," I replied, mollified. Maybe he had been letting off steam. Or maybe he'd just cursed. Was I too anxious for him to prove me wrong? Maybe. But I had to give him a decent chance. "Very well, Marine, do your job."

"Aye, aye, sahgent!"

SIXTEEN

As Hunter had given me his word, and as I was allowing him to stand watch, I returned to The Hole, parked my suit, and climbed out. I lay back down. But though as tired as before, I didn't sleep well.

Hunter had given me his word and according to my grandfather I must trust him until he proved otherwise. But I still didn't trust him. I couldn't. My instincts told me otherwise.

Yet, I slept.

Until Ruby awakened me.

"You going to sleep all morning? Or are you faking it so you can spy on me again?" she snarled at me.

"When did I spy on you?"

"The last time I woke you up. You commented on my personal appearance. How can a woman Marine have any privacy when the men in her team are always watching her behind her back?"

"Who's been watching you?"

"All of you," she claimed. "Every single day. When I relieve myself, I feel everyone's eyes on me. Even at base camp. You're all trying to figure out what I look like without my clothes on. You're all perverts!"

"What are you talking about?" I whined. "What kind people do you think we are? What's up with you, Ruby? We're not perverts. We watch out for you, not spy on you. We're your friends, your family. We're here for you. We're not after to you."

"I know," she said, a twinkle in her eyes and a little smirk on her face.

"Ruby! Why did you just do that to me?" I replied, angry at her deception.

"A woman's got a right to a little mischief now and then, doesn't she?"

I shook my head in disbelief. My Marines were nuts. "Where's Hunter?"

"That's just what I'm wondering," she said. "And why are you here and he's not?"

"I let him stand watch."

"You did what? How could you do such a stupid thing?"

I stood up. "Enough."

"What did you say?"

"You heard me, private. Hunter gave me his word and I'm honor-bound to respect it until he proves otherwise."

"What proof do you need, Lion?" Ruby demanded, ignoring my rebuff. "He's a loud-mouthed, rude, ignorant good-for-nothing son of a bitch! What more do you need to know?"

"That's just your opinion."

"And yours, too," she snapped.

"No. He gave me his word and I have to respect it. Both as a man and as a Marine."

"What a pile of Gorgon shit!"

"Ruby, you and Kamal are part of our original team. We've been together for almost two years, long before this war started and our coming here. We acquired Berk and RC after suffering severe casualties in our first weeks here. Yet they fit right in and now we're a family."

"Are you saying that Hunter should be part of our family? Because if you are, I'm transferring out as soon as we get back to the platoon."

"I'm not suggesting anything like that. As far as I know, he's just temporary. What I am saying is that for now I'm choosing to trust him and I want you to do the same thing."

"You don't know what you're asking me to do."

"I do."

She turned away. "Shit, shit, shit!"

I waited. When she turned back around, she seemed tired. "Just for now, Lion."

"Lye-un," Hunter called. His voice echoed from my suit. A couple of quick steps and I was in my suit. It sealed up. My stomach growled and my bowels said something else.

"What is it, Hunter?"

"Somethin's odd about them Gorgons down there."

"Such as?"

"Such as Ah don't know. Could yew come and take a look-see?"

"Give me a few moments."

"Yew got it."

SEVENTEEN

A FTER I FOUND A **clean toilet to relieve myself, and wonder** of wonders, a sink still with water in its lines so I could wash my hands and face and fill my water bottle, I returned to my suit and re-entered it. Inside, I opened a meal packet and ate breakfast. Ten minutes later, I reached Hunter. "What's up?"

"Nothin'."

"Why'd you call me here then?"

"Because nothin's goin' on."

"I don't follow you." Was this how he was going to prove himself unworthy, by behaving like an idiot?

"They're not movin'. Ah've watched them fo' hours now an' they haven't budged a centimeteh. No wigglin', no lookin' around, no nothin'."

"And that's bad?"

"Think about it, Lye-un. If we were pinned down in all that rubble, wouldn't we move around some? Wouldn't we want ta figure a way out? Wouldn't at least one o' us be movin', testin' the enemy, wonderin' what was goin' on, tryin' ta find a way out?"

"Maybe. But we don't understand how the Gorgons think."

"Ah've fought them almost as long as yew have, Lye-un. They always move. An' when they do, we suffer. But they're not movin' an' that bothers me. It bothers me a whole lot."

I said nothing. I didn't know if their sitting still should bother me or not, or if it was normal for the Gorgons to sit so quietly, which such patience.

Ruby came up and joined us. "Lion, I really, truly, absolutely hate to say it, but I think Hunter's on to something."

"Thank yew, little darlin'," he said. He sounded serious.

"Shut up!"

"Yew got it."

"Lion," Kamal called. "I was just listening in and I agreed with Ruby and Hunter. Something's not right. They're sitting too still down there. Could they have gotten away in the night and we didn't notice?"

"How?" Ruby said. "Why are their suits still down there if they're not. Did they just shed them like the snakes on Earth shed their skins?"

"I don't know," Kamal said.

"Neither do I," I remarked. "Something could be up. But what can we do? Our best course is to wait and see what happens."

"We could move a probe over to them," RC suggested. He had joined the conversation, too. I forgot I had my comm on the team channel. I had supposed my conversations with Ruby and Hunter had been private. But apparently not.

"That's a good idea," Hunter said.

"Kamal, you do it," I ordered. "We'll watch. Berk, get down to The Hole. We lost contact with one of the probes in the sewers last night. It might be a coincidence and it might not be. Watch The Hole and check the other probe."

"Got it, Lion," Berk replied.

"Should I go with him?" RC asked.

"He'll be fine, RC," I said. "You keep an eye on Kamal. Watch his back."

"Got it."

"Ruby, keep an eye on things down there. You too, Hunter," I told them.

"Got it," they echoed.

Through my sensors, I watched as Kamal separated a probe from its hiding place in front of the building. I changed my view to that of the probe as it floated across the street, maneuvering around rubble. It dodged from one place to another, keeping as out of sight as possible. Some of its sensors scanned the sky above. Nothing threatened it from any direction.

The probe spotted a Gorgon almost hidden by a pile of broken masonry. It slipped over to it. From a little to the left, it scanned the alien.

Its transparent helmet was opaque. None of the probe's sensors penetrated the Gorgon's armor. The alien didn't move. Not a centimeter.

"It's got to know the probe's there," Kamal said. "We're using active scans. Why isn't it responding?"

"Maybe it's already dead," Hunter suggested.

"But why?" Kamal wondered.

"And how?" I added.

"If Ah could jist get a better angle, Ah could shoot the damned thing."

"Move the probe closer. Let's see what happens," I said.

The probe drifted closer. Nothing happened.

"Touch it," I ordered.

Kamal instructed the probe to touch the Gorgon. It moved slower and slower, until it bumped up against the alien's helmet. The moment it made contact, the Gorgon's armored suit, minus any occupant, turned to dust and disappeared down through a body-wide hole in the pavement it had covered.

"What the hell!" Kamal and I both exclaimed.

"Play that for the others," I commanded Kamal.

He repeated it for the rest of the team.

"Impossible!" Ruby said.

The others swore.

"Hunter, shoot one of those things," I said.

"Ah can't from heah."

"Then float out there, get some height, and shoot something. Got it?"

"Got it, Lye-un."

"Kamal, RC, get over here. No. RC, go cover Berk. Kamal, you get over here."

"On the way," he said.

Hunter drifted out a little way. He rose up a couple of meters. It was a bright sunny morning, but the sun was behind the building. Hunter remained in the shadows.

"Target acquired," Hunter said.

"Shoot," I said.

He shot. Another suited dissolved into dust.

"Can you shoot any more of them?" I asked.

"Ah can shoot all of 'em," he said.

"Do so."

One after another, as Hunter fired on the aliens, their suits turned to dust. The aliens were gone. After twenty shots, Hunter gave up and re-entered the building. All that remained of the Gorgon suits he shot was a slowly expanding gray dust cloud.

"Ah ain't killin' nothin' but phony suits. Ah never seen anythin' like that trick before. It's pissin' me off an' confusin' me at the same damned time. What's goin' on, Lye-un?"

"I haven't a clue."

"We gotta go look," Hunter said.

"We don't have to do any such thing," I retorted.

"He's right, Lion," Kamal said. "We need to know where they've gone."

I wanted to curse, but controlled my emotions. "I suppose so."

"So it comes down to who's going out," Ruby said.

"I suppose so," I repeated.

"I could go," Ruby suggested.

"An' Ah could cover her."

"No," I said.

"We've got to do something, Lion," Ruby said.

"Not yet. I'm going to report in first."

No one said anything. The situation was just too bizarre for us to think clearly at the moment. A little time to clear our heads while I reported in was a good idea.

I contacted the outpost and again Mo answered. "What is it now, Lion? The lieutenant's busy."

"Watch." I sent my suit's recording of what had happened.

"What the hell?" he said.

"Our sentiments exactly, Mo," I said.

"I see. Or don't see. What are you planning on doing?"

"Sending someone to check it out."

"Good idea. Send Kamal and Ruby. Or Berk and RC. Don't go yourself and don't waste our sniper. By the way, how's he doing?"

"He's doing fine," I said. "He killed at least eight of them yesterday. Their gunboats hosed down all the buildings except ours. One of them circled it but it couldn't detect us. Hunter's laser rifle worked quite well. If we had engaged them with our plasma rifles we'd have been in a losing duel."

"I'll let the lieutenant know. She'll be ..."

"Lion," Berk interrupted.

"Not now, Berk. I'll get to you in a moment."

"What's the interruption?" Mo asked.

"Nothing that can't wait a moment."

"Lion," Berk interrupted again.

"I'm speaking with the outpost," I snapped, anger and frustration in my voice. "I'll get to you in a moment."

"No!" Berk growled back. "Lion, our other probe in the sewer just disappeared."

"What do you mean it 'just disappeared'? Do you mean it's malfunctioning?"

"I mean it's gone. Before it disappeared a massive infrared image appeared in the sewer. It looked like dozens of bodies with waving hair."

"Are you sure?"

"Definitely."

"What's going on?" Mo demanded.

"One of our probes in the sewer beneath us just died. Looks like the Gorgons might be coming this way through the sewers."

"Get out of there! Get out now!" Mo ordered.

"Got it, Mo." I cut communications with the outpost.

"Holy shit!" RC exclaimed.

"What's happened?" I demanded.

"Someone or something just blasted a plasma burst up The Hole. There's another."

"Get out of there, you two. Move. Right now!"

"Got it, Lion," Berk said. "Look out, RC!"

"Report!" I growled. But they didn't report. I turned toward Kamal. He took off.

"What's going on?" Ruby asked.

"I just lost communications with Berk and RC. Kamal's gone to find them. The Gorgons are coming up The Hole."

"What?"

"We're bein' sideswiped," Hunter said. "The enemy's comin' up our ass."

"Do something, Lion!" Ruby said, her voice full of fear.

My suit's sensors began detecting multiple plasma bursts and my exterior speakers caught the sounds of masonry exploding. Then, within seconds, Kamal, Berk, and RC burst out of a nearby stairwell.

"The Hole's been compromised," Kamal said.

"How close are they?" I asked him.

"Fifteen seconds and they'll be here."

"What're we going to do, Lion?" Ruby asked.

"Leave."

"Where to?" RC inquired.

I pointed toward the street where seventy or so empty alien suits sat amid the rubble. "Down there. Ruby, Kamal, lead the way. Berk and Hunter, follow them. RC and I will follow you. Let's go."

Ruby and Kamal floated out the wound in the building's side. They dropped to the street below and began scooting away through the rubble.

Hunter and Berk followed them, just seconds behind.

"Go, RC. I'll be along in a moment."

"What are you going to do?" he asked.

"Slow them down."

"Then I'm coming along."

"No," I replied. "You're going to get down on the street and cover me because when I come, I'll be coming down hot."

"Lion, we're a team."

"We are, but I need you down on the street. Got it?"

"Got it," he said, sighing. "Be careful."

"Always," I said.

He disappeared over the edge. I moved back through two rooms until I found the door that led to The Hole. I waited a moment. I needed to know how close the aliens were. If they were too close, staying might be fatal.

My team was my family and I wasn't going to let anything happen to them. The enemy needed slowing down. My team needed time to get away.

Something moved.

Two masses of wiggling snakelike hair appeared. Each mass moved a little higher, revealing a bald, pale scalp.

Wildly waving clawed hands grasped the edges of The Hole as one of the aliens dragged itself up with its wiry arms. Another pair of arms belonging to the same monster scooted a plasma weapon over the edge. Then the second Gorgon, maneuvering as the first did, began climbing out of The Hole. It also carried a plasma weapon. Both creatures wore the same clothing, covered from neck to foot by a gray suit. Across the surfaces of their suits squirmed black patches, some sort of moving camouflage.

As the first Gorgon moved away from The Hole, it turned about, its rifle pointing at various doors and rooms around The Hole.

Now the second monster climbed from The Hole and a third started climbing over the edge. I fired three quick, fatal plasma bursts. Each Gorgon's head exploded in a mass of vaporized mucous and flesh.

Two headless bodies fell to the floor while the third disappeared down The Hole. Almost immediately wild plasma bursts erupted from The Hole. Then a plasma stream blasted an emergency door away from a stairwell off to my left. That was my cue to leave.

I turned and scooted back the way I came. I stopped at the wound in the side of the building and glanced back. None of the Gorgons followed me. But my audio sensors picked up the loud buzzing of mosquitos. However, there weren't any mosquitos on Eos. The Gorgons were talking to each other, in their weird buzzing manner, no doubt discussing their next moves. They'd be along soon.

Leaning away from the building, I glanced left and right. As far as I could tell there weren't any Gorgon gunboats around. A quick glance down revealed the exterior of the tower clear to the street below. I saw RC squatting behind a huge rubble pile, keeping an eye on the streets stretching away from the building.

Looking along the street that led in the direction of where the enemy's armored suits sat, waiting to powder away when touched, I saw the rest of my team darting off, one pair watching while another zipped for cover. Kamal was my assistant leader and a fine one, too. He'd get the rest of the team to safety. Then he'd hide and cover RC and me while we joined them.

Masonry exploded beside me. I spun around and snapped a shot behind me toward where the Gorgon shooter stood. My shot blew it backwards.

Time to go. I glided out, nullified my grav disc, and plummeted to the street below.

EIGHTEEN

I FELL FASTER THAN I imagined possible. And as I fell, I started wobbling as the air pushed against my deactivated grav disc. I lost stability. It felt like I might flip over and that could be fatal. As strong and powerful as my armored suit was, I couldn't survive a fall from more than one hundred stories up.

The street flew up at me. Or, rather, I flew down at it.

RC looked up and saw me shooting like a giant bullet down at him. He screamed, "Lion!"

I snapped my grav disc back on. It's antigrav field energized and my descent slowed. I managed to restore my flight attitude. As I straightened out, I began curving out of my fall into a more horizontal flight path. RC ducked as I zipped over him, coming to a stop several meters beyond him.

"You scared the hell out of me, Lion," he said.

"It scared me, too. Anything following me?"

"Negative," he replied.

"Got it. Where is everyone?" I asked, remaining where I had landed, scanning for the rest of my team.

"Down the street. Hiding," he said. He glanced all around. Then he looked upward. "Oh, shit!"

RC zipped past me as the rubble pile he'd hidden behind just exploded from multiple plasma shots. A piece of the rubble caught him in the back and he fell forward, sliding face first across the street. His grav disc acted like a giant brake as it scraped along the pavement behind him, slowing his slide.

Small bits of rock and rubble bounced off of my suit. My energy screen popped on and further debris deflected away from me. Moments later, my screen was engulfed by brilliant bluish-white plasma streams.

I darted away, zigging and zagging as plasma shots sought me. I avoided most of them, though some struck me. I continued maneuvering. I had left just in time. If I'd stayed, I'd have been dead.

I checked my sensors. RC was still down. None of the aliens were shooting at him, however.

"Kamal, RC's down and I'm drawing fire. Can you help us?"

No response.

"Where is everyone?"

Again, no response.

Growing tired of being shot at, I found cover inside a cracked and crumbled corner of a damaged building. From there, I saw where RC lay, unmoving, back up the street. He was stretched-out on the pavement, his grav disc holding his ankles twenty-five centimeters above the pavement.

Glancing around while checking my sensors, I couldn't see the enemy anywhere. The Gorgons had gone to ground. I wasn't taking fire anymore.

I examined my suit. My long-range communications seemed to have failed. I tried short-range communications. "RC, are you okay?"

"I'm here, Lion," he responded.

I breathed a sigh of relief. "Are you hurt?"

"Negative, but I can't get up."

"Why not?"

"My grav disc isn't working."

"How come?"

"I think it's busted."

That didn't make sense at all. Our grav discs were as tough as out suits. "Is your suit functional?"

"Aye, Lion."

"Good. Release your disc."

"It's not responding."

"How's that possible?"

"I don't know. It's like it's not even there."

While RC struggled with his grav disc, I checked the area around me with my sensors. Where had the Gorgons gone?

"Any luck releasing?"

"No."

"Try telling your suit to disconnect from your disc. If that doesn't work, then nudge the emergency release with your chin. If you remember, it's located beside your left shoulder. If that doesn't work, pull your right arm out of its sleeve and press it."

"Lion, I can reach it with my chin, just barely. I'm free."

"Good job, Marine. Now, don't let your feet drop just yet."

"Why not?"

"The moment you pop off of that disc, it's going to flop onto the deck. When that happens, if any Gorgons are watching you, they'll fry you with their plasma rifles."

"Got it."

"Now, you're certain your suit's fully functional?"

"It is, Lion. Why?"

"Because you're going to have to get up and make a break for cover."

"Got it."

"Is your rifle functional, too?"

"Aye, Lion."

"Good."

"Lion, I don't think I'm going to be able to get up in time before they kill me."

"You will. You have to. You are one of my best Marines and I'm not going to let you die out here, RC. Got that?"

"Got it, Lion."

"Now, here's what I want you to do. I want you to order your suit to reduce your apparent weight to one-fourth of normal. This will increase your agility by a factor of four. When you hop up you'll soar up a few meters. The Gorgons won't expect that. When you land, run like there's no tomorrow. Pull out your rifle and be ready to fire. Come right to me, zig-zagging as you run."

Our armored suits, designed for spatial combat outside a planetary atmosphere without grav discs, came with their own micro-gravitic generators. When we use our gravitic generators on a planetary body we can change the apparent weight of our bodies by reducing gravity's pull upon us. While this change of weight allows us to move as if we were on a small planetoid, such as an asteroid, it doesn't increase our true strength. Our body mass remains the same, as does the suit's mass. We are no stronger than before, but rather moving a lighter body.

"Got it, Lion."

"I'm in the corner of the building on the left side of the street just after the intersection, the cracked-up one."

"Got it."

"Ready?"

"Aye, Lion. My apparent weight's reduced."

"On the count of three," I said.

"Got it."

"One." I checked my sensors and looked everywhere. There wasn't any sign of enemy movement.

"Two." I took a couple of breaths, as RC was most likely doing.

"Three!" I said.

RC pulled his hands and feet under him. With a shove, he was airborne, his disc falling away. He sailed several meters upward and forward.

Plasma streams from The Slab shattered his disc and melted the pavement where he had lain.

He hit the deck, stumbled, and ran for his life. From behind the rubble pile stormed a dozen unarmored Gorgons, their plasma rifles aimed at him.

"Break right!" I yelled.

He dodged right. Most of the plasma shots missed him, aimed at his left. Two shots hit him and he fell. But he rolled, got up, and kept moving, his energy screen scattering molten metal every which way.

I glided from my hideout. "Break left!"

RC zigged left. Behind him, closing, came the Gorgons. I fired into their mass. Though they wore some sort of protective gear, which absorbed most of my fire. But their heads and arms were bare. My shots vaporized their exposed flesh. Most of the aliens hit the pavement, some in great agony and the rest dead. The survivors took cover in the rubble scattered about the street.

RC ran over and darted inside the building beside me. As I stepped inside, I shot a Gorgon unfortunate enough to poke its head up. Its head disappeared in a cloud of super-heated steam.

Then I saw the most horrifying sight I'd ever seen: scores of unarmored Gorgons boiling out of The Slab. And from behind the building, and coming down along the side streets, hundreds of armored aliens charged at us.

We were out-numbered and surely dead.

NINETEEN

I SHOVED RC TOWARD THE interior of the building. "Inside, or we're both dead."

RC hurried in, but a fallen metal beam blocked his path. He planted a foot on the beam and shoved hard. The beam remained in place, but RC didn't. He sailed backward, crashing into me.

We both stumbled out onto the street and fell on our backs. Metallic plasma streams hissed over us. I fired multiple times to my left. So did RC. The Gorgons took cover. They didn't return our fire.

I shoved RC off of me. "Get inside and get that beam out of the way. And return to your true weight."

"Aye, Lion," he replied, bouncing to his feet, stumbling, then darting toward the door. A plasma shot sent him spinning sideways, away from the door, his energy screen protecting him from damage.

I killed the author of that shot. Then, rolling onto my stomach and reducing my own apparent weight by two-thirds, I thrust myself up and I zipped over to RC. "Run. Out into the rubble. I'll cover you."

He ran. From the way he moved, I knew he'd returned his weight to normal. I returned to my true weight as well. We were all use to moving around Eos with our weight normal. Playing with our apparent weight in combat could be fatal.

I zipped ten meters up and hosed the enemy as they darted from cover to cover. I killed and maimed many. But I noticed that the armored aliens were replacing the unarmored ones.

Darting down the street, I bobbed up and down. Most of the Gorgons' shots missed me. The rest glanced off of my energy screen.

From somewhere, I heard RC's panting voice. "I'm at the next intersection. I'm among the empty Gorgon suits. No sign of the others."

"Got it." Where was everyone?

I flew down the street at max velocity: one hundred kilometers per hour. At the next intersection, I spotted RC. I turned a wide arc in the air over him, scanning the buildings. A plasma stream flashed past me. I fired wildly, blindly. I missed.

Dropping to the deck, I scooted over behind a burned-out vehicle. RC knelt behind it.

"We're not going to make it, Lion. Not with me on foot. Leave me. I'll cover your rear."

"Be quiet," I growled.

"Got it."

Scanning down the street, I spotted dozens of Gorgons, all armored, dodging from rubble pile to rubble pile, or seeking cover behind the occasional burned-out ground vehicle. They were good and they'd be here soon.

Besides the troops in front of us others must be coming, too. No doubt they ran down the side streets, trying to get behind us. When they finished encircling us, we'd be dead.

I could get away on my disc, but what about RC? He was stuck on the ground.

Where was the rest of my team?

"Lion. Just leave me."

"No." I looked around. Five meters behind me sat an empty Gorgon suit. Dozens of other empty enemy suits were scattered along the street toward the next block.

"RC, holster your rifle. Reduce your apparent weight again to one-fourth and then climb onto my disc. And hold on tight."

"We'll be a bigger target," he said. "We won't be able to move as fast and we'll both get killed."

"Be quiet and do what I told you to do," I said.

"I'm better on the ground," RC replied. "You know that."

"You're dead on the ground and you know it. Now do what I said and be quick about it."

RC stepped onto my disc. He wrapped his arms around my waist. "What about our energy screens? Yours won't cover me, Lion, and mine won't cover you."

"Good point. Direct your suit to project your screen around your back and sides and I'll do the same for mine, but from the front instead. Don't cover your arms and I won't cover my waist."

"We'll be vulnerable where we're not covered."

"It's the best we can do," I said. "It'll have to do."

"Aye, Lion."

"Ready?"

"Ready."

We lifted off. My grav disc didn't have any problem with the added weight. The problem was in maneuvering. RC's rear stuck out over the back of my disc. His heels hung over the disc's edge. And while his hold was solid, it wasn't that solid. A sudden maneuver up or down, left or right, at maximum velocity could toss him off.

I rose just high enough to clear the rubble. I kept close to the buildings and moved along at thirty kilometers an hour. We were in the air maybe fifteen seconds when another plasma burst hit RC square in his back. The superheated metallic mist splattered against his energy screen. He wasn't hurt, but as the plasma engulfed us momentarily we both felt it through our suits where we were unprotected by our screens.

"See what I mean, Lion?" RC exclaimed.

"I felt it too. Hang tight. I'm crossing that intersection."

"Got it."

I increased our velocity to one hundred kilometers per hour. We shot across the intersection. Both side streets were filled with armored Gorgon troops. Their weapons weren't pointed toward us, but I knew they noticed us. Behind them, several blocks back, RC and I both saw troop transports on the ground disembarking hordes of troops. And behind the transports, in the air, gunboats protecting the landings.

"Jesus Christ, Lion, did you see that?"

"I did."

"They're going all out to get us. Looks like they got a whole battalion looking for us."

"It does." I scooted as close to the street as possible, decreasing my forward velocity below thirty kph. "RC, do you have long range communications?"

"Negative, Lion. I had it for a little while, back when I was on my face on the deck. But I couldn't reach the team."

"Did you try connecting to the outpost? Did you try getting Gunnery Sergeant Kano?"

"Sorry, Lion, but I didn't even think of it."

"It's okay. You had enough to think about."

"What about you?" he asked me.

"My comm's down, too. I thought it might be damaged from all those plasma streams that hit me. But now I'm thinking it might be something else."

"Like what?"

"Jamming. Or even something much worse. My suit has tried many times connecting to Kamal and the team. And it's tried to reach Sergeant Kano. But it's unable to contact anyone."

"What could it be, Lion?"

"I don't know."

"How about a virus?"

"Our suits are too well protected for that," I reminded RC. "No programing virus can harm us."

"Maybe not," RC replied. "Yet those wormhead suits all turned to dust. And easily, too. We know they have nanotube armor similar to ours. Maybe the purpose for that dusting was to infect our gear with a virus."

"Hang on," I said. We had reached the next intersection. I popped us up to ninety meters, and sped through at one hundred kph again. We didn't see any aliens or their vessels anywhere.

Where were the Gorgons? They had seen us a block back, but none had fired at us. And they hadn't pursued us. Why not?

After we made it safely through the intersection, I dropped us to the street and stopped.

"What's going on, Lion?" RC asked.

"A moment to think," I requested.

"You can think while we're getting out of here, can't you?" he suggested.

"Dismount."

"Okay," he said.

"RC, why aren't they following us? We're less than one hundred meters away. There looked like several hundred Gorgons back there. They could've kill us at any time."

"They still can," he reminded me.

"Yes, they can," I agreed. "So why aren't they after us?

"Beats me."

"Listen, RC, you just had a brilliant thought about their dissolving suits releasing a nanite plague against us."

"So?"

"So, why don't you put that brilliance to work and help me figure out why they're not following us."

"I'm more interested in why we're not high-tailing to the outpost, Lion. If they're not following us, that's a good sign."

"No, it's not a good sign. And as to why we're not heading back, if our suits are infected then we'll infect the rest of the platoon when we get there."

"I hadn't thought about that. So, what are we gonna do?"

This was typical RC behavior. He was intelligent and capable of moments of brilliance, but he let everyone else do most of his thinking for him. Some Marines were that way. And it was why they became Marines, so someone else could do all of their thinking for them.

Yet, his question was valid. What were we going to do? If we waited for the Gorgons to catch up to us or if we looked for them, then they'd slaughter us. They out-numbered us several hundred-to-one. Yet they didn't seem interested in us anymore. If so, where were they and what were they doing? Might they be searching for someone else besides us? Who could that be, other than the rest of my team?

"I don't like it out here," RC said.

I pointed toward a pile of rubble over beside a battered building. I floated over to the opposite side of the street and settled down. "Keep an eye on your sensors."

"Got it."

"How's your suit doing?" I asked.

"Most everything's working," he replied, "but my suit's no longer scrubbing the water from inside it. It's getting a bit steamy in here and I'm getting thirsty."

"Don't you have any water?" Besides dehydrating its interior air and turning that moisture into drinking water, each suit carried several pints of water.

"Yeah, but I'm afraid to drink it. I don't want to run out and then need it when I don't have it."

"Good point," I replied. "Keep me informed about anything else that has stopped working."

"Aye, Lion."

We waited. Nothing moved in the street.

I turned to go. But I didn't turn and I didn't go. Not anywhere. My grav disc was unresponsive.

I tried various different things to get it going, including switching circuits and trying to reboot its systems. Nothing worked. I didn't know what was wrong and neither did my suit because, as far as it knew, my disc didn't even exist anymore.

Yet I stood on my disc.

I tried disconnecting from it so I could get off it. Nothing happened. I tried the emergency release above my left shoulder. It clicked but failed to release me.

"RC," I called to him.

No response.

I called him again.

He still failed to respond.

I began to panic. If I was stuck on my disc, I couldn't move. The enemy could pick me off at any time.

I increased the gain in my comm unit. No answer. I doubled its output.

"What is it, Lion? You sound like you're a long ways off."

I doubled the output again.

"I'm receiving you fine now," he said.

"I need you to cover me," I said. "My disc's dead. The emergency release failed. I'm going to step out of my suit and manually release myself from my disc."

"Go for it," he said, sounding tinny and far away.

I took a moment to prepare myself. This was incredibly stupid. Leaving the safety of your suit in a combat environment was like stepping out of a starship in deep space, naked. It was a bad idea, but it was the only one I had.

My suit parted behind me, reluctantly. I just squeezed out.

After several tries I managed to kick the connection clamps open. I re-entered my suit. It slowly closed. But everything else worked. I stepped off of my disc.

I jogged over beside RC. I pointed up the street.

"What are we gonna do now?" he asked, as we walked away from The Slab and the enemy.

"Find our team. And hope nothing else goes wrong."

TWENTY

WE CAREFULLY MANEUVERED DOWN the street, all the while keeping an eye on our sensors. Several long minutes passed before we reached the next intersection. I motioned RC toward a large pile of rubble. Then I stepped into the intersection and glanced up and down the side streets. I spotted neither movement, nor threat.

I waved RC forward.

Our broadcast communications had now failed us. But our basic comm system still worked. However, for it to work, we had to touch our suits together. This simple task allowed us to talk in a basic close-range fashion. I kept this form of communication to a minimum.

As we crossed the intersection, RC kept tapping his suit, indicating he wanted to talk. I waited until we were across the street before pulling him inside a damaged building. We leaned together.

"Myf stuit nez getteh wurz," RC mumbled.

I knew what he said. His suit was getting worse. I waited a few moments and then said, "How bad?"

"Not too bad yet, Lion," he replied. Our suits had adapted to our new form of communications. Where at first RC's voice had been muffled, now it was adequate.

"My emergency systems have kicked on. My air's clean and my suit's temperature and humidity are better," RC continued. "But everything's working slower. I don't know how long it'll be before I have to exit my suit. What'll happen if it won't open? How will I get out?"

"I don't know, but we'll figure it out if it gets that bad."

"Got it. But I'm scared, Lion. I don't want to be trapped inside my suit. I don't to die in here."

"You won't," I reassured him.

"How do you know?" he demanded. "Has anyone ever been trapped inside a suit before? If all the systems have crashed is there even a way to get out?"

"I don't know, but we'll figure a way to get you out."

"I'm counting on you, Lion."

"I won't let it happen."

"You better not."

I didn't respond. What more was there to say? Besides, what if I couldn't even get out of my suit or it completely stopped functioning when the time came to save RC from his failed suit? What would happen to us then?

If the Gorgons found us trapped inside our immobile suits? There was a simple answer to that, they'd fry us.

To say I wasn't as frightened as RC would be lying. I was terrified. No Marine wanted to be found helpless by any enemy. It was the most terrifying possibility of all.

We moved on.

Every Marine learns that the best way to overcome fear is to keep busy. If you're too busy to think about it then fear cannot harm you. It can neither victimize you, nor terrify you.

The block we proceeded down was as empty, as unoccupied, and as quiet, as the last one. And the next intersection and next block were as quiet as the ones just behind us. And the next further block was quiet as well.

We stopped.

RC came over, holstered his rifle, and spread his arms, as if to say: "What's going on?"

I tapped my suit. He leaned his suit against mine. Our emergency comm systems had to compensate a little more as they were starting to fail just as our other systems had.

"What is it?" he asked, his voice like a whisper.

I shouted back, my voice hurting my ears. "We've come almost a kilometer, more than half of it without any pursuit. If they're not following us, where are they?"

"Maybe they're busy elsewhere," he whispered.

"Talk louder," I shouted.

"Can't you hear me?"

"Not much."

His voice came back louder, clearer, even more frightened. "What are we gonna do?"

"Stay in our suits as long as we can," I said.

"And then what?" he asked.

"Run as fast as we can."

TWENTY-ONE

LYING, FIGHTING, AND RETREATING we'd covered about a kilometer. We had headed more or less straight toward the platoon's hidden outpost. Keeping along this course, we'd lead the enemy straight to it. And if our suits held together long enough for us to reach the outpost, then we'd infect the platoon with the same plague that infested our suits. We couldn't do that.

Crossing another intersection without pursuit, we continued down another rubble-filled street. Climbing the rubble made me breathe harder. My suit should've compensated for the climbing by enriching my air supply with more oxygen. And it should've automatically adjusted my apparent weight, making me lighter so the climbing would affect me less. But it did none of that. My only conclusion was that more systems had failed. The plague was spreading.

Sweat beaded my face. The temperature in my suit had increased.

A new, greater danger occurred to me. What if my micro-fusion power plant shut down? Or worse yet, what if the containment field failed and released the superheated plasma from inside my power plant? I wouldn't need a Gorgon to fry me: my own power plant would accomplish the same thing.

Again, fear knocked at my door. The only thing I could do was to keep moving. But as I climbed a large rubble pile, I found it took twice as much effort to scale it.

I barely reached the top of the pile when I lost my balance and tumbled down the far side. Rolling, bouncing, bumbling, fumbling, I caught glimpses of my arms and legs flailing. At one point, I spotted RC bounding down the pile beside me. He seemed reasonably balanced. He had his rifle out, prepared to protect me. When I rolled to the bottom my butt bounced off the pavement. But the pavement gave way and I fell through into a darkened space below.

Splattering spread-eagle, I stared up at the bright blue sky above me. My visual systems still worked. However, my suit was as stiff as a board.

A shadow crossed over the hole in the pavement above me. A moment later, something landed beside me. Something reached down, grabbing me, rolling me over.

It was RC. He began trying to open my suit. In fact, I was hoping I could still open it.

But nothing happened. I was trapped in my own personal coffin. Then, I felt air on my back. It stank of sewer, but I didn't care.

With effort, I managed to remove my arms from the sleeves of my suit, folding them under my chest. Then I drew my legs out and managed to arch my back enough to get them bunched beneath me. Ducking my head, I slithered out of my suit.

Standing, I fell forward.

But RC caught me.

Stepping away from my suit and turning around, I saw that RC had exited his suit as well. "Status report?" I requested.

"Your suit's toast, Lion, just like mine," he said.

Grimly, I nodded. "Can you help me get my suit up?"

"Sure. But, why?"

"I don't want the Gorgons finding our suits. Too much technology to lose."

"Got it." With an effort, we manhandled it up. It weighed nearly fifty kilograms. Minutes later, our suits were hidden behind debris.

"Lion, where are we? Is this the sewer?"

I shook my head. "I imagine it's some sort of service tunnel beneath the street. The sewer system is several levels down."

"What about that smell?"

"There must be a broken sewage pipe somewhere nearby."

He nodded. "Makes sense."

Whatever it was, this tunnel was too low for me to stand up in. Only the hole I had fallen through allowed me to stand upright. When we moved our suits I'd had to hunch over. Even RC, whose eyes only came up to my shoulders, had to duck a bit when moving about.

"Lion, there's something odd about this hole."

"How so?"

He pointed toward it and then at the rubble beneath it. None of the pieces seemed to have broken upon impact with the deck below. As we picked up some of the pieces and held them together we noticed that they fit snug within each other.

"How odd," I said.

"Look here," RC said. From the light shining through the hole I noticed a large, square piece of plastic board on the deck. Beneath it were two damaged wooden beams.

"It looks someone has used this for an escape route."

"Or," RC suggested, "as a means to visit the city when there aren't any wormheads about."

"Could be. Must be." I walked over to my hidden suit, removed some of the debris hiding it, and with effort pulled the back apart enough to lean inside. I removed the five water bottles it carried, along with five food packets. I also retrieved the first aid kit and the only weapon available, my Marine combat knife. I also removed a webbed vest for carrying these items, and a flashlight.

Stuffing myself into the vest, I filled its pockets with food packets and water bottles. Then I said to RC: "Get your stuff."

RC obeyed. His equipment duplicated mine.

While he gathered his supplies, I flicked on my light. Its power supply was good for at least forty hours. If we didn't get back to the outpost by then, we'd be in the dark. Literally and figuratively.

I shined my light all around. The tunnel ceased just a few meters past us, where the massive rubble pile had collapsed through the street. Back the other way, it stretched away for hundreds of meters.

I turned back to RC. He had just finished hiding our suits again behind the debris we had gathered. He pointed at the hole.

"We'll put it back together," I said. "Someone went to a lot of trouble to create this hatchway. We should keep it as we found it until we know whether or not its builders are still around somewhere. And whether or not they are human."

"I doubt the wormheads built it."

"So do I. But let's play it safe."

"Got it."

As we hefted the pieces up to the hole, we noticed that the street's pavement adhered to each piece. It was like the pavement was alive and welcoming the return of missing bits.

"They've got the good pavement here," RC said. "Not like the stuff they have on the poorer colonial worlds where it's made out of oil and rock."

"Apparently so," I agreed.

After we had all the pieces in place, we replaced the plastic board, propping it up from underneath with wooden beams. They were just long enough to hold the board and pavement firmly in place.

Done, we turned around. RC flicked on his light.

"We'll use one light at a time," I said. "That way we'll conserve energy."

"Got it." He switched his light off.

"I'll go first. Keep your knife sheathed. I don't want you stabbing me in the ass."

"Got it. Besides, it's not like these knives will do us any good if we run into any wormheads."

"Probably not," I agreed. Hunched over, I led the way down the tunnel. In one hand, I carried my light. In the other, I carried my unsheathed combat knife.

We both wished we had our plasma rifles. But they depended upon our suits' power plants, which we had managed to deactivate before abandoning our suits. Attached by operating cords to our suits, our rifles were little more than clubs by themselves. As tight as this little tunnel was, we wouldn't be able to swing about them anyways. Our knives were better weapons than our rifles, though neither would protect us from Gorgon plasma rifles.

Walking hunched over in the tight tunnel took a toll on our stamina. I called a rest after about two hundred meters. We slipped down onto the deck.

Panting, RC fumbled for one of his water bottles. He sipped from it and put it back in its web pocket. "It's hot down here."

"It is."

"What time of the day is it now? Is it midday or afternoon?" RC asked.

"We left The Slab less than two hours ago. It's still morning."

"Is that all?" RC exclaimed. "It seems like it's been hours and hours."

"It hasn't, though."

"I know," RC said, nodding. His head was half-illuminated by my light. "Lion, if it's been such a short period of time, where are the others? What happened to Kamal, Ruby, Berk, and Virgil?"

"I don't know."

"I hope they're safe." He paused and stared at me. "Could it be that the reason the wormheads stopped chasing us is because they got into a firefight with the others?"

"Possibly. But I don't know."

"What do you know?" he asked me.

I took a deep breath and let it out slowly. "I know that if we don't make it back to the platoon, we'll never know what happened to the others."

"Seriously?" RC said.

"Seriously."

He got to his knees. "Then we better move on."

I got up. I banged my head on the overhead. I cursed.

"I don't think I've ever heard you curse like that, Lion."

"Get used to it. It's a new world."

"Okay."

We moved on. The tunnel continued onward, as confining as ever. Thirty more meters and we came to an intersection. Another passageway crossed through it at a right angle, while a shaft dropped straight down.

"Lion?"

"What is it, RC?"

"I'm thinking this might be an air shaft. Like for those big maglev trains in the subway system. They don't operate in a vacuum. The air they're pushing in front of them has to go somewhere and it has come from somewhere to fill in behind the trains, too."

"I think you're right."

"Thanks. Which way?"

"I don't know."

"How about down?" he suggested.

"How do we get down?"

"This shaft splits the intersection," he said. "There's probably hand holds in the shaft for access."

"Good idea. Unless the maintenance workers used an antigrav disc similar to ours for getting around."

"There's that," RC agreed. "How about shinning your light down and around the inside of the shaft?"

I said nothing. I was tired, sore, and concerned not just for the two of us but for the rest of my team as well. All this made me annoyed at RC's take-charge attitude, something I normally would've welcomed in him.

"Well?" he asked.

"Well what?" I snapped back.

He gaze dropped. "Nothing," he muttered.

I cursed myself. We were in a tight situation. I was his sergeant and it was my job to keep up his morale. And it was my job, and only mine, to keep up my own morale as well.

Sighing, I shined my light around the inside of the shaft. There were indented handholds leading downward on all four sides of the shaft.

"Turn your light on," I said.

"You got it, Lion," he replied, his voice a little happier. He switched his light on.

"I'll go first. My light will be off. Keep things illuminated for me. After I'm down and I've checked things out, I'll light the shaft for you."

"Got it."

I switched my light off and stowed it away. I sheathed my knife. Then I sat down, rolled onto my stomach, and backed my legs out over the shaft. Just as my torso reached the rim, RC grabbed me.

"Wait."

"Why?" I snapped, my annoyance gaining the better of me again.

"I hear something," he whispered.

"What?"

"Shhh!"

An angry retort was on my lips, but I heard something, too. It sounded light and bubbling.

"What is that, Lion? I can't make it out."

I couldn't make it out either. It drew closer. What was it? It seemed familiar, but alien. It sounded like something from long ago.

"Lion!" RC exclaimed in a whisper. "It sounds like kids."

TWENTY-TWO

"**K**IDS? DO YOU MEAN goats?" I asked.

"Goats? No, kids! Children. What do goats have to do with kids?"

I stared at him. His light blinded my eyes. Reaching out with a hand, I shoved his light aside. "Baby goats are also called kids."

"I didn't know that," he said. "I don't hear anything now."

"Me neither."

"Was it just my imagination?"

"I heard it, too. We can't both be insane. I think it was people."

"But, how? This city's empty. There are only Marines and monsters here. Unless it's...No. No."

"Get a hold of yourself!" I snapped. "There's no such thing as ghosts, except for maybe some alien races. You're not hearing the ghosts of anybody down here and you're not insane, unless you make yourself that way by fearing something that doesn't exist. Focus. I need you in the here and now."

"But what could it be?"

"Maybe it's the way the air moves around in these tunnels."

"But what if it's not?" RC demanded.

"Then it's people."

"But..."

"We're never going to know until we get down there and find out. Shine your light down there so I can see what I'm doing. Got it?"

He shined his light toward the shaft. Dangling my legs over the edge, I searched for a foothold. Finding one, I placed both feet on it.

Squiggling over the edge, my butt hanging over the open shaft, I reached down, searching for a handhold. I found one just centimeters beneath the edge. I grabbed it and began my descent.

RC crawled closer and shined his light on my hands and feet. Occasionally, he swept his light down the shaft to make certain all was well.

It was a long way down. My hands and arms ached as I descended. Sixty hand holds later, I reached the bottom.

Panting from my exertion, I leaned forward against the shaft. After a moment's rest, I stepped back and switched my light on. Four tunnels opened before me. Beside each opening was a set of handholds rising to each of the intersecting tunnels above.

"Come on down," I called. He switched his light off and I cast my light's beam upward. After several long minutes, he dropped down beside me.

"Whew! What a climb," RC gasped, breathing hard from the exertion of the descent.

"Yeah," I agreed. "We've gotten too soft flying around in our armored suits."

"You can say that again."

"Why?" I retorted, smirking at him. My light cast weird shadows on our faces, making us look wicked and demented.

He stared at me. I laughed, and he laughed, too.

"Which way?"

Shrugging, I shined my high beam down each of the four tunnels. They all looked the same.

At the last, I said, "We'll take this one."

"Why?"

"Why not?"

He shrugged. "Lead on, Lion."

"Thanks." I hunched over and stepped inside, my knife again in my left hand, my light in my right. "Another long tunnel to crawl down," I groused.

"For you, maybe," he joked.

I glanced back at him. He could almost stand straight up. Lucky for him.

"Why the hell aren't these tunnels bigger?"

"Lion, do you think your mother will appreciate language you've learned in the Marines?"

I glared at him. He grinned back. We shared another moment of laughter.

I turned back and caught my breath. Before me, illuminated in my light, stood a dirty little girl. Terror filled her eyes.

She screamed.

TWENTY-THREE

BEFORE I COULD REACT, she turned and ran down the tunnel. We pursued her as fast as we could.

"Don't be afraid!" I cried out. "We're Marines. We're the good guys. Wait. Wait." We chased after her.

She ran fast. As fast as we could move was not fast enough to catch up with her. She disappeared. My light shined down the tunnel. We couldn't see her, couldn't find her. She was gone.

"Where'd she go?" RC exclaimed. "Where'd she come from? What's she doing down here?"

"I don't know."

"How'd she survive all the killing? Why haven't the Gorgons found her?"

"I don't know."

"How are we going to find her?"

"I don't know, but we have to. If she's survived all this time, there might be others as well. There have to be others. And if there's others, then there's hope for us, too."

"But, Lion, how have they survived down here for so long? Where do they get their food? What about water?

What about the wormheads? How do they evade them? How can this be?"

"I don't know, I don't know, I don't know!" I exclaimed. "The only way we're going to answer any of those questions is by finding her and any others like her. Now, let's get going."

"Got it."

We scurried down the tunnel, our lights illuminating it. We ran hundreds of meters until the tunnel ended, finding no sign of her.

"Where is she?" I snarled. I had run through the tunnel hunched over while RC only kept his head down a bit. I panted and gasped for air while he just breathed hard.

"Maybe there's a side tunnel we didn't see," he said.

"How is that possible?" I snapped back at him. "We shined our lights on everything. We didn't miss anything."

"Then maybe she's not real."

"You think we're insane?" I demanded.

"Maybe she's a ..."

"There's no such thing as ghosts!"

"Then maybe she's a hologram."

Exhausted, I sat down on the deck. I put my knife away and motioned for him to do the same. "Why would she be a hologram?"

"To mislead the wormheads, if they come down here."

The air seemed too thick to breathe. I lay back on the tunnel floor.

RC sat beside me. He pulled one of my water bottles out of my vest and opened it. "Sit up, Lion. Have a sip."

I sat up and sipped some water. "She can't be a hologram," I gasped, still breathing hard.

"Why not?"

"Because I don't want her to be, that's why."

"Then where is she?" he asked.

"I don't know. But she's not a hologram. And we have to find her. Got that?"

"I've got it."

I took my water bottle from him and put it back in my vest. He helped me up. I banged my head on the overhead and cursed.

"Sorry," he said.

"Where could she be?"

"Maybe..."

"Maybe what?" I demanded. I was tired of his ghost stories and fantasies about holographic children. I wanted reality. I wanted a living, breathing child I could touch and know she was real.

"Maybe there's a hidden entrance somewhere," he offered.

"Now you're talking smart," I said. "Let's find it."

"How will we do that?"

I drew a circle with one of my fingers and, with difficulty, we turned around in the narrow tunnel.

"Now what?"

"I'll run my right hand slowly along this side of the tunnel and you run your left hand on that side."

"Got it. But we've come three or four hundred meters. This could take hours."

"You got something better to do?" I snarled at him.

"Not really."

"Then let's go."

We moved back the way we came, slowly, our hands feeling the sides of the tunnel. After an hour or so we reached the access shaft again.

"Nothing," I said, exasperated. "Nothing, nothing, nothing!"

"Maybe we missed something."

"How did we do that?" I demanded.

"I don't know, Lion, but we both saw her run that way and now she's not there. We must have missed something."

"But, what?"

"I don't know. Maybe she went through the end of the tunnel."

"RC, you're a genius."

"Oh, Lion, stop making fun of me," he groaned.

"I'm not making fun of you. Somehow, RC, you manage to think of things that I never do."

"You would've thought of it at some point, Lion."

"Now you're making fun of me," I said. He started to protest, but I stopped him. "I'm just kidding. You're right, we didn't go all the way to the end of the tunnel. Maybe there's a hatch there, somewhere. Let's go find out."

"You mean something like the one you tumbled through on the street above?" he asked.

"Exactly!"

We sprinted back down the tunnel again. Slowing before we reached the end, we abruptly found ourselves falling through another hidden entrance.

There was no bottom as we dropped into darkness, our lights fallen from our hands. We slid on a slick slide and tumbled out onto an invisible floor cloaked by the darkness around us.

Abruptly, blinding lights came on. We covered out eyes.

A female voice from beyond the lights snarled at us. "Who are you and what do you want?"

"We're Marines, ma'am," RC said.

"What's that to me?" the voice spat.

"We're looking for a little girl," I said.

"What do you want with her?" The hostility in the woman's voice scared me. Why was she so angry?

Before I could answer, I heard feet scraping all around me. I instinctively reached for my knife.

"Touch that knife and you're a dead man!" the woman yelled.

TWENTY-FOUR

FROZE. I WAS KNEELING on the floor. Somewhere to my right was RC.

My eyes were growing accustomed to the light. Before me stood a silhouetted form: a human form.

I started to get up.

"Don't move."

I finished standing up, pleased that my head didn't bang into the ceiling above me. "Listen, we're Interstellar Marines. We've been cut off from our forces. I'm trying to locate the rest of my team. If you don't want us here, then we don't want to be here. Just show us how to get out and we'll leave you be."

"You're not Marines," the voice said. "I've seen Marines before and they wear big ugly armored suits. You look more like scavengers to me. You're not going anywhere."

"You're going to kill us?" RC asked.

"I never said that."

"Well, we're going anyways," I replied. "Let's go, RC."

The woman hefted something up. It looked like a rifle. "My plasma rifle might be an antique," she said, with deadly intent, "but it'll fry you just as well as any Marine rifle would."

"It'll also fry everyone behind me and some of those to either side of me as well," I said, stepping forward. "Please, put it down. I won't hurt you."

"Get back. I'll shoot," the woman cried out. "I will."

"I think not." I grabbed the barrel and pointed it towards the ceiling. Then I pushed the woman through the crowd beyond the bright lights. Blinking my eyes to adjust them to the dimmer light, I saw children holding powered lighting units to either side of me.

The woman's features became visible.

"Who are you?" I asked.

"Lucy Brannon. Let go of my gun." She was shorter than me and a bit shorted than RC. Her shoulder-length hair was almost black. Her features appeared Asiatic, with high cheekbones. She wore tan overalls and boots.

She smelled musty. The whole place smelled musty.

"It's dangerous to play with a weapon you're not familiar with," I said. This particular rifle possessed a backpack power unit. It looked a century old. I noticed that the rifle's power setting was turned to the maximum and that the safety was off. However, a glance at the backpack revealed that the power unit had not been activated. Whether this was an error on her part or planned, I didn't know. I was just grateful it wasn't on.

"Let go of my gun," Lucy said.

"It's not a gun, ma'am, it's a rifle," RC retorted.

"Give it to me, please. We are Marines. I'm Sergeant Thandiwe Biyela and that's Private First Class Raymond Carlyle. You can call him RC. And you may call me Lion."

"I'd like to call you something else."

"I understand. Please, give me your weapon. The safety's off but so is its power plant."

"And if I don't give it to you, will you take it by force?" she demanded.

"Yes," I replied. What choice did I have if I didn't want her to kill RC and me, most of the children as well?

"All right, take it!" She removed the backpack and dropped the unit on the deck.

"RC, come get this."

"Aye, aye, Lion."

"Ma'am, could you ask the children to turn some of those lights off?" I requested.

"Barry, Denise, leave your lights on. The rest of you turn yours off."

"Okay, Lucy," a girl said.

But a boy asked: "You okay, Lucy?"

"I'm okay." Lucy looked at me. "I am okay, aren't I?"

"You are," I confirmed.

"Now what?"

It was a good question. With less light around me, I could see that the chamber was filled with children. Some of them were little, maybe five or six years old. Others were older. Some even appeared to be teenagers.

"I asked you a question, Mister Marine!" she snapped.

"Is this everyone?" I replied.

"No."

"How many children are there?"

"Many."

The whole situation bewildered me. A quick head count gave me thirty children. How could so many have survived so long?

I shook my head.

"What's wrong now? Trying to figure out how to rob us? To take from us what little we don't have?"

"Miss Brannon, we're not here to take anything from you. We're just trying to survive," I said.

"That's Mrs. Brannon. Go survive somewhere else."

I just stared at her. I didn't understand any of this and I certainly didn't understand her attitude. Why was she so belligerent?

"Mrs. Brannon, is there somewhere we can go and talk?"

"No, there's not," she said. "You said you were going. So go."

"Why are you so angry at us?" I asked.

"You attacked Annabel Li," she accused us.

"Who?"

"The little girl you tried to kill. She told us how you came after her with your knife. Why would we trust someone who wanted to kill a child?"

"Lion never did that," RC calmly explained. "We were trying to find a way out and as we moved down the tunnels, Lion led with a light in one hand and his knife in the other. We didn't know what we'd find down here. Some wild animals might be lurking around here, or maybe even the wormheads."

"Liar, liar, pants on fire!" one of the kids chanted.

"He's not lying," I said. "Look, our suits malfunctioned and we had to abandon them. A knife's not much of a weapon against a plasma rifle, but it's all we've got. We're just trying to find our way back."

"You chased after her."

"What would you expect me to do?" I growled at her. "We just escaped from the enemy with barely our lives. Four of our friends are missing. We stumble upon these tunnels and then we come across a little girl all by herself? And the first thing she does is scream and run away?"

"You terrified her."

"And I'm truly, truly sorry for that," I replied. "I haven't seen a living child since arriving here. We've been fighting for this world for almost a year now. We're dying so others may live. And you hate us for trying to survive? For being shocked at finding a living child beneath the ruins of this city?"

"Fancy words."

I'd had enough. I took the archaic plasma rifle from RC. I spent a moment examining it and then switched on its power plant. I handed it to Mrs. Brannon.

"Here," I said. "Kill me. It's what you really want to do. You want to blame someone for this war and for those monsters out there. You want to punish someone and now you've found him. So go ahead and kill me."

I turned my back on her and pushed my way through the crowd of children. "Come on, RC, let's see if we can find a way out of here. There's nothing for us down here."

"Okay, Lion."

We crossed the chamber. A small figure stood before us, blocking our way. It was the little girl, Annabel Li, who we had chased through the tunnel.

"Don't go," she said. "I'm sorry I ran away. I was scared."

I knelt down in front of her. "I get scared all the time."

A boy, a bit bigger and older than Annabel Li, came over. "You get scared? But you're Marines. Marines don't get scared."

"Everyone gets scared," RC said.

"I'm sorry I was scared," Annabel said. She placed a hand on my arm. Her grimy little face looked up at me. "Don't go."

"Why not?" I asked.

"Because I don't want you to."

"Why?"

"I don't know. I just don't want you to go."

Reaching into my vest, I removed a handkerchief. I unfolded it and then pulled a bottle of water out. After opening the bottle and pouring a little of the water on the hanky, I gently washed her face. "You're beautiful," I said, smiling at her.

"Really?"

"Really." All of a sudden, she leaped into my arms. And I wanted to cry. I don't know why, except holding her made me think of my family back on El Diablo Verde. I had never held a child before in my life. I started to put her back down but she struggled in my arms. Holding onto her, I carefully stood up.

"RC," I said.

"Got it." He gathered up my water bottle and hanky, closed the bottle, and stuffed both items into my vest for me.

Mrs. Brannon came over to me. I noticed that the plasma rifle's power pack was switched off. "I guess I was wrong," she said.

"Not entirely," I replied. "You're protecting these children. I can't fault you for that."

"Thanks."

"Don't mention it."

"I won't. Come with me. I'll show you where we live. I think you'll find it interesting."

"I'm certain I will," I replied.

"And by the way, you can call me Lucy," she said.

TWENTY-FIVE

LUCY AND THE CHILDREN lived in a large underground facility. The central station for the maglev trains that cruised the city's subway system, it consisted of various rooms, including quarters for workers, robots, equipment storage, spare parts, and everything one could imagine necessary for operating and maintaining the subway system. There was running water and fully functional lavatories, a fusion power plant for powering the trains, the lights, air purification, water purification, and much, much more. There was also a kitchen and cafeteria, with still operating freezers.

It would have been perfect except for the fact that after the Gorgons had ravaged Belden and moved on, small groups of survivors had scavenged almost everything they could from the station. After wandering the subways, hiding from scavengers who took everything, and avoiding the rare Gorgon patrol, Lucy and her band of children had found the station still operational, but empty.

So they settled here. And waited, not knowing for what. Maybe they waited for the war to end. Maybe they waited for someone to rescue them. Who knew what they waited for or why, but they waited. And while they waited, they hid. And while hiding, they searched for food, for medicine, for clothing, for tools, for weapons, for whatever was left.

And all the while they hid underground, the Twenty-fourth Marine Brigade took back Belden from the Gorgons. And then the Gorgons took it back from brigade. And then the brigade took it again; but only part of it.

Now, after months of fighting, RC and I had found this little band of refugees. But we didn't know what to do with them.

"How did you shepherd all these kids together?" RC asked. "How did you survive with all these mouths to feed, all these bodies to keep an eye on, while avoiding the Gorgons?"

"The Gorgons were the least of our problems," Lucy replied.

"The scavengers?" I asked.

She nodded. "Yes. Once decent people, they fell so far and fast that survival is all they know. Even the rats are better creatures than the people we met."

"I like rats," a little boy said. "I love roasting them, they taste so good!"

RC stared at the boy. We sat in the cafeteria, surrounded by Lucy's flock. "He's joking, right?"

"No. The scavengers left little for us, except the rats. And there are plenty of rats down here. We've lived on them for almost a year now. And there's enough of them that we could live on them for many more years to come."

"I see," I said. I toyed with the idea of asking for some rat to eat. Except for our field rations, made of compressed grains injected with vitamins, minerals, and extra calories, we hadn't had any real food for months. Even rat would taste better than our current rations. At least, I hoped rat would taste better.

"Would you like to try some?" Lucy asked, smiling.

"Hell no!" RC exclaimed.

I glanced at him and then turned back to Lucy. She smiled, her eyes twinkling with amusement. "Maybe later," I said.

"Lion!" RC protested. I ignored him.

"So, these are all the children?" I asked.

"Yes. Mike and I could only handle so many. There were a few more, mostly teenagers. The scavengers got some of them. The Gorgons murdered many more."

"Who's Mike?" I warily asked.

"He was my husband."

I didn't like the sound of that. Her phrasing sounded final and I was afraid that it meant he was dead.

"What happened to him?" RC asked.

Lucy looked away. After a moment, she looked back at us. "Mike led some of the older boys, mostly teens, after a group of scavengers who had taken Valerie."

"Who was Valerie?" I asked.

"A fifteen-year old girl who we had rescued. When she disappeared it became evident to Mike and me that maybe some scavengers had been watching us."

"Why'd they want her?" RC wondered.

"Why do you think?" Lucy growled. "She was a woman and they didn't have any."

"Son of a bitch!" RC said. "Did you get her back?"

"No. We never saw her again, not alive, anyways."

"They killed her?" RC asked, anger in his voice.

"In a manner of speaking." Lucy stopped and looked at the children. "They abused her until she couldn't take it anymore and then she died."

RC stared at the floor. He didn't ask any more questions.

I reached out and touched Lucy's arm with my hand. Lucy looked at my hand and said, "Thanks."

I withdrew my hand. "What about Mike and the others?"

"The Gorgons found them. Two of the younger boys followed Mike's group. Everyone loved Valerie and these boys wanted to help get her back. Actually, they just wanted to kill the men who had stolen Valerie from us.

"Well, the boys hung back a bit. They took cover when the Gorgons ambushed Mike and his guys."

"So they fried them?" I said.

"No! Mike and the others died like so many of the others in this city died!"

"I don't understand."

"Have you seen the tall building, the one that part of the top has been ripped from?"

"We have. We call it The Slab."

"That a good name for it. The rest of us know it as the slaughterhouse," Lucy said.

"The what?" RC said.

"After the Gorgons conquered Belden, they rounded up the survivors. Not everyone had been fried and not many had managed to evacuate," Lucy explained.

"The Gorgons rarely take prisoners," I stated. "Our very existence drives them insane. How many survivors were there?"

"Thousands. Mike and I were among the captured. So were Annabel's family, her parents and grandparents, her brothers and sisters, including twin baby brothers."

I didn't like how this sounded. Her voice trembled. There was fear and anger in it, intense anger, the kind of anger that led to acts of extreme violence and retribution.

"Valerie and her parents were among them, also. But Val was only fourteen then. Age didn't matter. What those monsters did burned holes in our souls forever."

I didn't know if I wanted her to continue or not. There was a morbid fascination to her story. But I saw how the memories affected her. She had paled. Her voice had cracked and her eyes widened, but anger, as much as fear, filled them. I could almost hear her heart pounding.

"They took us onto the roof. Dozens of guards lined the sides. Gunboats hovered in the sky. They could only fit a few hundred people on top at a time. But they kept the rest of the prisoners inside the building. They made us stand at the windows and watch."

She paused. I glanced at RC, who was staring at the children. They trembled in terror.

"RC, take them outside," I said. "Do it now."

RC stayed where he sat.

"You heard me, RC. Take the children out."

"You got it, Lion. Let's go, now. Everyone! Move it."

Lucy waited until RC and the kids were gone. While she waited, she trembled, tears running down her face. A wild, animalistic expression covered her face. She breathed short and fast, at times gasping for her breath.

"It's okay, Lucy," I said. "You're safe. You're safe."

"The children!" she exclaimed.

"They're all outside. RC! Keep them out there. Close the doors. Got it?"

"Got it, Lion." I heard a squeak in RC's voice. I'd never heard it crack like that before.

"You don't have to tell it," I said.

"I have to," she said. "I have to tell it."

She stood. Her body shivered and shook. I stood, too, ready to catch her, to comfort her, to save her if I could.

"They started with the babies. They pitched them from the building. Even inside the building we could hear the babies screaming. Then they threw some of the children off. I watched as they fell. They fell and fell and fell and fell!"

"Easy, Lucy," I said. "It's over."

"It'll never be over. Never! They fell. And when they hit the ground they exploded into bloody, bloody sprays."

She stared at me and I felt her terror. In fact, her eyes terrified me.

"We were screaming now inside the building. Women and mothers were screaming and crying, the men yelling, cursing, and crying out for their children, for all the children. Bodies rained from all sides of the building. Children, adults, even some of the monsters. They fought for their lives on the roof. They fought. And we fought inside. People burst into flames from plasma fire and we grabbed whatever furniture we could and smashed the Gorgons' heads. And then the gunboats opened fire, first against the roof and then through the windows at everyone inside. It was insane, horribly insane!

"We ran. Mike and I ran. There was a little girl on the floor, screaming and crying. I picked her up. She kicked me and grabbed my hair, pulling and tearing at it. Mike grabbed another girl at the door. She was older and terrified. We were all terrified."

What was there to say at such horror?

"The walls exploded around us. We rushed the guards on the floors below. They burned us down by the hundreds.

Mike and I, with Valerie and Annabel, escaped. We caught a few terrified boys and girls on the way. We ran out of the building. We ran and ran and ran. And we got away."

I nodded. Nothing would ever matter to her again after this. Nothing at all could ever matter again.

"We survived. Somehow. After that, Mike and I made it our task to save as many as we could. We could have saved more. We should have saved more."

"So, the boys saw Mike and the others tossed from a building?" I asked. I shouldn't have asked this question. I should have waited until later. But I didn't. I should have waited, but I didn't.

Lucy screamed. "Yes, yes! They took them to the slaughterhouse and tossed them away. They tossed them away like trash. Like they were nothing of value alive. Like their lives didn't matter."

She collapsed on the floor. I dropped beside her.

She looked up at me. "The boys came back and told me. They found Valerie. They said they buried her. The scavengers were gone. They had taken everything from her, including her life. They tossed her aside like the Gorgons tossed Mike and the others aside. The boys guessed what had happened to her. They cried all the way back and couldn't stop crying when they told me what had happened. They cried for weeks."

I stared at her. She trembled, her whole body shaking from her memories, from reliving the most horrible experiences of her life; perhaps the most horrible things anyone could experience.

I marveled at her. Her strength, her stamina, her will had kept her alive. She lived for the children more than for herself. Alone, she might have descended into the primitive savagery of the scavengers. Or she might have just wandered about until the scavengers took her like they took poor Valerie.

What can you say to someone who has suffered so much? What can you say to someone who has seen such horror? What can you say when the world was twisted inside out by so much terror?

In a way, she was like a Marine. She kept busy, and in keeping busy she kept the horrible memories at bay. But it wasn't enough to just try to keep those nightmares away because at some point they come after you. Traumatic events such as Lucy had experienced haunt you forever unless you deal with them. And the only real way to deal with them is to tell others about them. If you don't, those experiences will consume you and everyone you love, too.

However, Lucy had made a start at dealing with her horrific experiences. She was on her way to healing. But she would need much more therapy than just sharing her horrors with me.

Yet, the best therapy for her surrounded her. Lucy had thirty children to protect and take care. She had a reason to live. And that was reason enough to survive.

TWENTY-SIX

WE SPENT THE REST of the day and that night with Lucy and the children. I wanted RC and me to stand guard while they slept, but Lucy said no. She showed me a series of automatic sensors that kept the compound secure. She had installed them after Valerie was stolen from them.

Many of the children wanted to sleep near RC and me, but Lucy forbade it. Like any good gunnery sergeant shepherding her Marines, Lucy maintained firm discipline among the children. They slept in their usual places. But she promised them we'd be there when they awoke the next day. That calmed them down.

Even so, many of them talked well into the night, excited by our presence. Most of their conversations concerned if we were here to rescue them.

After the last of the children fell asleep, Lucy rose from her bed and came over to sit beside me.

"You're the best thing that has happened to them in such a long time. I don't know how I'm going to tell them that you're not here to rescue us."

I sat beside her. "I wish we could. But we have to find the rest of our team and get back to our outpost. Besides, two knives and an almost worn out old plasma rifle aren't any protection against the Gorgons."

"You're right." She paused and looked at me. "I'm sorry about my earlier behavior."

"I already told you that I understood and that I didn't hold it against you. And you promised not to bring it up again."

She laughed, softly. "I did, didn't I?"

"You did."

She pulled her knees up and wrapped her arms around them. "It's been months since I've had another adult to talk to. Some days I almost felt like I couldn't go on anymore. But the children give me strength and energy."

"So I've noticed," I said.

"There's still plenty of food to eat, though nothing fresh. We can last another year, if necessary. You're welcome to take some of it with you."

"We have our own."

She laughed again. "I've seen it. Even as old as our frozen food supplies are, what the scavengers never found, ours is still much better than yours."

I laughed. "It is. But ours is easier for us to carry than yours is. Besides, you extended our supplies by a whole day. And I have to say, I can't remember when I last had beef, even frozen beef."

"Thanks," Lucy said. "But I'm not much of a cook."

"You're better than any of the robot cooks we have!" RC blurted out, his back to us. He lay on his left side and I'd thought he was asleep.

"Go back to sleep," I growled. "And mind your own business."

"Got it. And I will!"

We chuckled. One of the children stirred and we hushed up. Everyone slept in the cafeteria, the largest and most secure room.

"Well," she said, "I should get some sleep."

"Don't go. Not yet."

"Why not?"

I reached out and caressed her face with my hand. Her face was oily, her skin rough, but I didn't mind.

She leaned in close and kissed me. "That's for letting me tell my story. I couldn't tell the children. They all lived through it, anyways. But I needed to tell someone. Thank-you."

I kissed her. We slid underneath the blanket she had provided me. We kissed some more.

"I shouldn't," she whispered. "The children might wake."

"Shhh," I whispered. I slid a hand underneath her shirt. She moaned as my hand brushed across her stomach and then found her breasts. She helped me out of my uniform and I helped her undress. I climbed on top of her.

"Oh, god," RC said.

"Mine your own business," I hissed at him.

"How can I, with the two of you fornicating right next to me?" he hissed back.

Lucy and I started giggling. We couldn't control ourselves. She kissed me again and slid out from underneath me.

"Don't go."

"Another time," she said. "I've lost the moment."

We dressed, as quietly and quickly as we could.

"Thank you for a wonderful evening," she said, giggling.

"You, too." We kissed again. Then she crawled back to her spot, careful not to disturb a single child.

I rolled over to RC. I heard his breathing, slow and rhythmic. He was asleep.

I sighed and stretched out on the floor. From my knees down to my feet, I stuck out from under my blanket. After a little while, I fell asleep.

A few hours later, we left. It was the best way. No long and hard goodbyes to suffer through. No clinging children begging for us to take them with us. No sorrow, no pain, no fear expressed.

It was hard not to say goodbye. But it was the best way.

RC and I stopped just outside the cafeteria's entrance and watched the children as they slept. They had caught our hearts. But we couldn't do anything for them.

Closing the doors, we crept down the hall. After we found our way out, disabling one of Lucy's sensors along the way, RC said, "You think they'll be okay?"

I shook my head. "I don't know. I hope so."

He nodded. "Where to now?"

"Back to the outpost, I guess."

"Got it."

We moved on.

TWENTY-SEVEN

WE FOUND A SECURED hatch, which we opened. We entered it and secured it behind us. In darkness, we switched on our flashlights. Before us stretched a ladder high up into a shaft, ending at a hatch far above us. I directed RC to shine his light upward while I climbed the ladder. It was a long way to the top, longer than any of the other ones we had so far encountered.

At the top, I discovered a locking wheel on the bottom of the hatch. I gave it a hard twist, but it didn't move.

"RC, come up here. I need your help," I called down.

"Coming up, Lion."

I shined my light downward, making sure the light was away from his face. It took him a while to reach me. As he drew near, I wiggled to the side and wrapped my legs around one of the ladder's guide poles. Once up, he wrapped his legs around the other guide pole. With two big men at the top of the ladder, space was tight.

"What now?" he asked.

With difficulty, I hooked my light to my vest. It pointed upward. He followed my lead.

"Now," I explained, "we'll grab the wheel and turn it to the left."

"Got it. But are you sure it's a righty-tighty, lefty-loosey type of wheel?"

"I sure hope so."

We grabbed the wheel and heaved. It didn't budge. We twisted harder. It still didn't move.

RC climbed closer to the wheel. He ducked his head and shoulders down and grabbed the wheel with both hands. Our legs touched and were in each other's way, while our bodies were crammed against the hatch and wheel.

We twisted hard. A little movement happened. We twisted harder, grunting. Some more movement occurred. We put our all into it, grunting and yelling while twisting and turning. The wheel gave a little way.

We stopped and gasped for air. Panting, we attacked the wheel again. Panting and gasping, twisting, turning, cursing, yelling we moved the rusty wheel. Again and again, we twisted and turned it, until it gave way.

"Now what?" he asked, gasping for his breath.

"Climb down beneath me and shine your light up here," I said, also gasping for my breath.

Moving down, he shined his light on the hatch.

"Be ready for anything," I said.

"I'm as ready as I'll ever be," he replied.

I shoved against the hatch. It barely moved.

I climbed closer, bending my back and pressing it against the wheel and the hatch. The position was awkward and painful. Shoving up with my legs, barely keeping my balance, I pushed. Pain seared through my neck, my back, my groin. I kept at it until the hatch popped open.

I had to twist and grab the wheel to keep my balance as the hatch flipped over onto its top. I climbed up out of the shaft, RC quickly following me.

We were on the street. The sky was purple, the stars above shining brightly. I crawled away from the hatch while RC closed it. My body ached. I remained motionless while my nanites repaired the damage done to me. It would take a lot longer than the few minutes I rested for the nano-machines within me to repair me, but I didn't have time to spare.

RC helped me up. I motioned toward the open hatch. With an epic effort, he closed it. There was no locking wheel on this side. The two-meter wide hatch lay even with the pavement. We scooted loose debris onto the hatch, covering it up.

I had no idea where we were in relation to where we'd been. The buildings were too tall, the darkness too pervasive, for me to see The Slab, the only reference point I had without my suit's guidance system.

Half a block away there seemed to be a clearing among the buildings.

"Wonder what that is," RC said.

"Let's go take a look."

"Is it safe to do so?" he questioned. "We might be surrounded by Gorgons."

"We probably are."

We walked toward the field. My body ached with pain, but I felt a slight warmth within me as my nanites repaired the damage inside me. Nonetheless, walking hurt.

As we neared the open area, we saw light emanating from the nearby buildings. It illuminated what seemed to be a wide, open field about a city-block square. It had a sort of yellowish-orange cast to it. It appeared to be covered with dried and flattened grass.

I motioned RC toward a large, fallen block of masonry near the field. We stopped behind it.

I stifled a groan.

"You okay?" RC whispered.

"Just a little pain," I lied.

"But you're getting better, right?" he asked, concerned.

"I am," I groaned.

"Good. What's a big field doing here in the middle of the city?" he asked.

"Maybe it was a park."

"What kind of park?"

"I don't know. Maybe it was for sports, or children. Or maybe it was a nature park."

RC stared at it. "It doesn't make sense to me. There's no equipment for sports or children. It's just a flat field."

I shrugged, which hurt.

"And why is it lit?" The lights illuminating the field were four stories above us.

"That's a good question." One I had no answer for. "Let's see if we can get into one of these buildings."

RC nodded. Carefully, we moved to our left. The first building was too shattered for us to enter. We skirted in front of it, hidden in the darkness.

An alley separated us from the next building. Glancing down it, I saw movement. Stepping back, I reached out and grabbed RC's shoulder, stilling him.

I put a finger to my lips. He nodded. Just enough light reflected from the orange field for us to see each other.

As he looked at me, I drew my knife. He drew his. I nodded and turned back toward the alley. The shape coming this way wasn't human.

I had never killed anyone, or anything before, with a knife, but I knew what to do. One of the beauties of the Marines was training for anything and everything, including killing an alien with a knife.

My heart pounded, both from the repairs occurring within me, and from nervous anticipation. From what I could tell, my victim was unarmed and unarmored. But it possessed more senses than me in those wormlike tendrils on its head. Could it sense what I intended for it as it came down the alley? Could it smell my fear, hear it, even taste it? If so, was it ready to kill me? Was it planning my murder, as I now planned its murder?

It moved closer.

I held my breath. My body, filled with adrenalin, trembled. My grip tightened on my knife.

It came into view.

It turned toward me!

I leaped at it. My knife shoved toward its chest. Its body armor deflected the blow.

The Gorgon bounded backwards. I stumbled. I heard a loud buzzing sound. RC leaped past me, his arm raised.

The buzzing became a shrieking whistle. The creature's four arms flailed at RC and he fell to the ground.

Tackling the monster, I knocked it down, landing on it. I slashed my knife at its head. A rubbery, tentacle-like arm knocked my hand back, my knife spinning away. We rolled over and it landed on me, pinning me beneath its body. It battered me with its arms, its tiny claws pinched at my flesh. I glanced into its faceless face, the worms on its head waving wildly.

Thrusting my knees up and toward me, I flung the thing over my head, onto the ground. It hit with a wet slap.

Rolling over, I jumped up. My knife laid on the ground, several meters away, to the creature's left.

The Gorgon popped up, a strange, dark liquid streaming from the lower of the two orifices on its face; what everyone supposed was a mouth.

It charged me, its arms wind-milling above its head. The shrieking whistle became a screeching whistle. I leaped at it, my legs stretching out in front of me as I rolled onto my side while still airborne. My feet slammed into the Gorgon's armored chest and it tumbled backwards while I crashed to the ground, the wind knocked out of me.

I gasped as I struggled to get up. I heard a wet smacking sound. And another. And yet another still.

Gasping, I made it to my feet. I glanced at the alien. It lay on the ground, its legs twitching. Two large pieces of masonry covered its head. Some of its tendrils waved and wiggled, but the rest were dead.

RC, his face bruised and bleeding, tottered toward it, a large piece of masonry in his hands. Stopping beside the Gorgon, RC lifted the large block up and slammed it down onto the other blocks covering the alien's head.

The Gorgon's whole body shivered. The last tendrils stopped moving.

Using the dusty sleeve of his field uniform to wipe the blood from his face, he smiled a bloody smile at me. He spat blood on the ground. "Just like squishing a bug."

I shook my head. It hurt. The nanites in my body would be working on me for a long time.

Glancing around, I didn't see any other aliens. I walked over and picked up my knife. I examined it. It seemed fine, so I sheathed it. I went back to the Gorgon's corpse.

"Those things are hard to kill."

"You just have to use the right tools for the right job," RC said. He began laughing, stopping to spit blood and then laughing some more.

I laughed, too. But it hurt too much and I quit. "Let's get out of here."

"Where to?"

"Anywhere but here."

"What about that?" he said, nodding toward the corpse.

"Leave it."

"But what if they find it?"

"Let them."

"How is that good, Lion?" RC asked me.

"It's not. But it doesn't matter."

"Why not?" he demanded.

"Because I'm leaving. You coming?"

"I am," he replied.

TWENTY-EIGHT

WE WALKED ACROSS THE orange-colored field, our destination one of the buildings in the far corner. What did it matter if the Gorgons saw us in the illuminated field? We had barely survived an encounter with an unarmed Gorgon. How might we fair against two, ten, a hundred of the monsters?

Fortune sometimes favors the bold and our audacity was all that kept RC and me alive as we trudged across the field, its orange grass, wet with dew, sticking to our boots.

"Why are we doing this?" RC asked. "Why aren't we hiding in the shadows?"

"Because, if they're going to kill us, going to fry us with their plasma weapons, I want them to see that we're Marines and unafraid of them."

"But isn't it better to survive than to throw your life away for an empty moment of vanity?" RC asked.

I stopped and turned to look at him. We were only meters from the shadows at the far end of the field. "You amaze me," I said.

"Why?" he asked. "Is it because I'm not a good enough Marine for you?"

"RC, you are by far the best Marine I've ever served with."

"Then why do I amaze you?"

"Because of your moments of brilliance."

"I don't follow you," he replied.

"You have this ability to pierce right through all the crap around us to the truth behind it all. Just now I was angry and sick of all this fighting and dying and wanted to make a statement. But I was only making that statement to myself, that's who. And what good is that, if I get us killed? It was my vanity, my anger, talking to me. And you saw through all that, even if you didn't know you were doing it. You reminded me of my duty as a Marine and that displaying vanity was not part of it."

RC stared me. "If that's so, then why are we still standing out here in the open?"

I laughed, turned, and sprinted into the shadows, RC right behind me. Once covered by darkness again, we slowed down, picking our way through the broken masonry and debris. Sprinting through this kind of terrain in the darkness was an accident just waiting to happen.

Keeping low, we crept inside the nearest building. From what I could tell, it was fairly intact. Though darkness still filled the sky, in a few short hours the sun would rise. I hoped this building might be tall enough for us to get our bearings, to locate The Slab and know, more or less, where we were.

We flicked our lights on, keeping them on low power, conserving battery life. There were lots of fallen metal supports, broken furniture, and masonry scattered about. All the lift shafts were destroyed. In the center of the building, in a great common area, we found a huge hole in the floor. When we shined our lights down it, it disappeared deep beneath the ground. Shining our lights upward, we saw the hole extended high into the building, maybe all the way to the roof.

"Looks kinda familiar, doesn't it?" RC said.

"It does," I agreed.

"Think it might be a pattern with the wormheads?"

"I think it's a definite pattern. I think the Gorgons maneuver through the sewers until under a building and then blast their way through the center so they can slaughter the occupants."

"How do they know where they are when they're in the sewers?" RC asked. "I mean, how do they know when to blast outward and upward?"

"The same way we would," I said. "They probably have sky craft or maybe just micro-probes orbiting above. When their sensors tell them to, then they start blasting away."

"Well, what're we going to do now?"

"Find a way up and wait near the roof. When the sun comes up, maybe we'll locate a pathway home."

He nodded. We were tired and sore and bleeding from the small wounds inflicted upon us by the alien. But we kept going. We didn't want to rest until we found a safe place to hide. Then we could care for our wounds.

After ten minutes of searching, we located a stairwell in reasonably fair condition. We climbed it for seven levels until we came upon a great hole in the side of the building that obliterated the stairwell. Our lights revealed upon the shattered stairs human skeletal remains.

Backtracking down a level, we located another stairwell. We managed to climb higher until another hole opened before us. We backtracked again. Finding yet another stairwell, we climbed it. When it ended, it was because a still intact piece of the roof blocked it.

We wandered around the top floor. Finally, we found a blasted-out corner that allowed us to look across the city as Thea arose. In the distance, maybe eight blocks away, stood The Slab. From the angle it presented to us, we realized we had traveled about a kilometer to its right.

"Lion, I think where Lucy and kids stay is further this way than straight back from The Slab," RC said.

"I agree. But how do we get back to the outpost from here?"

RC said nothing. He just stared out across the shattered city.

I stared, too. Even with all the destruction, it was still a beautiful city.

I scanned the skies. I didn't see any enemy sky craft flitting about. For the moment, we were safe from aerial attack.

"Lion," RC said. "What's going on down there?"

I glanced down. In the big square beneath us, about fifty floors down, rested four Gorgon troop ships.

"When did they get here?" RC asked.

"Probably while we were busy climbing inside this rotting building."

"Yeah." RC pointed. "Look."

I looked where he pointed. Hundreds of Gorgons traversed each of the side streets and alleys leading to the square. They carried strange-looking gray sacks, like bean pods. Along the sides of the alleys and streets lay thousands of these pods.

"Were those there when we came through last night?" he asked.

Shrugging, I replied, "Maybe."

"How did we miss them?"

"I have no idea."

"Maybe they weren't there. Maybe they came in with the troop ships."

"Maybe," I agreed. "But what are they?"

"Good question."

"RC, I need to sit down somewhere, back away from this opening. I feel dizzy and tired. I need rest, some food, and to clean my wounds."

"I feel the same way. But, Lion, I'd like to keep an eye on the wormheads down there."

"Go ahead, but don't fall out, it's a long way down."

He chuckled. "It is."

I moved back from the hole, found a good place behind a broken table, and sat down. I realized my light was still on and I switched it off. Then I called to RC and told him to make certain his light was off.

Pulling a bottle of water from my vest, I opened it and drank half of it. Then I opened a food packed and devoured its tasteless contents. Finished, I ran my fingers over my face, neck, and ears. Wherever I found a wound, I washed it out with a moistened handkerchief. After I cleaned all my wounds, and there were many, I opened a small bottle and rubbed its antiseptic, medicated lotion on the wounds. Done, I stretched out my body as best I could and slept.

A rumbling inside my abdomen awakened me. After a moment, I realized I wasn't hungry but needed to empty my bowels. Standing, I noticed the blown-out room was filled with growing darkness. Thea was setting.

RC was nowhere around. I called his name. No answer. I left the blown-out corner and wandered about until I found a filthy looking little spot I could relieve myself in. When

I was done, I used antiseptic lotion to clean my hands. Then I went looking for RC, but he wasn't anywhere to be found.

So I left the top floor and wandered the building, all the while calling his name. Floor after floor, I looked for him. But I didn't find him. With care, and after a long descent, I returned to the street level. It was dark out by then.

Where had he gone? What had happened to him? He wouldn't have left me behind. Had the Gorgons grabbed him?

I didn't know.

TWENTY-NINE

EXITING THE BUILDING, I stayed in the darkest areas beside it. Not knowing what had happened to RC ate at me. But I had an obligation to return to the outpost and report everything that had happened to us since exiting The Slab. It was my duty.

Yet my real duty was to RC. Marines don't leave anyone behind, if we can help it. And while I didn't know what had happened to the rest of my team or where they might be, if RC was anywhere close by, I had to find him. I couldn't leave him behind.

I made my way back into the building. Filled with a darkness deeper than death, filled with broken furniture, human remains, shattered dreams and debris, this was where I searched for one of the best Marines I had ever known. But where should I start?

At the beginning, of course. As quietly as possible, my light shielded by one of my hands, I searched the bottom floor. I found nothing.

Coming upon the big hole stretching downward and upward, I wondered if he had fallen into it. If so, he might have tumbled against one of the sides, bouncing onto any of the floors above me. Or he could have dropped down into the deep darkness below. Whether it was the former or the latter, he might be dead by now. If he wasn't, he might be before I found him.

If I searched every floor as thoroughly as I had just searched this one, it'd take days to find him. If he was injured, how long could he survive before it was too late? This building was too large for me to search by myself.

I sat down. I had to think, to consider, to plan for how to find RC before it was too late.

Where was he? And why had he left? Had he heard a noise and gone to investigate it? No, he was a trained Marine. He knew better than to leave me behind.

So why had he left?

If the Gorgons has seen him and fired at him, I'd have heard it. In fact, I'd have been killed, too. So that couldn't be it.

And if they had spotted him and come up to get him they'd have seen and taken me, too. That hadn't happened, either.

So what had happened?

Maybe he had needed to relieve himself, just as I had. If so, he'd have moved away from me, out of courtesy and sanitary concerns. He probably found a little corner to make his deposit. Maybe a couple of floors down?

It was a long, tiring climb back to the top. At least I knew the way, having traversed it twice.

On the second to last floor, my legs aching, my breath short, I began my search. I was careful not to let my light reflect off of anything or shine out any of the windows or holes in the wall. In a slow and cautious manner, searching every little nook and cranny, I sought RC. After almost an hour, I came up empty.

I dropped down to the next floor. Another hour of wasted searching.

On the fourth level down, I stopped to rest and have a little food and water. After I finished eating, I sat back and leaned my head against a wall. My eyes closed.

Then I heard something. My eyes popped open. I listened. It sounded like moaning.

Was it the wind? No. There wasn't any wind.

I scrambled up. "RC?" I whispered.

"Over here…" a voice whispered back.

"Where?"

"Here…"

I swallowed. He sounded bad. "Keep talking. I'll find you."

"Okay…"

Over in a corner, beside a battered desk and broken window, my light revealed blood—too much blood—and a body lying face down, its head turned away from me.

I stepped over and knelt beside the body. "RC?"

"Oh…"

I turned the man's body over. He cried out. "Please, don't move me anymore!"

"I won't." I shined my light on his face, keeping the beam out of his eyes. It wasn't RC. Whoever it was, he stunk of dirt, excrement and death. "Who are you?"

"No one."

"What happened? How did you get here?"

"Do…do you have any water? Please," he gasped. His face was badly bruised. Blood poured from a head wound, a wound filled with dirt and bits of masonry. His clothing consisted of rags.

Fumbling in my vest, I produced a half empty bottle of water. I held it to his lips. "Drink just a little."

"I'll drink all I want," he said, then gasped for breath. "I'm dying and I know it."

"So you are," I agreed. "How did you come to be here?"

"My brother and I saw the two of you come in here. This is our building. We followed you. We wanted your water, your food, your clothes, anything that you had that we wanted for ourselves. You were in our building. That made your possessions ours now. Your lives meant nothing to us."

"I see. You're a scavenger." The very word left a bitter taste in my mouth. This man had fallen beneath even the level of animals. He, and others like him, had treated survivors, such as Lucy Brannon and that teenage girl that had been kidnapped, raped, and murdered, like they were commodities for their own personal use. They didn't see them as fellow survivors and victims but as things, objects.

"We didn't want this war!" he cried out suddenly, blood bubbling from his mouth. "We had lives, families, homes. The wormheads took all of that from us. We were alone. Others found us and we joined them. But what was there for us to live on? No food, no life, no future? We survived. It was all we could do."

He emptied the water bottle. "More."

"Tell me, what did you do to my friend?"

"Him? We waited until your bastard baby killer came down here. Then we rushed him. My brother hit him with a chunk of wood and your son-of-a-bitch friend went down. My brother towered over him, intending to finish him off. But your shit-eating friend did something to him and my brother flew backwards, crashing onto a broken desk. When he screamed, I ran over to him. But he was unconscious."

He glared at me, hatred in his eyes. "So I picked up a chunk of wall and threw it at your friend. He ducked away and came at me with a knife. A knife! I hadn't seen a knife in such a long time. I charged him and he slashed at my head. Then he did this to me," he said, pointing at his side. There was a deep wound there. The scavenger had stuffed dirty rags inside it. The rags were bloody and more blood oozed from the wound.

"He left me here to die, like I was the piece of useless meat instead of him!"

"Where is he?" I demanded.

"Dead, I hope. I saw my brother get up and stagger toward your friend. I heard fighting sounds. I heard John scream. Then it was quiet. A long, empty kind of quiet. I hope your friend is dead. Just as I hope that you die."

I dropped his head onto the floor. There was a loud thunk. Silence rewarded my action. I got up and walked away.

Looking around, I found another body. It wasn't RC, but his knife stuck out of the man's chest. The knife was buried all the way to the finger guard.

Searching more, I located RC. He was unconscious. I called his name, splashed water onto his face, gently shook him. He didn't wake up.

He bled from his mouth, his nose, his ears. He had several small cuts on his face, as well as multiple bruises.

I washed the cuts and rubbed the antiseptic cream on them. Then I wiped the blood from his mouth, nose, and ears. With great effort, I managed to get him onto my shoulders. He was heavy, but I balanced his weight. Then I began the long journey back down to the ground floor.

THIRTY

IT WAS A LONG descent downstairs, longer than it took to ascend. I stopped several times to catch my breath, check on RC's condition, and rest. By the time I reached the ground floor, the sky was light again. In an hour, Thea would rise.

Exhausted, I found a safe place behind some debris a short distance from the entrance. Setting RC down, I dragged more debris over to better protect us from view. Then I inspected him again.

He remained unconscious, and I didn't know if it was a blessing or a curse. His nanites were probably busy repairing his injuries. But I didn't know how severe his injuries were, nor whether or not his nanites could fix them.

In other words, I didn't know how close he might be to dying. I only knew I had to get him back to our lines.

Sitting beside him, leaning back against a wall, I closed my eyes and slept.

I dreamt of people I hadn't seen in years. One of them was a young woman I knew when we were both teenagers. I loved her as much as anyone could love someone. But I was young. I didn't know who I was. I had no purpose, no path, no promise.

She had light brown hair, with skin less dark than mine. Her eyes were brown and she had a smile that lit up a room, a campus, a world. More intelligent than me, her grades were perfect while mine were so-so. She had personality and was liked by everyone. I had few friends and even less personality. She loved sports and I didn't.

She was a city girl, while I hailed from the wide ranch lands beyond the suburbs.

One day, I wrote her a love letter. We were both fifteen. I sent it to her, telling her of my deep feelings for her. Immature, embarrassed, shy, I had told her of my deep, genuine love for her.

She saw me from across a classroom one day and smiled warmly at me. But embarrassed and shy, I turned away. I never spoke to her, I never could. I never kissed her. I never touched her. I loved her all those long years ago, and still did. I loved her so much and yet never said anything to her.

The day I turned away from her, I turned away from myself. A slow, deep hatred for myself filled my soul. Every day for three years, I watched her and loved her. And every day that I loved her, I hated myself for being a coward. For not taking the chance that she might love me, too.

One day, when I returned home, angry and disgusted with my cowardice toward the woman I loved, I climbed into my mother's ground car and contemplated killing myself. But I couldn't do that to my parents or to my grandparents, nor to my siblings. So, to survive, for the sake of hope and personal salvation, I promised myself that the next day I would talk to my beloved. But I never did. I never did.

The last year of school, I let go of her. I still loved her from afar, but I learned to love myself again.

When Marine recruiters came to our campus, I decided I wanted to be a Marine. I found a purpose and had a plan. I improved my grades, got an appointment to the Naval Academy, and from there, I found friendship and myself.

I woke from my dreams. I thought of her, briefly wondering where she was now and if she was happy. I hoped she was safe. I prayed she wasn't here on Eos.

When RC moaned, I placed the past behind me and tended to him. He was still unconscious. I inspected his wounds. Some of the cuts had healed. His nanites were hard at work helping him.

I fed myself, got up, checked out our hiding spot, glanced outside, Thea stood straight overhead, and sat back down beside RC. He didn't move, but he was alive and he was healing. I closed my eyes and slept again.

I didn't dream of the past anymore.

So focused was I on survival and saving RC, that I stopped thinking about my own pain and didn't notice when it was gone, when my nanites had finished fixing my own injuries.

THIRTY-ONE

THE SUN SET. TWILIGHT preceded the growing darkness. I moved a short distance from RC and relieved myself.

Cleaning myself up, I tossed two empty water bottles away, stuffed food wrappers beneath debris, made certain I had my knife and that it was handy, and glanced outside. I saw nothing but night.

Gathering up RC, I lifted him onto my shoulders. Though his breathing was regular, he remained unconscious. I wondered if the microchip in his brain had ordered his nanites to induce a coma. True or not, I felt both lonely and relieved that he remained unconscious.

It had been three days now since we had evacuated The Slab. I hoped the rest of my team had made it back to the platoon's outpost and that they were safe. And I wondered if Lieutenant Kwung and Sergeant Kano had written us off as missing in action, if not dead. My only hope was of getting us safely back to the outpost.

As I moved toward the exit, I felt a cool, soft breeze flowing from the illuminated orange field. The air smelled moist. Dust and decay seemed mixed in the air. There was also a strange, nasty smell, almost like decaying animal odor. I wondered if it might come from the Gorgon RC and I had killed out there across the field. Having always fought safely within an armored, airtight suit, I had never smelled decaying alien flesh before. Did I now? I didn't know.

Yet, how could the smell be of Gorgon death? Earlier today the field had been filled with Gorgons and their flying machines. They would have found their murdered fellow. Wouldn't they have gathered him up?

Stepping outside, I crept with care through the debris near the building. Coming to an alley, I paused, put RC down. Then I glanced down the alley. The stars above provided a faint illumination. I saw a wide path leading away from the field and in the direction of my course. Retrieving RC, I entered the alley.

Moving maybe fifty meters, I became aware of large, long tubes on either side of the alley, set against the battered buildings. They looked almost like giant bean sprouts. We had seen the Gorgons placing them among the alleys today.

Though it was an old joke about pod people and aliens, humanity had never encountered any pod aliens. Might this be the first such encounter?

I doubted it.

However, I eased RC down again. He weighed a lot and I was grateful to have him off of my shoulders. Besides, he smelled. It might just be days of unwashed body odor, but it stank worse than that. Maybe, in his unconscious state he had relieved himself. Whatever the cause, I gagged while carrying him.

I turned my attention to one of the pods. It wasn't of a material with which I was familiar. Not a pipe, a tube, nor a pod, it seemed more like a blanket or tarp wrapped around something.

Glancing up and down the alley, I saw neither movement nor enemy. Switching on my light, I examined the object. It looked like a bag with a folded-over cover.

Unfolding the cover, I found a headless Gorgon soldier inside. I closed the bag and opened another, finding a second dead alien within. The third bag contained the Gorgon RC and I had recently killed.

Now I knew that the enemy gathered their dead just as we did. And that they smelled as bad as we did after we died.

I switched my light off and picked up RC, gagging at his stench.

I had never considered the enemy would gather up their dead like we did. The concept seemed so human. Knowing how much the Gorgons hated everything human, it puzzled me.

I walked through alley after alley that night, carefully traversing streets and intersections, and in almost every alley there were body bags, dozens in each alley, hundreds in all. And the more I saw of them, the more I was amazed and awed.

THIRTY-TWO

BY THE TIME DAYLIGHT came, we were hiding inside a blasted-out hole in the wall of a tall building on one side of an alleyway. The hole formed a cave in the building's side. Rubble had collapsed the only entrance into the building proper.

I managed to fill the hole with rubble high enough to block us from outside view. Then I collapsed beside where I had laid RC down. From this location, I could glance through gaps in the rubble out into the alley. Bright sunlight filtered into the darkness, filling it with gloom rather than with oblivion. The sunlight cheered me a little. I didn't feel so alone and lost.

And lost we were. During the night clouds had overcast the city. Running across intersection after intersection, darting this way and that, I had lost all sense of direction. I couldn't locate The Slab and all the streets seemed the same.

In the past months, I had probably patrolled and fought over much of this part of the city. But everything appeared different from a couple of hundred meters up while scooting around at sixty kilometers per hour. Down on the ground, nothing looked the same.

I didn't even know if I was going in the right direction toward the outpost, if I had by-passed it, or if I had somehow gotten turned around during the night and had proceeded back into enemy territory. However, with the fluid nature of the fighting in Belden, enemy territory was everywhere.

So I settled beside RC. I kept a lookout through the rubble for the enemy. And I kept an eye on RC. Meanwhile, I yawned, tired, needing rest. Needing delivery from this constant nightmare.

I hardly thought about my team anymore. Alive or dead, it was irrelevant to me now. All that mattered was getting back and getting RC medical attention.

His minor wounds continued to heal, but I couldn't tell anymore if he were alive or dead. He smelled really bad now. He could be dead. The truly bizarre and odd thing about nanites inside our bodies was that they continued to keep parts of the body alive even while the rest of it had died. The brain and major organs could be dead but our nanites kept repairing the body until they ran out of power and died themselves.

I could be carrying a dead man and not know it.

Four days had passed now since we had lost contact with our teammates and the platoon. Four days of wandering around out here, virtually naked, unarmored and unarmed, at the mercy of scavengers and alien monstrosities alike.

I had used up most of my water and food. I still had RC's water and food. He wasn't swallowing anything, but I kept wetting a cloth and placing it in his mouth, trying as best I could to keep him hydrated.

I needed strength to carry him. He wasn't consuming his food and he utilized little of his water, so I appropriated both.

My yawning was getting the better of me. My eyes grew heavy, my breathing slowed, and I fell asleep.

THIRTY-THREE

A SCRAPING, SCRATCHING SOUND AWAKENED me. I struggled to consciousness, wanting to keep sleeping. But the noise occurred again and abruptly, I was wide-awake.

I glanced around my gloomy hideout. RC lay where I had placed him. I rolled over and listened for his breath but couldn't hear it. I held his wrist. If he had a pulse, I couldn't detect it. His face felt cold.

Again, I heard the scraping and scratching. Rolling onto my other side, I realized the noise came from the rubble piled in the cave's opening. Something moved out there.

I peered out a slight opening in the barrier. Dark shapes move out there. Alien shapes.

Before I could guess what they were doing, I heard a thunk. A hole appeared at the top of the rubble pile. They wanted to see what was inside!

All I had was a knife. Even if they weren't armored, I was dead. As was RC.

Panic clawed at me. I got up, crouching low, ready to spring. When the wall came down, I'd jump them. I'd take them by surprise. I'd toss rubble at them. I'd beat on them until they were dead. Pound and run. That was my plan.

Pound and run.

My breathing accelerated. I grew dizzy. I swayed. Sweat covered my face, got in my eyes.

There was no way I wasn't dead.

What was I going to do? What about RC? He's dead. You don't know that. I'll leave him behind. No you won't. I must. Why? To live, that's why. What's life without honor?

Another piece of rubble crashed outside. Shaking my head, I caught my breath. I couldn't even handle one, even if I took it by surprise.

I had to think, to think!

Fighting wasn't any good. In a few moments, they'd be through. If RC weren't dead, he soon would be. And so would I.

More rubble fell.

I had it! I knew what to do.

Crawling over to RC, remaining on the deck, I pulled RC's body on top of me. He stank badly, but I dragged him over my head. Pulling my knife out, I placed it flat between my body and his.

Throwing one arm back, I let it rest in a haphazard fashion, my fingers splayed open. My other arm rested by my body but close to my knife's handle. I turned my head such that one eye was hidden by RC's body while the other saw the opening. When the last piece of rubble fell, I closed my free eye just enough so that my eyelids formed a slit. I saw the opening, barely.

Slowing my breathing, I parted my lips just enough for air to past through them. I lay as still as possible. To seem dead, I thought of myself as dead. No movement, no life, no thought, just observation.

The Gorgons entered. Their wormlike sensory tendrils waved about. Not knowing what they saw, if they saw at all, I remained still.

There they stood on bowed legs, the pasty flesh of their arms and heads ghostlike. Their torsos, legs, and feet were covered in some sort of camouflaged material, the camouflaged patterns constantly moving about on their clothing. Their feet were wide and flattened, more like terrestrial ducks than human feet. Their sensory organs didn't turn forward like eyes but I knew they took in every detail of our little cave. Did they see me? Could they? Did they smell me, hear me, sense the heat from my body? What senses did they have? Could they detect magnetic or electrical fields? Could they see the infrared frequencies?

So little was known about them, about how they saw, how they eliminated waste, how they procreated. We knew nothing of their society. What we did know of them was that our presence drove them insane. And that they were determined killers.

But I knew something more. I knew that they cared for their dead, just as we did.

The two aliens weren't armored, though one of them carried a plasma rifle connected to a power pack on its back. The other appeared unarmed. It moved closer.

As it approached, I saw small axes in the upper pair of its rubbery-looking arms. The lower pair dangled by its body.

I kept from moving, but I felt sweat on my forehead. If they noticed my sweat, then I was dead.

After a moment, the axes-bearing Gorgon turned and headed toward the opening. The other one let it pass. Then it aimed its rifle at me!

A faint buzzing sound came from outside. The nightmare lowered its weapon, turned and exited.

I almost breathed again, but held my breath and listened. I heard movement outside. They moved away. I remained motionless under RC's stinking body until the light changed. Evening approached.

Sliding RC off of me, I rolled over. Gathering up my knife and my meager belongings, I checked on RC. I still couldn't tell if he were alive or dead.

Moving to the opening on my hands and knees, I peeked around the corner. I didn't see anything.

Turning, I got into a crouch and grasped RC's shoulders, dragging him outside. Weak from lack of rest and from constant fear and tension, I barely managed to load him onto my shoulders.

Straightening, I staggered under my load. I leaned against the building across the alley to keep from falling over. After a moment's rest, I started down the alley.

The sky was darker know. A faint glow from the passing day filled one horizon. From the other horizon came deepening darkness. Stars appeared over me.

I clicked on my flashlight, but nothing happened. Its power was gone. Tossing it away, I removed from my vest RC's light. It glowed brightly, its charge nearly full.

I moved on.

THIRTY-FOUR

I HADN'T GONE TWO BLOCKS before I heard movement behind me, sort of a rasping, rustling, muffled movement. I didn't know what was coming but it sounded large. And it grew closer.

Fear edged me toward panic. But I wasn't going to panic again, I commanded myself. I had panicked enough for today, maybe for my whole life. Even so, I strode forward quickly. I wanted out of there.

Finding a smashed door in the side of a building, I switched off my light and pushed against the door with RC's body. It gave a little and I pushed harder.

It opened wide. I stepped inside.

I didn't know if it was filled with boxes, bodies, or enemy troops waiting for me. It provided cover and that's all I cared about. I stood far enough back to be hidden by the darkness, but close enough to see through the open door.

Down the alley came armored Gorgon troops in a column of twos. Twenty in all, they shuffled down the alley on their wide feet.

Were they after me? Was I ever going to be free from this nightmare? Was I meant to die here?

I shook my head, tired and terrified. I waited, but heard nothing. I stepped out. The alley appeared clear.

I moved on, following the enemy soldiers. As long as I was behind them, I was safe. Or so I hoped.

Moving quietly, I entered another street, glancing up and down it. Half a block away on either side of the street more Gorgon troops hurried forward. What was going on?

Flashes of bright light illuminated the sky up ahead. I recognized those flashes. The Gorgons were fighting somebody and I bet they fought my fellow Marines. But I couldn't proceed forward. If I did either the Gorgons or the Marines would burn RC and me down.

A small rock clattered on the pavement beside me. I looked around. Behind me stood a wormhead. It held two hand axes in its upper set of claws. I stared at it. It stared back at me. At least, I thought it did.

The Gorgon made a low buzzing sound, almost like the buzzing of insects. I stayed still. It made the sound again.

I remained still.

The alien leaned its head and shoulders forward. Then it made a wide circle to its left, backward, to the right and forward again with its head and shoulders.

I didn't move.

The alien leaned down and grabbed some more rocks with its free claws. I thought about kicking it in the head but wondered what good it would do. It took both RC and me to kill that other one a few nights back.

It tossed one of the rocks over my head and out into the street, to my right. Then it tossed another rock in the same direction. It landed past the first one and close to a broad, broken doorway in the building on the opposite side of the street from me.

It seemed like it wanted me to go that way. But for what purpose, other than to kill me? It had two axes and I had RC on my shoulders, while my knife was in its sheath, attached to my right hip. It could kill me at any time. Further, it could call out or contact the Gorgons in the intersections on either end of this street. They would gladly come down and roast us, if called.

I had nothing to lose, nothing to gain. I turned and proceeded toward the center of the street, off to my right.

The Gorgon followed at a discreet distance, maybe four meters behind me. I stopped at the doorway. My captor came up behind me and used the top of one of its axes to shove me inside. It followed me inward.

I stood in a gloomy, deadly darkness. I knew I was going to die in here and maybe quite horribly. But instead, twin shafts of bright light illuminated the interior. Turning, I saw two small white light discs in the Gorgon's upper claws.

The Gorgon pointed past me with one of its axes. Turning around, I spied a long, empty corridor. I went down it, my captor following me.

The corridor ended at a stairwell, the door burned away by plasma fire. I entered it. I climbed the stairs upward.

At the first landing, I turned to climb the second flight. I suspected my captor intended to shove me off of the top of the building. If I planned it right, maybe I could shove it off instead.

Outside the building, I heard the sizzle of plasma rifles being fired. I couldn't tell if they were ours or theirs.

A tapping behind me caught my attention. Turning, I noticed my captor tapping an axe near the exit from the stairwell on this landing.

Grimacing, I walked through it. I came out into a hallway narrower than the previous one. Doors lined either side.

Moving forward, I stopped when I again heard tapping behind me. I turned into an open door leading into what once must have been a large apartment.

I heard tapping on the floor behind me, to my right. Rotating around, I noticed the entire wall on that side was missing. I moved to the edge. Below me was an alleyway filled with debris. Armored Marines crouched behind the debris, occasionally firing down the alleyway!

I turned around intending to stare at my alien captor but it was gone!

I was stunned.

One of the monsters that had butchered humanity so brutally had led me to freedom. How was that possible? What about the insanity we invoked among them? Was that real or a lie? What had just happened?

Putting RC down, I went to the door. I glanced out into the hall. No alien.

I heard a groan. I turned and went back inside. RC's eyes were open. His mouth moved but nothing came out of it.

I knelt beside him. Opening our last bottle of water, I dribble some into his mouth. He choked on it, coughed, and said with a raspy, dry whisper, "What's going on?"

"A miracle," I replied.

Standing, I went to the missing wall and leaned out. "Hey, down there, could you give me a little help up here? I have an injured Marine with me," I called out.

The Marines below heard me on their exterior microphones and several of them glanced up at me. Then two of them floated up on their grav discs. The taller of the two moved closer, pointing his plasma rifle at me. His companion turned and pointed his rifle down the alleyway.

"Where the goddammed hell did you come from?" the taller Marine asked me.

THIRTY-FIVE

SOMEONE WAS SCREAMING. OR yelling. Or cursing. Or all of them.

Opening my eyes, I saw above me a white ceiling, known as the overhead in Marine and Naval parlance. Not just the overhead was white, but everything was white. Even the soft light illuminating everything around me was white.

My head seemed to rest on a soft pillow, probably all white. I felt soft clothing covering my body. Apparently, a soft white sheet covered me, from my shoulders down to my feet. Moving my feet slightly, I noticed the sheet seemed tucked into the bed I was resting on.

Where was I? I couldn't remember how I got here. For that matter, I couldn't remember what happened before I got here. Or even before that.

I sat up. To my left and right, white beds stretched away from me, twenty to my left and nineteen to my right.

Across the aisle were forty more white beds. All but mine were empty.

I heard the screaming again, mixed in with crying and babbling.

Someone seemed in trouble and I decided to go see if I could help. I drew back my white sheet and pivoting, swung my legs to the right and out of bed. My bare feet touched the soft white floor.

The movement made me dizzy, so I rested a bit, firmly grasping the edge of my mattress so as not to tumble to the deck. As the dizziness faded, I tried standing. A knee buckled and it was all I could do to keep from crashing down.

Why was I so dizzy and where was I? I had made it all the way across Belden with RC on my back without falling and now here I was… where exactly, I didn't know…and I couldn't even stand.

Belden. RC. Where was RC? I began calling his name.

At either end of the beds were white partitions, with rectangular openings leading elsewhere. Through one of these hurried a robot nurse.

"Sir," the robot said, "I am pleased you are well, but you must stop crying out and get back into bed. Though you have slept many days, your body is not quite fully functional yet. You must continue recuperation. "This requires rest".

"I heard someone crying out. It's my duty to help him or her."

"Sir, that is not your purpose. It is my purpose. I am designed to care for the damaged and disturbed. Your present purpose is to rest."

Struggling back into bed, I instead collapsed onto the deck. The robot nurse hurried over to me. It was both gentle and strong and carefully helped me into bed.

Robots possess no sexual characteristics. They are neither male, nor female. But most pick a gender, desiring to relate to humans more genuinely. This one seemed female, both from the tones of it voice and from its behavior.

"But what about the Marine calling for help? It might be my friend, RC," I said, lying back down.

"Your supposition is correct. It is a Marine. But it is not your fellow Marine, RC. His recuperation is completed. He has been returned to the surface."

"I'm on a ship?"

"Correct. This is the hospital ship *Rainbow of Heaven*. You will return to the surface in a few more days."

"But I wasn't badly injured," I protested.

"Sir, you were."

"Stop calling me sir. I'm a Marine sergeant, not an officer."

"Affirmative, sir."

"And my injuries were being repaired by my nanites."

"Your nanites are designed to help you reach sufficient care. Your nanites kept you mobile. Your damage was severe and plentiful, sir."

"Stop calling me 'sir'!"

"Sir, I exist to care for humanity. It is my right to pick the profession best suiting my individual purpose, as is dictated under human law. I am thus programed to respond in a friendly and respectful manner. I will always address all male humans as 'sir', regardless of their chosen gender affiliation. In a similar fashion, I will always address all females as 'ma'am'. As I respect you, I expect you to respect me. Affirmative, sir?"

I sighed. "Affirmative. What about the screaming Marine?"

"He suffers from acute emotional trauma, sir. He is being attended to. Beside robot doctors, human doctors and counselors are also present. With continued care, he will recuperate and return to his warrior profession.

"Now, please rest, sir. Sustenance will arrive soon."

"How long have I been here?"

"Two Earth weeks, sir."

I lay down. Two weeks? Would I even have a team, let alone a place to return to? How did I get here and what happened? How did I get RC and myself out? I remembered finding Marines from another company, but my memory ended there.

What happened to me?

THIRTY-SIX

MORE DAYS WENT BY before I was released. A transport shuttle took me from *Rainbow of Heaven* to a field hospital fifty kilometers north of Belden. There my brigade's second battalion rested and reformed after suffering heavy casualties fighting on the West Coast. Along with the field hospital were secondary units of the Twenty-fourth Brigade, including headquarters and support units. Dozens of supply and personnel shuttles arrived daily. The Brigade's base was situated one hundred meters underground, as were the shuttle hangars.

Before leaving the hospital ship, I received a new uniform. After reporting in at the Brigade's secondary base, I received orders to return to Chaos Company. Three train tubes connected with First Battalion's Belden base.

As my maglev zipped along, I passed hundreds of chambers where Second Battalion recuperated. I was glad I was returning to my battalion and also glad I hadn't fought with Second Battalion. What First Battalion had suffered in the last year was enough for me. I couldn't imagine what had so decimated Second Battalion.

Upon arriving, I reported to the First Battalion's Sergeant Major's office. She was in charge of all the battalion's returning non-officer personnel. She welcomed me back and sent me over to an ordnance unit where I picked up a new suit. All the suits are similar and conform to the size of each individual Marine. My suit was a bit tight, but I knew it would stretch to accommodate my extra-tall size. The robots there saw to it that the suit was powered up and fully supplied.

Twenty minutes later, I floated into Chaos Company's landing bay. Locating my slot, thank goodness no one new had been assigned to replace me after being gone for almost three weeks, I settled my suit down, exited it and sought out my platoon.

It was good to be home.

Reporting to First Sergeant Jones, the company's senior sergeant, I was welcomed back and informed that Second Platoon had rotated back from the company's outpost and was in the mess hall. I thanked him and proceeded there, only to be instantly noticed and assailed by happy voices and yells upon entering the hall.

Marines are rowdy people, and they're at their most rowdiness when their long lost fellow Marines return. Most members of my platoon were happy to see me. However, Staff Sergeant Dana Sinclair, Second Squad's leader, wasn't among them.

"Well, if it isn't the prodigal Marine," she said. "Did you forget something or someone?"

I glared at her. She was a bit shorter than me, but as mean and nasty as ever. She referred to my team and especially RC.

"No," I replied. "Did you?"

The nasty look left her eyes but the meanness remained. "What d'you mean, Marine?" she snapped.

"Did you ever replace April Bond's team?" I asked.

"You son-of-a-bitch, don't you ever talk to me like that again!" she screamed at me.

"Likewise."

Turning red, she cocked her right fist by her side, ready to strike at me. She stepped closer. As the crowd of welcomers formed a circle around us, I stepped back. I brought my hands up in a defensive posture.

"Now, now, children, play nice." We both turned and saw Gunnery Sergeant Kano stepping through the crowd. Our platoon sergeant, he out-ranked us both.

Mo stepped between us. He faced Sinclair. "Dana, go find someplace to cool off. Got it?"

Glaring at me, she nodded at him and left.

Mo turned to me. He clapped my right shoulder. "Glad to have you back, Lion! Just wish you'd mind your tongue a bit around Sinclair. She still feels guilty about losing Bond's team. As I know you would feel if you'd lost your team."

"Speaking of my team, where are they?" I asked.

"Out on patrol, with Saunders. They'll be back soon. They'll be glad to see you. Settled in yet?"

"I just arrived."

He nodded. "Stow whatever you need to and then get up to the CP. The skipper and lieutenant are waiting for you."

"Got it."

"Good."

I found my quarters in my team's bay just as I had left it weeks before. My room was just a cubicle cut out of the bedrock beneath Belden. When I wasn't on duty, my cubicle was my fortress, my home.

But it wasn't really my home. My home, before coming to Eos, had been aboard the destroyer *Sulu Sea*, along with the rest of my squad. I spent three years aboard that ship, rising from private to sergeant and team leader. Chip had been my team's corporal, then sergeant, until I took over Team B. So Chip had taken over Team C after its sergeant, Jim Thur, took over the squad.

The Twenty-fourth Marine Brigade was the Sixth Fleet's Marine Force, with squads scattered aboard destroyers, platoons aboard cruisers, and companies aboard battleships. The Fleet patrolled the billion cubic lightyears of the Sixth Region, headquartered on the planet Garten Veldt, almost three thousand light years from Eos. When war came to Eos, the Twenty-fourth Brigade was called up, with every part of the brigade reforming before shipping out.

It had seemed so glorious for all of us to come together. However, at the time there was only enough transportation for the First Battalion, so we reached Eos long before the rest of the brigade did. Then the glory ended as we were thrown into the hell of war.

Everything was where I'd left it, with the exception of a small black box on my pillow. Opening it, I found a new decoration for me to wear on my dress uniform. I already possessed two blue Distinguished Service ribbons and a green and gold Gallantry Commendation. But now, as I removed the little holographic projector from the box, a small crimson nebula appeared. Within the nebula was a single bright white dot, representing a star. It was my first award for wounds received while in combat.

Deep pride warmed me. For Marines, only those who have won a Crimson Nebula have truly proved their courage in battle. Too bad so many recipients of the award earned it by dying. So few of us have earned it and lived.

"If you're gonna cry, now's the time, before anyone else sees you."

I spun around. "Chip!"

"Good to see you, Lion," he said. "Good to see you."

THIRTY-SEVEN

"So, you're back," Chip said.

"I am."

We stared at each other. Then we stared at the walls, the deck, the overhead, anywhere but at each other. We were friends, the best of friends, but we weren't lovers.

At last, Chip broke the silence. "Hungry?"

"Not really."

He grunted. "Thirsty?" he asked, his eyebrows lifted in expectation.

"A bit."

"Good. Let's go over to the mess hall."

"I just want water."

"You can have water. I'll have something stronger."

"I can't," I said, yawning.

"Tired?" he asked.

"Some," I replied.

"Well, then you should rest. But first, let's go get a drink."

"Can't."

"Why not?" Chip demanded.

"The skipper and the lieutenant are expecting me at the CP," I replied, yawning again.

"Well, why didn't you say so before?"

I shrugged.

"We better get going. We'll stop and get you some water along the way."

"We?"

He nodded. "I've got a billion questions."

"I might not have enough answers."

"So what? I'll ask them anyways."

I nodded, stifling another yawn. We left my room, Chip leading the way.

"You seem very sleepy," Chip said, as we moved down a well-lit corridor. "Didn't you get enough sleep?"

"I thought I did. I don't know what's wrong."

"Maybe it's the excitement of being back."

"I doubt that."

We walked in silence for a while.

"What happened out there? After Mo ordered your retreat we lost all contact with you."

"We ran into some problems."

"I gathered that." Chip turned into a side passageway.

"Well, for one thing, there were Gorgons all over the place, anxious to get at us."

"To kiss you?" he asked, a mischievous twinkle in his eyes.

I punched his shoulder, just hard enough to show my displeasure with him but not enough to hurt him. He grunted in a satisfied way.

"Well?" he said.

"I sent most of my team ahead. Then RC and I followed. Almost immediately, his suit started having problems."

"This that nano plague we've heard about?"

"You could call it that, I guess. By the way, anyone come up with a cure for it?" I asked.

"Ruby did."

"Ruby?"

"What's so amazing about that? You've got a lot of good people in your team. Well, mostly anyways," he said, grinning at me.

"Shut up."

"Make me."

I rolled my eyes. We kept walking. "What'd she come up with?"

"Blood."

"Blood?"

"Her blood, to be exact. She said she wondered if her body's nanites might be able to counteract whatever the problem was. So, once they lost all control of their suits and dismounted, she cut her palm with her survival knife and smeared her blood inside her suit before her nanites could close the wound."

"And it worked?"

"More or less. Took a few hours, according to Kamal, but her suit came back online. Not all the systems worked perfectly and her grav disc wouldn't work at all, but she had found a solution. So they all smeared their blood throughout their suits and two days after leaving The Slab they came home."

"So you're telling me they all cut themselves and bled into their suits?" Such a simple and bizarre solution. I was disappointed that neither RC nor myself had even thought to try something like it.

"They did." We reached the mess hall. Chip led the way to the food bar.

"We are closed, sirs," a robot attendant said.

"We're not sirs," Chip said. "Sergeant Biyela would like a cup of water and I'd like a beer."

"Sir, I can give the sergeant his water but I cannot serve you any beer. Captain Vang has closed the bar for the day. Would you care for some coffee?"

"All right," he growled.

"Make that two coffees," I said.

I asked the robot to cancel the water.

Just a little while ago, the mess hall had been full of people. Now, beside the robot server, we were the only ones here.

I'm use to how quickly things can change in the field, especially in combat. But I had forgotten how fast the world rotates while back at base.

"Very good, sir."

"We're not sirs," Chip growled.

"Very good, sir."

Chip glared at the robot, which turned its back on us as it proceeded to fill two cups with steaming, black coffee.

"That smells good," I said. "The Navy's getting pretty good with what it can do with bean curd."

"It's not bean turds," Chip replied. "Brigadier General Clarke, our new brigade commander, made sure that the Navy gets us good food now. Eight months of bean shit is too much for any Marine to think of eating!"

"Really?" I said, referring to General Clarke's care for us, his Marines and his brigade, and also referring to the new food, the possibility of good food.

"Would I lie to you?".

"You would," I replied.

"Only in jest," he said. "Only in jest."

"Well, then I'm glad I returned before things changed back to the way they were."

"What makes you think things are gonna go back to the way they were?" Chip demanded. He turned around just as the robot server handed him two cups of coffee. He offered me one and then lifted the other to his lips.

"Careful, sirs, the coffee's hot," the server said.

"We're not sirs," Chip muttered. He sipped the coffee. He hissed. "The damned stuff's hot."

"You were warned," I said, smiling at his discomfort. Everyone, from time to time, ignores good advice and does what he or she wants to do, usually with bad results. It's a matter of ego, I suppose. We all want to control our own lives. And if someone or something ticks us off, we ignore safety and good advice just for spite. The results are never pretty.

He reluctantly nodded. Leading the way to a table, Chip sat down and motioned me to join him.

"There's not really time for this," I said, sitting across from him. "I'm expected at the CP."

"Take a few moments off," he said. "What's the worse they can do to you, fire you? Stick you in the brig and demote you to private? Kick you off of Eos? We're just simple sergeants, Lion. We're as poor as poor comes. Privates and corporals are only slightly beneath us. We have the right to a little life for ourselves, a few minutes of peace before we're thrown back into the meat grinder." He sipped his coffee and winced again from its heat.

He leaned across the table toward me. "Think about it, Lion. We've been here for almost a year, during which time none of us have had any leave. Nor are we likely to get any, either. Where could we go? The whole planet's a war zone.

"Officers get to go up north to the cities far from the fighting. Sometimes they go up to the warships in orbit. Some of those ships, like the carriers and battleships, have recreational facilities, including gymnasiums and lounges. Hell, the most fun we've had was that food fight a while back.

"We've lost too many friends since coming here. Half of almost everyone we've known is dead now. So what if we take a few minutes to catch up? The skipper and the lieutenant can wait."

I stared at him. "I didn't know you felt so strongly about all this."

"I usually don't. But when we lost all word from you I assumed we'd lost you, too. That left me pretty much alone here. Seeing you again has given me hope I might make it through this war."

I nodded, sipping my coffee. It was cool enough to drink now, so I took a big swallow.

"So," he said, "your suits started having problems."

"Yes, they did. The Gorgons swarmed out of The Slab like bugs. Dozens came after us. RC lost his grav disc. I carried him on mine. Then mine ceased functioning and we got off it. After that, the Gorgons stopped chasing us. But we kept running. Eventually, my suit malfunctioned so much that just climbing a rubble pile proved almost impossible. Then..."

Chip leaned forward. "Then what? What happened?"

I shook my head to clear it. "I'm not sure. It seems kind of confusing. I remember tumbling down the rubble pile, RC running beside me, covering me. I fell through the pavement..."

"You fell through the pavement? Hah! I said you were eating too much, that it'd make you fat. You must've been as big as a battleship by then."

"I wasn't fat!"

"So you say."

I stared into my coffee. It was deep black and reflected the overhead's lights. "I fell through the pavement."

"You said that."

I nodded. "Underneath was a room. It had a trap door leading to the street above. RC followed me inside. We removed our suits, gathering up our knives and emergency gear. Then we hid our suits. I think we did. Maybe we replaced the trap door, too. I can't quite remember that part.

"It was low in there. We both had to bend over as we made our way. RC bent less than I did."

"Bet that ticked you off," Chip quipped.

"It did."

He chuckled and then asked, "So what happened next?"

"We wandered around for a while." I stopped. For the life of me, I couldn't remember what happened next.

"And?"

I exhaled heavily. "I think we somehow descended deeper down underground. I remember finding a door leading to the surface. Only we had to climb a tall ladder and at the top was a rusted hatch. I think we dangled from a ladder while we twisted the hatch open. Yes, that's what happened."

"And then?"

"Then RC climbed down a bit and using my back and legs I pushed the heavy thing open. I must have torn myself up inside because I remember hurting for a long time. We got out and closed the hatch. Then ..."

"Yes?" Chip inquired, with exasperation and expectation.

"We got into a hand-to-hand fight with an unsuited Gorgon."

"You did what?" Chip loudly exclaimed. The robot server turned to look at us. We looked back. After a long moment, it returned to whatever tasks it performed.

"Yes. Its arms or tentacles or whatever they were pounded at us. I found myself on the ground, unarmed, with it on top of me, flailing away at my face. Somehow, I managed to shove or push it off of me and then RC crushed its head with a couple of big blocks of rubble."

"Holy hell!" Chip exclaimed, louder than before.

"Yes, hell it was, though I don't know about the holy part. After that we had an encounter with a couple of human scavengers. Well, RC did. They beat him pretty badly but he managed to kill one of them and mortally wound the other one. RC was unconscious when I found him. I carried him around for days, hoping he wasn't dead but wondering if he was, wondering if I was toting around a corpse.

"Then, somehow, we found our way to where a platoon from Binary Company was involved in a firefight. I don't remember how we got there. The next thing I remember is waking up in a sickbay somewhere, in a ward.

"I was surrounded by empty bunks, forty of them. The ward was huge. I tried standing and almost collapsed. A robot nurse came along and insisted I get back to bed. It kept calling me sir and I kept telling it I wasn't an officer. Finally, it told me that it was trained, as a nurse, to address all humans either as sir or ma'am, depending upon gender. It said it was what made it a professional, and as a Marine, I should respect its dedication to its professionalism."

"Doesn't that beat all?" Chip exclaimed. "After fighting with robots all of our lives as Marines over whether or not we're sirs, it comes down to professional courtesy?" Chip shook his head. Then he grinned. Then he laughed: a loud, boisterous, long laugh.

The robot server came over to us. "Sirs, you must keep your volume down or I will have to ask you to leave."

Grinning, Chip turned around to the robot. "You got it, buddy. You got it."

"Thank you, sirs," the robot replied and turned away.

THIRTY-EIGHT

CHIP LED THE WAY to the CP. "So, you can't remember what happened underground or how you got to Binary Company or where you went after that?"

"I should, but I don't. I got an okay from the docs just before they discharged me. I've these gaps in my memory and I don't know why."

"What did the docs say?"

"They said I was fine. They couldn't explain my memory lapses and thought maybe I dreamt it while I was recuperating."

"Do you believe that?" Chip asked.

"I don't know what to believe."

We kept walking.

"Maybe you were so exhausted that when you slept, you dreamt all those experiences up," Chip suggested. "Maybe you stumbled upon Binary Company half asleep rather than wide awake."

"It doesn't feel like a dream. It feels real."

He shrugged. "Well, maybe it is. I don't have any answers for you and don't even know how you find any."

"That's what I'm afraid of, that I'll never know what happened to me or why I can't remember it."

He shrugged again. "Maybe it's that machine plague which infected your suits. Maybe it messed with your nanites or memory. Maybe the docs can't figure it out because they're used to healing organic plagues rather than machine ones."

"It's scary not knowing what happened," I said.

"I'll bet. But put it behind you. You're safe now, relatively speaking. You're back with us." He stopped talking and grunted. "We're here."

Looking around, I realized we had reached the Command Post. Nothing had changed since I'd last been here, except maybe they had more floating holographic imagers. First Sergeant Jonah Jones met us at the door.

"Where the hell have you been?" he bellowed at me. "You shoulda been here fifteen minutes ago. The skipper and the major are mad as hell!"

"Major?" Chip said.

Sergeant Jones turned, startled, at Chip's comment and presence. "What the goddammed hell are you doin' here?"

"I'm along for moral support," Chip quipped. "And to clean up any blood that gets spilt."

"Well, you're not invited. Get out!"

"You got it, First Sergeant." Chip turned to me. "Behave yourself now."

"Where's the fun in that?" I replied, grinning.

"Get out!" Jones bellowed.

"Sheesh, what a loud mouth," Chip complained as he left.

The first sergeant fumed as Chip disappeared down the corridor. He turned to me. "What are you waitin' for, an invitation? Get in there."

Nodding, I entered the CP. I proceeded to the center, where I spotted my platoon leader, Second Lieutenant Kwung. She stood beside Captain Vang. Both of them were short, but powerful and tough. They were fine Marines.

Beside Captain Vang stood a man almost as tall as me. He dwarfed Vang and Kwung. He had thick blond hair and a muscular build.

"Biyela, here you are. I want you to meet Major Bennett here," Vang said. "He's with the brigade's intelligence group, the IG. He has a mission for you."

I came to attention.

"None of that now, sergeant," the major said. He stuck out his hand and I took it. We shook, his grip painfully tight. He wanted me to know who was in charge.

His eyes were bluish-green. But they were cold, as cold as an ice planet. When he smiled, it was as cold as his eyes.

"How can my team help you, sir?" I asked.

"Not just your team, but you as well," he said.

"I don't understand, sir," I replied.

"He means, Lion," Lieutenant Kwung explained, "that your recent experiences in the field have caught the attention of General Clarke and the brigade's staff."

"I still don't follow," I said.

The major smiled a big, toothy smile. He seemed amused at my denseness. "I'll take it from here, lieutenant."

Kwung nodded. She glanced at Captain Vang. "Skipper, if there's nothing more you need me for, I'll return to my platoon."

"Go ahead," Vang said. "I just wanted you to know why Biyela and his team will be unavailable."

"And how long will I be short a fire team?" Kwung asked.

The captain glanced at the major. He sighed. "As long as it takes, Lieutenant Kwung. One never knows how long an operation will last or when it will end. It ends when it ends, that's just the way of it."

"I see," Lieutenant Kwung said. Coming to attention, she addressed her seniors: "Skipper, major." Then she spun curtly around on one heel and exited the CP.

I looked at the two officers before me. "I'm still at a loss as to why you need me, sirs."

Again, the big, toothy smile flashed at me. "You see, Sergeant Biyela, may I call you Biyela?"

"Most people address me as Lion, sir."

The major smirked. "Well, I'll just call you Biyela, if you don't mind." He didn't wait for a reply from me. As my superior, he could address me however he wished to, just so long as he didn't use any foul or derogatory words.

"You see, Biyela, you've learned more about the Gorgons in the few days you were out there than anyone else has learned about them since this conflict began. Hell, you've learned more than anyone else has about them since we first encountered them more than a century ago."

I looked at him, then at Captain Vang.

"Lion," she explained, "we've long suspected they had officers, that they weren't gobs of mindless warriors, like Earth's ants, for instance. But in your first few days in The Slab you found out how their officers were differentiated from the rest of their troops."

"Actually," I replied, "Lance Corporal Hunter figured that one out, ma'am."

"Whether Sergeant Hunter figured that out or you did is irrelevant," the major interrupted. "It happened on your watch."

"Sergeant Hunter?" I asked, surprised.

"Don't sound so incredulous, Biyela," the major said. "We gave him back his previous rank. He proved himself worthy on your last patrol."

I just stared at him.

"He's going to organize a sniper training program for us. It'll be a separate unit within the brigade," Major Bennett explained. "But for now, he'll be part of this operation."

"Will he still be part of my team?" I asked.

"Not exactly," Bennett replied. "But your team will still be responsible for protecting him."

"Got it."

"Good. Among the other things that you learned was where these holes running from the sewers through to roofs of the tall buildings came from. No one ever considered that the Gorgons might have created those tunnels so they could attack from underground up into the buildings. They never did that in the past. We've always thought of them as a slow and deliberate race, taking time to consider every possibility before moving forward. After all, when they first conquered the planets of their star system it took them two thousand years to reach the stars. We did it before we finished settling the Solar System. And that only took us a few centuries," Bennett explained.

"You also discovered they gather up their dead, Lion, like we do. A whole year and more of fighting and we never knew they even honored their dead," Vang added.

"Also," Bennett continued, "unarmored and barely armed, you spent days wandering through enemy lines carrying an injured Marine. You upheld the finest traditions of the Marines. You've proven that you can think on your feet, adapt to changing conditions, and still accomplish your mission, reporting back.

"Plus you possess considerable experience patrolling all over Belden, while neither I, nor my team, have much of any such experience here. You're dedicated and intelligent. You're the kind of Marine I want on this operation."

I looked at him. He still grinned that big, white grin of his. "Major, sir, I think you're laying it on a little thick, don't you agree?"

He guffawed. "Maybe so," he said. "Maybe so. But I specifically asked for you and I've got you. You've got eight hours. Eat and rest. We'll meet at the landing bay at Oh Four Thirty. Your company's first sergeant will brief you. Dismissed."

I came to attention. "Sir. Ma'am."

"I'm glad you're back, Lion," Vang said, smiling. "Be careful out there."

"Thank you, ma'am. I'm always careful." I glanced at the major. We stared at each other for a moment. His eyes were hard and cold. Then I exited the CP.

THIRTY-NINE

Found Lieutenant Kwung waiting for me outside the CP. As I came to attention she waved her hand and I relaxed. Stepping closer, she looked into my eyes.

"Lion," she said. "You're one of the best Marines I have. That number continues dwindling, though it's still a good list."

She had never said anything so personal as this to me before, so I was a bit perplexed. She was all about the mission and getting it done. Kwung usually kept her distance, avoiding personal relationships within the platoon. Hers was a difficult and lonely job. Her survival on Eos was a testament to her courage, caution, integrity, and intelligence.

Our original platoon leader, Second Lieutenant Francisco Gonzales, who commanded our disjointed platoon for more than a year in space, had lasted but three weeks before he'd been killed trying to rescue three Marines surrounded by the Gorgons. He had charged in, all by himself, blazing away at the enemy. His actions allowed the Marines to escape but it cost him his life. He had received a posthumous Scarlet Nova for exceptional heroism, a posthumous Crimson Nebula, and a posthumous promotion to first lieutenant.

He hadn't thought things through. He had charged forward fueled by his emotions and adrenalin, and it cost him his life. He'd had enough Marines with him to come up with a quick plan to out-maneuver the enemy without losing anyone, yet he failed to do so.

To his credit, Gonzales never asked anyone to perform any task he wasn't willing to perform himself. But survival in war requires more than physical courage, it also requires quick wits and intelligence. Gonzales was an intelligent man, but he let his emotions get the better of him.

Two weeks after Gonzales' death, Lieutenant Kwung had arrived. She was fresh from a rear echelon job as a quartermaster's assistant. Though out of the Naval Academy for more than a year, she had never commanded a platoon nor led any Marines into combat. Even so, she willingly listened to Gunnery Sergeant Kano as he shepherded her throughout her first months leading the platoon. He had vowed never to let another member of our platoon make the same mistake that Gonzales had made. And Kwung never did. As a result, our casualties remained low.

As low as total warfare allowed, anyways.

Her kind words for me surprised me. "Thank you, ma'am," I replied.

She nodded. I was too tall for her to look over my shoulder so she leaned to one side and glanced back at the CP. "Walk with me, Lion."

"Aye, aye, ma'am."

She led the way down the corridor. Ten meters beyond the CP she said, "I have a bad feeling about this mission, Lion. I've an even worse feeling about Major Bennett. He troubles me."

We walked a few more meters before heading down a side passage to our right. We proceeded toward the enlisted quarters.

After a long silence, I asked, "Is there something more I should know, lieutenant?"

She nodded. "Bennett's up to something. And I don't think the mission is his top concern. Be careful."

"I always am, ma'am."

"I know that, Lion. It's one of the qualities that we all value in you."

"We, ma'am?"

"The skipper, the XO, myself, Mo, and most of the platoon. We feel safe around you."

"Thank you, ma'am."

She stopped, turned, and looked up at me. "Bennett graduated two years before me and already he's a major. I've been a platoon leader for a year and I'm still a platoon leader. The skipper's been a captain for four years and she graduated ten years ago. Bennett reached major in five years and he's never commanded a platoon or a company."

"Ma'am, maybe he just went right into Intelligence." Major Bennett had been a year ahead of me in the Academy. I hadn't known him. Though Lieutenant Kwung had graduated a year after me, I had never known her, either. I had seen her around the Academy's campus a few times but that's all I remembered of her. It was strange having officers around me that were so close to my age and yet I had never known them at the Naval Academy.

However, I was only a noncommissioned officer while they were officers. Whether I had known them or not was irrelevant.

"Yes, he did enter Intelligence right away. And he's excelled at it. Make no mistake about it. He's proven himself many times in combat. But I think he's a ladder climber and I feel this mission's more about reaching his goal of commanding a battalion than about gathering intelligence or bringing back everyone he takes out with him."

"Does he leave people behind, ma'am?"

"I don't know, but I'm afraid people might be expendable to him. Watch out for him. I think we're all just tools for his ambitions. He's got a powerful agenda, Lion. Be extra cautious."

"I will."

"You'll be short two Marines in your team. RC's not scheduled to return from the hospital for at least another week, if not longer."

"How's that possible, ma'am? He should've been out before me. His nanites did most of the repairing while I carried him around Belden and while he was in the coma."

She shook her head. "I don't know. Maybe there were complications."

"Could the major be behind it?"

"I don't know. But I think that anything's possible with him."

"If he's as clever as you think, ma'am, then maybe he can do whatever he wants," I suggested.

She nodded in agreement. "I'll look into it. But as I said, you'll be short two Marines. Sergeant Hunter's no longer part of your team. But you'll be responsible for his safety."

"And no doubt the success of the mission."

"No doubt."

"What is the mission, ma'am?" I asked.

She shook her head. "I'm not cleared for that, Lion."

I grunted.

"Your team's waiting for you in the mess hall. Go see them and get something to eat."

"I'm not sure I'm hungry now, ma'am."

She laughed. It sounded like water bubbling over rocks. I loved hearing it. "I've seen you eat, Lion. You'll find your appetite once you connect with your team. Get going."

"Aye, aye, ma'am."

FORTY

I THOUGHT I'D BE EXCITED to see my team again, to know that they were well and safe. But after what Lieutenant Kwung had said about Major Bennett and this upcoming mission, I wasn't so sure about wanting them along. Did I want to lead them into harm's way for someone else's petty agenda? Did I want to go out there, not knowing if the major had our backs, or if we were just cannon fodder?

Every day, every hour, every minute, was a lifetime in this war. Everyone who fought here knew his or her life was on the line. Anyone could die at any moment. But they fought for duty, for glory, to defend the weak, to save humanity, for their honor and their friends. Not one single person wanted to sacrifice his or her life for someone else's personal ambitions.

But as I walked into the galley and saw Kamal, Ruby and Berk sitting at a small round table in a corner, chatting with Chip and Corporal Sami Souza, I felt relief and that I'd really, truly come home. This was my family!

Striding across the room, I caught them unawares. "Partying without me?"

"Lion!" Ruby and Berk exclaimed, coming to their feet. Their smiles were so big that they looked almost like little kids.

Kamal, ever cool, stood and offered me his hand. "Glad you're back."

"I'm happy you all made it back safe."

"I'm glad you're back," Ruby said.

"So am I," Berk said. He gave me a hearty bear hug, one that almost choked the wind out of me. When he let go of me, he glanced around. "Where's RC?"

"Still in sickbay. The docs decided he needed more rest."

"That lucky bastard!" Berk exclaimed. "We get back in record time, with only a little fire fight here and there and after a quick physical they send us right back out to fight again. And RC gets to sleep. Some guys get all the breaks."

I nodded. "Some do."

"Sit down," Kamal said, gesturing toward the table. "The first sergeant came in and told us all about the new mission. We're up to date. But we want to know everything that happened out there."

"Yes!" Ruby exclaimed. "Sergeant Saunders told us what you told him, but we know that can't be everything."

"Rube, how do you know that's not everything?" Berk teased.

She glared at him. "Shut up."

"Ruby, manners," Kamal said.

"What manners?" I said.

She punched me in the shoulder.

"Ouch!" I said.

"Everyone, sit down," Chip said, grinning. "Your mission begins soon enough."

"It does," I said, sitting down. "So, Ruby, blood? How'd you come to that conclusion?"

"I told you it'd come back to bite your ass, Rube," Berk said.

"Shut it!" Ruby said to him. To me, she said, "I don't really remember how that idea came to me."

"Yes, you do," Kamal said.

Glaring at him, she turned back to me. "We were trying to figure out what was going on."

"We sure as hell were," Berk interrupted.

"I told you to shut your mouth. Got it?"

"If I was you," Corporal Souza said. "I'd do what she said."

"Sounds like a plan to me," Chip agreed.

"And to me, too," I added.

Berk closed his mouth.

Ruby continued. "Like I said, we were trying to figure out why our suits were malfunctioning."

"Even Hunter?" I asked, winking at Chip.

"You're not so big that I can't take you down," she growled at me. "Let me finish what I was saying!"

Chip and I laughed while the others snickered.

Ruby growled in frustration. "You want to hear this or not?"

"Please, continue," I said.

"All right." She glared at all of us.

We had our fun pushing her buttons, but if I wanted to hear her story, I knew I had to control my desire to trick and tease. And from Chip's slight nod, I knew he felt similar.

"After abandoning our failed discs, we discussed the possibilities," she explained. "Kamal pointed out that whatever the problem was, it started as we flew through the clouds of micro-debris released by the dissolving Gorgon armor. Hunter pointed out that it wasn't affecting us but only our suits. Berk thought it was some sort of signal broadcast by the wormheads to our suits. I felt his idea was a little out there."

"Actually," I began, "RC and I agreed on the first two items but we never even considered it being some sort of signal broadcast by the enemy. And, really, RC came up with most of these ideas, anyways. He had quite a few moments of brilliance out there."

"I can see that," Kamal said.

"Moments of brilliance surrounded by many more moments of stupidity, I'm sure," Ruby said.

"Why do you say that?" I asked.

"Because I've worked with him enough to see more stupidity than brilliance," Ruby said.

"I concede the point."

"Anyways, as our suits slowed down more, more things malfunctioned at an alarmingly rate. All the while I kept thinking how was it happening that our suits were malfunctioning but whatever it was wasn't affecting us? Finally, when my suit broke down completely and I barely got out before it froze up, I wondered if the reason we weren't affected was because our nanites might be stronger than whatever virus or plague was affecting our suits. So, when I retrieved my survival knife, I wondered if my blood, filled with millions of nanites, might slow or even stop whatever infested our suits. I never thought it would regenerate them."

"She was also afraid of being stuck out there with a Gorgon company surrounding us and our only weapons consisting of our field knives," Kamal said.

"So maybe I was. But what good are field knives against personal force fields and high energy plasma weapons?"

"None," I said. "You did the right thing, Ruby. We never thought of it. And we almost didn't make it back."

"Thank-you, Lion."

"So, after your suits fixed themselves, with your own nanites, what happened next?" I asked.

"Well," she continued, "after a night of wondering what would happen to us if the wormheads caught us without our suits, during which we worried about you and RC, we found that our suits were fine. Re-entering them, we walked back toward the outpost."

"And right into a pack of Gorgons!" Berk exclaimed.

"Quite true, Lion," Kamal agreed. "We ran out of the bottom of a broken building into this large, dry orange-colored field surrounded by four buildings."

"RC and I were there, probably that night!" I exclaimed. "What are the odds of that?"

"Pretty huge, I think," Chip said.

"You're right."

"I am," he agreed.

"You guys done?" Ruby demanded.

We nodded.

"Good. Then let me finish talking," she growled at us.

"Go for it," Chip said.

"We literally stepped out into a street filled with wormheads. In fact, as Berk came out, he collided with one of their officers in his shiny blue suit. Knocked it right down. A dozen of them turned around to see what had happened."

"Two dozen," Berk corrected her.

"Kamal and I were right behind him. Kamal opened up immediately, scattering them all over the place."

"Did you get any of them?" I asked.

"A couple," she proudly replied.

"Five, to be exact," Kamal stated.

She shrugged her shoulders. "I think Kamal got five."

"And what was Hunter doing?" I asked.

"Wetting himself, probably," Ruby spat.

"Rube, you know that ain't true. He was lookin' for a place to shoot from," Berk said.

"More like hiding until we chased them off," Ruby growled.

"I'll take over from here, Ruby," Kamal announced. "She's a little prejudiced against Sergeant Hunter."

"So I've noticed," I said.

"We fired and ran across the courtyard, ducking whenever the enemy fired at us," Kamal explained.

"Everything except our force fields worked," Berk said.

"He's right," Kamal continued. "We took some damage and made it almost to a building on the far side of the orange-colored field. And then the enemy stopped firing at us.

We ran into one of the buildings, took cover inside, and turned back to cover Hunter as he followed behind us."

"Only the bastard wasn't following us," Ruby snarled.

"And it was a dammed good thing, too!" Berk snapped back at her. "If it weren't fer him, we would've been dead."

"What do you mean?" I looked from Berk to Ruby and then to Kamal, wondering what was going on while at the same time knowing what their answers would be.

"He found a secure location to fire from. When we glanced back, prepared to repel a massive attack, we saw the courtyard filled with bodies. Only a few were burned while the rest looked relatively unharmed."

"But they sure weren't movin'," Berk added.

"They were dead, as far as we could tell. We couldn't see where Hunter shot from, but we saw the effects. The Gorgons pressed toward the building. But as they drew closer to his location, they fell. And when they fell, they never rose again. Some tried rushing him in twos and threes. They fell, too, never to rise again."

"He mowed 'em down like they were weeds!" Berk exclaimed with enthusiasm.

"Exactly. We knew eventually they'd get to him as more and more of them swarmed in from side streets. But the more that appeared, the more that Hunter killed.

"While watching him slaughtering the enemy, I realized the sky was darkening. So, I checked my suit and my screen was available. Berk and Ruby checked their screens and they were fully charged and ready for use. I contacted Hunter, explaining we were running out of time. I told him we were going to attack the enemy from behind. We'd push them toward him. He agreed."

"With a lot of swearing and foul-mouthed comments," Ruby complained. "What a mouth he has on him!"

"Maybe you'd like to kiss him," Berk quipped. "You're always talking 'bout him. Maybe ya love him!"

"Maybe you'd like to lose your teeth," she replied.

"So," Kamal continued, ignoring them both, "we attacked from behind and after a few minutes of being caught between an invisible killer and our lethal rifles, they scattered and fled every which way. "We made a quick inspection and found six officers among the three dozen dead Gorgons."

"Nearer to four dozen," Berk corrected.

"Perhaps so," Kamal agreed. "After taking stock of our killing spree, I led us out of there. A few hours of hard walking and we made it back to the Outpost."

"Where they were havin' the same problems we'd been havin'," Berk said. "Ruby told 'em about the blood thing and we stood watch all night while their suits came back online."

"It was a long walk home with Berk and Hunter," Ruby complained. "They compared notes on the day's massacre. They were like two teenage boys, comparing how many girls they'd bedded and how big their cocks were."

"Ruby!" Kamal exclaimed. "When are you going to learn to act like a lady?"

"When I leave the Marines," she snarled back at him.

"And there you have it, ladies and gentlemen, the definitive answer," Chip said, standing and straightening his uniform. "You have a little more than seven hours to rest and gather your gear before meeting Major Bennett at the Landing Bay. Best get going, children."

"Aye, aye, your majesty!" Ruby snarled, standing and bowing low to Chip. "And may the winds of fortune blow your farts back into your face."

With that comment, Ruby turned and marched from the galley.

"There you have it," I retorted to Chip. "Proof positive that not all Marines can keep their tongues in their mouths when they should. Especially, when a woman of Ruby's temperament is around."

"You're quite right," Chip said. We all laughed as we left the mess hall.

FORTY-ONE

MY ALARM AWAKENED ME an hour before departure. I showered, who knew when I'd have another opportunity to bathe, and dressed. I met my team in the galley. We were the only ones there. A robot served us real eggs, real steak, real bacon, real bread, real vegetables, real fruit! No more artificially made food. No food made from bean curd.

Real food, that's what we ate, wholesome food, food that tingled and tantalized our taste buds, food we could sink our teeth into and be happy about it. It seemed so unreal, so incredible, so absolutely welcomed and wonderful.

Half an hour before departure, First Sergeant Jones arrived. He got a cup of coffee in a big white mug from the robot server and sat down among us. Grinning, he said, "My, my, aren't the four of you feasting like royalty? Or the condemned."

"What d'you mean by that?" I demanded.

He sipped his coffee. "Do you want the sanitized story that Major Bennett gave me, or the real one the skipper told me to tell you?"

"The real one?" Kamal asked.

Jones nodded. "The real one."

"So there's a difference?" I asked.

He nodded.

"Better tell us both," I said. "So we can have the official version if we're questioned by the major as well as the real one told by the captain."

Jones laughed. "That's what I love about you, Lion, you're smarter than the average Marine."

I said nothing.

"Well, the official briefing is that Brigade Intelligence, of which Major Bennett is the new director for the Belden area, wants to gather up some recently killed Gorgons and take them back for scientific study. Your job is to provide the victims. Now, blasting their heads off leaves a mess and doesn't give us enough information on what makes them tick."

"That's where Hunter comes in," I interjected.

"You're absolutely correct there, Lion," Jones said. "We've noticed how surgically precise his laser rifle is in killing the enemy. A head or a body shot still leaves enough to dissect. Whereas vaporizing the head eliminates that part of the body and burns a lot of the rest of it."

"I don't get it," Berk said. "We've collected the dead and examined them before. Don't we have enough info?"

"You'd think so," Jones agreed. "But apparently not."

"But, still, sergeant, we're pretty good at killing them now," Berk continued. "Why do we need to get more info about 'em?"

"Why? Because you're ordered to, that's why!" Jones growled.

Ruby grunted.

"Don't approve of that, Private Johnson?" Jones asked.

"I don't. Aside from your unhelpful attitude, why the hell do we need to know anything more about them?"

"Because we know so little," I said.

"Well, apparently, you know a lot more than anyone else does, Lion," Jones said.

"What do you mean?" I asked.

"I mean," he continued, "that Bennett doesn't know what you know."

"And it's his job to know," Kamal said.

Jones jabbed a finger at Kamal. "You got it. This mission is about ego. Lion has upset the balance of intelligence in this war. He knows things no one else knows, things that the men and women in Marine Intelligence should know, but don't. And that's pissing them off. A lowly sergeant knows more than all of these experts, from scientists up through generals. It makes the lot of them look like fools."

"But, why should they?" I asked.

Jones threw his hands up in exasperation. "Because it's your job to fight and maybe die and their job to figure things out and make good use of it. That's why!"

"And they don't enjoy being upstaged by you," Kamal said.

"That's absolutely correct, Corporal Kamal!" Jones exclaimed. "However, that said, the skipper thinks there's more going on here than we can see. She wanted me to tell you just that."

"Lieutenant Kwung feels the same way," I said. When Jones and the others looked at me, I told them how she had expressed her concerns to me.

"Good for her," Jones said. "She's a smart one. Someday, this'll be her company."

"What will happen to the skipper then?" Berk asked, concerned.

Jones grinned. "She'll be running the brigade."

"Or at least First Battalion," Ruby quipped.

"You got that right," the first sergeant agreed.

"So, officially, we're going out to hunt and kill Gorgons and try to bring them back whole?" Kamal summed up.

"Exactly," Jones replied.

"And what's the captain think?" I asked.

"Well, Bennett's not taking along containment tanks for freezing the enemy's corpses but capture tanks."

"What!" Ruby exclaimed.

I shook my head. "So he's going out to capture live Gorgons?"

"Well, it ain't worth a damn capturing dead ones, is it?"

"That puts us all at a greater risk than just harvesting corpses," Kamal said.

"It does." Jones picked up his coffee mug, stared into it, lifted it to his lips and slurped up whatever moisture remained. Then he set his mug down and shoved it across the table.

"And that's the reason for Hunter coming out here and dragging us out on this patrol," Kamal said. "So he can wound them rather than kill them."

"Could be," Jones replied.

My team looked at Jones, but I knew him better. He understood Hunter as well as I did. Hunter enjoyed killing. That made him even more dangerous than the enemy. But did it make him more dangerous than Major Bennett?

"You got twenty minutes to get to the landing bay," Jones said. "Use it wisely."

FORTY-TWO

THE LANDING DOCK WAS empty save for a handful of robots performing maintenance tasks. None of the robots paid any attention to us but rather kept busy with their work. We walked past them to our suits.

"Where's this major?" Berk asked.

"I don't know," I replied. I hoped that at the last moment Bennett's operation had been cancelled and he'd been recalled to the brigade's headquarters.

"Seems lonely here, doesn't it?" Kamal said. We looked at him. He smiled a bit. "After all, usually, day or night this dock's filled with activity. Why not this morning? What's different about today?"

I shrugged. Looking around, I noticed there were a lot fewer suits present than there should've been. Third Platoon occupied the outpost, which should have left more than a hundred suits in the dock, enough for the First and Second platoons, plus the Headquarters and Support Platoon. Even with a patrol or two out and the fire teams guarding approaches to the company's base, there still should have been many more armored suits present.

"I thought Virgil was joining us," Berk said.

"Count your blessings if he's not," Ruby grouched.

Berk grunted. "I think I'll suit up."

"We should all do that," Kamal agreed.

"Indeed, you should!" a voice commanded. It came from beyond where our silent suits stood.

From the exit tunnel, Major Bennett moved toward us, his head exposed above his suit. Behind him floated six more Marines. Five floated in enclosed suits while the sixth Marine's head was also exposed. It was Hunter.

"Hey, Lye-un, good ta see ya agin!" Hunter cried out.

I nodded.

Bennett's suit settled beside mine. The back of his suit opened and he stepped out. "I see you're all bright-eyed and bushy-tailed and raring to go!" he exclaimed. His smile was big and wide and white, and as cold as ever. When he smiled, I felt like his mouth was filled with ice instead of teeth.

Berk, Kamal, and Ruby stared at him.

"Come on," Bennett whined. "That was a good line! You should've at least smiled. Laughter would've been better, though."

"Ya think?" Ruby replied.

That got a laugh out of me. The major turned around with a sour glare. Then he grinned. "I guess I fell into that one. Well, is everyone ready for the mission? Did the good company sergeant fill you in?"

"He did," I said.

"Good. There'll be four robots with us, carrying the containment tanks for the bodies. If we're lucky, maybe we can stuff two corpses into each one. We'll try, anyways."

"Got it."

"Good," he replied. "I'll lead us out of the base, Sergeant Biyela. Your team will accompany me. Once we reach the outside, your team will lead the way. Sergeant Hunter will stay with my team. Two of my Marines, corporals Conway and Hats'ma, will protect the containment tanks. Questions?"

"Yes, sir," Berk replied.

"Very well, ask away," the major said.

"Where'd you get that funny-looking suit? I mean, major, with your head exposed like that you wouldn't last a minute in combat," Berk stated the obvious. "You'll be the first one any wormhead burns."

Bennett laughed.

"Well, you see Marine..."

"Lance Corporal Umar Berk, sir," Berk interjected. "But people just call me Berk."

"Yes, of course. Well, Berk, this is the new 5200 SCM2S model. Most Marines here on Eos, including you, operate the older 5147. My team operates the more recent 5175. But this newer model has better sensors, better capabilities, including the ability to retract its headgear, better power, better protections against alien nano viruses, better everything. In fact, my rifle even has a larger magazine, providing me with fifty percent more shots than your rifles. All in all, it's a nicer ride than yours." The designation SCM2S stood for Space Combat Marine Support Suit, with the 2S referring to the words support and suit.

"When you pull your headgear on, sir," Ruby asked, "is it big enough for your head?"

With his eyes closed, Bennett shook his head. Then he chuckled. When he opened his eyes, he said to Ruby, "You're Private Johnson, right?"

"Aye, aye, sir!" she replied, coming to perfect attention.

He nodded. "I'm going to have to be careful around you, aren't I, private?"

"Aye, aye, sir!"

"Very well. Any other questions?"

Berk nodded his head.

"Well, lance corporal?" Bennett asked Berk.

"When will we be gettin' our 5200s, sir?"

The major smiled his iceberg teeth. "Not for a long time. They're only being given to officers and special units, such as the newly forming sniper teams, for the moment. A few rifle companies in the heaviest fighting areas are also receiving them. Unfortunately, at the present time there's none available for the rest of you."

"Aye, aye, sir," Berk replied, disappointed.

"But don't worry," Bennett said, smiling again, "when we get back you should be receiving newer suits. You'll receive either the 5160 or the 5175. They'll not be much different from your 5140s, except for better screens and somewhat larger rifle magazines."

"Yes, sir," Berk replied.

Bennett turned to me. "You have a good team, Biyela. Suit up."

"Aye, sir!" I said, coming to attention. "Mount up!"

FORTY-THREE

After securing ourselves in our suits and performing our pre-mission assessments of our supplies and suit systems, we took one of the supply routes heading north and away from Belden. We traveled for several kilometers before zagging down a side tunnel, moving westward. Almost an hour later, we zigged north again.

I wondered, as did my team, why we took such a circuitous route away from our destination. The major never told us. But eventually, we exited from underground into a fading purple sky, a few fading stars still present. We were thirty kilometers northwest of Belden. After a few minutes gliding through low steep hills, hills still covered in healthy trees and with the white stringy stuff that passed for grass on Eos, the major settled us down on a steep hillside.

We were widely scattered among the trees. To our east, a golden streak chased the purple from the sky, replacing it with a growing blueness.

"What's going on, sir?" Kamal asked.

Major Bennett turned his suit around so it faced south toward the distant city. "We're just getting out of the way, corporal."

We all turned and looked at the city, far away from us. Using our suits' visual systems to enhance our view of distant Belden, we saw little dots moving above the city. Some of these dots meandered about while others flew tight figure-eight patterns.

When I zoomed in my visual system I saw that the highest dots, those flying figure eights, were Sky Command fighters. Four fighters flew HI COP over the city. Beneath the fighters, closer down and almost among the buildings, drifted a full squadron of Marine gunboats.

As we watched, a single larger craft, much bigger than the fighters and even the gunboats, lifted up out of the ruins. Immediately, our gunboats surrounded the larger craft and escorted it away from the city, in our general direction. The fighters followed for a few moments and then veered up and away into the sky.

A few moments more and the craft, a troop transport, raced over our position. It streaked northward, the gunboats following, until it disappeared from our sensors.

"What was that all about?" I wondered aloud on the general communications channel.

"A simple rescue mission, Sergeant Biyela," Major Bennett said. "Most of Binary Company's First Platoon was out there, securing the rescue."

"Who was being rescued?" I asked.

"A woman and thirty or so children that had hidden out in the underground operations center for Belden's subway system. Haven't you heard about them?" the major asked, his voice accusatory.

I didn't know what he was talking about and told him so.

"Are you absolutely certain, sergeant? You were out there for several days. You might have run into them."

"Sir, I still don't know what you're talking about. I'd have a memory of doing so, but I don't. I'd remember finding a bunch of women and children survivors hiding beneath the city if I found them. I'm certain I would. In fact, I know I would."

"I didn't say 'women and children', sergeant. I said a woman, singular, and children, plural. Got that?"

"Got it, sir."

"And you're certain you don't remember them at all? You know nothing about them?" Bennett inquired of me. For some reason, he couldn't let it go.

"Not a thing, sir."

"Well, it's your memory. I'm sure you'd remember them if you'd met them," the major said.

"I'm sure I would, sir."

"Very well. Get organized, people. We're moving out, heading back to Belden as carefully and quietly as possible. Got that?"

"Aye, aye, sir," everyone acknowledged.

FORTY-FOUR

B ERK AND I TOOK the lead, with Ruby and Kamal following about twenty meters behind us. Major Bennett, Hunter, and three of Bennett's Marines followed fifty meters further back. Behind them came the robots carrying the capture tanks, guarded by the two corporals Bennett had mentioned before.

We were stretched out over more than a hundred meters of terrain. Out here in the hills, behind our own lines, we were safe. However, when we reached the city such a long formation could be easily ambushed.

The four robots carrying the capture tanks, which the major continued calling containment tanks, had their own antigrav units attached to their backs. Their units were less maneuverable than our grav discs but as they were just muscle and only needed to carry the tanks, it didn't matter. They weren't going to engage in combat. Other than computerized plasma cannons, the Marines didn't use combat robots. That age had come and gone in humanity's history.

Even though the robots carrying the capture tanks possessed limited glide maneuverability, they still kept up with us. I monitored them just as I monitored everyone on this mission. I not only led the vanguard, I needed to know where everyone else was in case anything went sour.

It took us less than fifteen minutes of dodging trees, of darting down into draws and gullies, of popping over rocks and scooting below ridgelines before we reached the outskirts of the hills. As the hills flittered away, I pulled my team closer behind me until we reached the last low, rolling hill, where I reformed my team again. I halted them while I drifted up until just the merest millimeter of my suit poked over the hill's crest. My sensors scanned the terrain beyond the hillside. What I saw beyond me was several kilometers of gutted farmland before the first low ruins of the city's perimeter appeared. Stretching straight from the hills to the city was a wide, wrecked road. A few burned-out farmhouses littered the landscape.

There was no cover to be had.

"What's the holdup, Biyela?" the major asked as he drifted up beside me.

Dropping beneath the crest, I sent Bennett my recording of the terrain on the other side. His fancy headgear bobbed up and down as he studied my recording.

"Well, I guess we'll just have to fly as fast we can into the city," he said.

"The Gorgons might see us, sir".

"They might," he agreed. "However, Binary Company controls that part of the city. I'll let them know that we're coming through and ask them to watch out for us."

"What if they're in no position to do so, sir?" I asked.

"They know their part in this operation. It'll be fine."

"Aye, sir."

"Send your recording to everyone else, including our mechanical men," he said.

I sent the video.

"We're going to cross that?" Ruby grouched on our team's channel. "Does he know what he's doing?"

"I sure hope so," I said.

"So do I," she replied.

"Okay, listen up," I said to my team. "We'll all go out at once, abreast. Move as fast as you can. If you come under fire hit the ground and take cover. Once we make it into those burned-out houses, we'll spread out. Ruby, you and Kamal cover the others as they come across. Berk and I will proceed in a little distance and set up a perimeter."

"Oh, yeah, a two-Marine perimeter," Ruby growled. "What a great idea."

I ignored her. "Everyone ready?"

They confirmed they were.

"Let's go." We drifted close to the crest. When my suit cleared the top by a millimeter, I performed another quick scan. Nothing had changed. "Now!"

The four of us popped over the hill. We zipped down the other side and raced across the destroyed farmlands.

Kamal and Ruby flew down the right side of the blasted-out road while Berk and I flew down the left side. I was closest to the road while Berk was twenty meters to my left. Across the road flew Ruby. Twenty meters beyond her flew Kamal.

Our screens were down. I didn't want the energy signature from them drawing enemy fire.

We kept low to the ground. Blackened trees, burned-out buildings, ruined crops, and crisped corpses of animals and even people littered the farms. It sickened and enraged me.

Nervous, taut time passed. Finally, we had crossed the farmland to the city's edge. We were now in among the wrecked houses. Kamal and Ruby spread out on either side of the road as we entered the ruins. Berk and I dodged melted ground vehicles as we scooted low among the destroyed homes. Half a kilometer in, we stopped.

I pointed past Berk's shoulder toward where the remains of two blasted houses formed an unnatural barrier. He sped over to it, disappearing among the debris.

I found cover on the other side of the street inside the brick and plastic remains of a store. While we waited, our passive sensors listened for enemy activity. Time passed. No contacts occurred.

"Biyela," the major called, "we're all here."

"Got it."

"I'm sending Sergeants Greiner and Hunter up to you. Once they've arrived, continue forward."

I moved into the open. A minute passed while I felt completely naked. Then Hunter, in his new suit, and the other Marine, Sergeant Greiner, arrived. I motioned them to cover and then called Kamal and Ruby up. They arrived half a minute later.

"Okay, I don't know how far we're going, but keep close. Hunter, you know the drill," I said.

"Ah got it, Lye-un," he replied.

"Good. Sergeant Greiner, you stay close to me. Berk, you stay with Hunter."

"Got it," they chorused.

I led the way, Greiner five meters to my right. Berk and Hunter followed close behind, with Kamal and Ruby bringing up the rear.

We edged down the road, sensors still passive, still listening. One hundred meters, two hundred meters, five hundred meters, with nothing happening.

We were among taller structures now. None of them resembled the giants in the city center but they stood taller than the crushed houses further back along the city's edge. The tallest structure stretched five stories high.

I directed everyone to cover. Then I checked where Bennett and the rest of the patrol were located. They remained five hundred meters back, still among the destroyed homes.

"Biyela, you've stopped. What's wrong?" the major called.

"We're waiting for you to catch up, sir," I said.

"I know what I'm doing, Biyela. Follow your orders and move out."

"Aye, sir.

We moved forward.

FORTY-FIVE

B Y MIDDAY, WE WERE among the skyscrapers of the city's center. While we scooted along, several blocks to my left I spotted the building we called The Slab. It made me queasy.

A lot had happened around that building, though I couldn't recall most of it now. Somehow, it brought a brief shadow or ghostly dream of bodies plummeting from the building before the top portion had been sliced away. I didn't know if it was real, or fanciful. I just knew it meant something to me.

Marines don't feel much fear in the field. It's not that we're incapable of being afraid, because we do feel fear. A lot of it has to do with our constant hours of training for almost every contingency. We depend upon our training when we're in combat to get us through it, and it does.

Yet, upon seeing The Slab, I still felt frightened. Something much more than our fighting and fleeing from the Gorgons had happened there. I just wished I could remember it!

We were well ahead of the rest of the patrol. The major and the others were at least two kilometers back.

They meandered along, slowly but surely. Yet if we were attacked, or if they were, we'd be hard pressed to support each other.

"Hunter, Bennett's far behind us. Can you find a good hide or two?" I asked.

"Yeah, 'bout a kilometer ta our right an' a block back."

"We're not going back there. Find something around here."

"Got it, Lye-un. Come on, Berk, we got ourselves some searchin' ta do."

"Got it, Virge," Berk replied.

They sped away. I directed the others into a tall, battered building. A huge Gorgon-made hole ran from the sewers far below straight to the roof above. We steered clear of it. We kept near the street but out of view.

"Everyone still here, take a few minutes," I said. "I'll stand watch."

"Got it," they replied.

While the others powered their suits down, I continued searching with my passive sensors. I caught the faint blips of Hunter and Berk's recognition signals. They were a block away, searching a building similar to the one we rested in, but across the street from us.

I also picked up the faint blips of the rest of the patrol, slowly moving this way. However, I didn't detect any enemy activity. Nonetheless, I kept searching for the Gorgons.

Sergeant Greiner's suit glided up beside me. I had yet to converse with the sergeant.

"How you doin'?" a friendly feminine voice asked me.

"Fine. How about you?" I replied.

"I'm good," Sergeant Greiner replied.

"Good. How long have you been with the major?"

"Long enough. My name's Maria, but everyone calls me Em Gee. For my initials, you see."

"Got it."

"Good."

"So," I said, "is the major always this slow? Does he always split his forces up like this?"

"No. We usually keep a tighter formation. I don't know what's going on today."

"Neither do I," I replied. "But if he doesn't close up, and soon, we could get ambushed. Anything can happen out here."

"Maybe that's what he wants," she said.

"I don't follow you."

I heard an exasperated sigh from her. "Maybe he wants us to get ambushed."

"Why would he want that?" I asked. It would be the worst tactic possible. Only an inexperienced officer would seek to expose his Marines to an ambush.

She grunted. "I've heard from a lot of people that you weren't the brightest bulb around, but I thought it was a joke. Now I see that they were right."

"What are you talking about?" I demanded. There's nothing like being insulted to sour your opinion of someone. Up to this point, I had felt comfortable with her. Now I doubted that estimation.

"Don't you get it, Biyela?" she said. "If we get ambushed, it'll draw the enemy out. Then we can grab a few prisoners and get out of here. The mission would be over with, quick and simple."

"Grab a few prisoners?" I replied, my voice sharp. "I thought our mission was to bring back corpses?"

"That's what it is," she said. "It was just a slip of the tongue, that's all."

"I see. It's still a stupid idea." So she was lying to me, just like the major.

Greiner grunted again.

"So we're some sort of sacrifice for this mission?" I asked. "We're just bait."

She threw her suited arms upward in exasperation. "You gotta do whatever it takes to gather the intelligence needed for crushing the enemy."

"Even if it means getting people killed?"

"Yes," she growled. "Even if it means getting people killed. It's all about the mission."

"And you're okay with that?" I said. "You're okay that he's willing to sacrifice you for the mission?"

"I'm used to it," she said.

"Are you?"

"Yes. Some people might think that the major's more interested in position and promotion," Em Gee said, "but he's not. Maybe a little bit, but not much. He genuinely cares for his fellow Marines and for civilians."

I grunted.

"You don't believe me?" Greiner demanded.

"I don't know what to believe," I lied. After the warnings from Captain Vang and Lieutenant Kwung, I wondered if Bennett's only mission was the advancement of his career. But would he sacrifice anyone and everyone for it?

"I've seen him dismount from his armor to cradle the burned remains of children," Greiner declared. "I've seen him weep. He's a man of deep feeling."

"He might be," I said. "But he better not get any member of my team killed."

"What if it's not his fault?" she asked.

"At the moment, it will be his fault. He should be up here, not way back there. He's endangering us all. And that I cannot abide."

"Well, remember this, Marine, you're still a sergeant, like me, and he's a major. Your duty is to obey him. And that's it!"

"You're wrong," I snarled back at her. "I take it you've never commanded a fire team before?"

"No, I haven't. I'm only an intelligence tech. But I'm also a Marine and expected to fight at any and every moment. I've seen almost as much combat as you, I think. But it's our duty to obey orders. You better not forget that."

"You're still wrong," I repeated. "As a fire team leader, it's my responsibility, my duty, to make certain my team makes it back alive and in one piece. And it's my further responsibility, to my squad, my platoon, and my company, to report back in and give as accurate and correct a report as possible."

Her suit lifted up and she glided away. "I see we'll always be on different sides of the same bulkhead here. I'll admit that you have different responsibilities from me. But you better follow orders or it's your ass."

"I will. But only those that are lawful."

"And whose concept of lawful are you talking about?"

"The one that puts others above self-interest."

"Then we agree on at least that," she said, before switching her comm unit off. She settled her suit down over by the hole in the floor.

I went back to keeping watch.

FORTY-SIX

HALF AN HOUR PASSED, and still the major and his patrol hadn't arrived. But Berk and Hunter had returned.

"Lye-un, there's nary a good hide out there," Hunter said.

"What about this building?" I asked.

"We'll give it a look-see, but don't hold yer breath."

"Understood."

They glided over to the hole vertically traversing the building and went up. While they searched, I checked on the major's location. He was less than a kilometer away, but moving even slower.

Ruby walked over. "What's with Miss Pissy Pants over there?" she said, referring to Sergeant Greiner.

"We disagree about the major's methods, that's all."

Ruby grunted. For Marines, a grunt was one of the most effective and direct forms of communication. And for some Marines, it was practically the only form of expression.

"By the way, where's your disc at?" I asked her.

"Back behind you in one of the corners. I felt like leaving it for a while and walking about. My legs need some exercise."

I didn't say anything. I decided I needed a little exercise, too, and dismounted from my disc.

"Cover this spot for a bit," I said. "I'm gonna look around."

"Have fun."

It was my turn to grunt now. It felt good to move. I understood why she wanted to wander about.

I made my way across the main floor of the building. It was little different from the rest of the ruined buildings I'd seen here in Belden. Blasted-in holes, their edges melted from the extreme heat of plasma fire, pockmarked the walls. Debris lay everywhere about the floor. Shattered doors lay beside offices or led to stairwells. Burned and broken furniture was scattered everywhere. And, of course, under the debris and furniture lay the occasional charcoaled corpse.

Nowhere was there any Gorgon remains. We knew now that they retrieved their dead.

On the far side of the building, which covered a quarter of a city block, I found Kamal. He stood beside the shattered remains of a window, staring across the alley behind where the wrecked remains of another building stood. The window he looked out was a meter square.

"Hello, Lion," Kamal said.

"Seen anything?"

"Just another destroyed building. Just another lovely, exciting day in the beautiful city of Belden."

I snorted at his sarcasm.

"Lion, do those tube-like containers out there contain Gorgon remains?" Kamal inquired.

I glanced out the windowless window. "Maybe."

"Shall we investigate? It is part of our mission, after all, securing intelligence."

"Just a moment," I replied. "Ruby?"

"Yes, Lion?" she responded on the team channel.

"Go pound on Sergeant Greiner's suit. Wake her up and tell her to help watch the front. Kamal and I are going out back to check something out."

"You got it, Lion."

"And get her to turn her comm back on," I added.

"I'll do that," she replied.

To Kamal, I said, "Dismount. It's too crowded out there for flying about. We'll be more maneuverable on foot."

"Got it." He dismounted and drew his rifle from behind his right shoulder and inspected it. I drew mine, too. I checked its magazine load and tested the energy feed from my fusion power plant. Everything seemed fine.

"What about our shields?" he asked.

"It might attract unwanted attention. We'll go naked."

"Good! I always enjoy much freedom while walking the back streets of any major metropolitan city without clothes on."

"You're in good spirits today," I said.

"I just finished praying."

"How's that work, anyways? I've never asked you."

"What do you want to know?" he asked.

"Well, the big question..." I began.

"How do I pray towards Mecca? When it's on Earth, thousands of light years away?" he said. "And where in the sky would Earth be right now? That's three questions, Lion, not one."

"You're right. Those three."

"A fatwa, which is a religious edict or declaration of sorts, was made way back when the first Moslems travelled beyond the Solar System's outer planets. It suggested that when in doubt, always pray to where the sun rises on a planet, symbolically representing the location of Mecca. After all, we pray to where the sun rises on Earth because Mecca is always to the east."

"And what about when you're in space or hyperspace?" I asked.

"Then you pray aft, assuming that you're always moving away from Earth and Mecca. Or, if you're returning to Earth, pray towards the ship's bow, as you're travelling toward Mecca."

"I see. So you prayed to the east just now?" I asked.

"I did," he said. "Acknowledging the supremacy of Allah always eases my heart."

"Good to know."

"You should try it sometime. I understand your ancestors were Moslem."

"Mostly they were Christian. My grandparents attended The Church of the One God. It accommodates all religious beliefs from Earth."

"Not all. There are some radically fanatical beliefs that The Church of the One God doesn't accept."

"Such as?" I asked. We still stood beside the window glancing out into the alley.

"There are some that worship Satan. Some believe that evil is more powerful than good."

"I thought that God was both good and evil."

"Some think that. I choose to see Allah as only good and His goodness as all-powerful. He provides for and cares for those who come to Him in humility, with an honest heart, seeking only His will and His blessings, and accepting the good he gives to those who genuinely seek to follow him."

"I never thought of it that way."

"There's more about it all that we could talk about sometime," Kamal offered.

"I'd like that," I said. "But for now if we're going to go outside and check out those tubes, we better move before any Gorgons show up."

"Yes. How do we go about getting out there? This window's too small for us to climb through with our suits on," he explained.

"Good point." I looked around. Broken shelves and smashed cooking equipment lined the walls beyond. I hadn't noticed before, but this looked like a small café or perhaps a commissary. There were tables and chairs scattered about, burnt and broken. To my right was a blown-out door leading into another room. I went through it and found a smashed door leading out into the alley.

"Over here," I said to Kamal. He made his way into the room. Because of our big suits, together we barely fit inside it.

"A back door," he said.

"So it seems." I kicked debris away from the door and then, with one hand, while I held my rifle in the other hand, I yanked the smashed door open. Part of it fell to the floor and I kicked it outside. Then I stepped through.

Kamal followed me.

FORTY-SEVEN

GRASPING MY RIFLE WITH both hands, I swung around and looked down the alley, my legs spread wide, bracing myself against enemy plasma fire. Kamal did the same behind me, oriented toward the opposite direction. But no aliens fired at us.

"Well, that was thrilling," Kamal said, followed by a laugh.

"Too much so."

"What now?" Kamal asked.

"Keep your rifle ready and follow me."

"Got it."

I walked over to one of the tube-like containers. Peeling back the cover, I glanced inside it. Before me lay a dead Gorgon, half its head missing. "Take a look."

Kamal did. After a moment, he straightened. "Something's odd."

"Like what?"

"It's head, it doesn't look like it's been hit by a plasma weapon. There's no burn marks or damage. It just appears to be half missing."

First glancing up and down the alley, I then looked back at the alien corpse. "You're right. I wonder why?"

Before Kamal could answer, Ruby called, "Lion."

"What's up?" I asked.

"Major Bennett's here. He's looking for you."

"Be right there." I pulled the cover back over the dead Gorgon. "Time to get back inside. Once you're in, remount your disc and keep an eye out here. I'll send Ruby to keep you company. When she joins you, pile some stuff by this back door. Make anything that wants to sneak in this way work for it."

"Got it."

After we re-entered the building, I left Kamal behind. I quickly walked back to the front of the building. I had just climbed back onto my grav disc when I spotted Major Bennett drifting over the cracked and battered remnants of the wide sidewalk in front of the building. He had his headgear retracted. His rifle remained holstered on his back. With his gloved fists upon his hips, his arms bent, he surveyed the city before him.

I shook my head, glad that no one could see my motion due to the stiffness of my suit. This guy was going to get himself killed, moving around without his headgear on and striking dramatic poses all the time. He was just inviting a Gorgon to take a shot at him.

I glided over to him. He spotted me as I approached. "Sergeant Biyela, why have we stopped here?"

"To let you and the rest of the patrol catch up with us," I replied, surprised by his comment.

"That's commendable, sergeant, but you didn't need to do so. We're perfectly capable of protecting ourselves."

"I understand that, sir," I lied. I had no idea how capable he was of defending himself or his people. I had never seen him in combat.

"You should be looking for a place for us to settle in and wait for the Gorgons to show up," he added.

"Aye, sir. We stopped for that reason, too. Sergeant Hunter and Lance Corporal Berk are seeking sniper hideouts even as we speak."

"Indeed?" he asked, his eyes colder than ever. I was glad he couldn't see my face or my eyes. Otherwise, he might see the contempt I felt for him. "And what makes you think this is a good place to stop?"

"This is the general area, sir, where we've had the most contact with the enemy during our recent patrols."

"Really?" he said. "From what I've studied of your patrols around here, this is where you let yourself be ambushed, costing the life of a new member of your team."

Before replying, I concentrated on maintaining my self-control.

"Well, Biyela?" he growled. "Is this where you think we'll get the best hunting done?"

"Aye, sir."

"Why?" he hissed.

"Because out in the alley behind this building, sir, are dozens of dead Gorgons in their coffin cocoons," I replied.

"I'm looking for whole bodies, Biyela, not maimed corpses."

"At least one of them has a partial head," I said.

"I see. You've inspected them. You think we can grab a bunch of bodies out of those cocoons back there and then skip back home before anyone gets hurt? Well, Biyela, I want whole corpses, not bits and pieces of the aliens."

He entered the building. I followed him inside.

"Sergeant Greiner!" He called on the patrol channel.

"Yes, sir!" she responded, drifting over to us.

"Take a detail out back and burn all those alien bodies out there. Don't let one little bit survive."

"Aye, aye, sir," she said.

"No!" I growled. "I mean, sir, don't do that."

"Why not?" he snarled. "Are you afraid to offend whatever god or demon the Gorgons worship? Or are you just afraid, sergeant? Like you were when your listening post, what did you call it, oh, yes, The Slab, was invaded by gobs of Gorgons? You abandoned The Slab and split your team up and then you abandoned your suits so the enemy could get ahold of them.

"You seem to abandon everything. Do you want to abandon this mission, too? Admit it. You might be a great warrior but you're only good at it when you're running away."

Though his headgear was down his suit mike was on, and he had it set to the general broadcast frequency for everyone in the patrol. Everyone could hear what he was saying to me and what I said in return.

I steadied myself. "No, sir."

He glared at me. Then he said to Greiner, "Burn them all, sergeant. That's my order."

"Sir, the Gorgons will be back for those bodies. How are you going to get any corpses if you destroy the bait?"

He continued glaring at me with his glacial eyes. Then his face softened. His mouth quirked into a little smile.

Relaxing, he shook his head. "Biyela, you're always thinking ahead. You're right. If we destroy those bodies they probably won't come back here. Then the mission will take longer, if it doesn't end up a bust. Sergeant Greiner, disregard my last order."

"Aye, aye, sir," she responded.

FORTY-EIGHT

MAJOR BENNETT TURNED BACK to me. "Sergeant Biyela, show me where these coffins you found are."

"This way, sir," I said, jerking my gloved thumb over my right shoulder.

"Lead on."

I spun around and glided toward the back of the building, floating across the rubble-covered floor towards the rear rooms. As we skirted the Hole extending down into the sewers and up into the top of the building, Hunter and Berk drifted down.

"Hey, Lye-un," Hunter called to me. "We found some good hides up there. This is a good place fer snipin'."

Before I could reply, the major said, "Glad to hear that, Sergeant Hunter. Next time, report to me."

"Yew got it, majuh. Ah had no idea yew was heah already."

"Now you know. Do you need anything else?"

"No, suh."

"Get your report in to Staff Sergeant Waldau. When you're done, return to your 'hide'. Got it?"

"Aye, aye, majuh."

"Good."

Hunter drifted off. Berk, however, floated above us, not knowing where to go or what to do.

"Need some guidance, lance corporal?" Bennett said to Berk, without raising his head up to look up at him.

"Yes, sir," Berk replied.

"Well, if Sergeant Biyela has assigned you to Hunter then I suggest you stick to him like glue. And make sure nothing happens to him. He's too valuable an asset to lose."

"Aye, aye, sir!"

"Get going."

Berk scooted after Hunter.

"Some Marines are like little children, Biyela," the major explained. "They want you to hold their hands. But you can't do that, not if you want them to function efficiently within a fire team. You make suggestions and if those don't work then order them where to go and what to do. It's the only way. Anything else is less than professional."

"Yes, sir." I turned and led Bennett toward the building's back. Berk was a good Marine and knew his place and his job. After surviving a year of almost constant combat it'd be surprising if he didn't know what to do. Berk's problem was he was intimidated by Bennett, which was the major's intention. He wanted everyone scared of him.

But I wasn't interested in being either intimidated or scared. Rather, I was wary of the major. The more I saw of how he handled this patrol, the less I trusted him.

FORTY-NINE

FOR THE REST OF the day we remained where we were. Major Bennett called the building we were in Location One. But after a while, Hunter and Berk started calling it Bennett's Place and that's the name that stuck. Soon everyone, even the major, called it such.

While the major and Sergeant Greiner inspected the cocoons out in the alley, Staff Sergeant Hana Waldau, Bennett's team leader, set up camp. She went upstairs with Hunter to inspect his hides and made some suggestions. One was for Hunter to find cover on the roof, where he could watch the street below and yet scurry to the back of the building to watch the alley as well. She directed him to gather ruble and debris so as to cover his movements from the sky and from observers in the taller buildings surrounding Bennett's Place.

I knew all this because she kept her comm on the patrol frequency so the major could hear what she suggested. So, while I watched the street from below, and while my team was scattered about the building, I heard everything. I was kept from participating yet I knew what was going on.

How odd it seemed to me, to be sidelined like this. I had led my team on the most dangerous portion of our mission so far: crossing the open terrain outside the city and then scouting ahead until we picked a place to set up a base camp and observe the enemy's movements. But though my team and I had risked our lives getting us here, now we were nothing more than glorified guards while others took over and led the way.

The last to arrive in the patrol were the four robots moving the containment tanks. They were the most odd-looking robots I'd ever seen. While most robots mimicked people in almost every way, from appearance and motion to voice and personality, these four looked like they'd been assembled from water pipes and left-over agricultural equipment. They sported pipes for arms and legs, with thick joints at the shoulders, elbows, wrists, knees and ankles. Their heads had a conical shape to them, as if assembled from antique steam whistles. Their chests appeared to be flattened barrels and their hips seemed like a cartoon rendition of the human pelvis. Their feet looked like heavy metal boots while their hands seemed to be made of three-fingered gloves.

And their faces? They hadn't any faces. Even the Gorgons possessed the semblance of a face, with orifices for eating and breathing. But these robots had electronic bulbs for eyes, and nothing else.

All in all, they seemed cartoonish and comical, as if from an ancient animated video or an Industrial Age dream of mechanical men. And yet, strangely enough, they appealed to me.

I enjoyed watching them move about in their oddly mechanical manner, lacking all the artifice and dignity of the more sophisticated robots interacting with humanity. Yet these robots seemed more real and acceptable to me.

Sergeant Waldau, back from the roof, showed the robots where to go and what to do. After stacking the containers in a corner, the four mechanical men sat crossed-legged on the floor, just like real people, and became inanimate. They powered down.

While I watched the robots settle, the two corporals guarding them glided in beside me, settling to the deck.

"Curious things, aren't they?" one of them said. His suit identification said Hatsuma.

"They are," I replied.

"The major likes them. He got 'em on Tengaku when he was stationed there a few years ago," the other corporal, Conway, said.

"I'm Sergeant Biyela," I said. "You can call me Lion."

"We know," Conway said. "I'm Charlie. And this is Masaaki Hats'ma."

"Hats'ma?" I asked. "Then why does your suit say Hatsuma?"

"On Tengaku, we're more traditional," Hats'ma replied. "Whereas on other worlds my name might be pronounced as it's spelled, on Tengaku wherever there's an 'S' followed by a 'U' in a name, the 'U' is silent."

"Got it," I said. "Hats'ma it is."

"Good." Hats'ma drifted over to a nearby corner. He used his disc to scatter debris out of his way. Then he rotated around and settled down, his suit facing toward the hole in the wall where a great doorway, now blasted away, had been. That doorway, that hole, I now guarded. Backing out of his suit, he joined me.

"Me and Charlie'll guard this hole," he said. "You're relieved. You've done enough today."

"Thanks."

"It's the major's orders. He told us when we arrived we were to relieve you," Conway said.

"Again, thanks."

"Any time," Conway replied. He remained suited, standing watch while Hats'ma went exploring, no doubt looking for his other teammates, or maybe for a clean toilet.

I drifted away. A quick scan revealed that my team, minus Berk, who watched Hunter, had gathered together on the third floor, near the back of the building. I scooted over to the Hole and popped up two floors. A minute later, I exited my suit.

Kamal and Ruby were both out of their suits. Ruby combed her hair while Kamal heated rations for the three of us. Carrying a blanket and a self-inflating cushion removed from my suit, I spread my gear out beside theirs and settled down.

"A long day," Ruby said.

"Indeed," Kamal agreed.

Glancing around, I saw several blast holes in the nearby walls and a still intact window frame, minus its pane, in the back corner. Crossing the room, I glanced through a shattered door into the stairwell. Though mostly dark inside, the late afternoon sun peeked through a hole in one of the stairwell's walls. The stairs looked remarkably intact. However, the skeletal remains of several people draped down the stairs to the floor below.

What a world. What a war.

Moving away from the stairwell, I walked to the window. I examined it. The heat of several plasma bursts had warped the frame and had melted the glass away.

Through the empty window I saw the alley below. The alien cocoons remained intact and undisturbed. The major hadn't felt the need to disturb or destroy them. Not yet, at least.

"Food's ready," Kamal called.

I returned to our tiny campsite. It seemed so odd, camping out in a broken building. I stood above my friends as they ate. After a few moments, they looked up at me.

"Not hungry?" Kamal asked. "Or just tired?"

"The latter," I said and sat down. Kamal handed me some food on a plate. Ruby offered me hot coffee.

Pulling a spoon from a pocket, I stared at it. My field uniform had automatically cleaned spotless the shiny steel utensil. I dug into my food. It was beef stew, with real beef and real vegetables. It was nothing like the very disappointing tofu we had eaten for most of the year.

Praise to Brigadier General Clarke, our brigade commander, for supplying us with real, tasty, decent food!

When we finished eating, we relaxed. We lay back on our bedding and drank our delicious coffee. After a few minutes, Ruby looked at me in a serious way.

"What?" I asked.

"Why is the major being such an ass with you?" she asked.

I shrugged. "I have no idea."

"And why does he keep asking you about some woman rescued today and the many children rescued with her? D'you know who she is? What's your relationship to her?"

"None, as far as I know."

"Why not?" she asked.

I set my empty cup down and stretched out on my matress.

"Well?" Ruby demanded.

"I don't remember any woman or any children."

"He seems to think you do," she said.

"I can't help that," I said. I looked toward the window and the long shadows on the buildings out in the alley. "Sun's going down, Kamal."

Rising, he grabbed a little colorful rug from his nearby suit and trotted over to the window. He glanced out. Then, turning, he went toward the other side of the building, beyond the Hole and into a back room.

Ruby looked at me and raised an eyebrow in question.

"Prayer time," I explained.

She nodded. "How stupid of me."

I got up and went to the window. Ruby joined me.

"Difficult to image such a lovely sunset on such a horrible world," she said.

I concurred.

As the shadows lengthened and finally dissolved, Kamal came back. Without words we walked back to our bedding. No one had asked us to stand watch. No one came to see how we were doing or to give us any orders for the morrow.

A good leader always checks on all of his Marines. He'll see if they need or want anything. He'll care about them. But Major Bennett ignored us. We were forgotten, unneeded, unwanted. We were nothing to him.

We slept, fidgeting the cold night away.

FIFTY

A BEAUTIFUL MORNING, AND A **beautiful** sunrise, filled our floor with warmth and sunshine.

There'd been no enemy contacts during the night. No ambushes, no firefights, nothing but solitude. A perfect night, without any bad dreams, except for one about a woman I'd never met and children I didn't know. And they, the woman and children, were faceless images, more like blobs than human beings.

A strange dream it was, inspired no doubt by Major Bennett's ruthless accusations.

I rubbed my eyes and crawled out of my bedding. I groaned as I stood. Sleeping on a hard surface wasn't necessarily the best thing for your back.

Looking around, I noticed that Ruby and Kamal must have gathered up their gear and stuffed it in their suits, because both of my Marines and their suits were gone.

By my bedding, I found a cold cup of coffee and a food bar. I ate breakfast.

When I was done, I packed away my cup, bowl and spoon in my suit, which automatically cleaned them, then gathered up my gear and stowed it inside my suit.

Our armored suits, designed for extra-vehicular spatial combat, were virtually miniature spacecraft. Our bedding, cups, plates, limited amounts of food and water, air supply, literally everything we needed to survive in space or on a planet for limited amounts of time, was stored within our suits' leathery walls.

After I loaded my gear into my suit, I found a battered bathroom, relieved myself, found that there was some soapy water present in a stopped-up sink, and washed up before re-entering my suit, my second skin, my home away from home.

Then I contacted Kamal and found out that he and Ruby were with Hunter and Berk, three more floors up. So I joined them.

FIFTY-ONE

Gathering up Hunter and my team, we dropped down to the main floor. The rest of the patrol, from Bennett down through the five Marines in his team and the four robots carrying their burdens, was assembled. Every Marine was suited up. Hunter and the major had their heads enclosed in their suits.

"Glad the rest of you could make it," Bennett began over the patrol channel. "We didn't see any enemy activity last night, nor this morning. This area is contested but inactive at the moment. So we're moving forward. We're going deep into enemy territory. Be ready for anything."

"Why are we doing that, sir?" Kamal inquired.

"Because we need whole bodies to take back for examination," he replied. "We're not going to find them in those cocoons behind this building."

"Sir," I interjected, "let's be honest. Everyone here knows those aren't containment tanks but rather capture tanks. You're looking for prisoners, not corpses."

"You're right, Biyela, I am looking for prisoners."

His reply both surprised and pleased me. I was grateful for his honesty but also surprised that he had given it.

No one said anything. I remained quiet as well.

"All this fighting and no one's been successful at taking Gorgon prisoners," the major explained. "Every time we capture them, they kill themselves. And often when they do, they kill their captors, too. But this time will be different. It has to be different.

"We're slowly losing this war. We have to find better ways of destroying the enemy. If we don't soon, then we'll have to withdraw from Eos and we don't have enough ships to remove the hundreds of millions of colonists."

He paused. We remained quiet.

"So," he continued, "we're moving into enemy territory. We want prisoners. We want them as whole and healthy as possible. We'll stick them in the capture tanks, activate the suspended animation fields, and get out of here as fast as possible. Everyone clear with that?"

"Aye, aye, sir!" we all responded.

"Good. Biyela, your team will lead the way. Sergeants Greiner and Hunter will follow you closely. The rest of us will tighten up and stay close behind you. We won't spread out like yesterday.

"Move slowly and carefully, everyone. I don't want us getting ambushed. I want us to be the ambushers. Got that?" the major demanded.

"Aye, aye, sir!" we responded.

"Good," Bennett said. "Sergeant Biyela, move out."

FIFTY-TWO

BERK AND I DARTED across the street and took cover in a broken building twenty meters down from Bennett's Place. Ruby and Kamal followed us but kept on the other side of the street. We continued in this fashion until we reached an intersection fifty meters down. There we stopped.

I checked my sensors. They didn't detect any enemy activity, but that didn't mean that the Gorgons weren't around us or watching us. I did detect Hunter and Greiner moving down the street on Kamal's side. They kept about forty meters back.

Bennett and his senior sergeant, Waldau, exited the building next. They climbed about halfway toward the rooftops and slipped along, providing top cover for us. Behind them, along the sides of the street, came the robots carrying the capture tanks. Just behind the robots floated corporals Hats'ma and Conway. With them was the last member of the major's team, Sergeant Ludoslav, whom I had to yet meet.

We continued for half a kilometer down the street and then zigged left over a block to the next street. Another half kilometer and we zigged another block left again. We encountered neither friend nor foe.

We kept this pattern for several hours. By mid-afternoon, we had traversed three kilometers to the left and all the way across the city. We saw nothing but ruins. No Gorgons attacked us. The city appeared empty.

On the far side of Belden the forward elements of our patrol, Berk, Greiner, Hunter, Kamal, Ruby, and myself took refuge on the roof of the tallest still standing structure, an almost untouched sports arena. Fifteen meters high at its walls, it towered above the flattened suburbs around it. Circular in design, it covered four city blocks. Its windows and doors were blown in: burn damage around them indicated plasma weapon fire. The roof consisted of a frosted translucent dome. The dome, though cracked, towered ten meters above the edges of the roof. Atop the dome, at its peak, rested a communications platform, its antenna array melted away by enemy fire.

All around us stretched flattened suburbs. They were unlike the suburbs on the farther side of the city we'd encountered the day before. Those suburbs had consisted of smashed and broken buildings, of homes and schools, of businesses and recreation facilities, all crushed, burned and broken. Yet here, nothing was left but ash and dust, bits of glass and plastic, melted metal and crushed ceramics. And beyond all this, beyond the city's edge, stretched burned and charred farmlands for dozens of kilometers.

Nowhere did we see any living sign of the enemy.

I directed Hunter to the communications platform atop the dome, with orders to flatten out as best he could and establish a sniper's hide there. Then I sent Kamal, Ruby, and Berk to the roof's edge, where a meter-high wall encircled the dome. I positioned them exactly one hundred twenty degrees apart around the dome from each other. Their mission was to provide security for us and for the rest of the patrol when it arrived, which would be quite soon.

"And what are we going to do?" Sergeant Greiner asked me.

"We're going to check out the interior," I said.

"By ourselves?" Greiner said, a nervous knot in her voice.

"You got it. Kamal," I called to him, "you're in charge while we check out the inside."

"Got it," he replied. As always, he was ready for anything and everything.

FIFTY-THREE

"LET'S GO, EM GEE," I said.

"Only my friends call me that," she replied.

"Whatever you want."

"I'd rather be somewhere else right now, rather than with a crazy, glory-hunting sergeant ready to get himself and any companions killed by doing it the 'easy way'," she snarled.

"Well, you're here right now and we're going inside. Get used to it."

She made an obnoxious sound, then said, "How are we going to get inside without getting fried?"

"We'll go back down over the side and go through a door," I said. "That's what they're there for."

Since she didn't reply, I floated over the arena's edge and dropped to the ground. My sensors reported nothing. The building and the surrounding ruins seemed deserted. I didn't even pick up the heat signatures of any rodents or small animals. Everything here was dead but us.

Greiner settled beside me. We had our weapons at the ready. The nearest opening large enough to accommodate our suits was twelve meters to our left. I floated over to it.

It had been a large picture window. A few meters before it was a smaller window.

Though the interior was dark, enough light filtered down through the dome for our suits' sensors to translate it into a viewable image.

"How are we going to do this?" Greiner asked me.

"I'll cover you from here and you zip inside," I said.

"Hell, like that's going to happen!" she snarled. "You go first. I'll cover you."

"Okay, I will." I drifted to the left of the hole where the window had been. Glancing inside, my sensors revealed nothing. Nothing living, nothing dead. Nothing moving, nothing waiting. Nothing.

"No, wait," she said. "I'll go."

"You sure?"

"I'm sure."

"Okay. Go for it."

Greiner stood to the right of the opening. After a full minute of waiting, I said, "You okay?"

"I'm fine," she said. "I'm just checking things out."

"Got it."

Another minute went by. "Well?" I demanded.

"Give me a minute."

"You've had two minutes," I said.

"Oh. Yeah. Got it." She shifted her position, but didn't go inside. Something was wrong.

Leaving my covering position, I scooted inside.

"What are you doing?" she demanded.

"My job, protecting my partner."

"We're not partners," she snapped back. "I can handle myself!"

"So I imagined."

"Then why didn't you let me do my job?"

"You still can," I said. "Get in here and cover me while I scout out the building."

Her reply sounded almost inaudible, but nasty and negative nonetheless. I ignored it. She entered the arena and slid off to my right.

I glanced around the interior. Pieces of wood, bits of glass, plaster, plastic, fabric, paper and who knew what else, littered the arena's floor. The interior walls, those not supporting the dome, appeared shattered and broken. Bleachers, chairs, desks, drinking fountains, doors, cabinets, countertops, kiosks, viewing panels, athletic equipment of every kind, lay smashed, burnt and broken all around us. Only the exterior walls, with stairs leading to second floor offices and viewing booths, and support beams holding the dome in place, remained mostly intact. The flooring revealed the presence of a possibly short and vicious firefight, with scarred and blackened patches and deep gouges caused by plasma weapons fire.

What seemed missing was the evidence of any recent human or Gorgon presence. No food containers, no missing personal objects, no clothing, no broken tools or replaced parts, no water bottles, no bodily waste. And no remnants of bodies, human or alien.

But what stood out in clear evidence of the sports arena's importance was the gigantic hole in center of the floor. Easily three times the size of any other hole found in Belden, this monstrous opening indicated how the aliens had gained mastery of the entire city so quickly.

"All clear," I said.

"No shit."

Ignoring her comment, I drifted over to the hole's edge. "Wish I had a microprobe right now."

"Wouldn't that be nice?" she replied, sarcastically. "But then we don't want to give our patrol's presence away by tossing probes willy-nilly about, do we?"

"I guess we should descend and check it out."

"Or not."

"Why not?"

"Let's wait for the major to make that decision."

"Got it," I said, not a bit disappointed.

I drifted away from the monstrous gaping hole.

"Now what?" Greiner asked.

"I should check on my team. You stay here and keep an eye on that hole."

"Oh, not me, Mister Lion. I'm not waiting all alone in here for whatever monsters come out of that thing. You do it. You seem quite capable of handling monstrous hordes of aliens all the time."

"I was just lucky."

"Whatever you want to call it."

"It is what I want to call it."

Scooting away, I glanced back at the Hole. My scans revealed nothing from over here, other than it was big, and deep. "We'll both keep an eye on it. Two Marines are four times as much force as one Marine."

"I doubt that the inverse square law works where esprit de corps is concerned," Greiner said.

"Where Marines are concerned, I think it does."

She laughed. It was a nice laugh. "Have it your way."

"You say that a lot," I said. "Usually with less sincerity and more cynicism."

"Really? Goes with the territory, I suppose."

"And what territory would that be? Do you mean warfare? Or just being a Marine?"

"A little of both, I suppose. Mostly I mean from being in the Intelligence Group. You get used to being detached and unemotional when considering information and its sources in regard to saving or expending lives."

Expending lives. How easily and simply that phrase slipped from her lips. "I never thought of it that way," I said.

"Most people don't."

I remained silent for a few moments. Afterwards, I said, "We should keep it covered, anyways, until the rest of the patrol arrives. Find a spot over to the right of that big empty window. I'll do the same to the left of it. If any Gorgons come out of the hole, blast them and then get out of here. I'll cover you while you move. Once you're ready, cover me."

"You got it," she said.

FIFTY-FOUR

W E ASSUMED OUR POSITIONS and waited, ready for anything. Our suits tightened around our legs, hips, and buttocks, taking the weight from our muscles. It was as if we sat rather than stood. Our suits completely supported us.

After about five minutes of waiting, Sergeant Greiner spoke up. "This is incredibly boring."

"It is," I agreed. "Pardon me while I check in with my team." I called Kamal. He reported that everything was fine. They neither saw, nor had any contact with the Gorgons. Hunter from his high perch reported the same. The arena was like a small, hollow hill surrounded by a vast desert of pulverized civilization. In every direction, there was no cover.

Next I checked the location of Major Bennett and the rest of the patrol. They were still a few minutes out.

"Are we just going to stand here with nothing to do except sleep?" Greiner asked me.

"I hope you're not asleep. I'm not." My last words betrayed me as I yawned in the middle of them.

"Yeah, I'm sure you're not," Greiner replied, rather sarcastically.

"I'm a little bored and tired, too," I admitted.

"Good," she said. "Honesty is important in everyday relationships."

"In that case, I have a question for you."

"I'm sorry I froze," she blurted out, both resentment and regret in her voice. "I've been in a lot of combat situations, usually with lots of people that I know and trust all around me. But I don't know you. And I've never been asked to take point and be the first inside a darkened building all by myself. I was nervous and frightened. I couldn't bring myself to step through."

"It's okay. You don't trust me yet. You don't know if I have your back or not."

"I still don't know if you do," she said, her voice more controlled, harder, colder.

"And I don't know if you have my back. I know that my team, Kamal, Ruby, and Berk do, but not if you do, or if anyone else in your team does."

"Including Hunter?"

"He's dangerous. He enjoys killing things and this war gives him the legal right to do so."

"Do you enjoy killing?" she asked.

"No. Does the major?"

"I told you he's a good man!"

"Maybe and maybe not. He seems to have it in for me for that woman and those children that were rescued. He feels I should know them, though I have no memory of them. In fact, he makes it sound like I abandoned them. But how could that be when I don't even know what he's talking about?"

"I haven't any answer for that," she said. "You know, on your last patrol you gathered so much more intelligence about the Gorgons than we've ever had about them, that maybe he thinks you should've encountered these survivors. Maybe he thinks that you're holding out on him."

"And why would he think that?" I snarled at her. "Why would he think that I'd hesitate to save lives, especially those of children?"

"I don't know!" Greiner growled at me. Then her voice softened. "You have to understand that cynicism and paranoia are unfortunate side effects of being in the Intelligence business."

"How is that possible?" I demanded. "How can anything be worse than being a grunt in the field? We watch our friends die. We wade through destruction and death on a daily basis. We never know what's waiting for us around the next corner, in the next building. How can anything you do be as traumatic as what we experience every single day?"

I hadn't meant to explode at her like that. Usually, I could tuck all that anger and fear deep down inside of me, rarely releasing it in front of anyone. But for some unknown reason, maybe because of the wrong way that the major rubbed me, I just couldn't contain myself.

"You get to experience it all the time," she replied, her voice as angry as mine. "But we go out on patrols almost as frequently as you do. Like right now, if you may have noticed. And we get to see and experience what you get to see and experience. But we also sort through tons of data, including unlimited video feeds of everything everyone sees and experiences out here. And it gets to us, too. You understand me, Biyela? It gets to us. I don't know how bad it is for you, but I know how bad it is for me, for all of us!"

I didn't know what to say. And she, apparently, had nothing more to say. We stood watch in silence. Until Major Bennett called us.

"Where are you, Biyela?" he demanded.

"Sergeant Greiner and I are inside the sports arena," I said. "The big, circular building that's still standing, sir."

"And what are you two doing there?"

"We're guarding the mother of all Gorgon holes," Greiner replied. "You could fly a small starship inside it."

"Interesting," he replied. "I'll be right down. Remain where you are."

FIFTY-FIVE

THIS WAS ONE OF the few times the major was as good as his word. He arrived only moments later.

He came through the same big empty window Greiner and I had entered through. Sergeant Waldau and one of the corporals followed him.

Bennett went straight over to The Mouth, as we called this monstrous hole, wandering around the edge for a few moments. Then he, the corporal, and Sergeant Waldau all dropped into it.

Immediately, and without a word to me, Greiner scooted across the dusty and debris-covered floor and dropped into the hole after them. Her action startled me.

"Kamal," I called to him. "Keep an eye on things. We're apparently going exploring."

"Got it, Lion. Be careful."

"I will," I replied.

"Lion," Ruby said. "You come back to us. We're barely a team as it is and we can't afford to lose you."

"You know me, Ruby. I'll be fine."

"That's what worries me," she said. Berk and Kamal both laughed. Who really receives respect from peers in the Marines?

I lifted off and zipped over to The Mouth. Before I could drop down it, Bennett and his team returned.

"Going somewhere, Biyela?" Bennett asked, his voice as cold as ever.

"No, sir."

"Good, because there's nothing down there except darkness and a dozen tunnels stretching away from this monster."

"The Mouth," I replied.

"What did you say?" he demanded.

"Nothing, sir."

"Good. Pull your team inside here, Biyela. We're setting up for the night. Waldau, everyone comes inside. No one outside. And no one leaves."

"Aye, aye, sir!" Waldau replied.

"What about security, sir?"

"You really are so droll, Biyela," Bennett replied. "The Gorgons cannot attack us if they cannot find us."

"Maybe, sir. Yet if we're all in one place, then we're trapped if they do find us."

He spread his suited arms wide. "In this huge building and with a gigantic hole in the floor through which we can escape? No, sergeant, we're as safe here as anywhere on Eos. Bring your team inside. Now. That's my order."

"Aye, sir!" I responded, though not as curtly or quickly as Sergeant Waldau had. He was wrong. However, the only way I could prove it was if the enemy attacked us during the night. And this once, I didn't want to be right.

FIFTY-SIX

We spread out around the arena. Major Bennett instructed Staff Sergeant Waldau to set up security for the night. She assigned everyone but the major, and my team, to stand watches. Each of the two corporals would stand a watch with a sergeant. Corporal Hats'ma and Sergeant Greiner served the second watch. Waldau and Corporal Conway served the first and last watches. And Hunter and Ludoslav served the third watch.

I still knew nothing about Sergeant Ludoslav. We hadn't spoken and I didn't know if I wanted to, or even cared. All I knew of him was that he was of average height, looked quite muscular, and that his eyes were colder than the major's iceberg smiles.

Since neither my team, nor the four service robots, had any instructions, I settled us all on the far side of the arena. There was a big wall back there with no windows and no doors. If anyone attacked us from behind, they wouldn't be coming through that wall. At least, not without at first making a lot of noise.

The four robots settled their containment tanks near The Mouth. Then they dropped into their ubiquitous cross-legged sitting positions, drooped their heads, and powered down.

"Wish I could tune out as quickly as that," Ruby commented.

"Who wouldn't want to?" Berk concurred.

"Me," I replied.

"Let's clear some of this garbage from the floor," Kamal said to Ruby and Berk. "I want as clean a floor as possible to sleep on tonight."

"You just take the fun outta being a Marine," Berk complained.

"Ditto," Ruby agreed. But she got to work, along with Kamal and Berk, using the leading edge of her grav disc as a plow to push the detritus and debris away from the area we claimed for the night.

After the deck was cleaned, Kamal informed Ruby and Berk that, though we hadn't been assigned watches by Staff Sergeant Waldau, we would still stand watch. He assigned Berk to the second watch and Ruby to the third. Then he let them see to their personal comforts.

Floating near the back wall, they rotated to face The Mouth, landed and dismounted. Afterward, they had unpacked their sleeping gear and foodstuffs, and set-up on the deck by their suits.

Kamal drifted over to me. Over his comm system he said, "I imagine you wish to serve a watch."

"I'll take the fourth," I said. "You take the first."

"Got it," he agreed.

"You can dismount for now. We won't be standing watches until it's dark out. From the angle of Thea, that probably won't be for a couple of hours, minimum."

"Good. I need time out of this suit before I re-enter it. You should dismount, too, Lion. We all need a little down time together."

Kamal was right. I followed him over to the wall and positioned my suit beside his, in the same manner as Ruby and Berk had theirs. Shortly, I dismounted and spread my sleeping gear across from Ruby, Berk, and Kamal, just far enough to maintain a professional separation from them and yet close enough to be part of our little team and community, as well as jump into my suit if things went sour.

Before exiting our suits, we had each set all the necessary combat protocols. Each suit would alert its owner of impending danger. Then the suit would power up and wait while its owner mounted up.

As usual, Kamal had a cup of hot coffee waiting for me before I was finished distributing my gear. He handed it over to me.

"Thanks," I said. Kamal nodded and claimed a cup for himself and settled on the floor. "You'll make someone a good wife someday."

Kamal snorted. "Thanks!"

"You know," Ruby began, "this is just like camping with my family back on Earth, about a trillion years ago."

Berk nodded. "Maybe two trillion years ago."

I stared at my team but said nothing. We'd had these kinds of conversations several hundred times since arriving on Eos. It was how my team handled stress.

"I'm disappointed 'bout this patrol," Berk said.

"You sad that Hunter hasn't killed anything yet?" Ruby replied, her lips twisted into a smirk.

Berk glared at her. "No. I just thought we'd have filled those capture tanks by now and would be on our way back to the company."

"It is a bit too quiet," Ruby commented. "Where are all the fucking Gorgons at?"

"Ruby!" Kamal exclaimed with indignation. "Your language."

"Oh, my apologies. Or condolences. Can I help it if the fricking Gorgons are fucking up my language skills?" she snarled at Kamal.

"Young lady." Kamal's voice took on a severe fatherly tone. He stood up and stared down at her.

Ruby glared up at him, then glanced down at her coffee. She swigged a mouthful and swallowed it. "Sorry," she muttered.

He continued staring at her. Kamal was older than all of us. I imagined that he was at least ten years older than me, maybe even fifteen or twenty years. I knew little of his background. I only knew he joined the Marines late in life. He was one fine Marine and really more officer material than grunt material.

But by the way Kamal fathered and mothered us, like all good corporals should, I often wondered if he'd been a parent before joining up. And I wondered, ever so carefully and only to myself, what had happened to his family and why he'd joined the Marines.

If he had a family, he never spoke of them. In fact, he rarely spoke of his past at all.

"I'm sorry," Ruby repeated. "It's just that where the hell are the Gorgons? They should be swarming over us by the thousands, but they're not. Why? Have they abandoned the city? Is the war over? What's going on?"

"I doubt the war's over," I said. "And I sure don't know what's going on. But we must keep alert. I want us all to go home."

"I don't even know where home is anymore," she said.

"Neither do I," a voice said behind me.

The others gazed past me. I turned around. Standing behind me, dismounted and wearing field fatigues, stood a female Marine Sergeant. Her nametag said, "Greiner." I'd never seen her out of her suit before.

Shoulder-length light brown hair, cut in bangs over her forehead, fell around her face. Her skin was lightly tanned. There wasn't enough light for me to see her eyes. She had a very pretty face.

FIFTY-SEVEN

"MAY I JOIN YOU?" she asked.

"By all means," I said, standing up and offering her my sleeping gear to sit on. She chose to sit on the deck instead. However, she sat close to where I had sat. So I sat back down beside her.

"You were saying about home," Greiner reminded Ruby. "By the way, what's your name? Mine's Maria, but everyone calls me Em Gee, because of my initials."

"I'm Ruby."

"Berk."

"You can address me as Kamal, though my first name is Khalid."

Greiner nodded and smiled, ever so small and gentle a smile. "And, of course, I know Lion," she said.

We all looked at each other for a few moments. Then, seemingly out of nowhere, Kamal produced yet another cup filled with coffee. He offered it to Greiner. She smiled and thanked him.

"About home?" Greiner reiterated.

Ruby drained her cup. She wiped her mouth with her fatigue sleeve. "I've just been gone for so long," she said. "Earth's so far away. It's a year's journey from here. I haven't seen any of my family for such a long, long time. And this war just doesn't quit."

Ruby stopped and drooped her head. We said nothing. We all felt the same way.

When Ruby's head came up, tears filled her eyes and streamed down her cheeks. And I found my throat choking up. Moisture gathered in my eyes and I struggled to keep them from filling and flooding and revealing my own humanity and my own loneliness and sorrow.

Ruby wiped her face and eyes with her hands. "I don't know if I'll ever see my mother or father again. And I don't know if they'll ever see me again. I'm not even sure, if I even live through all this garbage, if I'll be able to go home. Or if I'll be able to ever face them again after what I've seen and done here."

Ruby stood. She glanced at the deck. "Shit," she said. She walked away, over to her suit, where she just stood, her back to us, and stared at it.

I started to stand up, with the intention of going over to comfort her, but Kamal moved first. Up before me, he walked to her, turned her around and held her in his arms, comforting her.

I watched him and I knew that, whatever his past was, whatever had happened to his family, if he had even had one at all, that right know he had a family. He took care of us better than anyone else ever could. And as I watched Kamal comfort Ruby I only saw a father comforting his daughter, not two Marines from different worlds and different backgrounds comforting each other.

It was starting to darken in the sports arena. I asked Berk to take Kamal's watch. Then I ordered my suit to provide a bit of low-level light for us to see by.

Abruptly, I was startled by something touching my hand. I glanced down and saw one of Greiner's fingers brushing against my hand.

I glanced at her.

"Sorry," she said. "We've all experienced a lot of crap and misery. We all get a little too tight sometimes. I hope you can forgive me."

Before I could answer, she stood and walked away.

FIFTY-EIGHT

YET ANOTHER NIGHT PASSED uneventfully. We had no contact with the enemy. They never appeared anywhere within our vicinity. They didn't even come up out of The Mouth, though my team guarded it all night long.

Even though I'd jumbled Berk and Kamal's watches around, I still took the last watch. I'd gotten maybe six hours of sleep. Even so, I still managed to fall asleep immediately. When on patrol, in combat, or otherwise, you learned to take whatever sleep you could, as fast as you could. Your suit could provide stimulants to keep you going when sleep was short, but sleep was still the best answer to exhaustion.

The bay window we'd all come through into the dusty, dirty sports arena faced roughly southeast. From deep in the farthest reaches of the arena, in the almost Stygian darkness near The Mouth, I saw the first faint glimmers of the morning's light. Much later, while I stood in my suit, I saw Thea's light as it streamed through innumerable small windows on the eastern side of the structure.

The camp came awake. Greiner and the other Marines of Bennett's team stood and stumbled around, shedding the last bits of sleep as they prepared for yet another day of activity. The two Marines guarding the bay window remained motionless, but I knew they were alert and action-ready.

Even the robots, silent all night, stood. After a few motionless moments, they moved as one toward their burdens: the capture tanks they toted.

Most civilians think of combat patrols as unending battles. They cannot envision what a real patrol is like. As you move along, say down the broken streets of Belden for instance, your nerves sit on edge. Your heart beats a bit faster and your adrenalin pumps while your nanites struggle to keep you as calm as they can.

All might be quiet, like the last two days. But you don't know that it will remain quiet. You don't know when the enemy's going to swarm out from nowhere. You don't know if the enemy's going to fry you with a plasma rifle. You don't know if you're going to live or die, or if any of your friends are going to die. You only know that you're encased in an armored suit and that there are only two ways out: on your own or when the medbots remove your charcoaled corpse from your ruined suit.

Life is precious: especially your own life. But you never know how long you have. The mission comes first but the fear, even when shoved deep down inside you, is always there.

The best mission, then, is the uneventful one. Even if you spend that mission moving around full of suspense and fear, it's much better than the terror and cruelty of combat.

Behind me, my team struggled awake. Sometime yesterday evening Kamal had found a mostly undisturbed and undamaged bathroom. Each member of my team relieved themselves there. Going inside your suit isn't as bad as it sounds when you know that your suit will absorb and recycle all your waste. But there's nothing like exiting your suit and relieving yourself in an empty toilet stall behind a closed door. Doors are nice.

After my team had freshened up, I dismounted and took care of my own personal needs. We then ate breakfast and gathered up our gear. Afterwards, we re-entered our suits and joined the others on the far side of The Mouth. Everyone was lined up in a semi-circle, except Greiner and Hats'ma, who guarded the bay window.

Major Bennett stood across from us. His headgear was closed and secured.

"Well," he began, speaking over the team channel, "at this very moment it might look like this patrol's a bust. We've come all this way and there's no sign of the Gorgons to be found anywhere. But for those of you in the Intelligence Group you know that just because you turn over a lot of rocks and don't find any worms underneath doesn't mean they're not around you."

"It just means we haven't found dem yet," Sergeant Ludoslav said.

Bennett jabbed a gloved finger at Ludoslav. "Exactly right, Marek. Our job is to find them. And until we know where they are and have some sense of what they're up to, we haven't accomplished our mission."

"Sir," Kamal spoke up, "I was under the impression the mission was to take prisoners."

"Right you are, corporal. But the primary objective is always gathering intelligence about the enemy. And since entering the city two days back we haven't found any evidence of the enemy except for those corpses back behind Bennett's Place. Now, I suppose, from the intelligence Sergeant Biyela gathered some weeks back, the Gorgons will return to recover those bodies. So, we could hide there and wait for them to return, which would be good for acquiring prisoners and for killing the enemy. But it wouldn't explain where they've gotten to or what they've been doing. So we'd accomplish my personal mission, maybe, but we wouldn't accomplish the primary objective.

"So, what should we do?"

"Go home," Ruby suggested.

The major laughed. "I can always count on you for the logical suggestions, can't I, Johnson?"

"Always, sir!" Ruby retorted. I was glad Ruby was back to her feisty, aggressive self.

Bennett laughed again. "We'd all like to go home. But we still have a mission to accomplish."

"You mean two missions, sir," I said.

"You're right, Biyela, two missions. One, locate the enemy. Two, take prisoners. Very good, Biyela."

I said nothing.

"So, what do we do?" he asked. "Well, we could float down into that big hole over there. The only problem with that is there are at least a dozen tunnels branching out from it at its bottom. And those could each branch out a dozen more times. And each of those branches could split open into a dozen more tunnels. And so on and so on.

"Ten Marines cannot search all those tunnels. We'd quickly get split down to individuals. And each of us might encounter dozens, if not even hundreds or thousands, of Gorgons. Our deaths would be quick and quite meaningless."

"What are we gonna do, majuh?" Hunter inquired.

"Good question, Sergeant Hunter. For now, for this mission, our area of operation is limited to Belden. To that affect we will circle around the city until we ascertain whether or not the enemy has left Belden.

"Now, we cannot circle the whole city. That would take days and even then we might find nothing. And, we'd probably run into our own troops patrolling their designated fronts. So what we'll do is circle to the west. When we come up parallel with Bennett's place we'll scoot over to it. We'll then set up for the night. If the wormheads haven't already recovered their corpses, we'll stake them out and wait to see if they do. Everyone got that?"

"Aye, aye, sir," we all chorused.

"Very good. Sergeant Greiner will lead the way. She'll take Biyela's fire team. Sergeant Biyela, I want you to travel with me. There are some things I want to discuss with you. We'll bring up the rear and guard the robots. Questions?"

I had tons of questions, but kept quiet.

"We'll leave in fifteen minutes," Bennett said. "We will remain on combat alert at all times until we're back at Bennett's Place. Let's move."

FIFTY-NINE

I WATCHED, UNCOMFORTABLY, AS SERGEANT Greiner led my team out of the arena. Greiner was a good person and a good enough Marine, though I had my concerns about her combat effectiveness after her freezing yesterday afternoon. However, I trusted my team and knew they'd take good care of her. Yet it was my team leading the way, with me remaining behind. I belonged out there leading them, not her.

Less than a minute after my team left, Sergeant Waldau led her team out, which consisted of herself, Sergeant Ludoslav, corporals Conway and Hats'ma, and Sergeant Hunter.

Another minute went by and the robots exited, carrying their burdens. And just after them, Major Bennett and I exited. It was a combat formation, with all the combat power out in front and the patrol's senior member and a lowly sergeant bringing up the rear. If we were attacked from behind, the others might not make it back to us before we were roasted. But I had so many questions to ask him that such an opportunity, while far from ideal, was too good to miss.

Greiner had led my team around the building and past several barren blocks until we were back among the still standing buildings of Belden. She waited for Staff Sergeant Waldau's team to catch up before moving on. However, the staff sergeant didn't wait for either the robots or us to come up before continuing onward. She just kept going.

Neither the major, nor I, had spoken to each other since leaving the sports arena. But once we were among the semi-tall buildings of Belden, the major broke the silence.

"Biyela, I imagine you have some questions to ask me," he said. "Well, ask away."

"Why have you been torturing me with questions about a woman and children that I don't know nor have ever met?" I asked, unable to contain my frustration and anger as I spoke to him.

"Wow! Right to the point. Good for you."

"I take it from your response you're not going to tell me anything. Is that correct?" I snarled at him.

"On the contrary, I will tell you everything," he said.

"When?"

"Now. You do know them. You and PFC Carlyle found them. You spent part of an evening with them. And then while they slept, you abandoned them, finding your way to the surface. You wanted to get back and report in, like any decent Marine would. You did your duty."

We came to a corner and stopped. I checked my sensors, as I was certain Bennett did. Halfway down the street the robots sauntered along. Two blocks further down, Waldau led her team. A block beyond them my team stretched around a corner, making a turn to the left.

"How could you know that, when I don't know it? I don't remember meeting any woman or children. I don't remember spending time with them. I don't remember abandoning them. How can you tell me such things when I have no memory of them, when they must be absolute lies?" I yelled over my comm at him.

"Because your memories of the encounter were deleted," the major explained.

I stopped. "What the hell are you telling me?"

"The robot docs and the human doctor on the hospital ship *Rainbow of Heaven* felt that particular memory was disturbing you too much. So they had your nanites remove it. After you returned to your company you were immediately sent to the auxiliary hospital back at Second Battalion's location, where you suffered intense emotional dysfunction from feelings of abandoning those children in the midst of an enemy occupied city."

"You're lying!"

"It's true. I brought along a recording from the auxiliary hospital."

He floated inside a dead building. I followed him. Then he sent the recording to my suit. I watched a small image of RC staring at me from across a table in the hospital's mess hall.

"You sonuvabitch!" RC yelled. "You left them behind. We left them behind. All those scared, trapped little kids. When the Gorgons find them... oh, God! What have we done?"

In the recording, I stared at my food, moving it around with a spoon. RC reached across the table and grabbed hold of my hospital robe. He stood and dragged me up with him.

"We're murderers," he screamed. "Baby killers! You made us leave them and now they're probably dead, burned alive by those monsters. You made us murder those kids!"

I brought my arms up roughly between his arms, breaking his hold on me. Then I cocked my arms back and thrust forward with them, palms open. My attack struck him hard on the chest and RC tumbled backward, falling over his chair and onto the deck. My face held a terribly angry look. I grabbed his food tray and threw it at him.

"So what?" I screamed at him. "We did our duty. What else is there to do?"

"What about our duty to those kids? What about our souls? Why, oh why, did we have to leave them behind?" RC cried. "I'm a monster, just like the Gorgons. Somebody kill me. Please, somebody kill me!"

"Kill me first," I snarled. "Or, maybe I should kill you first. Would that make you feel better?"

There weren't any knives or forks on the table, just spoons. My image must have known that because I picked up my chair and walked around the table. I raised it over my head. "I'll end your pain. But who will end mine? You? You'll be dead. And then what will I do? Tell me, you cowardly son of a bitch. Tell me!"

"You bastard!" RC screamed. "You bastard, you bastard, you bastard..."

A bright flash of light washed out the image. A moment later the image returned. RC and I were both on the floor, unconscious. My chair had fallen from my hands and landed on RC's face. Blood covered him.

Beside us stood two robot orderlies, one with a stun weapon.

The image faded. I wanted to sit down and my suit started to conform it's shape to allow me to sit. But my sensors revealed that the robots carrying the capture tanks were turning the corner where my team had changed the patrol's direction from northerly to due west. The two teams were several blocks ahead of the robots, who dutifully followed them.

I remained standing. My suit re-conformed to my position.

"So…how's RC?" I whispered. Was the recording true? Had I said those things? Had I acted that way? Did I really abandon those kids and that woman? How could I do that?

"Fine, for all I know," Bennett replied, concerning RC. "The docs kept him on the hospital ship to fix his face."

"How did they remove my memories?" I asked.

"With your nanites, as I mentioned. The doctors programed them, through your microchip, to locate the disturbing memories and the feelings of guilt and sanitize them."

"Sanitize them? But, how?" I knew from one of the history courses I took at the Naval Academy on Earth that in the 20th Century—way back when—that electricity was used to purge memories. Later, in the 21st Century, chemicals were used to accomplish the same treatment, but without the intense physical suffering. However, I didn't know how they wiped memories now.

"I have no idea," the major replied. "My best guess would be that your nanites used some sort of pico-static charges to remove the memories. Or, maybe they surgically removed the cells containing them. I don't know. What's done is done."

"What do you mean, what's done is done?" I demanded.

"I mean all those memories are gone. You can try, for the rest of eternity, to find them, by seeking medical or spiritualistic help, but they're gone. For both you and PFC Carlyle."

"Why did we end up on *The Rainbow of Heaven?*" I inquired.

"Probably because the auxiliary hospital is not equipped for memory surgery," Bennett explained.

"And RC? Will he still hate me?"

"No. He'll be himself again. He won't remember any of that, neither the woman and children, nor the brawl in the mess hall. What you now remember is what he'll remember," Bennett said. "More or less."

"What do you mean, 'more or less?'"

I heard him sigh. "As I understand it, no one's memories are exactly the same as anyone else's memories. We all pick and choose what to remember. So PFC Carlyle's memories are, or were, most likely different from yours, to some extent. But generally speaking, what memories you share in common concerning the events with the castaways, and in the hospital with Carlyle, those memories will have been purged."

"It's incredible what technology can do nowadays," I remarked. I wished I could sit down. I wished to vomit. But my nanites, those little bastardly memory thieves, were no doubt tending to my emotional agony right now and how it affected my stomach's activity.

"Hell, sergeant, that tech's a couple of centuries old. We haven't found any better way to remove bad memories that I know of, so we kept the best tech around for such treatments."

We started down the street. We were far behind the rest of the patrol now.

"You okay, Biyela?" Bennett asked, after a few quiet moments.

"I don't know, sir. Why'd you bully me so much about remembering a memory I don't have anymore?"

"Because I wanted to see if it was really gone. I wanted to know if anything remained."

"Why?"

"I wanted to see if there was some sort of recoverable memory. Apparently, there isn't."

"I still don't understand, sir," I said. My head and my stomach felt better, but I still felt abused.

"It's my job, sergeant. I'm supposed to learn everything I can about everyone and everything. That's our purpose in the Intelligence Group."

"Right," I said. "What about that woman and all those children?"

"You saw," he said. "We watched as Sky Command fighters and our own gunboats, and about half your company, rescued them two days back, swiftly moving them to a more secure location. We saved them all, Biyela. We saved every single one of them."

"How did that happen?" I asked.

"With a lot of planning. You reported their location and a team from your company's third platoon located them. They remained with them until we had all of the assets in place for the operation. And then we executed it."

"So RC and I suffered for nothing?"

"It's a bitch, isn't it?"

"So, why am I here? I mean, why are my team and I with this patrol?" I demanded.

"You're lucky, Biyela. Whatever you do, wherever you go, whatever happens to you, you always come through," he explained. "You have luck and lots of it and I wanted some of that luck to rub off on this patrol and upon me."

"I'm not lucky, sir. I believe in getting my people back."

"But you are lucky, Biyela. You are. We'll discuss that another time, though. We better haul ass now, sergeant, if we don't want to be left out here all by ourselves. Looks like the patrol's more than a kilometer ahead of us. We're going to need some of your famous luck now to catch up with everyone else."

"Aye, sir."

SIXTY

HOW BIZARRE, HOW UNREAL, how sick it all seemed. How could I be in that recording when I didn't even remember being there, let alone saying and doing the things I did? How could I threaten RC like that? What kind of man was I?

I blindly followed the major down the street, ignoring my surroundings, ignoring the potential dangers in every shadow, every corner, behind every wall.

My suit's sensors scanned around me but I ignored them. I obsessed over a drama of which I had no apparent knowledge. That was RC and me in that recording, but how could it be?

We reached the corner at which the patrol had turned left. Major Bennett stopped. However, in my daze I continued forward.

"Biyela, what are you doing?" he demanded.

I stopped in the middle of the street. "What?" I said.

"Are you still considering that recording I sent you?" Bennett asked. "Let it go. We are still in a potential combat situation. Pull it together, Marine."

"Aye, sir," I said. I rotated around and floated back to the corner he hovered behind.

The major grunted. "It's no good joining me now. Any wormheads about will have seen you by now."

"Aye, sir," I replied, not quite paying attention.

"Stick close to me. And screw your head on tighter."

"AYE, sir." I shook my head to clear it. Yet I couldn't let go of the melodrama I had witnessed. It was so captivating, so hypnotic, to see yourself in a situation you know you hadn't experienced. For all I knew it was a computer construct. Yes, that's what it had to be!

A construct.

My suit continued scanning the streets around us with passive sensors, listening, looking, sensing, detecting. And it detected nothing.

The major glided around the corner, his plasma rifle at the ready. I followed him.

My suit's comm system picked up the IFF—identification friend or foe—signal from my team and the rest of the patrol. It was a tiny, encrypted and compressed, nanosecond burst of radio energy emitted by every armored Marine suit. It located the patrol in relation to us. It hid itself in the planet's background radiation and unless the Gorgons knew what to look for, which they might, it remained hidden from them. The patrol had stopped two kilometers west of our present location. It waited near the west edge of the downtown area.

Three blocks down from where we had turned the corner the major changed our course. He popped up on top of a five-story building, except there wasn't any roof, only four lonely walls.

I followed him.

The building was but an empty shell surrounding a huge area of destruction reaching downward into the ground. The structure's four outer walls stood intact. What remained of the building was a bit of sagging flooring hanging down towards the next sagging floor beneath, and the next after that, and the next and the next and finally down through the ground floor and basements below into whatever abyss had been created by the hole in ground below. It didn't look like a Gorgon Hole but as if either a gunboat or several such craft had blasted into the ground through the building's roof with their many plasma cannons.

From up here, as we floated over the abyss and looked downward into the devastation beneath us, we presented a perfect target for any Gorgons hiding hereabouts to blast us out of existence.

Before I could suggest this to the major he must have considered the same thing. He dropped down inside the hollowed-out building to the first floor beneath the missing roof and floated over to the glazed remains of a window.

Again, I followed him.

He said nothing to me. Nor did I have anything to say to him. His suit faced the fried window. After a moment, he turned and popped up and out of the building.

I pursued him and came up just as he disappeared over the edge of the wall and down into the street beyond. He kept above the debris and burned-out ground vehicles littering this new street. Coming down behind him, I arrived just as he zipped through a narrow alleyway between two twelve-story buildings.

The alley indeed was narrow and tight as I maneuvered behind Bennett. Ahead, as he exited the man-made gorge, he turned sharply and disappeared. I came out a moment later. He was nowhere to be seen.

I checked for his IFF signal. He was half a block away, up on top of yet another tall building, maybe nine stories tall. He must have quickly zipped along to get beyond me so soon.

When I arrived on the roof, he was waiting for me.

"Having trouble keeping up with me?"

"A little."

"Good. I don't want us too close together if we get jumped. A bit further apart and we can cover each other better."

"Got it."

"Good. By angling this way we've cut the gap between us the rest of the patrol almost in half. Seven more blocks and we'll come out just two blocks behind them."

I said nothing. I did the calculations and found out he was correct. It didn't make me happy. Zipping down alleys, popping over buildings and generally gliding all over the place didn't mean the two of us might not run into a superior enemy force. All it would take was a couple of lucky shots from a couple of the enemy and one or both of us would be at the Gorgons' mercy, and their concept of it was brutal, and quite final.

We moved on. Just as we glided across a street my sensors picked up several large targets low in the sky coming from the southwest, approaching from enemy territory. As he continued toward an alley, I reached out and grabbed one of his arms.

"What the hell are you doing, Biyela!" he yelled at me over his suit's comm.

"Check your sensors, sir!" I yelled back, tugging him toward cover. He was silent. Abruptly, he shook loose from me and bolted through a big hole in the side of an even bigger building. Once inside, we turned and peeked outside at the sky.

Two vics of Gorgon gunboats, each vic three gunboats strong, drifted across our view. Next came one of their big troop transports. Then came a somewhat smaller supply transport. And then another vic of three gunboats.

"What's that all about?" I whispered.

"I don't know, Biyela, but I do know that where they're going we're going, starting now."

I kept quiet. He spoke over the patrol's comm channel.

"Waldau, a large formation of Gorgon sky craft just drifted over us. They were heading toward Bennett's Place. I believe it might be a retrieval team coming to pick up their dead. Turn the patrol around and head straight for the aforementioned location. Got that?"

"Aye, aye, sir," Waldau replied. "We're moving out now."

"Converge with us two blocks due west of Bennett's Place."

"Aye, aye, sir."

"Let's go, Biyela." We turned about, climbing up among the tall rooftops, and sped after the receding vehicles. I felt more nervous than ever.

"Kamal, Em Gee," I called to them "the major and I are following a large formation of enemy sky craft, including one of their troop transports. Watch out for foot patrols and be careful."

"Got it, Lion," Kamal replied.

"Yes, got it, Lion," Greiner hesitatingly concurred.

"Em Gee," I added, "follow Kamal's lead. We've encountered this kind of formation before, though not with as many gunboats. Be careful or else Graves Registration may not find enough of anyone to send home to their relatives."

"I'll be careful, Lion."

SIXTY-ONE

WE WENT TO GROUND several blocks from Bennett's Place. We had no choice. Three Gorgon gunboats flew lazy figure-eight patterns just a few meters above the tallest buildings near Bennett's Place. Had we arrived at roof top level, these gunboats would have burned us from the sky.

Scooting from building to building, seeking cover as we shot forward, we watched the gunboats above us. Our suits detected all kinds of active electronic and magnetic signals as the aliens searched for intruders.

Major Bennett sent a short, highly compressed message to Sergeant Waldau informing her of the area's tight security. With effort and stealth, we made our way to within two blocks of our destination. We found a sixteen-story structure, more shambles than building, and gingerly entered it. Taking turns covering each other, we ascended shattered stairwells and empty lift shafts until we reached the second floor from the top. The roof had been battered down onto the top floor, leaving more destruction and less than adequate cover from enemy detection.

Stepping off our grav disks, we walked over to the nearest windows and carefully peered out. Fifteen floors beneath us we watched as teams of lightly armed Gorgons activated small antigrav lifters beneath each cocooned corpse. Mobs of heavily armed Gorgons in full battle armor guarded the teams retrieving the dead.

"I knew I should've ordered the destruction of those bodies," the major whispered. There was no reason for whispering, our transmissions were protected from enemy detection.

"For what good, sir?" I said. "You'd only be destroying the dead and angering the living."

"Good enough reason in a war such as this," he replied.

So many Marines sought such violent responses to the deaths of their friends and the slaughter of the innocent on Eos.

"Major Bennett," Sergeant Waldau called. "We're close by. Where do you want us?"

"Good question. Sit tight and I'll instruct you momentarily," he replied. "Suggestions, sergeant?"

"Do you intend capturing prisoners?"

"I do."

"Then you'll have to set up a crossfire. Plus, you'll want Hunter to wound the ones you wish to capture."

"Correct again, Biyela," the major exclaimed. I detected a gleeful joy in his voice, an anticipation of success and triumph.

"Then you'll want Hunter where he can fire with clear discrimination at his assigned targets," I said. "We should place him a few floors down from us, sir."

"We will so do," he replied. I imagined that inside his suit he grinned a big, wide, toothy iceberg grin. He was in his element, that of power and pride.

"You'll want my team dispersed nearby, up here somewhere or in another building close by, for top cover. You may want to assign someone to guard Hunter and you might even want to stand with him and pick out the targets you wish shot," I suggested.

"Indeed I will," he said.

"And you'll want Waldau and your remaining Marines to cover the robots as they dart out to retrieve your prisoners."

"Very good, Biyela," he said. "You're an excellent tactician."

"Now," I said, "what kind of prisoners do you want?"

"What do you mean?" he asked, his voice more serious.

"Well," I said, "for instance, do you want the lightly armed technicians removing the bodies below?"

"No," he sharply replied. "They're nothing more than rear echelon fodder. They know nothing."

"How about the armored soldiers down there?"

"They know even less than the techs."

"So, you want officers and leaders?"

"I do."

"Have you spotted any?" I inquired.

"No!" he spat. "How do I find them? How did you?"

"Hunter found them. Adjust your view to filter out some of the UV. Look for a glittering blue in their armor."

"I don't see a single one," he growled at me.

"There are at least five officers within easy view."

"Five. Huh! Where are they? Wait. I see them!" Bennett's voice went from disgusted anger to an almost childlike joy in spotting his victims.

I kept quiet.

"You're forgetting something, Biyela," the major said.

"What would that be, sir?" I asked.

"A distraction. We need to distract the guards and gunboats. We need to draw their strength away. That's your team's job."

Like hell, I thought. My team belonged to me, not to him or anyone else. There was no way I'd let any of them die for cold-blooded Major Bennett. "Four Marines cannot do that, sir. They'll die before they can get away."

"Success often requires sacrifice. We need those prisoners."

"I'll do what I can," I stated.

"No, you'll be with me, protecting Hunter. Sergeant Greiner can guide your team."

"Sir," I exclaimed, "it's my team and I'll lead it."

"I've said what I've said. Expedite my orders."

"Aye, sir," I snarled. The major was a self-satisfied, glory hog sonuvabitch!

SIXTY-TWO

THE MAJOR HAD INSTRUCTED Hunter to join us where we overlooked the street. Now, I watched as Hunter inspected his pulse laser rifle, scouted his hide, and began checking out targets down below. I watched the major, too, as his headgear retracted. With excitement, he took in the scene. I also watched, in horror, as my team took up their positions two blocks down, at street level.

Somehow, Kamal and Berk had crossed the street without being detected. Greiner and Ruby took cover across from them, hiding inside some blown-out storefronts.

Staff Sergeant Waldau reported her team in place, down at ground level, beneath us in the same building. The robots and their capture tanks hid with her team.

It all came down to how much havoc Hunter could create among the aliens and the distraction my team would make when they attacked the Gorgons.

SIXTY-THREE

W E WATCHED FOR FIFTEEN minutes while the Gorgons below stood around. Their technicians had gathered together twenty-two coffins and waited while other techs moved coffins from other nearby alleys. The troops guarding them appeared alert, moving their wavy tendrils every which way in their transparent, bubble-shaped helmets.

The major wanted prisoners. We couldn't capture any Gorgons while they were so many below us. We needed them thinned out.

While we waited, we noticed from time to time that the enemy's gunboats drifted overhead. The first time that happened, I waited until the gunboats had passed by and then glanced down the street toward where my team crouched on either side of the street. But they were gone. I called Kamal. He told me each of them had found cover inside their respective buildings.

Though relieved, I wondered how long the waiting would last.

"Biyela, get up on the roof and see what you can see. But don't let the Gorgons see you."

"Aye, sir." It took me a minute to get to the roof. There was no cover up there.

I floated near to the edge of the roof. My active sensors were off so as not to draw any attention to me. My passive sensors revealed that six of the gunboats had separated into individual units. They flew close to the rooftops. I calculated that the next nearest would pass overhead in about five more minutes.

The remaining three gunboats drifted at a distance. They seemed attached to a point over the ground. I decided it must be where the troop transport had settled and possibly where the cargo shuttle sat as well.

As I watched, I noticed near the horizon another vic of three gunboats approaching, a single cargo shuttle flying behind them. They approached the area where the current formation drifted. Abruptly, the grounded cargo shuttle lifted off. The three gunboats, which had protected the first cargo shuttle, now formed up around the departing vessel and escorted it away. After a few moments, the new shuttle landed. Its vic assumed the stationary guarding position the departed formation had occupied.

While the gunboats and cargo shuttles traded locations and while the patrols were still ninety seconds away, I drifted over to one of the roof's sides and glanced down. Beneath me, twelve Gorgon technicians moved twelve coffins down an alley toward the street we watched. A dozen Gorgon soldiers guarded the techs and their cargo. But twenty other Gorgon soldiers moved down the alley in the opposite direction from their comrades.

A warning chimed in my suit. I glanced down at the interior corner of my viewing system and saw that one of the orbiting gunboats approached the roof while flying its patrol pattern. I popped over the edge and settled into the shadows one floor down, close to a back corner.

While the gunboat drifted by I looked down and around. The breakaway Gorgons had gone around a corner and now moved down the street behind our building. They had separated into four teams of five. They moved carefully and deliberately. I didn't know what they were looking for but they headed toward the building where Em Gee and Ruby hid. Were they on to my Marines or merely patrolling for protection?

As soon as I knew the sky was clear, I found my way back to the major. I reported what I saw.

"Twenty enemy soldiers isn't all that much," he said. "Sergeant Greiner and PFC Johnson can easily take care of most of them."

"Twenty well-armed and experienced soldiers are a lot for two Marines to handle," I retorted. "Once the enemy makes contact with them, every Gorgon down there will be onto them."

"Then the plan's coming together," he said. "Sergeant Waldau, are you ready?"

Waldau, hidden on the first floor with her team and the robots, answered, "Aye, sir."

"Good. Hunter, you know what to do?"

"Ah know, majuh. Ah'm ready."

I reached out and grabbed Bennett's shoulder, yanking him around toward me. "Those are my people," I said. "Don't sacrifice them for your own glory."

"It's for the mission, Biyela," the major snorted. "The mission comes first. We need prisoners."

He shook his shoulder loose from my grip and moved closer to the empty window in the wall that gave us access to the scene below. I began drifting back from him with the intention of going to my team's aid.

"Remain where you are, Biyela. This is your post," he said, still staring out the opening. "Abandon it and I'll have your ass in front of a court-martial board when we get back. Got that?"

"Got it." But I didn't like it.

"What was that?" he responded with an ice-cold voice.

"Got it. Sir."

"That's better."

SIXTY-FOUR

"T HEY'RE LEAVING," WALDAU CALLED from below.
Bennett and I both moved forward beside Hunter. The Gorgons below had started guiding their coffins down a side street. The five officers Bennett and I had previously noticed moved with the technicians and the coffins.

I glanced up the street where my team hid. The four Gorgon teams of five marched around the corner further up from my team. They moved away from where Greiner and Ruby hid.

"Now, sergeant," Bennett said.

"Aye, suh." Hunter twisted around and leaned out the window. He fired his laser up the street. Its three-shot pulse hit a Gorgon, first pounding through its energy shield, then punching through its armor, then killing it. The wormhead collapsed onto the street. Hunter fired again and a different Gorgon died. His third was directed away from where the Gorgons were. It struck the building where Em Gee hid.

Greiner popped out into the street, her suit damaged by Hunter's shot. Eighteen enemy soldiers pivoted and fired at her.

"What're you doing, you sonuvabitch!" I screamed.

The first four shots flared against Greiner's screen, knocking her backwards onto the pavement, her grav disc flipping up, scraping against the street, catching on rubble and stopping her slide. The sixteen remaining plasma streams more or less missed her, though a lucky shot wrecked her grav disc. The other shots struck the building where Ruby hid. The building exploded outward, propelling rubble, and Ruby, onto the street. Before the Gorgons could fire again, Kamal and Berk flew forward and fired, dropping two Gorgons. Then they darted back into their building as the remaining Gorgons opened fire.

I zipped forward, intending on exiting the building and diving down to assist them. But Bennett lunged against my side, sending me sliding sideways into an interior wall. The impact knocked the major backward as well.

"You go out there, Biyela, and I'll have Hunter drop you. Got that?" Major Bennett growled. "This mission continues." He righted himself and moved back to the opening. I did the same.

Below, the last of the coffins disappeared into an alley. Three of the five officers went with them. But the other two, along with twenty more enemy soldiers, moved towards the fighting up the street.

I was helpless, trapped with a killer Marine and a maniacal major.

Movement on the street below brought my view back to where the Gorgons had disappeared into the alley. One of the other officers had come back and seemed like it was glancing up into the buildings. Hunter saw it, too, and poked through screen and armor before shooting it in the leg. It collapsed.

Four Gorgons in the second wave turned back to help the fallen officer. Two fell from laser pulses from Hunter's rifle while the other two soldiers' heads exploded in clouds of vapor. Four plasma streams from Waldau's team had hit them. As the four Gorgons died, and as the injured officer watched, one of Bennett's robots burst into the street carrying a capture tank. Before the wounded Gorgon could respond, the robot grasped it, stuffed it into the tank, and activated the tank's suspended animation system.

The firefight continued up the street. Two Marines lay on the street, unmoving. The Gorgons and the rest of my team exchanged shots at each other.

The officers leading the reinforcements split their forces. Eight Gorgons and an officer continued forward and the eight other aliens and their leader turned back. Two Gorgons aimed and fired and the robot that had captured the officer exploded. White-hot metal fragments cascaded everywhere.

Hunter hit the remaining two officers. Waldau's team killed four of the returning Gorgons. One of Waldau's Marines screamed as four plasma streams collapsed his energy screen and fried him. Hunter killed two of the remaining four Gorgons. The other two aliens died at the hands of the rest of Waldau's team, but not before another robot, carrying its tank and rushing toward another wounded alien officer, was destroyed.

The final two robots rushed the nearest wounded Gorgon officer and before it could fire at them or kill itself, the robots stuffed it inside their destroyed comrade's tank and activated it. A second prisoner had been successfully captured.

"Hunter, kill that other officer," Bennett ordered. "Then follow us down. Let's go, Biyela."

Hunter shot the last Gorgon officer.

I followed the major down and into the street. We passed by the burned remains of a Marine. A quick check of the signals from the other Marines' suits in Waldau's team told me this had been Corporal Conway.

The remaining eight Gorgons in the second wave had joined the fourteen Gorgons of the first wave. They gained ground on my Marines.

Major Bennett quickly scanned the situation. "Biyela, you take the lead. We've got to get these capture tanks back. Waldau, you and Hunter guard the robots. Ludoslav and Hats'ma, bring up the rear."

"I'm going to help my Marines," I said.

"You'll obey my orders. You know the consequences if you don't."

I turned to Hunter. "I gave you a chance. I trusted in you. You owe me."

"Ah do owe yew, Lye-un. Yew're safe. Yew got mah word."

I turned to go.

Major Bennett glanced at Hunter, then at me. He leveled his rifle at me. "I can't let you go, Biyela. I need your assistance getting these prisoners back."

I glanced at Bennett's rifle. "Do what you have to do, sir. I'm going to save what's left of my team."

"You'll die," he said. "You're disobeying orders and deserting while in combat. I have the authority to stop you by any means."

"Ah wouldn't do it, if'n Ah were you, suh," Hunter said. He leveled his pulse laser rifle at Bennett.

"Are you going to kill me, Sergeant Hunter?" Bennett inquired. "Are you going to throw your future away for a deserter?"

"Ah gave him mah word, majuh. Besides, the wormheads'll probably kill him anyways, suh."

The major looked toward me. "Have it your way, Biyela. If you make it back I won't press charges," Bennett said. "Ludoslav, take the point."

SIXTY-FIVE

DRIFTED DOWN THE STREET. I felt a hole burning into my back. But my sensors revealed my suit as intact, with all systems operational. Besides, my energy screen was active.

Still, I didn't trust Major Bennett.

I was surprised at Hunter, though. I thought he'd have certainly sided with Bennett. But he had remained honorable and watched my back.

As I moved up the street, two Gorgons popped out of the building on my right and fired at me. My screen flared red and purple. I returned fire. One of them staggered back while the other collapsed to the ground. I had only fired at one of them.

"That's fer yew, Lye-un, fer trustin' me at The Slab" Hunter called. "We're even."

"Got it." I zipped across the street as the surviving Gorgon climbed up and shot at me again. I was so close that its plasma stream flared off my screen and washed onto its own screen. My velocity took it by surprise and I collided with it. We bounced off of each other. It got up before me. It aimed its rifle at me. Nothing happened. I fired at it, twice, from the ground. My first shot weakened its energy screen. My second shot, fired so close, penetrated its screen, blew its clear helmet apart and vaporized its head.

The Gorgon's headless body collapsed into the alley.

I got up. My sensors revealed that the fighting had moved several blocks down the street. "Kamal, where are you?"

"We're good, Lion. They're on foot and we're not. We're keeping ahead of them and taking shots at them. We've wounded a few. They're still coming at us, minus their wounded, but we can keep away."

"Good. How many are after you?"

"All who survived and can fight," Kamal said. "Did the major get his prisoners?"

"Two of them. Two robots were destroyed. One of his corporals didn't make it."

"A shame," Kamal said. "I liked the robots and both Hats'ma and Conway. Which one got it?"

"The latter."

"Sad. What do you want us to do? We can circle around."

"Good idea. Make it wide. We'll meet on the western edge of the city and make it back to the company."

"Got it," Kamal replied. "Be careful."

"You, too."

I glanced back down the street. I saw nothing moving. I floated up over the rubble and the enemy's bodies.

Approaching Greiner, I couldn't tell if she was alive or dead. Settling to the ground, I debarked from my grav disc. I kneeled close beside her and touched my headgear to hers. "Em Gee, are you alive in there?"

No response. Standing, I looked around. I held my rifle ready. My sensors revealed nothing. But the enemy could be lurking anywhere, their suits powered down so that I couldn't detect them.

I knelt down again, releasing my grip on my rifle and grasping her shoulders with both hands, I shook her hard. Then I touched my suit to hers again. I heard groaning.

"Em Gee, are you okay?"

"What a stupid thing to ask someone!"

"Can you move?"

"My suit's dead. Wish I was."

"Don't say that!" I said. "You're lucky to be alive."

"Who's talking to me?" she demanded.

"Lion Biyela."

"Where's the major?"

"Gone."

"The mission?"

"Successful."

"He got his prisoners then?"

"Two."

"Good." She paused. "How're you going to get me home?"

"I'll think of something."

"You're insane."

"Maybe so."

"Anyone else hurt?" she asked.

"Conway's dead."

"He was a nice guy. And a good Marine."

"I barely knew him."

"Too bad," she replied. "Ruby hid near me. Is she okay? Where is she? And what about Kamal and Berk?"

"Kamal and Berk are in the middle of a running firefight. But the enemy's on foot, and they're not. They'll be okay."

"Good," she said. "How's Ruby?"

"She's nearby."

"She okay?"

"Don't know yet. She hasn't moved since the building blew up around her. I'm going to check on her now."

"Do that." There was a long pause during which I thought maybe Em Gee had fallen asleep or even passed out but then she spoke again. "I hope she's okay."

"So do I."

"Lion?" Em Gee said.

"Yes?"

"Don't be too long."

"I won't be." I took a deep breath and stood up. I checked my sensors again. Nothing. If the enemy was around, it was playing it safe, not giving its position away.

Ruby lay in a pile of rubble ten meters off. I walked over to her. Some big blocks covered her. I wiggled them off of her. She didn't move.

Reaching down, I touched her shoulder with a gloved hand. My suit searched hers for signs of life. It found nothing.

I returned to Em Gee. I knelt down and touched my suited head to hers. "She's gone."

After a moment, I heard Em Gee crying. I sat beside her and cried, too.

SIXTY-SIX

TIME PASSED. I STOOD up and stepped back onto my grav disc. A sensor sweep still revealed nothing. The fighting had long since left this area.

Parking my suit, I backed out of it. The suit's sensors remained on full scan. If danger presented itself my suit would alert me.

With great effort, I managed to disengage Em Gee's boots from her grav disc. Then, straining, I rolled her onto her stomach. With greater effort, I managed to pry open her suit and help her out. Standing, she swayed. I steadied her.

"I'm okay," she said.

She looked like hell. Her eyes were puffy, her face wet. I probably looked similar. I guided her toward my suit.

"What're your intentions?"

"I thought we might climb inside together."

"And do what?"

"Not that."

"Do you think we can get out of here jammed into one suit? We won't fit."

"We might. What else can we do? I can't leave you here and you can't ride on the back of my disc without a suit on. If we got attacked, you'd be fried. And if I activated my energy shield, it'd knock you right off. Aside from a hard fall, you'd also suffer serious burns."

"We won't fit," she reiterated.

"So?"

"Leave me some rations and I'll hide out until you can come back for me."

"No deal. I've already lost one Marine today. I'm not losing another one."

She shook her head, a motion that unbalanced her. She caught hold of me and said, "We don't have any other choices. Give me some rations and your combat knife. I'll be fine."

"You won't. Get in. It's the only way and I'm not leaving without you."

"You'll have to get inside first. You won't be able to operate the suit with me squeezed in front of you."

"Make certain you get in," I ordered.

"I promise."

I climbed inside my suit. She ran off. My suit closed and I popped up into the air, catching up to her before she had gone five steps. Landing in front of her, I reached out and grabbed one of her arms. She struggled, but I held her tight.

Exiting my suit, I instructed it to keep hold of her.

"Why are you doing this?" she demanded.

"Unlike Major Bennett, I'm not going to throw your life away."

I touched my suit and it let go of her. Grasping her arms, I guided her to my suit. "Get inside."

"How will you operate it with me stuffed in front of you?"

"I'll figure it out. Get in."

"Okay," she said, climbing inside. I followed her, closing the suit behind me.

Though my suit stretched to accommodate us, it was still quite a tight fit. We had a little trouble breathing. Increasing the oxygen content of the air helped. Our breathing slowed and we relaxed.

I had a little trouble seeing over her as she was shorter than I was. She barely reached my collarbones. But my long arms did not stretch out to my gloves. However, my suit reduced my sleeves' length so I could slip into my them. They fit fine.

Everything seemed operational and we lifted off. Gliding away, I managed to get my rifle into my hands again. I couldn't see my sensor display but Em Gee could.

"All clear," she said. "We are moving and everything seems fine, so I was wrong. But the Gorgon that gets us will get the two-for-one daily special."

"I don't know what that means."

"Never mind. It's a bit warm in here."

I nodded and my chin bounced off of the top of her head.

"What the hell was that for?" she yelled. The loud sound bounced around in our ears and we both cried out in pain.

"Don't do that again," I admonished her.

"Then don't pound the top of my head!"

"Right."

We floated over to Ruby. I looked down at her body. Em Gee couldn't see it. "What's going on?" she asked.

"I'm looking at Ruby."

"What are you going to do about her?"

"What can I do? I've got to get you to safety."

"Her family will never see her again."

"It happens."

"You don't seem very broken up about it."

"You cried and I cried," I explained. "Part of my family is gone now. There's nothing I can do about it. You get use to minimalizing it. You have to, to survive. You save living for when it's convenient and fighting for survival when you have to. You do the same thing for sorrow. There's nothing else to do and nothing else to say."

"All neatly wrapped up, isn't it?" she said, her voice harsh.

"Like us," I quipped.

"Like us," she agreed. "Let's get out of here."

"You got it."

SIXTY-SEVEN

W E GLIDED WEST, AWAY from Ruby's body. I kept us halfway between the street and the rooftops but close to the buildings on my right. We had traveled five blocks when Em Gee screamed, "Take cover!"

The sound banged around in my eardrums, causing me great pain, but I obeyed without hesitation. We dived into a blasted-out window in a ten-story building beside us. Our suit's exterior lights popped on as we zoomed through the darkness. Zipping through a large room filled with smashed furniture, we exited into a narrow hallway just as the room behind us and its exterior wall exploded in a fiery blast.

"What'd you see?" I demanded, my voice low, my ears ringing.

"A Gorgon gunboat."

I started to nod but stopped myself before banging against her skull again. An empty lift shaft stood down the hallway before us. We zipped into it as I cancelled our disc's anti-grav field. We plummeted as another fiery blast ripped open more of the building and part of the hallway.

"Switch your lights off," Em Gee said. "The gunboat is probably detecting the energy from them."

"Got it."

Moments later, we crashed into a lift car. The collision jolted us into the shaft's walls. We rested against the wall while I quickly checked my systems. Everything remained fully operational.

"That hurt."

"Ya think?" she replied. "Get us out of here before they find us."

We felt vibrations through the shaft's walls. The gunboat plastered the building, tearing it apart with broadsides from its plasma cannons.

"Why didn't they hit us sooner?" Em Gee asked.

"I don't know. They sure seem to want us now, though."

"Yeah. What about getting us out of here?"

"I'm working on it." When the next broadside shook the building, pieces of debris cascaded down upon us from above. I sent a quick, single radar pulse upward. It came back negative. "No way out above."

"I'm not going to die like this!"

"You're killing my ears."

"I don't care. I don't want to die down here."

"Neither do I." Another blast shook the building. Then another. And another. Each blast dumped more debris upon us, eventually covering us completely.

The firing stopped. We waited a couple of minutes.

"What's going on?" she whispered.

"I have no idea," I whispered back. There wasn't any reason for us to whisper; nothing outside of our suit could hear us.

"Maybe they've given up."

"Probably not."

"Probably not," she agreed.

We waited a few more minutes. No more broadsides hit the building.

"Think they're searching the building?" Em Gee asked.

"As far as I know, gunboats don't carry troops."

"But ground troops could've joined them." I heard the fear in her voice. I felt afraid, too.

"I sure hope not."

"Then let's get out of here," she insisted.

"We've got a good pile of debris on us. Anything looking down here may not see us."

"That's the best idea?" she hissed at me. "Stick around and hope they don't see us? Play dead and hope we don't become dead? We should run. Right now."

"We're staying here."

"Lucky for you, I don't have a choice in the matter!" she screeched, her voice tearing at my ears.

"Lucky for you, too." I kept my voice soft, hoping to ease her fear. My sensors detected movement above us. "Something's up there."

"I see it, too. What do we do?" Em Gee asked.

As tight as we were in my suit, I didn't think it was possible for us to get any closer. But Em Gee pushed up so tight against me it was as if we had somehow melted together. I could barely breathe. Her body trembled against me.

We were in a tight situation, both inside my armored suit and in the lift shaft as well. Three Gorgons were climbing down the shaft, spread equally apart around its walls. They seemed capable of climbing anything. They used three arms for climbing while the fourth arm supported a plasma rifle. They were almost upon us.

"We're going die, aren't we?" Em Gee whispered to me.

"We're not," I whispered back.

"Thanks for coming back for me," she said.

"Sure." I focused on the wormheads as one of them pushed at the debris pile with its rifle. It paused. Then it shoved a larger piece loose. The piece dropped and I leaned our suit back ever so slightly. The piece missed us by millimeters.

"I'm scared."

"Don't be."

"That's easy for you to say."

"Why?" I inquired, my voice ever so quiet.

"You seem to never be afraid of anything."

"I trust in my training," I lied. Though I never wanted to be scared in combat, I always was. Maybe not enough fear to paralyze me, but almost enough.

"I have trouble with that," she said.

"Shhh." The Gorgons leveled their rifles at the pile. They had come down without activating their energy screens. They were as vulnerable as we were. While they had climbed down, I had managed to get my rifle up by my right shoulder. The one that pushed against the rubble pile was just two meters away. When they fired, I would fire. They would be in for a fatal surprise.

They didn't fire. They cradled their weapons in their arms and climbed back up the shaft. We waited and waited and waited. After ten minutes of silence, I began shoving the debris away.

"I think they're gone," I said.

"I think you're right," she said.

Two minutes later, we drifted up the shaft. My rifle was ready. We came to another hallway. The walls were gone, blasted away with fire and force. Small flames burned in the remnants of rooms that had survived the bombardment. The roof was gone, blasted away. Above us floated a small troop transport and a gunboat. I kept us in the lift shaft. Somehow it had survived while the top of the building had not.

After a minute, the small troop ship sped away. The gunboat followed. I breathed a sigh of relief, as did Em Gee.

We gingerly exited the shaft. From where we floated, I could see the buildings around us. Their roofs remained intact but small fires and hot spots pockmarked them all. It had been an intense bombardment. We drifted higher, rising above the building.

"We're lucky to be alive," I said.

"We are," she agreed.

SIXTY-EIGHT

WE GLIDED ONWARD.

I kept us close to the street but not so close that I couldn't maneuver us to safety. The gunboat had spooked me. I didn't want another such encounter. My suit, energy screen, and plasma rifle were worthless against a gunboat. Another gunboat attack might not allow time to reach safety. In fact, it might roast us alive!

We traversed most of the city during the next hour. Eos's sun, Thea, dropped closer to the horizon. It sat low in the sky, dead ahead. My suit's optical system kept it from blinding me.

Em Gee stared at my sensor display, hidden from me by her head. She had moved away from me after the gunboat attack as much as she could, but not so much that we weren't still in close physical contact. She just wasn't shoved into me anymore.

"What did you have for lunch?" she demanded.

"Nothing."

"How about breakfast, then?"

"The usual rations. Why?"

"It's starting to stink in here."

"Oh." I directed my suit to increase air filtration. After a few minutes, the smell disappeared.

"The sun will set soon," she said. "Are we anywhere near to the rendezvous point yet?"

"I don't know. Do you detect any Marine units anywhere?"

"Not exactly."

"What does that mean?"

"Well, I don't detect anything or anyone in front of us. But a few blocks back, I'm getting indeterminate readings. It seems like there's a Marine flying behind us, but sometimes not."

"Could it be another gunboat?" I asked, a bit of a quaver in my voice. "Or Gorgons on grav discs?"

"It doesn't appear like a gunboat. Do the wormheads even have grav discs? Where would they even possibly get them?"

"We've lost a lot of discs in battle. A year of fighting and taking casualties must've scattered hundreds of them around."

"Maybe."

"Well, the Gorgons trade with some of the other alien races humanity trades with. Someone could've sold them grav discs. It's not like we're the only ones who could use them, is it?"

"Maybe. I don't know who's back there, or what," she said. "It seems more like we're being followed by a ghost."

"I don't believe in ghosts," I sharply said.

"Why not? There're lots of alien races that seem like ghosts, that even behave like them. Look at the Ilmatarans, don't they seem like ghosts? We assume they're made of living water but they're capable of leaving the surface of Ilmatar. They've been spotted in deep space and even interstellar space. They've even been detected close to the surface of stars. How is it, if they're made of water, that they're not frozen to death by the coldness of space, or vaporized by the intense heat from the stars they've drifted around? And how do they get around? How do they fly through space? And how do they enter hyperspace? What are they made of, really? What are they, if not ghosts?" Em Gee speculated.

"I don't know what they are but I don't believe in ghosts, human or alien," I replied. "Whether there's life after death or no life at all, I don't know. But if there is life after death, why would anyone want to come back?"

"Good point. But whatever is following us, it's gone again."

"Any contact ahead?"

"Negative."

I activated my comm and called Kamal. "Where are you?" I asked him, after making contact.

"About two kilometers to your left, among the trees of a city park the Gorgons forgot to burn down," Kamal said. "We've got both you and Ruby on our sensors."

"Ruby's dead," I said.

There was silence.

"Kamal, you still there?"

"Yes. You're certain about Ruby?"

"Definitely."

"I see. Veer to your left about thirty degrees. You should be here in fifteen minutes."

"Got it. Who's behind me?"

"I have no idea," Kamal replied. "I've lost contact with the target. So has Berk."

"What does the IFF say?" I asked, referring to the Identification, Friend or Foe broadcast from each Marine's armored suit.

"Unknown," Kamal replied. "I'm not receiving anything."

"Who could it be?" Em Gee asked.

"I don't know."

"Who's voice was that?" Kamal demanded. "Is that the voice of the phantom contact behind you?"

"Negative. Sergeant Greiner's suit was destroyed but she survived. She's crammed in with me."

"I didn't know that was possible."

"Neither did I," Em Gee replied.

"It sounds cozy," Berk interrupted. "Must be very, very nice having a woman so close to you, Lion."

"Shut-it, Berk." I snapped.

"Got it," Berk replied. "But I bet you got it more."

"Kamal," I said.

"Berk!" Kamal hissed. Berk shut up.

"We'll be there soon," I said. "Keep an eye out for visitors. And be careful. I don't want to lose anybody else today,"

"Got it," Kamal replied.

I veered to my left and kept going. "Any more contacts?" I asked Em Gee.

"Negative," she replied. "Whomever it was has stopped following us."

"Maybe he or she has circled around us. Maybe it's not the enemy we expect but a different one seeking our demise."

"What d'you mean by that?" she demanded.

"It could be Sergeant Hunter or Major Bennett."

"Why would the major want us dead? Or Hunter?"

"The major doesn't like me. He threatened me twice today. And he ordered Hunter to shoot you."

"He wouldn't do that!" she snarled.

"He did," I sternly replied. "He did it to precipitate a battle between the Gorgons and you and the rest of my team. It's what got Ruby killed."

"I cannot believe that. Major Bennett needs every Marine he has to get his prizes back to the brigade's headquarters," she reminded me.

"He evidently didn't need you. Or Ruby. Or the rest of my team. When Hunter shot you, you drifted out from cover. That's when a detachment of Gorgons saw you and opened fire. You were hit. You fell over. Your grav disc was destroyed and several plasma streams meant for you shot over you and blasted Ruby out of the building you both hid in. Ruby didn't stand a chance."

"If that's true," Em Gee countered, "how come I'm still alive? How come I'm crammed in here with you? The wormheads should've fried my ass out there. Why didn't they do that? Tell me that!"

"Because Kamal and Berk came out and opened up on them, drawing them away, so I could come see if you were..."

"If I was what?" she demanded.

"If you were alive. And you were, but Ruby wasn't."

Em Gee was quiet.

We kept gliding along. Finally, she said, "I'm sorry. I just can't believe I'm so valueless to the major."

"You're not valueless. At least, not to me. Major Bennett might not see you as anything but an expendable resource but trust me, not everyone is like that."

"Being jammed in here with you has proven that to me. So who might it be back there? Sergeant Hunter, maybe?"

"If it were Hunter, we'd be dead already."

"Then who's back there?"

"I don't know. But keep an eye on that sensor display. We're going to try something a little different."

"Okay."

We had left the taller buildings now and entered an area of burned-out and battered apartment buildings. I dropped down between these slaughtered structures, zig-zagging among them.

"Still no contact," Em Gee said.

"Go active," I said.

"Are you insane? That'll give our position away."

"We need to know who's following us and where he is."

"So, you think it's Sergeant Hunter?" she asked.

"Who else can it be?"

"Maybe somebody left over from a previous patrol?"

"I doubt it."

"Why?"

"A hunch."

"A hunch?"

"Haven't you had hunches? Haven't you listened to your instincts?" I asked. What Marine hasn't had hunches?

"I have," she said. "But never in such a situation."

"Hunches sometimes are the only things keeping us safe out here," I explained.

"I'll remember that, if we live through this."

"Active sensors on," I told my suit.

"Sensors active!" Em Gee reported. "No contacts yet."

I hopped over a small building, zipped around a market and then spotted a two-story building with a big hole burned straight through the ground floor. The hole was big enough to fly a gunboat through. I accelerated my disc to maximum, racing through the building at one hundred kilometers per hour. On the other side, I cut hard to my right, Gee forces slamming us against each other.

After the tight right, I cut our velocity and scooted around some burned-out ground vehicles. Then I took us into the shattered remains of the top floor of a five-story apartment building. Pivoting left, we entered a wide hallway, zipping to the far end. Spinning around to my right, I slammed through a closed door to find an apartment with its entire outside wall missing. I stopped there in the shadows.

"Now what?" Em Gee asked.

"We wait," I replied. It was dark out now.

Kamal called. "Wild maneuvering, Lion. We're two buildings away, right behind you. Your sensors are illuminating the area. Everything's clear. We finished scouting just as you entered your current location. Come on over."

"Got it," I replied. "Switching to passive sensors."

"No contacts," Em Gee said. "Maybe we lost the ghost."

"I told you I don't believe in ghosts."

"You should," a familiar voice said over the comm. "Because this one's going to kick your ass!"

SIXTY-NINE

"R UBY!" KAMAL EXCLAIMED. "YOU'RE alive!"

"And pissed! Lion, why'd you leave me behind?"

"I didn't receive any life signs from your suit. What else was I supposed to think?"

"You could've had a little faith in me. You could've waited a little longer. Why didn't you?"

"I had to get Sergeant Greiner to safety."

"You expect me to believe that? The back of her suit was pulled open and she's gone. I didn't see her on your disc and I've been following you for quite a while. The Gorgons got her."

"They didn't."

"You think I'm stupid?"

"I'm in Lion's suit with him," Em Gee said.

"What the hell!"

"Exactly," Em Gee quipped. "The way this guy drives, it is hell. Believe me."

"Rather cozy, isn't it?"

"You don't know the half of it. He's had a boner against my ass for the last hour."

"A what?" I said, embarrassed and shocked.

"A boner, a stiffy, an erection," Em Gee explained. "It's been a little scary and a bit pleasant."

"Lucky you," Ruby said. "I had to play dead, surviving on the reserve air until I was sure I was safe. It was hard not to move. I laid on my face while a Gorgon patrol came along after you left. They poked me with their rifles but left me when I remained motionless. They left after they examined your suit. They moved like their asses were on fire. Do they even have asses?"

I groaned.

"Ooh, I bet that's exciting for you, Em Gee," Ruby said.

"Ruby, you're embarrassing us," Kamal said.

"Good. I'm still alive, little thanks to all of you. All of you left me behind."

"I didn't," Berk said.

"Yeah? Where were you while I lay on the deck surrounded by Gorgons? I didn't know if they were going to fry my ass or not. And none of you, not even you, Em Gee, were there. I was scared. So scared. And alone. My team had abandoned me. How could you do that? How could you!"

"I thought you were dead," I pleaded.

"You left pretty quickly," she accused me.

"I had to get Sergeant Greiner away," I reminded her.

"Because she's more important than I am?" Ruby demanded.

"Because I thought you were dead. Because I'd already lost one Marine and I didn't want to lose another."

"So that makes it right?" she spat.

"I thought you were dead!" I said.

"My suit was rebooting. It was on minimal power. Did you think to check that? Did you even try to see if I was still alive?"

"No," I replied.

"Doesn't a good sergeant think of that? Why didn't you think of that?"

"I thought you were dead. I wasn't thinking straight."

Ruby didn't answer me. After a moment, her suit floated up in front of me. We were still in the blown-out apartment. Moments later, Kamal and Berk arrived.

"Lion," Kamal said, "we shouldn't stay here too long. We don't know what the enemy's doing and we don't know if they'll be coming this way."

"That's all you guys think about, isn't it? Saving your asses and running away!" Ruby snarled. "What kind of Marines are you?"

"Ruby," Kamal said, "it's just your nerves talking. Calm down. You're alive and well. We'll all be home soon, and safe."

"My home's on Earth, not with you no good sonsabitches."

I floated over to her and grabbed one of her arms, holding her tight. "I'm sorry about what happened to you. I thought you were dead. It broke me up. I couldn't take the chance of losing another friend and Marine. I should've made certain whether you were alive or dead, but I didn't. I can't change that. However, we have to get back to the company. Are you coming or not?"

"What if I choose not to?" Ruby said.

"It's your choice," I reminded her. "Maybe you'll make it back on your own. I hope so. But if you won't come, I'll slave your suit to mine. Got that?"

"Got it. This isn't over."

"Don't you know how happy we are that you're alive?" Em Gee asked her.

"Why would you be happy that I'm alive?" she growled. "You don't even know me."

"Maybe not. But you showed me what a real team is like," Em Gee said. "We're not a real anything in Intelligence. We're a collection of individuals looking out for ourselves. We obey orders but we can't count on each other to have our backs. Not really. We're not family. We're strangers that work together. But we're always thinking about ourselves first."

Ruby kept quiet.

"Being with your team was the greatest experience I've had since becoming a Marine," Em Gee said.

"So what?" Ruby snarled. "What do I care about what was the greatest experience of your life? What do I care if you've enjoyed Lion's dick up your ass? You're nothing to me."

"Why don't you care?" Em Gee demanded. "Everyone suffered grief when they thought you were dead. Even I grieved."

"So what!" Ruby's screamed, anger and pain in her voice. "You all left me behind. I was terrified. I thought I was going to die and none of you were there."

"I can't change that," Em Gee said. "But it still hurt me that you were dead. I cried for you."

"Come again?" Ruby's demanded. "What did you just say?"

"I cried for you," Em Gee replied. "I wasn't part of your team, but I felt a loss knowing that you were gone and I cried for you."

Ruby said nothing.

"So did Lion," Em Gee continued. "He sat beside me and wept. I don't know how long we cried, but it was several minutes. Then he got me out of my suit and convinced me to go with him, though I thought he was insane about me riding inside with him."

"He does do a lot of crazy things," Ruby agreed.

"So I've seen."

"When we get back, you should transfer to infantry," Ruby said, her voice less emotional. "We can always use another rifle wielder. But I don't think we'll see each other again. They don't let two sergeants serve in the same fire team. At least, I've never seen it happen before."

"I'll miss you, Ruby," Em Gee said.

"I'll miss you, too," Ruby replied. "It's been nice having another woman around. It's nice to know there're some Marines you really can trust."

"Aw, Ruby, you know you can trust me," Berk said.

"Not any further than if I spit into a three hundred kilometer-per-hour headwind," she quipped.

We laughed. Ruby was back. And alive, mouth and all. We were a team again.

"Lion," Ruby growled at me. "Are we going to get Em Gee back home or not? Or do you just want to keep her in there so you can molest her?"

"That'll be enough of that."

"Not hardly," Ruby quipped again.

We left the blown-out apartment. Kamal took the lead, followed by Berk. Em Gee and I were next. Ruby flew alongside us. We curved wide around the city, on a semi-circular course back to Chaos Company's base.

"Did he really cry for me?" Ruby asked Em Gee.

"Like a baby," she replied.

"Baby Lion," Ruby said. "I like that. Baby Lion. Where's the Baby Lion? Where's baby?"

I groaned.

SEVENTY

A GENERAL ON EARTH SEVERAL centuries back once said, "War is Hell." On El Diablo Verde, my home world, we have a saying, "Don't hunt anything you cannot kill." Both sayings more or less summed up the situation on the planet Eos. After more than a year of fighting we were no closer to victory than when we first arrived.

Everyone in our battalion knew this, from Lieutenant Colonel James Grunnig, our battalion commander, down to Private First Class Dan Bogan, the most recently arrived replacement and the newest member of my fire team. Kamal, Berk, Ruby, RC, and I had drummed it into Bogan's consciousness since he first joined our team. And we were doing it again today, trying to convince him that while we weren't losing, we weren't winning, either.

"But what d'ya mean we're not winnin'?" Bogan demanded. "We're killing the Gorgons by the thousands. How can we not be winnin'?

"We just aren't and that's all there's to it," RC said.

"But I don't understand. Civilian deaths are down and we're holdin' them at the defensive lines on the west and east coasts and here in the middle at the Asser Line. Sky

Command's kickin' the shit outta them in the sky. How can we not be winnin'? I call that winnin'."

"The Asser Line?" Berk guffawed. "Bet the troops holdin' it would love to know what it's called!"

RC stopped trying to convince Bogan and began laughing. He laughed so hard tears rolled out of his eyes. "Hold onto your assers!"

Ruby laughed, too. Between gasps for breath she said, "It's not the Asser Line."

"Whatever they call it," Bogan said. He glared at the three of them as they enjoyed his mistake. Even Kamal and I laughed.

"It's called the Auster Line," Ruby coughed, struggling with her words while laughing at the same time.

"That's what I said!" Bogan growled. "The Asser Line."

Ruby shook her head and laughed so hard I thought, for a moment, she might pass out from the lack of air.

We sat on our bunks, in our team's bay, at the company's new forward base. Chaos Company was no longer housed in the subway tunnels on the northern edge of Belden. Our sector was a quiet sector now. Since Major Bennett's Intelligence team captured two Gorgon officers a couple of months back there hadn't been a single contact with the enemy. Nor even a sighting of them in our sector within fifty kilometers of the city.

First Battalion's Headquarters, along with Chaos Company, now occupied what had once been the territorial governmental buildings in the city's center. Most of the buildings had been badly damaged or even destroyed. However, two of the buildings, low and wide, remained in fairly decent shape. The combat engineers platoon, part of the battalion's Headquarters and Support Company, had cleaned them up and established reasonable living quarters as well as strong defensive points.

The fire team's bay wasn't very big. It contained six bunks and a lavatory, known as the head, plus a place for Ruby to have some privacy away from the five men in her team. Each team bay was especially constructed for male and female Marines so that the women could have the privacy they needed for personal hygiene. Some teams had more women attached to them, while others consisted of nothing but female Marines. And sometimes teams only consisted of male Marines. But as a rule, teams consisted of both genders.

The Headquarters building had a decent galley. We spent our free time there, though sometimes we gathered in our team's bay to discuss issues, such as convincing Bogan of the seriousness of the situation on Eos. Soon, the chow bell would sound and we'd be on our way to the galley.

Apex and Binary companies were housed on the outskirts of Belden, to the West and East, respectively. However, the battalion's fourth rifle company, Deny, had been temporarily re-assigned to Second Battalion, along with two squads from each of the remaining companies. Second Battalion, restored to full strength and reinforced by Deny Company and the six squads from our three remaining companies, had rejoined the rest of the Twenty-fourth Marine Brigade on the West Coast, where the Gorgons strived to break through and destroy the human colonial cities located there.

"It's a good thing that this is a quiet area," RC said.

"Why's that?" Bogan demanded.

"Else the poor guys guarding the Asser Line would be up to their asses in deep..."

"That'll be enough, RC," Kamal warned. He had regained his composure, while I struggled to regain mine.

"Sure," RC said. "Just let me catch my breath and sit my asser on my bunk."

The laughter broke out again. But Bogan wasn't amused. "You're the dumbest Marines I've every served with! How could I have such bad luck to be assigned to you idiots?"

"Guess you're just a lucky asser," Berk said.

"Not to mention a cute one," Ruby said.

The laughter grew fiercer. Even Kamal turned to hide his grin.

Bogan stood. "Sons o' bitches." He crossed the bay and yanked the hatch open.

"Bogan," I said.

He spun around. "What?" he demanded, glaring at me.

"Calm down. We wouldn't be kidding you if we didn't like you."

"You call this likin' me? My whole life people have laughed at me. 'There goes Danny Boganny,' they'd say. 'He ain't much. Hell, he ain't nothin'. 'I joined the Marines to prove them wrong, to prove that I could be somethin'. But ever since I joined up people been laughin' at me.

"Bogan, you're nothin'," he continued. "Bogan, I've met fleas smarter than you. Bogan, you ain't smart enough to be a maggot. Well, I've had it with you assholes. If you don't want me, just say so."

The laughter had stopped. We all stood. "You're one of us," I said. "You belong here."

"Sure I do. I know how it works."

"How what works?" RC asked.

"How it works in veteran units. You ain't anythin' 'til you been shot at. 'Til then, you're just another asshole waitin' to die."

"I'll shoot you if that'd make you feel better," Ruby said. Berk and RC smirked. Kamal and I didn't.

Bogan glared at her. "Just what I expected from you."

I stepped over to Bogan. I towered over him, as I did over everyone in my team. "You're here now. We need you."

"And how can I prove myself worthy of you in this here quiet sector? What chance do I have?"

"A better chance than if you were in combat," Ruby told him. "Combat's the worst place to be. It's a nightmare."

Kamal nodded. "It is. Don't wish for combat."

"But how can I..." Bogan began.

"Do your job. Be there when we need you. Be ready for anything," I said. "You're one of us and you don't have to be fighting for your life or getting shot at to prove who you are. Just be there. That'll be enough for us."

"I've heard that before."

"Give us a chance," Kamal said.

"You?" Bogan asked.

"Us," Ruby said. "Give us the chance to prove ourselves to you. Give us a chance."

"Listen to Ruby," Berk said. "She usually knows what she's talking about."

"Usually?" Ruby growled, glaring at Berk.

"Stow it," Kamal said.

"I don't know about you guys," I said, changing the subject, and the mood, "but I'm getting hungry. I'm heading out for chow. You can stay if you want, but I'm not leaving anything for you."

"Got it," five voices replied.

"Let's go, then."

SEVENTY-ONE

IF THERE'S A GALLEY, that's where you'll find Marines. Whether aboard ship or planetside, the galley's the social center. Recreation centers have their place, but where the chairs and tables, the food and drink are, that's the place to be.

The galley.

The forward headquarters' galley was no exception. Designed to feed several hundred Marines at once, it occupied a converted and repurposed warehouse. Scores of tables filled its center while along the walls were food and drink dispensers and serving stations crewed by robot cooks dispensing hot food.

We entered the galley just as the meal bell banged away. Half of the Headquarters Company and most Chaos Company filled the room. Long lines reached from the hatches to the tables where the robots served food.

"How can this be?" RC said. "The bell's just ringing and already the place is packed!"

Ruby turned and glared at Bogan. "It's your fault. If you hadn't been feeling sorry for yourself, we'd have been here earlier. Now we have to wait while all these bozos eat."

"Bozos?" Bogan asked.

"Bozo," Berk began. "Any Marine that's between you an' what you want to eat."

"Or drink," RC said.

"Or anyone who's between you and whatever good is rightfully yours," Ruby added. "If you were in front of me right now you'd be a bozo, bozo."

Bogan sighed and looked at his feet. I reached past him and slapped the back of Ruby's head.

"Hey!" she exclaimed, turning on Bogan. "You want to be on my bad side?"

I cleared my throat and glared at her.

"You hit me?" she exclaimed. "Why the hell'd you do that?"

"Probably because you deserved it," Kamal said.

"And why the hell would I deserve it?" she growled.

"Think about it," I said.

She glared at me, grunted, and shoved her way past Berk and RC to the front of our little group. When she shoved two other Marines in front of her, both much bigger, out of her way, they stepped forward and blocked her.

"What the hell did you do that for!" the bigger one said.

"Mind your own damned business!" she snarled. The two big men stepped toward her. She glared back at them. They backed off.

Ruby could easily have taken them. But her attitude didn't make them back off. What made them back off was the looks on our faces, on Berk's, RC's, Kamal's, mine, and even Bogan's face. One spry, dangerous female might make them nervous but five glaring Marines was a whole different thing. She was our family and in the Marines you don't mess with someone else's family.

The two Marines sighed and left the line, crossing over to the far side of the galley where they joined the end of the other line.

I glanced around at everyone. Then I clamped my hand on Bogan's shoulder and grinned at him as he turned around. He grinned back.

Up ahead, Ruby seemed to have calmed down. She chatted with some female Marines from another squad.

"Isn't this paradise?" Chip quipped as he came up behind me. He held a two-scoop ice cream cone. One scoop was chocolate and the other looked like orange sherbet.

"Where did you come from?" I said.

"When you're in the forest it ain't so hard to find the tallest tree around, ya know."

I grinned. "You just can't live without me, can you?"

"You got it, baby."

"What'd you say?" I said. It had been two months since I'd thought Ruby had died even though she hadn't. After she found out I had wept for her, for a whole week she referred to me as 'baby'. I was afraid that Chip knew now, too. I didn't want him also rubbing it in.

"What d'you mean?" he replied.

I looked at him. He looked back. "Nothing."

"Good. Did I just witness a bit of family trouble?"

"Nothing we couldn't handle."

"Good, because those two are recent replacements in Bob Gaiman's Third Squad."

"Oh," I replied. "More family."

"Yep. Cousins."

I nodded. "Has Mo said what he's planning for us today?"

Chip shrugged. "Exercise. Study your manuals. Have some fun. Get some sleep. The usual."

"Don't you think we should be doing something else?" I asked.

"Like what? The war's on hold for us."

"Marines with nothing to do get fat and lazy," I reminded him. "You got to give them something to do."

"Take them running, up hills and stairs. Take them tree and rock climbing. Remember what our drill instructors told us at Basic: Nothing makes a Marines happier than when your sergeant work them into the ground."

I laughed. "You're a mean one, Chip."

"Damned right I am. A fit Marine is a fighting Marine," he said, smiling a big, happy smile.

"Did you memorize everything our instructors said to us at Boot Camp?" I asked.

"You bet. I knew I was going to be a sergeant some day and I knew I needed to know everything the corporals and sergeants at Basic knew. If you want the best, be the best."

I laughed so loud that my team stared at me, as did most of the nearest Marines. "Holy crap, Marine Corps maxims," I exclaimed. "Chip, you never stop amazing me."

"Be boring otherwise."

Laughing, I clapped him on the back. He smacked me back, and it hurt. But we laughed so much that we didn't care. We reached the food tables. Chip picked up a plate and filled it. I followed his example.

"Seconds?" I inquired.

"Thirds."

"What!"

"A well-fed Marine is a happy Marine and a happy Marine is a fighting Marine."

Laughing, I almost dropped my plate. "You're something else."

"Damned right I am. Let's find a table and I'll tell you what Mo told me this morning."

Most of the tables were filled with teams and squads. So we stepped into the hall and found a bench. With our coffees sitting on the deck beside us, and our plates on our laps, we ate in silence. After we finished, I asked, "What's up?"

"We're moving up tomorrow," Chip said.

"Moving up where?"

"Up front. We're moving forward. We're going to check out all those cities and towns south of here that the wormheads overran. We're going to find out what's there, then dig in and wait for the enemy to come back this way."

I turned and stared at him. My mouth hung open, a bit of potato salad falling from it. "You're joking?"

"Nope. The whole battalion's moving up, minus one platoon from Binary for Battalion Reserve. Colonel Grunnig will be setting up shop with us, though I don't know where that'll be. But the most important thing is we're moving up."

"I don't get it. Why do that? If we're spread out up there and I bet we will be, then anything could happen. A hundred thousand Gorgons could crawl out of the ground and if that happens they'll overrun us. We'll be toast."

"I like toast," Chip said.

"You know what I mean."

"I do. Hell, ten thousand Gorgons, or even five thousand, would be enough to crush us. But orders are orders."

"Whose orders?" I demanded. "The Colonel's?"

"Higher up than him."

"How much higher?"

"Much higher than you can imagine."

"I can imagine pretty high," I said.

"I bet you can. It's decided, we're heading out tomorrow. Pack extra rations. We'll be out there for a long time."

"Things were just getting to be fun."

"There's all kinds of fun."

"That's what I'm afraid of."

SEVENTY-TWO

WHENEVER CIVILIANS THINK OF **Marines, they think of glamour, glory, and adventure. Well, sometimes it's there. But there's also a lot of boredom, mixed in with sheer terror.

The two months of quiet in the Belden area was a relief to us all. Sure, we spent a lot of time patrolling and searching the city, but rest was what we needed the most. With the whole world at war, there was no place to go for leave, at least for enlisted personnel. So we rested. And trained, exercised, and received replacements.

And we partied, almost every day. I think Marines party more than any other human agency. And with parties came romantic relationships, and with romantic relationships came emotional entanglements, and with emotional entanglements came jealousy and fights. And with fighting came brig time and sickbay time.

Yet even with all this activity and fun there was always that tug, that little nudge in the back of your consciousness, reminding you that violence, danger and death waited for you just outside of the city. You could hide from this nudge for a while, but not forever.

You had to deal with that fear before it dealt with you. If it got the better of you, then you were useless as a Marine.

Maybe moving up right now was the best thing for all of us. After all, a lot of Marines were jittery now, afraid of what was to come, and I was among them.

As a sergeant, and a team leader, I had to lead with strength. I had to fight fearlessly, with a steadfastness I didn't always feel but that I must always project. I had to follow orders, but also make sure my team followed me. At no time could I run away in wild terror, even though I often wanted to. Not courage, but dedication and duty won the day.

Though jittery, I glided away from Belden, surrounded by my team, and eight hundred other Marines. We traversed the dusty, ash-filled fields south of the city in platoon-sized waves. Apex Company led the way, followed by Binary Company's two platoons. Then the various units of the Headquarters and Support Company came next, while Chaos Company's headquarters and our Third Platoon brought up the rear.

Our First and Second platoons, each minus a squad sent to Second Battalion for reinforcements along the West Coast battlefields, provided flanking patrols. First Platoon covered the left, while we of Second Platoon covered the right.

The first city we came upon, Farmington, had stood forty kilometers south of Belden. Its population had been around six thousand civilians, most of which had retreated long before the fighting reached them.

Records of Farmington revealed a peaceful town with indigenous trees and some genetically adapted Earth trees, such as poplar, willow, and ash, lining its streets. Homes and churches, temples and mosques, schools, recreational facilities, parks, government buildings, hospitals, stores, restaurants, and the parts and functionaries of colonial civilization had lined its streets. All were gone. The destruction had been fierce and final.

We stopped and spread out. Apex Company proceeded to the left, toward the east. Binary moved west, toward the right.

Chaos Company reformed around the battalion's headquarters.

"Whaddya think?" Berk asked. "This as far as the colonel's gonna go and then we head back to Belden?"

"We'll continue forward," I replied. "Kamal, take Ruby and RC and move a bit further to the right."

"Got it, Lion."

"Berk and Bogan, spread out a bit."

"Got it," they replied.

I instructed my comm to listen to my team and to patch me in with Chip and secure our conversation.

"Interesting morning," I said.

"Yeah," he replied. "I see you spread your team out a little more. Expecting trouble?"

"No more that you are. I noticed you're spread out, too."

"Better to be safe than sorry."

"Exactly."

My suit's sensors scanned the area. Nothing but ashes. "I hope no one remained behind when the Gorgons came."

"Someone always does. They want to defend their homes."

"Always cheerful, aren't you?"

"Just realistic. Better focus now, the lieutenant's coming."

"Got it."

I watched as Lieutenant Kwung and Gunnery Sergeant Kano floated on by, accompanied by the rest of the platoon's command team, Sergeant Jindal and corporals McCallister, Mpopi, and Xi. They sped up to James Thur's location.

"What do you think?" I asked.

"Displacement inspection. She just wants to make sure we know what we're doing."

I didn't answer.

"Okay. She just wants to be part of what's going on."

"That's what I thought. Everyone wants to be part of what's going on. It's tough to hang back and do nothing," I said.

"So it is," he agreed. "But not everyone wants to be part of what's going. At least, not all the time."

"I agree with that," I said.

"There are times when you want to be part of the crowd," Chip said, "and times when it's too crazy to join in."

"Especially, when joining in can get you killed," I said.

"Agreed."

SEVENTY-THREE

"So," Chip said, "what about your lost memories. Any luck there?"

"No."

"What about your trip a few weeks back up to the hospital ship?"

"None of the docs up there, human or robot, can find any way to restore them. They've decided they were completely deleted."

"What a strange way to put it," Chip said. "Deleted. Like you were some sort of machine."

"It's the way they think of it. They used my nanites to eliminate painful memories."

"But Association protocols require them to keep copies of a subject's memories in case too much is removed. What about those copies?"

"For some reason, they lost my copies. They don't know what happened to them."

"They lost them!" he declared. "How is that possible?"

"I don't know."

"Think Major Bennett had something to do with that?"

"I don't know. Maybe. But why? What would he gain?"

"Good question. What about RC? Were his memories of that woman and those children also deleted?"

"No. He told me he has most of his memories. But he doesn't remember ever being in a hospital cafeteria with me or arguing with me."

"Maybe it's not a real memory," Chip suggested.

"What do you mean, 'not a real memory'?"

"Maybe Major Bennett took images of you and RC and used them to make holographic representations of you two fighting."

"What for?"

"I don't know," Chip said. "But let's look at the situation. You have a lot of valuable memories missing. None of RC's memories are missing except for those of a fight between you two he says never happened. Furthermore, all copies of your missing memories, copies the naval doctors are required by law to make and keep for you, are missing. And, as you've mentioned to me, Bennett doesn't like you. He's good at manipulating people. Not to forget how self-seeking and willing he was to sacrifice a member of his own team for a mission."

"And don't forget he was willing to sacrifice my team for his 'mission' as well," I reminded Chip.

"That, too."

"As far as I'm concerned, he's not a very good officer. He's only looking to get himself promoted and as fast as possible. He doesn't care about strategy, safety, or his Marines."

"What you've told me of Bennett, I don't trust him, either. Here comes the lieutenant."

"For you, maybe. Looks like Mo's coming over to me.
"A lesser cut for a lesser Marine."
"Very funny."
"I liked it," Chip said.
"You would."

SEVENTY-FOUR

GUNNERY SERGEANT KANO AND his counterparts, corporals Laura McCallister and Ina Mpopi, floated over to where I stood on my immobile grav disc. The corporals had their plasma rifles drawn, but pointing downward. They were prepared and ready.

"Everything okay, Lion?" Mo called over his comm to me.

"All good, Mo."

"Good."

"What's the word, Mo?" I asked.

"We're moving up in twenty minutes," he said. "Keep your positions and intervals."

"I'm glad we're going to get out of here," I said. "But are we just moving up to more dust and ash?"

"Who knows?"

"What good is it to keep moving forward into more dust and destruction when there's no cover? Enemy gunboats could sweep down and cut us to bits. We're no match for that kind of firepower."

"I'm sure the colonel knows what he's doing," Mo replied, a bit of a warning in his tone. I ignored it.

"Maybe so," I said, "but being spread all over the place without cover isn't terribly smart. No offense, Mo, but we could have remained in Belden where there's plenty of cover and good escape routes. Here there's little chance of dodging gunboats."

"True," he concurred. "But orders are orders, aren't they? We're at the beck and call of the colonel, as well as the brigade commander and whatever grand strategy the planetary commanders have."

"But that's just it," I insisted. "What is their strategy?"

"I don't know. But I'm sure it's a good one." After a moment, he laughed. "Maybe we're just bait."

"Bait!"

"Maybe Theater Command wants to see if the Gorgon army's still here and if they're willing to come out and get us."

"Oh, hell," I said. "That's all we need, sacrificing an almost full battalion to find out what our probes and sensors cannot."

"It wouldn't be the first time," Mo said. "And it sure as hell won't be the last."

"What are we going to do?" I demanded.

"The only thing we can," he replied.

"And what's that?"

"Obey orders and do our job. We keep our wits about us, and be ready for anything, even a massacre."

"I knew you'd say that."

"Yes, you did. It's the only answer I could give you."

"Attention Second Platoon!" Lieutenant Kwung called to us. "We're moving up in a few minutes. Keep close to the Battalion's headquarters and support company. We'll be rejoining Captain Vang in the city of Gateway in an hour.

Apex and Binary will be closing in and joining us, too. They've reached the towns of Roundburg and Danburg, respectively, and found the same destruction as here in Farmington. That's all."

"Looks like we're moving out sooner than expected," Mo said. "McCallister, Mpopi, and I are falling back to ride herd on Gaiman and Third Squad. The lieutenant's staying up here. Keep an eye on her, will you, Lion?"

"You got it, Mo!".

Mo's suit spun around and lifted higher off the ground. He started away and then stopped. "Your team's gonna ask the same questions you asked me," he said. "But I don't know the answers any more than you do. I don't know why the enemy plastered these towns out here. Maybe they wanted to make certain no one could sneak up and ambush them. But why they didn't do the same to Belden, other than its suburbs, I don't know. Maybe there wasn't time to reduce it to ashes before we got here."

"Got it."

"So, I'm telling you to let this one go. And tell your Marines the same thing when they ask you why. Just tell them to let it go. There are some questions without answers, because they're impossible questions. Got it?"

"Got it."

"Good." Mo moved on.

SEVENTY-FIVE

WE CONTINUED ONWARD. BEYOND Farmington were wide, empty plains and we crossed them. All signs of life, of habitation, of fields, trees, farmhouses, barns, ground vehicles, were gone. Blasted, plastered, and otherwise destroyed. Where something could be turned to ash, it was ash. Where it could be melted, it had been melted. Where it had once been alive, it was charcoaled death now. Solar arrays, milking machines, farming robots, tractors, windmills, microfusion power plants, all were destroyed. Even irrigation canals were blasted full of holes. If it wasn't gray or white ash, then it was black ash. And if it wasn't blackened ash, then it was the gray remains of metal and plastic, and even carbon super-conductors.

Kilometer after kilometer, hour after hour, we passed through this depressing terrain. We reached another town. Not our final destination, of course, for this was the remains of the small city of Rio Verde, named not for a river of water but for the great green fields of engineered Earth grains grown here. Fields now annihilated. Once fertile land now sterilized by the intense heat of metallic plasma streams.

Rio Verde had once been a bustling burb of ten thousand people, now the ashen ruins of the two-hundred-kilometer-wide farming belt we had just crossed. It was the same kind of destruction as Farmington was.

"What are we going to do?" Berk asked.

"Nothing," I replied. It had all happened a year or more back, so what could we do?

"Nothing?" Ruby demanded.

"Just our job," I said. "We're moving forward."

"Aye, aye, sir!" she spat.

"You're going to have to clean up your suit now, aren't you?" Kamal asked Ruby.

"Mind your own dammed business!" she spat again.

"Ooh, it's gonna be nasty in that suit," Bogan said.

"Who said that?"

"Never mind," I told Ruby. "Just keep moving forward."

"Was that you, Bogan?" Ruby demanded.

"Maybe it was me," Berk said.

"Naw, it couldn't have been you," RC said. "You're not smart enough for such a witty comeback."

"I'll find out who said that," Ruby growled. "And when I do, I'll..."

"You'll knit me a sweater?" Bogan interrupted.

"It is you, Bogan, isn't it?"

"And what if it is?" Kamal interrupted. "He got your mind off of things."

"Yeah," Bogan said. "You should thank me for having your back. Maybe you should even kiss me."

"I'll kiss you with my foot!" Ruby bellowed.

"That's enough, Ruby," Kamal said. "Time to simmer down."

"And give me some sugar," Bogan said. Berk and RC burst out in loud laughter.

"Don't push it, Bogan," I warned. "Get back to work."

"Aye, sergeant," Bogan replied.

"Lion, don't you worry, I'll be pushing him, right over a cliff without his armored suit," Ruby cackled.

"What was that?" RC asked, referring to Ruby's cackle.

"Never you mind," I said. "Get back to work, Marines. Focus on your job and keep your eyes peeled for the enemy."

"Got it, Lion!" four of my Marine voices chorused. Ruby remained quiet.

"Ruby?" I inquired.

"I'm here," she said, anger still in her voice.

"Let it go," I suggested. I knew she wouldn't. She was tenacious in battle and worse when holding a grudge. She reminded me of the aighamuxa, mean little predators from the drier regions of El Diablo Verde. Half a meter tall, they were ambushers. Once they bit you, they never let go. You had to kill them and literally dismantle their jaws to remove them. Alone, they were a nuisance. But if they got hold of you, they released an evil-smelling odor that attracted every other aighamuxa for kilometers around. You could kill two. Three or four and you were dead. We killed them whenever we found them.

"I can't."

"You have to," I encouraged her. "I need you at one hundred percent effectiveness."

"I'm not certain I know how to let it go anymore."

"Find a way. I need your best game. Got it?"

"Got it," she said, albeit reluctantly.

"Do whatever it takes to keep yourself set in this moment."

"You got it, baby!"

I groaned. And she laughed with wild abandonment. She was back with us, but for how long? How much more of this war could she take? How much more before she snapped?

How much more before any of us snapped?

SEVENTY-SIX

A FEW KILOMETERS FURTHER ON we caught up with Captain Vang and the rest of Chaos Company. We stopped to rest while she reported to Colonel Grunnig. After about thirty minutes, the captain put Second Platoon on point. And Lieutenant Kwung let my team lead the way. We moved out, while First and Third platoons took over security for both the company's command post and the battalion's Headquarters and Support Company.

We scooted out two kilometers in front of everyone else and continued southward, skimming along at fifty kilometers per hour, while more than eight hundred armored Marines followed us. We flew in pairs, Berk and Ruby leading the way. We passed more and more ruined farms and fields. Then the terrain changed.

It got worse.

"What the hell?" Berk exclaimed, stopping.

The rest of us stopped beside them. What we saw I transmitted back to the lieutenant, who relayed it to the skipper, who sent it to the colonel.

We were all connected now.

Before us stretched a nightmarish scene, as if all we had encountered before had not been enough of a nightmare. Just meters away, stretching toward the horizon, lay a tortured, butchered, warped and raped land. Before us stood row after row, wall after wall, wave after wave of blackened, broken, burnt rock. All soil, even sand and grit, was gone. Between the walls and waves and rows were deep furrows of brutally blasted and compacted rock. It looked volcanic, but we were thousands of kilometers from the nearest of Eos's volcanoes.

"What did this?" RC asked, his voice low, as if at a funeral.

"I have no idea," I said.

"I do," Colonel Grunnig announced, the same awe in his voice as in RC's voice.

"What would that be, sir?" Captain Vang asked.

"Starships," he replied. "Cruisers and battleships and possibly everything else the Gorgons fly."

"But, why?" RC asked.

"To teach us a lesson," the colonel said. "To let us know just how powerful they are."

"But, to destroy the land like this?" I said, anger in my voice. "This land will never raise a crop again. It's sterilized now. It'll be centuries before anything will grow here again. They want this world for the same reason we do, to live on it. How do they hope to do that, when they do something like this?"

"I don't know," the colonel replied. "But don't get confused. The Gorgons are not human, they're alien. How they think, what they feel, is still unknown to us. They may share similarities with us, but they are not us.

"The fire power from their ships, the heavier cannons and higher temperatures, hotter than our plasma rifles can generate, tortured this ground apart, killing it just as they kill us. I believe it's a warning, letting us know that if they cannot have this world, neither can we."

We all remained quiet.

"We'll bivouac here for the night. Captain Vang, deploy your platoons. I want a fifty-fifty alert, half on guard duty and half at rest. Got that?"

"Got it, sir," the skipper replied. "Lieutenant Kwung, your platoon will occupy the scar. First and Third platoons will continue their mission of securing the headquarters."

"Aye, aye, ma'am!" Kwung said. "Sergeant Kano, deploy the platoon."

"Aye, aye, ma'am," Mo said. "Ladies and gentlemen, welcome to yet another nightmare."

SEVENTY-SEVEN

WITH OUR PLATOON OCCUPYING the rugged and unforgiving terrain around us, we remained in our suits. Fortunately, armored Marines learn to sleep standing up. Considering that our suits are so stiff, falling over in them while sleeping is impossible. However, it's not the most refreshing sleep.

Lieutenant Kwung placed every other fire team on active alert for the first four hours. Hence, First Squad's teams A and C were awake, along with Third Squad's Team B. My team was stretched out between our A and C. While most of my Marines slept, I had trouble sleeping, as did Bogan.

"Lion," he called, "you awake?"

"So far," I replied.

"I'm not bothering you, am I?"

"Nope."

"Good. I mean..."

"It's okay," I said. "What's bothering you?"

"A lot of things."

"I see. Why don't you start at the top of your list?"

"Okay," he whispered. "What's combat like?"

"Just like training, only more real."

"That's what everyone says, but what if I fail? What if I don't shoot when I should? Or freeze? Or run? Or do nothing?"

"You'll do fine."

"But how d'you know?" he demanded, an edge in his voice.

"Because you did well when you irritated Ruby today, helping to get her mind off of things. She needed the distraction and you took up the slack. That's how I know."

"But how did you know I wasn't being just mean?" he asked.

"I hoped you weren't being cruel. And you weren't."

"That's a lot different from fighting for your life," he said.

"So it is. But you did what I told you to do. You stepped in and took your share of the weight."

He was quiet for quite a while. "But what is it like, really?"

"You won't let it go, will you?"

"No."

"It's terrifying. And exciting."

"I don't understand," Bogan complained.

"You don't have to. Just trust training. It makes the difference. Now get some sleep, you'll need it."

"Got it, Lion."

"Good."

"You should get some rest, too," Chip said over the comm. "After all, you'll be replacing me in a few short hours."

"You heard the conversation?"

"All of it."

I cursed him.

"Your mother know you talk like that?"

"Shut up."

"I'm recording this," Chip quipped. "I'm sending it to your mother."

"The hell you are."

"What are friends for, after all, if not to take advantage of each other and torture them?"

I said nothing, but just thought it. "Did you hear that, too?"

"You mean what you were just thinking?"

"Yes."

"Nope," Chip replied. "Your thinking is too rusty and crusty and full of cobwebs."

"Yours, too, kiddo."

"Oooh, what a biting comeback. Oh, it's too much for me. I'm dying, dying. Oh, the misery and inhumanity of it all!" Chip said, laughing.

I was also laughing, too hard to say anything now.

"Gotcha, didn't I?" Chip said.

"You did," I choked out between laughs.

"Good. Get some sleep."

"Aye, aye, sir!"

"Don't call me sir," he said. "I work for a living. I run the Corps."

"You run something."

"Another biting comeback! Two in five minutes, a universal record."

"You win."

"Glad we got that sorted out. Get some sleep."

"Yes, mother," I said, yawning.

"And, by the way," he added, "your conversation with Bogan?"

"Yeah?"

"You did well."

"Thanks."

SEVENTY-EIGHT

CHIP LET ME SLEEP an extra half hour. When he awakened me, his team was already asleep and mine was up and bustling about. However, my first reaction wasn't gratitude but indignation.

"What the hell was that about?" I griped as my suit warmed a coffee packet for me.

"You're welcome," he hissed. "I thought you could use the sleep. Guess I was wrong."

"I didn't want it. You embarrassed me in front of my team."

"And you don't think the way you're behaving now embarrasses you more? I gave you the gift of more sleep. You could be grateful!"

"Alright," I snapped. "Thanks."

"You're welcome!" he hissed again. "You know, you wouldn't be embarrassed if you'd tell your suit to awaken you at a certain time. It's a simple little thing and then your best friend wouldn't have to accept all of this abuse just because you're feeling entitled to a moment of childish self-righteousness."

"You're the self-righteous one in this conversation!"

He said something rude and I called him the same. Without another word, Chip cut the communication.

After a moment, I cursed at myself. What an ass I was, behaving this way with my closest friend.

My suit chimed. A straw emerged from the lining of my suit. It angled upward past my chin, just brushing against my lips. I leaned forward and began sipping the coffee up. Finished, I pulled my hand from my glove and sleeve. I wiped my mouth, the straw withdrawing into my suit. Then I moved my hand down to adjust my suit's somewhat uncomfortable plumbing so I could vacate my own body's plumbing.

Done, I checked my sensors, inspecting my team's positions. They were where they should be. Next, I checked where Staff Sergeant Bob Gaiman's teams A and C were located. They, too, were where they were supposed to be.

All was well.

We kept on alert until nearly dawn. Then the entire battalion roused itself. In thirty minutes, everyone was up and ready to go. By that time, the sky was brightening. But we didn't need daylight to see by. Our suits' infrared and ultraviolet sensors aided us in seeing in the dark just as if we stood in bright daylight. However, our enemy probably possessed similar sensors, giving them the same advantage.

As Thea crept into the sky, as thin strips of white crystalline clouds drifted in from the west, the battalion moved forward. Chaos Company occupied the right flank while Apex Company covered the left. Binary Company fell back to protect the Headquarters and Support Company. With Apex and Chaos companies each fielding three platoons, and each platoon covering a kilometer, we were spread out over a six-kilometer front.

The burned and blackened rock, now called The Scar by all of us, stretched east and west for thousands of kilometers on either side. We drifted over it at five meters up, scooting along at about fifty kilometers per hour. In some places, the blackened walls rose ten or more meters with intervening trenches merely scratches between the walls. In other places, the trenches were several meters wide with the walls a meter or two high. But everywhere The Scar was an ugly wasteland. Whatever had been there before, be it farms, fields, or families, were long gone, obliterated by the hellfire from heaven.

After two more hours of flight, we reached The Scar's farther side. Beyond it, to our amazement, were untouched hills covered with the stringy white and silvery native grasses of Eos. Earth trees, genetically designed for the soils of Eos, dotted the hillsides.

We landed beyond The Scar, fire teams from various platoons scouted forward. In minutes, they were back and the battalion pressed onward.

Hundreds of Marines in our six-kilometer-wide front scooted through the hills, zipping along gullies and draws, popping over crests, covering each other, pausing for our Headquarters and Support forces to catch up, then again darting and dashing forward.

We found three small villages, burned and battered but basically intact.

Chaos Company's Third Platoon turned west, searching for more surviving towns. Apex's First Platoon moved east. The rest of us settled down and waited. In less than an hour, both scouting platoons found more towns, some of them entirely intact, though filled with burnt corpses.

The hills connected the Axial Mountains to the west with the plains and deserts to the east. These mountains were the North-South spine splitting the giant continental mass of Titanus. The mountains were five hundred kilometers to our west, while the plains stretched thousands of kilometers to our east.

"First Squad," Lieutenant Kwung called out. "The captain wants a patrol south. You just volunteered."

"Aw, shit," Ruby loudly said.

"What was that?" Mo snarled. Every Marine knew better than to quarrel with gunnery sergeants.

"What was what?" I replied.

"Nice recovery, Lion," Mo complimented. "First Squad, get yer asses in gear and get moving. Got that?"

"Got it," eighteen Marines replied.

"Well," Chip said, to no one in particular. "This war gets more interesting every day."

"It sure does," Staff Sergeant Thur replied. "Let's move, Marines."

SEVENTY-NINE

THUR LED US FURTHER into the wooded hills. We formed a tight line-abreast formation, with Thur's team in the center, Chip's team to the left, and my team to the right. We moved forward in pairs of two, each pair five meters behind the previous pair. Three teams in three columns, each column fifteen meters long, separated from its nearest neighbor by fifteen meters, the whole squad covering a front of just over thirty meters wide. The squad zipped through the draws between the hills, popping over some when necessary.

We traveled the hills at the reckless pace of five kilometers per hour. After twenty minutes, Mo called a progress report. Annoyed at our covering but two kilometers, he ordered us to pick up the speed.

"The lieutenant and the skipper both want you to cover more terrain and get to the river as soon as possible. Remember, if you get into a fight, the whole battalion's close by. So get going. Got that?"

"Got it, Gunny," Thur replied. "You brats hear that? Saunders, take your team to port two hills over. Biyela, do the same to the starboard. Got it?"

"Got it," Chip and I replied.

I twisted to starboard, my team following.

We scooted through a gully, darted up to the crest of a rather large hill, scanned about, dropped down into the space between our hill and next one to starboard, circled around that hill, and then dived into another gully and continued onward. At no time did we detect either humans or Gorgons.

We continued through the hills, moving quickly. In half an hour, we covered almost five kilometers.

"How's it going?" Mo called to me.

"We're about five kilometers further out," I responded. "We've found nothing."

"Kind of spooky?" he suggested.

"Kinda," I replied.

"Be careful," he suggested.

"Got it."

We continued forward, finding nothing.

"This place is starting to scare me," RC said.

"Me, too," Bogan agreed.

Stopping in a flat area between two tall hills, I split Berk and RC apart, sending each one halfway up the slopes of the opposing hills. Then we proceeded between the hills.

At the far end of the flat area, I stopped so suddenly that Bogan collided with me. We both hit the ground. Bogan and I levered ourselves up, regaining control of our grav discs.

"Just like babies learning to walk," Ruby teased.

"Shut up," I said.

"Oooh. An unhappy baby," Ruby retorted.

Exasperated, I continued forward. Ruby glided by my side.

The flat area, a streambed smoothed out by draining rain water, bent around another hill. It continued toward two more hills. But between them we found a meter-high rock wall, connecting with either hill. A large, gaping hole split its middle. Melted and long since cooled molten rock pooled everywhere. On the right side, were the blackened remains of two skeletons. Melted metal covered bits of the bones.

I floated over and stared down at the skeletons. Upon their backs were the remains of the power packs for their archaic portable plasma rifles.

"I hope it happened quickly," Ruby said. "I wouldn't have wanted such brave soldiers to have died in agony."

"I wouldn't have wanted them to die at all," I said.

"Oh, god," Bogan said. He and Kamal had just joined us.

"This your first sight of death, baby Bogani?" Ruby taunted. "Deal with it. You'll see a lot more before the war is over. If you live that long."

"Ruby, leave him alone," I commanded.

"Why? He wants to prove himself, so let him. Let him live with it. Let him see it and know what this is really about. It's not about manhood or womanhood. It's not about honor or glory. It's about survival. And survival's about fighting smarter than the wormheads. It's about knowing when to fight and when to run.

"You get that, Bogan? Testicles don't make you brave and running doesn't make you a coward."

"What does it make me, then?" Bogan demanded.

"Human," Kamal said. "We all want to run away, but we can't. We have a job to do."

"And that's killing Gorgons," Berk said. He and RC were still covering the sloping hillsides, watching for the enemy. But they were part of the conversation.

"Getting out of this war alive is also important," I said. "But the most important part is protecting the people of Eos."

"And how do we that, Lion?" Ruby snapped pointing at the blackened skeletons.

"That happened long ago," Kamal said. "Before we got here."

"These two were probably militia," RC said, "first responders to the invasion."

"Who cares what they were?" Ruby hissed. "They fought stupidly, thinking a wall would protect them!"

"Who knows why they made a stand here," I said. "Maybe they were protecting their families."

"They did a lousy job of it," Ruby said. "Their families probably died right after they were fried."

"Maybe," I said.

"You think their families survived?" Ruby asked. "Oh, my little baby sergeant, how can you think such a stupid thing?"

"Maybe not."

"Maybe? Maybe!" Ruby snarled. "There's no maybe about it. These guys are dead and whomever they defended are dead, too."

"Isn't that what this war's all about?" RC asked.

"Shut your mouth, Carlyle," Ruby snarled.

"Ruby!" Kamal commanded. "Calm down."

I heard a mocking whimper from Ruby. "Sure," she said. "You're right. You're as right as wrong is right!"

Before I could say anything, Kamal interjected: "Cut the double talk, Ruby. This isn't helping anyone."

"It might not be helping you, but it's helping me."

I tried easing the situation by focusing us away from her anxiety and hatred. "Maybe they weren't defending their families. Maybe they were buying time for their squad or platoon to get away."

"Lion might be right," RC said. "There's no thermal damage up here on the slopes. The trees hereabouts are intact. I bet a bunch of Gorgons came around that bend up ahead and these two got a couple of them. Then they over-ran these guys, frying them where they stood."

"You thought that up all by yourself, did you?" Ruby snarled.

"RC might be right," Kamal said. "It makes sense."

"It seems plausible to me," I said.

"You guys slay me," Ruby said. "That's the most ridiculous thing I've ever heard a Marine say."

"Children, children," Mo said over the comm system. "Behave yourselves. You've work to do. Thur has just called. He's reached the city of Monroeville and beyond that is the Axial River. Get over there and give him the support he needs. Got that?"

"Aye, aye, Gunny," we chorused.

EIGHTY

After Berk and RC rejoined us, we zipped away. We were twenty kilometers northwest of Monroeville and at top speed, which we couldn't travel through these high wooded hills without banging into things, we were at least thirty minutes away.

"Chip," I called, "how far are you from Thur's team?"

"Ten minutes," he replied.

"We're triple that."

"Don't worry, he's waiting for us," Chip explained. "He reported that the city's mostly intact. It's too big for one squad to clean out on its own. I just got word the lieutenant's bringing the rest of the platoon up. We're to wait until she arrives before proceeding forward."

"Got it. Where are we meeting?"

"A kilometer east of the city. You'll find us strung out along the north side of Tanner Ravine. Come up slow so no one shoots at you."

"Got it." I cut communications. I slowed us down a bit. Carelessness got Marines killed.

I didn't know what to expect but when you were as far forward as we were, deep in enemy territory, you learned to expect anything and everything.

And you planned for it!

EIGHTY-ONE

WE WERE FIVE MINUTES late and by the time we arrived, all of Chaos Company had come up. First Sergeant Jones met us as we drifted in.

"Glad you could join us, Biyela," he said.

"Sorry about that."

"No need," Jones replied. "Mo said you were the furthest out and had the most rugged terrain to get through. Second Platoon's moving up the center. The skipper's deploying First and Third platoons to port and starboard, respectively."

"Got it," I said. "Where's First at?"

"Mo said they're less than a hundred meters from the downtown. If you leave now, you can join them before they get there."

"Thanks, First Sergeant."

"Any time, son. Better get going."

I scooted away, my team with me. We zipped through scattered brush and open fields, moving toward the houses and homesteads of Monroeville, a kilometer away.

"What's going on?" Ruby demanded.

"They left without us," Berk said.

"Who left without us?" she asked.

"The platoon," Berk replied.

"Why'd they do that?" she said. "We weren't that late!"

"We were late enough," I said.

"But what's the whole company doing here?" Ruby asked. "It's not that big of a town."

"Big enough, I guess," Bogan said.

"We're deep in enemy territory," Kamal explained. "We haven't seen any sign of the enemy. A place like this is as good as anywhere to ambush and slaughter a lone platoon."

"Or a whole company," Berk added.

"Maybe so," RC said. "But a company's a bigger beast than a single platoon."

"Or even a fire team," I said. "Keep focused. Anything can happen at any time."

"Is it that dangerous, Lion?" Bogan asked.

"It's always that dangerous," Ruby said.

"Keep your intervals," Kamal reminded everyone.

We scooted through yards and alleys, past houses and apartment buildings, down streets, around trees and playground equipment. There was battle damage, yes, but almost everything stood solid and whole. Little was burned-out. Little was blasted away.

Here was a hole in a building. There was a burned-out house. Flipped-over ground vehicles lay in cratered streets. Over there was a shattered armored vehicle. Behind it lay the remnants of a squad of Eosian soldiers.

Violence had come to the river town but most of the people had fled before it had touched them.

"Why so few casualties?" Ruby wondered.

"Looks like the Gorgons moved fast here," I suggested. "Their victims, the city's inhabitants, fled before them. The Gorgons crave mankind's death. Yet rear guard forces kept the enemy from reaching their prey."

"You got that pretty much right, Lion," Mo said, from somewhere up ahead. "We found the site of a massacre a few kilometers back. It consisted of destroyed armored ground vehicles. Lots of them, maybe a battalion's worth. Scattered throughout the area were hundreds of blackened skeletons and corpses, all human. There were dozens of Gorgon tanks and even the crashed hulls of a couple of Gorgon gunboats. There were thousands of burn marks where plasma fire scorched the ground. The enemy probably paid as dearly as the Eosian Army did. However, we never found any Gorgon bodies."

"That makes sense," I said. "The Gorgons gather up their dead, just as we do. They were able to retrieve their fallen troops while we couldn't get back here to do the same thing."

"But now we can," RC said.

"When we've secured the territory," Mo corrected. "Until then those brave men and women will just have to remain where they rest. But soon, soon, the Eosian Army will gather up their dead and give them the honors due their sacrifice."

"Indeed," I agreed. "Families and friends need to know what happened to their loved ones."

"They do," Mo agreed. "Continue on your course. You'll reach us in a minute or so. Slide up beside Saunders's team."

"Got it," I said.

"Good. See you soon. By the way, a few wormheads have already taken pot shots at Gaiman's squad."

"Anyone hurt?" Kamal inquired.

"Negative. But be ready to fight."

"Always," I replied. "Always."

EIGHTY-TWO

SECOND PLATOON OCCUPIED ONE side of Monroeville's Main Street. Its Marines floated in the alleys and over the rooftops of the buildings lining the north side of the street. Sergeant Gaiman's Third Squad waited on the east side while Sergeant Thur and First Squad lingered on the west side. In the middle, atop the tallest building watched the platoon's Command Team. The team consisted of six Marines: Lieutenant Kwung and Gunnery Sergeant Kano, Sergeant Jindal, and corporals McClallister, Mpopi, and Xi.

Everyone awaited our arrival.

"Welcome, Lion," Lieutenant Kwung called to me.

"Thank you for your patience, Lieutenant," I said.

"Anytime," she replied. "You'll take wing position next to Saunders's team."

"Aye, aye, ma'am," I confirmed. I led us along the edge of Broadway Street, the next avenue north of Main. Corporal Sammi Souza met us and directed us down past an intersecting street to the next block. That would be our position for the advance.

"Watch yourselves," she instructed.

"Got it," we chorused. We buddied up in twin-Marine formations. Instead of five-meter intervals, we kept ten.

"Attention everyone," the lieutenant called. "We'll advance toward the river and the bridge crossing it. We know the enemy's here. We don't know in what strength, though. Watch yourselves. If you get into trouble, call us. The Command Team will be the reserve force. Everyone ready?"

Everyone concurred.

"Good," she replied. "Let's move."

By teams, we scooted across Main Street. Chip's team led the way, followed by Thur's team. Then Gaiman's team crossed, followed by his team B. Then his Team C zipped along. Next moved the lieutenant's team. We crossed last.

We moved down alleys and along rooftops. Our screens were up, our rifles ready. The enemy knew where we were.

Sniper fire flared against a Marine's screen. Return fire incinerated the alien sniper.

Slow and steady we moved through the city. First Platoon, moving along our port side, encountered an enemy squad. A Marine was killed. The Gorgon killers got away.

Second Platoon continued leading the way. First and Third platoons followed on either side, each a hundred meters back. We had no more alien contact.

After an hour, we reached the Axial River, the fifth largest on Eos. A single bridge crossed it. The bridge stretched more than a kilometer across the river. Located on the far side was the small town of Mike's Landing. A vast, semi-tropical rain forest spread along the southern bank of the river from east to west, disappearing into the distance.

"Look familiar?" Chip asked me. He floated behind a small building a hundred meters to my right.

"It does remind me of home," I replied. "Though whatever dangers lurk within can't compare with even the tiniest tropical forest on El Diablo Verde."

"Bet none of the forests on El Diablo Verde hide Gorgons."

"You're right."

"Which means to keep on your toes," Mo reminded me. "We might be crossing the river, if the captain and colonel can agree on what to do next. Let your Marines know."

"Got it." I told Kamal and the others. Then we waited. An hour passed, during which we watched enemy movement across the river. At first, we noticed troops gathering in clearings. Then we saw their robot tanks arriving in Mike's Landing. An occasional gunboat orbited over the far shore. After a while, several troop carriers floated down from the sky and into Mike's Landing.

"I don't get it," RC said. "They have plenty of firepower to hit us, so why don't they?"

"Who knows and who cares?" Ruby grouched. "We'll start killing each other soon enough."

Ruby wasn't the same person anymore. Since she'd been left behind a few months back, she had become more bitter and cold. The life had gone out of her. All she wanted now was to get on with the war, to kill the enemy whenever possible.

"Take it easy, Rube," Berk said. "We're all on edge."

"You don't even know what being on the edge means. You weren't forgotten. You weren't left behind with the enemy all around you! The only way to get out of this shit is to kill the enemy. And as long as we concentrate on that, the sooner it'll be over. I'll relax when it's over."

"Ruby!" Kamal exclaimed. "What's happened to you.

"Reality kicked me in the ass, that's what happened."

Kamal said nothing.

"That's enough, Johnson!" Mo growled. "Keep your opinions to yourself or get your ass back to the company command post. If you don't like it in Second Platoon, I'll see to it that you get transferred somewhere else, pronto. But it sure as hell won't be in Chaos Company. You got that, Marine?"

"I got it, gunnery sergeant!" Ruby growled back. "But it won't change my opinion."

"Fine," he agreed. "Now shut up."

She did as she was told.

EIGHTY-THREE

"ATTENTION, EVERYONE," MO CONTINUED, a little less sternly but with as much seriousness. "The Colonel has decided we're gonna go across. First Squad will lead, followed by Third Squad and the platoon's command team. The Skipper's bringing the rest of the company up and the Colonel's sending up Binary Company to support us."

After a moment of silence, Mo continued. "He's also sending up a couple of the battalion's robot plasma cannons. We're gonna have a good little fight on our hands.

"We're going to get slaughtered," Staff Sergeant Gaiman said.

"No, we're not," Lieutenant Kwung interjected. "First and Third platoons are going to provide cover fire."

"Cover fire?" Gaiman exclaimed. "Our rifles have a five-hundred-meter range. The river's a kilometer across, so how are they going to provide cover fire? Will we be tossing rocks across the river, too?"

"Rocks! Now why didn't I think of that?" Chip quipped.

"Can the comments," Mo growled. "Let the Lieutenant talk."

"There are two islands in the river, one on either side of the bridge," the lieutenant explained. "The larger one, west of the bridge, is called Big Easy. The smaller one, down river, is Little Easy. First Squad will take Big Easy and Third Squad will take Little Easy. Both islands are close to this side of the river, less than two hundred meters away. We're tasked with capturing and holding these islands."

"Do we know if the enemy occupies these islands?" I asked.

"We don't know," Mo replied.

"Nice," Chip said.

"The Command Team will cover the bridge," Lieutenant Kwung continued. "We'll also assist either squad if they get into more trouble than they can handle. The skipper has informed me that First and Third platoons will take and hold the bridge, but only after Binary Company joins us.

"Where will the colonel be during all this?" Gaiman inquired.

"He'll be establishing the battalion headquarters back on Main Street," the lieutenant replied. "Apex Company's going to provide lateral and rear security for the battalion."

"At least nothing will sneak up on our asses," Gaiman said.

"I hate it when that happens," Chip said.

"That'll be enough, Saunders," Mo snapped.

"It's okay," Lieutenant Kwung replied, laughing. "Let him joke all he wants. It helps ease the tension."

"Was that what I was doin', Gunny?" Chip quipped.

"Shut up!" Mo spat.

"There's someone else who's gonna need to clean their suit out," Bogan said.

Mo started to reply to Bogan but I quietly asked him not to.

"Why not?" Mo asked me.

"I'm still working on building up his self-confidence."

"Got it."

"So, while we're hanging our asses out over the water," Ruby asked, "where's the skipper gonna be?"

"I'll be at the company's command post, right behind Lieutenant Kwung's team," Captain Vang said. "The Command Platoon will cover First and Third platoons as they cross the bridge. We're family and we fight together. Agreed?"

No one dissented, not even Ruby.

"Good," the skipper said. "Binary will be here soon. Time to go. Gaiman, Thur, move your squads out."

EIGHTY-FOUR

MY SUIT'S SENSORS SHOWED where everyone in Second Platoon was, from where Staff Sergeant Gaiman and his squad waited downstream of the bridge, to where Lieutenant Kwung's team hunkered down in front of the bridge, to where our squad stood in the open, ready to attack Big Easy. Twenty-five meters back, hiding among the buildings and in the alleys between them, floated the Command Platoon, and the rest of Chaos Company. After we took the islands, the company would take the bridge.

"Move out," Mo commanded.

Thur's team led the way, scooting out over the slow-moving river. Their energy screens were up, their rifles ready to fry the enemy with superheated iron plasma.

As Thur reached the fifty-meter point, Chip's team readied to go. But before they moved, I led my team out. Chip immediately protested, "What the hell are you doing? You're supposed to bring up the rear."

"I thought maybe you'd like to do that," I replied.

"Why the hell would I want to do that?"

"So you can assess the situation and assist us as need be. And because my team's tired of arriving last."

"I see."

"Hope you do," I said. I chose to jeopardize things because Chip was my closest friend and I had a bad feeling about this attack. If we were about to be slaughtered, I didn't want to watch him die. So I put my team, my family, in harm's way to protect the closest friend I'd ever had. I hoped and prayed that I wasn't making a colossal mistake.

"Be careful," Chip said. From the sound of his voice, I knew he understood. True friendship is a precious commodity, one not to be taken lightly.

"We will," Kamal replied for me.

EIGHTY-FIVE

I KEPT MY TEAM LOW over the river. While Thur's team flew ten meters up, my team flew just a meter above the water's surface. I wanted to make certain that when the enemy opened fire, they couldn't just sweep their plasma weapons back and forth, killing us all.

If the enemy occupied Big Easy, which was two hundred meters long and fifty meters at it widest, then they were well hidden. My sensors detected nothing out of the ordinary.

We reached the fifty-meter mark. My sensors showed Chip's team gliding out over the river. They kept five meters up.

"What are we gonna do if they open up on us?" Bogan asked.

"Return fire," Berk said. "And fry some Gorgon ass."

"You'll do whatever Lion tells you to do," Kamal said.

"And try not to fry our asses," RC added.

"Or anyone else's," Ruby said.

"Focus," I ordered.

"Aye, aye, oh imperious baby master," Ruby replied, with a snort.

I sighed. If it kept my team's tension down, I could take a few more minor insults.

As Thur's team approached the island, they spread out. Five-meter lateral intervals became ten-meter intervals. His team was now less than seventy meters from the island.

"Spread out," I ordered my team. "Fifteen-meter intervals."

As we moved apart, I noticed Chip's team holding back a bit and expanding their intervals as well.

I didn't pay attention to what Gaiman's squad was doing now. Neither did I notice what the lieutenant and the command team did. All of my attention was focused on our approach to the island and what Thur's team did next.

Staff Sergeant Thur inclined his Marines down toward Big Easy, descending from ten meters to centimeters above the water. As they were about to beach, I heard Berk scream.

I turned my head sharply to my right. Forty-five meters away, the lower half of Berk's body—including his grav disc—was engulfed by a huge spherical head that connected to what looked a like a giant eel or snake's body, the body stretching up river about fifteen meters. Hundreds of sharp spikes, similar to the tendrils on a Gorgon's head, twisted and wiggled around the alien eel's head.

Berk continued screaming as he struggled to climb out of the creature's mouth, his energy screen keeping the thing's mouth from crushing him. His terror kept him from firing his rifle at the monster's throat.

"There aren't any predacious animals in Eosian rivers!" RC cried out.

"Tell that to Berk!" Ruby cursed. Both Marines broke ranks to help him.

And at that moment, dozens of enemy weapons opened up on Thur's team. Two of his Marines were engulfed by multiple plasma streams. They didn't even have time to scream as their energy screens flashed out of existence and they exploded into miniature suns, disappearing into the river in scalding clouds of steam.

Over the comm I heard Corporal Rita Peres, Thur's assistant team leader, crying out, "Take cover, take cover! Get on the deck, get down on the deck!"

RC and Ruby floated a meter from the monster struggling to swallow Berk. Their attention was torn between the monstrous creature and the brutal ambush on the island.

"Kamal, take Ruby and RC and get on the island," I commanded. "Cover Peres and keep your heads down. Kill anything that moves."

"Got it, Lion," Kamal said.

"Bogan, kill that damned alien eel and get Berk out of there. I'll cover you."

"Got it, Lion," Bogan said. One shot from his rifle killed the creature. The body disappeared into the river, surrounded by an ever-growing pool of black liquid, blood from the beast's body. As the thing sank into the river, it dragged its prey with it.

I dashed downward, firing. My shot split the creature's head open, releasing Berk. His energy screen created a bubble around him. It pushed the water aside, leaving a gap into which he fell.

"Berk! Berk!" I called to him.

"It's eating me alive!" he screamed.

"You're still alive!"

But he continued screaming, ignorant of my attempts to save him from his terror.

"Bogan, get over and join Kamal. Keep down," I bellowed.

"Got it, Lion."

"Berk, snap out of it. Marines are dying out here and we need you," I told him, my voice less strident.

He screamed again.

Chip's team raced past me, rifles blazing, hosing down the enemy on the island. "Need help?" Chip asked as he passed by.

"I've got it. Get us off that island."

"Aye, aye, skipper!" he retorted.

"Shut up!"

I dropped into the river, pursuing Berk. My screen created its own bubble but the water pressure pushed me along, as it did Berk.

"Berk! Marines are dying around us. We need your help."

"It was eating me," he cried. At least, he realized it wasn't still trying to consume him.

"Shut up!" I bellowed at him. "You're a Marine—act like one. Get your head on straight and come with me. Others need us."

"It was…" he began again.

"Shut up, Marine. That's an order."

"Aye, aye, sir."

"I'm not a sir, I'm your sergeant, now wake up."

"Got it, Lion."

"Good. Systems check." Checking his suit's systems gave him something to do, focusing his attention away from his terror.

"All systems nominal," Berk replied, his voice still shaky. "It was…"

"What did I tell you?" I demanded.

"To... wake up!"

"Then do so."

"Okay," he replied, meekly.

"Put it behind you. Marines are dying and they need our help. Got it?"

"Got it."

"Good. The current's pushed us past the island," I explained. "My plan is for us to pop out under the bridge, if I can time it right. We'll then zig-zag back towards the island. As we get close, kill anything that isn't a Marine. Got it?"

"Got it."

"Good." I checked my sensors. We were almost under the bridge.

"Lion?" Berk asked, his voice subdued.

"What is it?"

"Thanks."

"Anytime, Berk. Anytime." I glanced at my sensors. "Ready?"

"Ready."

"Now!"

EIGHTY-SIX

W E SURFACED JUST A bit downstream of the bridge. A quick check of my sensors behind me revealed that Staff Sergeant Gaiman's Third Squad was in as tight a spot as was our squad. Though he hadn't lost anyone yet, his entire squad, was pinned down along the edge of the island, half in and out. Standing close together, their energy screens sparking from contact with each other, enemy plasma fire cascaded off them. The dozens of Gorgon rifles, couldn't break through their screens. But likewise, Third Squad couldn't move without weakening its position and opening itself up to casualties.

"Should we do anything to help them?" Berk asked me. He had apparently scanned Little Easy to see how Gaiman's Marines were fairing.

"We have our own problems to deal with right now," I said. "We're going up to Big Easy at max velocity. Keep low and tuck down as much as you can. When we come under fire, begin zigzagging and bobbing up and down as much as you can."

"Got it," he replied. "But what if something more comes out of the water?"

"What did I say?" I demanded.

400

"If it's not a Marine, kill it?"

"That's right."

"Got it," he said, with more confidence now.

Without another word, I led him under the bridge. Just as we entered its dark shadow, the water behind us exploded in a superheated cloud of steam.

I checked my sensors, thinking we'd been fired on from Big Easy. But the fire came from above. Up in the bridge's understructure, a dozen Gorgon soldiers were located. Their clear, bubble-shaped helmets and camouflaged armor matched the bridge's concrete and steel beams. Tucked into niches, they fired at us as we moved.

"So much for surprise," Berk said.

"Yeah," I replied. Twisting and turning, making myself a more difficult target to hit, I began shooting them out of the understructure.

Berk copied my maneuvering and firing. When we exited from underneath the bridge, we had killed three of them.

"Mo," I called.

"Where are you?" he replied. "We're a bit busy out here, trying to cover both islands."

"Berk and I are just coming out from under the bridge. We're going to attack Big Easy from down river."

"Good! I thought that thing that got Berk got you, too. Glad you're both okay. We'll hold fire while you attack."

"Thanks. The bridge's understructure is crawling with enemy soldiers. We got three of them."

"Good. I'll let the lieutenant and the skipper know."

He cut communications, being a little bit busy himself. Out beyond the bridge, we increased our velocity to one hundred kph. We quickly approached the island. We continued twisting and turning, bobbing up and down, and zigzagging.

Less than half way to island, the river erupted in a wall of superheated steam. A Gorgon tank on the south side of the river had fired its four plasma cannons at us. But its aim was off. It had missed us. We flew through its wall of steam.

"Gettin' a bit hot out here!" Berk cursed.

"Got that right," I replied. A moment later, another burst of plasma fire crossed behind us. Brighter and hotter than the previous volley, it came from one of our robot plasma cannons. Binary Company had arrived.

No more tank fire crossed the river towards us.

We came up on Big Easy. Shapes moved in front of us. None of them were Marines. We opened fire. Racing across the island, we climbed to sixty meters to avoid the low hill in the island's middle. We continued firing at the mass of enemy troops below. Alien shapes, missing heads and other parts, tumbled to the ground.

The enemy shot at us. Most shots glanced off of us, but an occasional direct hit staggered us. We kept firing and kept moving. Moments later, we zipped past the island, flying upstream.

With Berk close beside me, we arced around to begin another pass over the island. But before we could, we were recalled.

"Second Platoon, fall back," the skipper called. "Repeat, fall back. That's an order."

As we retreated from the island, Berk and I continued maneuvering about, bobbing about and taking potshots at the island. Once the remainder of First Squad returned to Monroeville, we returned as well.

EIGHTY-SEVEN

RETURNING TO SHORE, THE skipper ordered our platoon to take cover among the buildings across the street from the river. As we moved into our new positions, one of Binary Company's platoons took over guarding the entrance to the bridge. Binary's other platoon deployed along the river, guarding a twin-barreled robot plasma cannon.

First Sergeant Jones directed us into various buildings. As I passed him, he said: "Sergeants call at the command post in two minutes."

"Got it," I said. To Kamal, I said: "Secure the team. I'll be back as soon as I can."

"Got it," he confirmed.

My suit's navigation system led me to the company's command post. It was located in a moderately tall building a block back from the river. A team of Marines from the company's Command Platoon maintained security. A corporal directed me to a wide room on the second floor. When I reached it, I realized it must have been some sort of restaurant in a previous life, though now it housed the Command Post. A row of wide windows overlooked a park below. My team had not passed it when we proceeded toward the river. Tall, genetically modified oaks created a perimeter around the park's green lawn. It seemed out of place.

Inside the room, tables had been pushed aside and stacked along the walls. The CP's staff, both human and robot, had set up tall holographic screens. Likewise, they had also emplaced along the windows and walls energy barriers protecting the CP from assault. The barriers and holo screens flickered, warning of their locations. A familiar faint blue light filled the room.

The only occupants, other than CP's robot staff members, were the sergeants from Second Platoon's two squads. Everyone but James Thur was present. No officers were present, but Gunnery Sergeant Kano was, as well as First Sergeant Jones.

"Dismount!" Jones barked. All of us, including the first sergeant, climbed from our suits.

I glanced around, looking for Thur. His team had suffered three killed, the last killed as we retreated from Big Easy. No doubt, with half of his team gone, he was seeing to his surviving Marines.

"Hey," a voice behind me called. I turned. It was Chip.

"Why'd you pulled that stunt with your team?"

"I told you, I'm tired of us being the rearguard."

"You're a bad liar. Besides, if you'd let us go first, we would've dealt with that river monster, not you."

"We did fine," I retorted.

"That you did," he agreed. "You're a lousy liar, but one hell of a Marine. Second to me, of course."

"Of course," I concurred. "I take it that Thur's consoling his remaining two Marines?"

"Thur was blown apart," Sergeant Jones said behind me.

I turned to face him, horrified. "What?"

"Last Marine off, he was last to die," Jones said.

I followed the first sergeant over to where the other sergeants stood. We were a small crowd. Mo stood with us. Chip and I stood to his left. Gaiman and his two sergeants, stood to our right.

"Let's bow our heads in silence for a great Marine," Jones said. We bowed, saying nothing, thinking nothing.

After a minute or so, Jones said: "What the hell happened out there? Biyela, why'd your team jump the gun?"

"I just wanted to get out there, I guess," I said.

"You expect me to believe that shit?" he growled. "You're a trained Marine, Biyela. You've never done that before. You ruined the entire advance. You cost us some good Marines!"

"Bull shit!" Mo exclaimed. "Biyela's not responsible. We should have hosed down those islands before attacking them. Preparation was called for. Whatever reason Biyela skipped out there before Saunders' team is irrelevant. The Gorgons lay in wait for us and we moved right into their trap.

"Hell, if anyone's to blame it's you and me. After a year of fighting we've grown complacent. We've won so many firefights just by charging down on the enemy that we've forgotten how to fight as Marines!

"But Sergeant Bileya hasn't. After that river monster attacked Berk, he organized his rescue and when Thur came under fire Lion sent the rest of his team to assist him. Then he attacked from the flank, out-maneuvering the enemy and breaking up the Gorgons' ambush. He did nothing wrong. We did."

Jones glared at Mo. "Or you did."

Mo shrugged. "Whatever."

Jones looked at me. After a moment, he turned back to Mo. "Re-organize your platoon. The colonel wants us to take the bridge. He's ordered the company to try again. Lieutenant Kwung is consulting with the skipper right now. You've got twenty minutes."

EIGHTY-EIGHT

MY TEAM RESTED IN a row of buildings across from the river. Between the river and the buildings, a highway stretched upstream and downstream. Most of the buildings consisted of shops and restaurants, but hotels and warehouses also dotted the kilometers-long highway.

First Sergeant Jones had assigned us to a warehouse. Two stories tall, the upper floor consisted of offices, while the lower floor was jammed with all kinds of boats, fishing gear, diving equipment and sundry items. Kamal had taken the team to the upper floor.

When I arrived, everyone had dismounted from their suits. They sat in comfortable-looking chairs well back from the windows, safe from observation by the enemy. They had out their rations and were relaxing.

As I floated up a stairwell, Ruby called to me: "Hey, baby, why don't you unload that thing and take a few moments with us?"

The team's suits were scattered about in a disorganized fashion, quite unlike their usual orderliness. I pulled up beside Kamal's suit, settled to the floor, and a moment later backed out, carrying a food packet and a bottle of water.

"Cozy place," I said.

"Ain't it, though?" Ruby remarked. "What's up?"

"Us," I replied.

"What d'ya mean?" Berk asked. "We're not going back out there again, are we?"

I nodded. "In about seventeen minutes. A robot with fresh supplies and ammo will be along soon. Then we're going to attack the islands again."

"But, why?" Berk demanded. "We lost three good Marines. One of them was Thur. Why risk another firefight? Let someone else do it. Maybe the Navy, or the Eosian Army. We've given enough for this world. Let the locals handle this."

"I'm with jughead here," Ruby said. "Unless we're going to fight this war right and just burn out the wormheads from space, then we should stay out of it. We've paid with enough blood for this rock. Let someone else fight for it."

"Someone else already is," Kamal said. "For every single life we lose the Eosians loose ten or maybe a hundred, or even a thousand. Without our help, millions more will die."

"So let them," she retorted. "They shouldn't have moved here in the first place. This planet's located right next door to the Gorgons. Our nearest world is hundreds of light-years away. These colonists knew what they were getting into, so let them pay the price."

"Even the children? Even the babies?" Bogan asked.

Ruby had been eating peaches. She spun around in her chair and threw the remnant all over Bogan's face.

"Shut it, you little prick! You don't know what it's like here. A few minutes of fighting and you think you got it all figured out. You don't. You don't know a fucking thing.

None of you do." She spun her chair around to face me. "Least of all our little cry-baby, do-as-he's-told sergeant."

I stared at her. She was so twisted now, full of anger, fear and hatred. It was getting harder to work with her all the time. She was a member of my team, like a sister, though a very irritating one.

"What a fucking little asshole you are!" she spat at me.

"Ruby!" Kamal exclaimed, exasperation and disappointment in his voice. "Control yourself."

"Oh, fuck it," she said to him. "You're nothing more than a corporal, little better than me. Shut up."

Kamal opened his mouth to respond, but I motioned for him to keep quiet. He did so.

"You think you're the only Marine disturbed by this war?" I demanded. "You think that you're the only one hurting?"

"I'm the only one that cares," she snapped at me.

"We all care," Kamal interrupted.

"Oh, yeah, you," Ruby said, her voice full of sarcasm and disrespect. "All you know is how to play daddy. Mister morality, that's you. You think you own the high ground, but no one owns it. Not you, not me, not baby sergeant here, none of us. We've all got blood on our hands. No one cares about anything."

"We care," Berk countered.

"Sure you do," Ruby snapped. "You only care about fighting. Men are that way. They get hard when they're killing things. There's so much shit running through your heads, you can't see anything but the mission, the kill, the victory. You're all insane when you're fighting."

"Aren't women that way?" RC asked.

"You're just as fucked up as everyone else," Ruby said, standing, glaring at RC. "Mister I'm-dumber-than-dirt. That's how you want everybody to think about you, that you're so stupid you can't even dress yourself in the morning. And then we hear words like 'predaceous' from you. How'd a clod like you learn such language?"

RC stared at her, then shook his head.

"Trying to clear the crap out of it?" Ruby said, laughing cruelly. "Open your mouth and let it tumble. Then you can say something intelligent again."

"Ruby," I said, tired off her meltdown, "I've known you for a long time…"

"That must really suck."

"It does."

"Whaddya know, something honest!"

"I don't know what I can do for you, how to help you."

"Help me? All you want is to make me a good little murderer again. You want me to keep killing and killing and killing, until all that's left to kill is me. That's what you want." She glared at me, her face twisted with rage.

Her rage burned me, burned my heart, my flesh, my soul.

We all felt like she did, full of anger and self-contempt. But as I couldn't help myself, how could I help her? How could I help any of us?

She marched past me to her suit, leaving her food and water behind. Climbing into her suit, she growled, "When's that fucking robot getting here?"

From the stairwell, a voice said, "I am here now, ma'am."

She backed out of her suit as the humanlike robot reached our floor. It carried two large bags of supplies.

"I'm not a ma'am, or a madam, or any such thing," Ruby growled. "If you ever call me ma'am again, I'll kill you."

"Yes, ma'am," the robot said as it walked over to my suit, where it stopped and began filling my ammunition hopper with iron pellets.

Even from across the room, I felt the heat of Ruby's hatred.

RC pointed at the robot and said, "I wish I was like that machine, without feelings."

"Me, too," said Bogan.

"And me," Berk concurred.

I turned and looked at them. Their faces were blank, as blank as the robot's face. I glanced at Kamal, who had his back to us. I heard him whispering. Whether he was praying, cursing, or just saying something else, I couldn't tell.

My team was falling apart and we still had a long way to go. After a year, we could barely hold it together. How long the war would go on, how much more suffering and terror we had to endure, I couldn't know. Yet I knew we had to stay together. We had our limits, but we had to stay together. Only as a team, fighting together, could we survive. If we stopped functioning as a unit, then we'd die.

When the robot finished re-supplying us, we entered our suits and moved out.

EIGHTY-NINE

OUTSIDE, WE MET CHIP'S team and what was left of Thur's team. Gunnery Sergeant Kano also waited for us. With Chip in tow, he approached me.

"As we're missing a squad leader," Mo began, "and as Saunders is senior to you, he's got the squad now. The colonel has promoted him to staff sergeant, with Brigade confirming it."

I grabbed Chip's suited shoulders with my gloved hands and shook him. "Congratulations!"

"Battlefield promotions are never a good thing," Chip said. "How can I be the company's smartass now?"

"You're more like the brigade's smartass," Mo said.

I burst out laughing. Mo quickly joined me. After a moment, so did Chip. When we heard Ruby growl, "What are those assholes laughing about?" we almost fell on the ground. We laughed, uncontrollably, for a good minute, until Kwung called.

"Time to go, gentlemen," she said. "Congratulations, Saunders. I realize it's not how you wanted to get the squad, but it's yours now. You'll do fine. Even so, I still expect you to be the platoon's jester. If not, then you're nobody's fool."

That comment brought on another fit of laughter, with a little snickering from the lieutenant. It continued until First Sergeant Jones told us to shut up and get with the mission.

That shut us up.

"Good hunting," Mo said, as he darted off to the lieutenant's location. "By the by, Corporal Peres and the rest of Team A is temporarily assigned to the Command Team."

"Got it," Chip and I replied.

"Now what?" I asked.

"Now we take Big Easy. And hold it."

"How will we do that?"

"With whatever works. We've got our orders."

"Got it."

"Any ideas?" Chip asked me.

"You're the squad leader."

"That doesn't mean I don't value your suggestions."

"How about we attack from underwater?" I said.

"Too slow. Besides, I don't want to tackle any other surprises the Gorgons might have for us in the river."

"Got it," I said. "What was that thing, anyways?"

"Battalion's Intelligence team thinks it was some sort of Gorgon shark. Apparently, down in the Gorgon territories, the water's full of them. They'll eat anything and attack everything."

"No underwater attacks. Got it."

"Any other ideas?" Chip asked.

"We could hit the island from two different directions."

"Such as?"

"Well, last time the Gorgons lost control of the situation when Berk and I out-flanked them. Maybe it'll work again."

"I knew I kept you around for some reason. Other than as a target of opportunity, of course."

"Of course," I concurred. "But you know you really kept me around because I'm a good audience. In fact, I'm probably your only audience."

"You're making it hard for me to be your new boss, you know."

"Sometimes new jobs are that way."

He grunted. "Want to come out from under the bridge again?"

"No. It's too heavily guarded. Berk and I barely escaped."

"I see. How about you come from up river while my team attacks it straight on?"

"Sounds good," I said. "Be careful out there."

"You too. Have a couple of your Marines ready for anything that comes out of the river. My Marines will do the same."

"Good idea," I agreed. "What about intervals?"

"Ten meters."

"Got it."

"Where the hell are you guys?" the First Sergeant growled. "Get your squad out here, Saunders."

"Aye, aye, First Sergeant," Chip replied. "Let's go, Marines!"

NINETY

A S WE CAME AROUND the warehouse, we saw the entire company lined up on the near side of the street. We could see the bridge and the far side of the river but we couldn't see this side of the river, nor the islands.

We pulled up next to Third Squad. "Welcome to the world, Staff Sergeant Saunders," Staff Sergeant Gaiman said. "Tradition requires we toss a squad leader into a bathtub full of gin, but where we'd get that much gin is beyond me right now."

"At least I've got something to look forward to," Chip said.

"Anyways, we're gonna play your favorite game."

"Throw up on an admiral's feet?" Chip asked.

Our whole squad laughed. Rank hadn't changed Chip.

"I haven't heard of that one," Gaiman said, after laughing. "No, we're gonna wait. Until someone figures out what they want us to do."

It wasn't long before the skipper addressed us. "Hello, Chaos Company. Here we are again. Asked to do the impossible with less than we have. But it's what we do.

We're Marines. We fight the battles we're given. We do what we're asked and we do it well.

"Let's get down to it. Second platoon lost three good Marines earlier today. But they didn't accomplish their mission, through no fault of their own. They still have the same mission, taking the islands on either side of the bridge. Once they have them and are holding them, First and Third platoons will take the bridge. And then they will hold it.

"Now, we're not crossing the river at this time. Our supply line is almost a thousand kilometers long. We've created a bulge in the enemy's line, but we're not strong enough to do more than that.

"Two Eosian Army divisions will be here within a few hours to help spread out the line. For now, though, we're on our own. And we still have a mission to accomplish."

There was silence while we took it all in. We were alone, so what else was new? It was nice to know that the Eosian Army was on its way, but we had little respect for them. We owned the battlefield, not them. But what about the bridge? We were supposed to take it, but not cross it? Why spend lives for such a frivolous goal?

"I'm sure you're all wondering why we're not going to invade the south shore," the skipper continued. "It's simple. We have a thousand Marines here while the Gorgons have maybe twenty times that many on the other side. We have to take the bridge, but we don't have to glide into a slaughter."

"Sixty seconds," Mo told us.

At that moment, our sensors caught the loud hissing and whistling sounds of the plasma cannons firing. And almost immediately afterward, we heard shrieking explosions as the cannons' eight-thousand-degree plasma streams struck the islands' land mass.

I quickly informed my team of our plan.

"Fifteen seconds," Mo said.

"Gotta get into position," Gaiman said, peeling his squad away and toward the east. "Good luck."

"You, too," Chip said.

"Five … four … three … two …" Mo counted. "One. Go!"

Leading my team to the right, we zipped west along the highway until we were well beyond Monroeville's city limits. We climbed upward as we moved, until our sensors revealed damage the plasma cannons were doing to Big Easy. Everything not melting into the river burned. Flames shot skyward dozens of meters. Everything living had been vaporized.

Turning left, to port, I guided my team high out over the river. We flew in teams of two. Bogan kept close to me. Kamal and Berk followed, with Ruby and RC bringing up the read. Once we were perpendicular to Big Easy, I turned us hard port again and we dived for the island, our shields up, our rifles ready.

Sporadic rifle fire from the island flared against our energy screens. As we wondered how anything could survive that fiery bombardment, our cannons focused on the attackers, vaporizing them. Then cannons stopped firing. Chip's team had reached the island. They advanced under heavy fire.

"How could anything survive that?" Bogan wondered.

"It's the way of the universe," Berk replied. "If you think the enemy won't survive, then they do."

"Keep quiet," I chided. "Make intervals ten meters and spread out. Kill anything that isn't a Marine."

"Got it," they replied.

We twisted and turned, bobbing up and down as we came in over the island. We moved fast and we cut them down faster. I flamed each one a couple of times, cracking their shields. Then Bogan finished them off with a quick shot.

We burned them down.

Chip's team, organized like mine, fought across the island. But as fast as they killed the enemy more came at them. The same happened to us. For every Gorgon we killed, two more took its place.

A meter above the molten ground, we advanced from the upriver side while Chip's team held onto the longer eastern side.

"Where are they all coming from?" Berk wondered.

"Kamal, cover Bogan and me. I've got an idea and I'm going over by the southeast side. I think they're coming out of one their infamous holes."

"Got it, Lion," Kamal said.

We popped high into sky, dozens of plasma rifles flaming at us. Weaving, tipping, and bobbing, we kept most of the molten metal streams away from us.

"Ammo check," I ordered Bogan.

"Forty percent," he reported.

"Me, too," I replied.

"What're you doing?" Chip called.

"Looking for intel."

"Be careful."

"Always," I said.

After a few tense moments of enemy fire and tight maneuvers, we found what we sought. A big hole just above the water line on the southeast corner of the island.

Looking down into it from above, I saw hundreds of bodies scrambling out of it. They were too close to activate their screens so I pumped several shots into them. Dozens fell back inside, knocking others down with them. Bedlam reigned below.

Then, while I gawked instead of retreated, dozens of plasma rifles fired up at me. My energy screen flashed to black and winked out before rebooting. I climbed fiercely into the sky, twisting away from the hole. Bogan flew right beside me.

"My screen's finished," he said. "I'm screwed."

"You're not screwed," I replied. "Try rebooting it."

"Done," he said. "It's back. Just barely."

Once our screens had returned to full power, we attacked again. But we didn't stay long. There were too many of them.

"Ammo check," I called.

"Ten percent," Bogan replied. "Fifteen rounds left."

"I've got twenty rounds left. Kamal, ammo check."

"We're all down to twenty percent," Kamal replied. "You found what you were looking for?"

"I did. A big hole full of hundreds of squirming Gorgons. We're not taking this island away from them today."

"Lion," Chip interrupted. "We're running out of ammo. How 'bout you?"

"Same." I told him about the hole. "A whole army's coming out of it."

"Got it. Mo, we're almost out of ammo. There's a Gorgon Hole on the southeast side."

"Understood," Mo said. "I've informed the lieutenant. She's talking to the skipper. Wait one."

How could we wait when death rushed toward us?

"Saunders, Biyela, this is Jones. The skipper says to hold at all costs. Gaiman has taken Little Easy. You can do the same with Big Easy."

"There's a Gorgon Hole on the other side of the island," I exclaimed. "An army's coming out of it. If we stay, we're dead."

"Do as you're told!" the first sergeant commanded. "Twelve Marines are more than a match for a thousand wormheads."

I was ready to curse out Jones, but Chip interrupted, "Don't do it. You'll just get into trouble. We'll figure a way out. Our honor as Marines is at stake."

I forced myself to calm down. Honor, duty, liberty, freedom, fraternity, all were buzz words for the Interstellar Marine Corps, but important nonetheless. Leave no Marine behind. Watch your back. Guard each other. Fight well. Die well.

Was this the day to die well?

With orders to hold an island without the means to do so, what could I do but obey? Yet when should orders be obeyed and when should they be disobeyed? When are twelve lives more important than a piece of molten ground? I knew that obeying my current orders meant sacrificing my team and myself for an unattainable goal. However, disobeying orders meant running away, saving my team and maybe Chip's team, too, if I could get him to go, and what would we get for it except a court-martial and a dishonorable discharge?

The future seemed bleak. Seconds slipped away. The enemy crashed towards us.

I made a last desperate call to Chip. "What do we do?"

"Fall back! The skipper's recalled us."

We fell back.

NINETY-ONE

AFTER RETURNING, WE RETIRED to our respective buildings. Chip and his team went to the shop across a small alley from us and we to the warehouse where we had previously settled. Out along the riverbank beyond us, one of the platoons from Binary Company set up for the night, guarding our positions. We were as safe as we could be when occupying forward lines.

As we settled on the second floor, all the windows darkened by protective force field generators, we dismounted. We arranged our suits in a neat row this time. Then we retrieved our sleeping gear and whatever water and field rations we still possessed. Tired, bewildered, disgusted, bitter, we claimed little places on the hardwood floor for ourselves.

After laying out our sleeping gear and rations, we located facilities for relieving ourselves. Fortunately, the Gorgons hadn't destroyed Monroeville's water and sewage systems.

Ten minutes later, as we rested on our sleeping gear, a pair of service robots from the battalion's support unit arrived bringing fresh food and water, and replacement ammo for our suits. They had brought a small stove with them. Within minutes, we smelled beef stew, with vegetables, cooking. There was also the wonderful smell of fresh coffee. Miraculously, one of the robot's produced a brownie mix and began mixing it into a batter.

"Sirs and ma'am," the robot baker inquired, "walnuts or chocolate chips?"

"Both," we all bellowed.

"And make it snappy," Ruby said.

"Serving you is my purpose," the robot replied. "I have been instructed to meet your every need tonight, if I can."

When the coffee was ready, it smelled so good, we produced our cups and the robot served us. "Sugar, cream, and mocha are available," the robot said.

"You're my new best friend," RC quipped.

"Thank you, sir. I have always wanted a friend." The robot looked almost human.

"Wonder what it meant by meeting our every need?" Berk said.

"Not that need," RC said.

"But what if it could?" Berk demanded.

"It might look human, but it's still a machine," Ruby said, smirking at Kamal and me.

"Yeah, I wouldn't want to ride that horse," Bogan said.

Ruby twisted around to stare at Bogan. "Do you even know what you're talking about?"

Bogan smirked at her. "There are a lot of different kinds of horses."

Ruby grunted.

Berk said, "Say, Ruby, maybe you'd..."

"Maybe my combat knife," Ruby snarled back.

"Maybe not."

We all laughed.

"Dinner is ready sirs," our mechanical chef said.

"And the brownies?" Berk asked.

"Imminent."

Dinner was fantastic. There was enough for all of us to have seconds. Then the brownies arrived. And more coffee, much more than we could or should drink.

"Man, I gotta visit the toilet again," Bogan said. "My back teeth are going under."

Our robot chef stared at Bogan. "Sir, that is physically impossible."

We laughed again. Except for Bogan, who hurried off to the head.

"Was my comment in error?" the robot inquired.

"No," Kamal said, "The private's comment was a metaphorical jest."

"Understood," the robot replied. "I do not know if I will ever comprehend human humor."

"Don't worry about it," Kamal replied.

Several minutes later, as we rested on our sleeping gear, Chip arrived. He came up the stairs just as the robot served another round of coffee and brownies.

"Chip!" I exclaimed. "How was your dinner? Would you like some coffee and a brownie or two?"

"My dinner was good," Chip replied. "And, yes, I'd like a brownie and some coffee."

"Good," I said. I glanced at the robot.

"Very good, sir," the robot replied.

Chip winced.

"Still can't get over being called 'sir' by a robot, can you?" I commented to him.

"Nope, but I'm working on it." As he sat down, I noticed that his insignia now indicated his new rank of staff sergeant.

"Why'd the skipper order us to fight to the last Marine and then recall us?" I asked.

"The lieutenant told me that the colonel wanted us to take the islands, and the skipper was torn between her duty to him and her responsibility to us. She finally chose us."

"I'm grateful for her choice."

"Me, too."

"What's next?"

"We try again."

"And how are we supposed to that? Even Gaiman, after he took Little Easy, had to leave it after he ran out of shot. He has eighteen Marines and we only have twelve, and yet he couldn't hold onto an island a quarter the size of ours."

"A third," Chip corrected me.

"A third, then. But what good is it to throw a handful of Marines against hundreds of enemy aliens?"

"I don't know," Chip said, shaking his head. "But what can we do? Orders are orders. Our job is to carry out the colonel's commands, even if it cost us our lives."

"So be it. It's a helluva way to die."

"It is." Chip stood up. "Thanks for the food. See you at sunrise."

"See you," I said, standing and shaking his hand.

He left.

NINETY-TWO

WE WERE UP BEFORE sunrise. Our robot chef returned and fixed us breakfast. Eggs and steak, with hash browned potatoes, the last meal of the condemned. We gobbled it down, with all the coffee we could get.

Unlike last night, conversation was absent. The sounds made were those of utensils against plates, of coffee sloshed into cups, of chewing and swallowing, and of the grunts of Marines stretching out their kinks after a quiet night of sleep.

Finishing off the meal, everyone made polite comments of gratitude towards our chef.

We used the facilities again. Washing our faces and armpits with cold water from the sinks was a last luxury before suiting up.

We mounted up, ready as we could be to return to the fight.

"Comm check," I said over the team channel.

Everyone reported to me. I switched to the squad channel. Chip said, "Good morning, sleepy head. Ready to kick alien ass?"

"Is Sinclair back, along with Second Squad?" I inquired.

"Nope. As far as I know, she's still at Brigade, four thousand kilometers west of here."

"Too bad."

"Agreed. Come on, let's get it over with."

"Got it," I said. Back on the team channel: "Move out."

"Got it," they replied. My team didn't sound unhappy, but rather tired. I could tell by the melancholy in their voices. We had fought twice now for the same island and we had accomplished nothing. It was a hopeless fight and here we were going back out to fight it again. What would happen today?

We drifted outside and onto the road. Chip's team was lined up, facing toward the river. Their grav discs rested on the pavement. They formed a perfect line, separated one meter from each other.

I formed us up into a duplicate line three meters behind them.

Beside us stood Gaiman's Third Squad.

"First Squad present and accounted for!" Chip announced to Mo and Lieutenant Kwung.

Two meters in front of both squads stood the Command Team.

"Second Platoon present and ready for action," Lieutenant Kwung announced.

On Chaos Company's channel I heard the skipper say, "Very well."

We stood there, supported by our suits, cool within them even as Thea's sub-tropical sunlight beat down upon us. We waited. Five minutes passed. Then ten minutes more.

Then First Lieutenant Gino Magliano, the company's executive officer, announced: "Chaos Company present and accounted for, skipper. All Marines ready for action."

"Very well," the skipper replied.

More time passed. It gave me the opportunity to scan our deployment. The entire company had joined us. We were all lined up again, like yesterday. Yet again we would have an audience to watch us fail.

We stood in perfect little groups. Squads separated from each other, blocked together with their command teams, forming platoons. Platoons formed larger blocks, with the company's command and support platoon blocked up in perfect line with the rest of us.

We waited.

"What's going on?" Bogan asked, his voice an unnecessary whisper over the team's channel.

"We're waiting while the big shots figure out what they want us to do," Ruby explained.

"Maybe it'll be a banzai charge," RC said.

"What's that?" Bogan asked.

"When we all charge the islands at once," Kamal replied. "It's an ancient form of attack from the middle Twentieth Century or maybe farther back. Frightening to its enemies, it was rarely successful."

"Then why do it?" Bogan asked.

"Why, indeed?" was Kamal's reply.

Bogan sighed.

"Easy, killer," Ruby said. "There'll be enough time to butcher the enemy."

"Last night was fun, wasn't it?" Bogan said.

"It was," Ruby replied.

"What?" Berk inquired.

"Mind your own fucking business," Bogan snarled.

"What the hell?" RC said. "You sound like Ruby."

"You heard him," Ruby snapped. "Shut your traps."

"Is, um, something going on between you two?" RC questioned.

I listened intently to this suddenly out-of-character conversation within my squad.

"What if there is?" Ruby growled.

"Well," Berk said, joining the conversation. "If you're giving out favors, I'd certainly like to be on the receiving end."

"How 'bout me shoving my plasma rifle up your ass?" Bogan snarled.

"Easy, children," Kamal said. "Save it for the enemy."

I foolishly joined the conversation and said to Ruby, "Did you and Bogan..."

"Shut up!" Ruby snapped back.

"Yes, ma'am," I replied.

"You did!" RC said, letting out a bellowing laugh. "You slept with him, didn't you? Bogan, you lucky bastard!"

"Ruby, how could you break my heart like that?" Berk said. His voice was anything but serious.

"You sonsabitches!" Ruby exclaimed. "When we hit land, I'm going to fry your asses."

"Hey, Bogan, aren't you gonna stand up for your woman?" RC quipped.

"I'm not his woman!" Ruby bellowed.

"Yes, you are," Bogan said, softly and sweetly.

"Yes, I am," she replied, just as sweetly and softly.

"Oh, oh, I love you so much," RC snickered.

"That's enough!" I growled. "What they do is their business and no one else's. Got that?"

"Got it," Berk and RC replied.

"Good!"

"Got it," they said again.

"Kamal, Ruby, Bogan?" I demanded.

"Got it!" the rest of my team chimed in.

"Good."

"Oh, Ruby, Ruby, Ruby..." RC groaned.

"I'm gonna kill you!" Ruby yelled.

"Not if I get to him first," Bogan said.

I sighed. Even when we were about to go into battle, even when we might all die, they behaved like teenagers. I apparently led juveniles to war. Oh, hell.

NINETY-THREE

"WHAT DO YOU THINK?" I asked. "What's taking so long? We've been out here an hour. Are we going to hit Big Easy again or not?"

"Don't know and don't care," Chip said. "Life's precious and I'm happy to wait right here, right now."

"You're right."

"I always am."

"Except when it comes to food."

"A Marine's gotta have a weakness or two."

"How about seven?"

"How about you shut up, kiddo?" Chip said, clearly growing annoyed at me.

"Kiddo? We're practically the same age."

"But not the same rank."

"Oh, I see," I said. "It's all gone to your head."

Chip laughed. "Not quite."

"I really didn't think so."

So we stood there and waited some more. And waited even more. My legs trembled a bit. Though my suit held me up, I had just enough adrenalin getting by my nanites that I needed to move about. I needed to get on with whatever awaited us. Soon my team and I would be wrecked, too stressed out by waiting to be effective in battle.

We waited so long that everyone in my team, myself included, had peed into our reclamation systems. The salts in our urine were processed out and dumped from our suits. The remaining water was purified and stored as additional drinking water for later consumption.

"Chaos Company, ten-hutt!" First Sergeant Jones bellowed.

"Good morning, Chaos Company," the skipper said. "I know you have all been standing here for a long time. That time is just about over. Colonel Grunnig has decided for a full company assault on the islands and the bridge. First Platoon will capture Big Easy. Third Platoon will capture Little Easy. Second Platoon and the Command and Support Platoon will capture the bridge."

The skipper paused to let it all sink in. We weren't attacking Big Easy today, but I imagined the bridge would be just as tough a nut to crack. First Platoon was the only one with three full squads. Second and Third platoons had each given up a squad to Brigade Headquarters out west.

"I hope you all understand your missions," the skipper said. "The plasma cannons will again blast away at the islands. But this time we will have gunboat support for the attacks on the islands. They'll crush those Gorgon Holes.

"The gunboats will also pulverize the far shore. They will be assisted by Sky Command fighters. Today, we will achieve our goals. Today, we will succeed. Today, we will win! Marines, ready?"

Motivated by her speech, we all replied: "Ready!"

"Good!" the skipper said. She floated out in front of the whole company, up on the road for all to see, even the enemy on the far shore, on the islands, and on or under the bridge. She was an easy target for Gorgon snipers, but none shot at her.

The plasma cannons began firing on the islands. We glided around into our positions. First Platoon moved up in front of Second Platoon, while we dropped back and joined up with the Command and Support Platoon. Third Platoon fell further back and drifted down opposite Little Easy. In minutes, we were in our new positions, ready to do or die.

Preferably, to do.

A full squadron of seven Marine gunboats appeared. Two attacked Big Easy and two more struck at Little Easy.

Meanwhile, the other three gunboats zipped across the river and began strafing enemy forces on the far side. When enemy gunboats raced up to strike at our gunboats, four Sky Command fighters fell out of the sky and blasted the Gorgon gunboats out of existence.

We watched the spectacle for several minutes. Then the plasma cannons ceased firing upon the islands and the two platoons began their attacks.

Third Platoon arced high over the river and quickly descended upon Little Easy. Rather than scoot across the river, their lieutenant had decided for a more vertical attack the moment the bombardment ceased. The forty-two Marines in the platoon dropped like leaves from a gigantic tree, blanketing the island. Each Marine fired at any surviving aliens as they dropped down among them. Within moments, the whole platoon was on the island, scattered about in fire teams, slaughtering the unprepared survivors.

Even as Third Platoon engulfed the Gorgons from every side, hundreds of more enemy soldiers swarmed from the Hole on the southwestern corner of Little Easy. But they were met with scalding plasma fire from the two Marine gunboats assigned to provide suppression upon the Hole. Besides raining plasma streams down upon swarming Gorgon ground forces, our gunboats also dropped micro-fusion warheads into the Hole, collapsing it in upon the thousands of alien troops trying to get out at us. Then a final plasma salvo from the gunboat turned the sealed hole into a lake of molten rock.

Soon, the fighting was finished. The two gunboats sped toward the far shore to assist their squadron mates. The Third Platoon Marines policed up what was left of the enemy.

First Platoon's advance had been more traditional. The entire platoon, in three close waves, had scooted across the river and attacked the north shore of Big Easy. In minutes, all sixty of the platoon's Marines were ashore.

The gunboats slaved to First Platoon quickly collapsed the Gorgon Hole on the southeastern side of Big Easy. After that, the fighting came to a sudden and effective conclusion. Both islands were secured without loss of human life.

Now it was our turn. We wouldn't have any sky support.

First Lieutenant Magliano led us onto the bridge. The Command and Support Platoon, forty Marines strong, popped over the end of the bridge and began shooting the alien soldiers hiding on the surface of the bridge. Magliano, besides being the company's executive officer, commanded the Command and Support Platoon.

Lieutenant Kwung led us beneath the bridge. Since Berk and I had previously engaged the enemy down here, my team led the way. Chip followed my lead, though he was in charge.

"Keep an eye on the support braces," I instructed everyone in the platoon. "Shoot quickly and don't ask questions. Watch the braces, the water, the kiron columns holding the bridge up, and anywhere else the Gorgons can concentrate. Keep moving and keep firing. Don't stop. Don't make a target of yourselves."

I scooted out. My team took the east side of the bridge while Chip's team took the west side. Behind us came Kwung and Kano, the three surviving Marines from Thur's fireteam, the Command Team, and one of Gaiman's teams. Gaiman and his other two teams followed Chip.

"Don't concentrate fire," the lieutenant warned. "The supports might be made of kiron and titanium, but concentrated plasma fire can damage them. The Eosian Army and the Colonial Guard need the bridge to cross to the other side. We don't."

"Got it," we all replied.

Multiple plasma streams sizzled from above. One of Gaiman's Marines was hit and fried. Her ruined suit, containing her burnt corpse, fell into the water. Several Gorgon river sharks grabbed her suit and dragged it beneath the waves. Gaiman sent her team mates after her remains.

Plasma fire struck at the Command Team. Sergeant Jindal and Corporal Mpopi were killed. In turn, Mo and the lieutenant cremated their attackers.

There were four sets of kiron pillars supporting the bridge as it stretched across the river. Each set consisted of twin pillars, about twenty meters apart, holding up either side of the bridge. My team made it to the first pillar on the left side where we came under intense fire. We couldn't move without being hit with multiple plasma bursts. Chip's team was pinned down in a similar fashion behind the pillar across from us.

The kiron pillars were surrounded by strong concrete, two meters thick. The concrete stretched four meters parallel to the river and two meters perpendicular to it. The upstream and downstream sides of the pillars curved to allow the river an easier path around the pillars.

Chip's team had taken cover along the eastern or trailing side of his pillar, while my team had taken cover along the western or leading side of our pillar. Sporadic plasma rifle fire licked at the edges of the pillars, occasionally striking the screens of the Marines nearest the edges.

Lieutenant Kwung had led the rest of the platoon into the support beams above us and they slowly made their way southward toward us. Since zipping upward among the supports, two more Marines from the platoon had fallen dead into the water below.

"We gotta get around these pillars," Chip called to me. "Any ideas?"

"No. How about you?" I replied.

"How 'bout I take my team up and swarm around the outside of my pillar while you do the same from the surface? Go outside."

"Got it," I agreed. "Be careful."

"You too."

I explained the plan to my team. "Bogan, you stick with me. Berk and RC, you follow closely. Kamal, Ruby, wait thirty seconds and then follow."

"Ruby and I want to fight together," Bogan said.

"I need you beside me," I said.

"No, we want to fight together," he demanded.

"Listen," I said to him, "If you want your relationship to be more than one night, you have to let her fight on her terms. Otherwise, she'll feel smothered by you. Then she'll think the whole thing's a bad idea."

"I want her safe. I want to protect her."

"I understand. But you have to let her take care of herself. She'll think you think less of her otherwise. It'll ruin your relationship."

"But what if she gets fried?" I heard the fear in his voice. He cared about her. I hoped Ruby cared as much about him.

"Fight hard enough and it won't happen," I said.

"How can you know that?" Bogan asked.

"Because she's precious to all of us. We'll fight for her, just as she'll fight for us. Do your job and let her do hers."

"I don't know if I can," he said.

"If you can't, there's not much hope for either of you."

He said nothing. The whole conversation had been on the team channel. The rest of the team had heard it.

"Daniel," Ruby said. "Do your job and it'll be fine. I can take care of myself. Keep Lion alive. He's really just a big baby anyways."

Bogan laughed. "Got it."

"Ready?" Chip called.

"Ready," I replied.

"Let's go."

NINETY-FOUR

As Chip's team floated upward, I maneuvered Bogan and myself toward the outer end of our pillar. Just before we reached the edge, my sensors detected several plasma shots blasting at Marines scooting through the support beams above and behind me. I looked back around and saw a brilliant flash followed by a Marine plummeting toward the river. It was the lieutenant, her screen shot away, her suit damaged. The rest of the platoon appeared too engaged to either notice her or fly to her rescue.

"Kamal, Ruby, get the lieutenant," I said.

Immediately, they replied: "Got it." As they zipped away from the pillar, plasma fire vaporized the river behind them. Return fire from the Marines above silenced their attackers.

I turned back to the end of the pillar. "Follow me," I said to Bogan and scooted around the corner. As I came around four plasma streams engulfed my energy screen. It flashed bright blue, then a violent violet, and then it was gone. Suddenly, I was defenseless.

Four plasma shots seared past me. In front of me four Gorgons died as their heads were vaporized. Bogan had killed them before they could kill me.

The Gorgons' defensive screens had been off. Their suits, like ours, were wonderful at hiding our presence from the other side's sensors. But once any of them, or us, activated our energy screens everyone knew where we were. There was no way to hide a defensive screen's energy signature.

So, with their screens off, there wasn't any way for our sensors to know that they had hidden themselves on the other side of the pillar. They knew we were coming because our screens were active while theirs were not. But Bogan, bless him, had been ready.

"You okay, Lion?" he asked me.

"Yes," I said. My screen was slowly rebooting itself. I looked across the river, behind the western pillar where Chip's team was busy engaging the enemy up among the support beams. Along the pillar's side four Gorgons climbed upward. They sought to ambush Chip's team as this group had ambushed me.

Without a thought for my safety, without even my energy screen rebooted, I zipped across the river, firing at the unscreened enemy soldiers. Bogan followed close beside me. He shielded me with his suit's energy screen when an enemy's plasma rifle fired at me from further away in the support structure. Before we reached the other pillar, however, we had fried the four ambushers.

Berk and RC joined us. We watched as the platoon surged forward through the support beams. They reached the second set of pillars, clearing the enemy from them without further casualties.

Chip's team had returned to the river and engaged more Gorgon soldiers at their next pillar. Meanwhile, Berk, Bogan, RC, and I had resumed our assault on our next pillar. We easily wiped out the unshielded defenders there.

By the time we approached the third set of pillars, Kamal and Ruby had rejoined us. The Gorgons had learned from their mistakes. The defenders along the river's surface were now fully screened. It became a brutal fight. But we beat them.

We lost more Marines. But my team was still intact. So was Chip's team.

My suit had taken more hits and now my energy screen flickered on and off. RC's screen was gone. So was Bogan's.

"Lion," Mo called. "Take Bogan and RC and return to the north shore. Collect any survivors who need help. Saunders will take charge of your Marines."

"Got it," I replied. "How's the lieutenant?"

"She's fine. Her suit's ruined but she's okay. A little dazed, a bit stunned, a bit cooked, but she'll be fine. There's a battalion aid station in Monroeville. She's there."

"Good to hear. I'll check in on her when I get back."

"You do that. Now get outta here," Mo growled.

"Got it." I led Bogan and RC back across the river. "Chip," I called on the squad channel as we retreated. "Take good care of my Marines."

"They're my Marines, too," he replied.

"Right. Be careful," I said.

"I will be," he said. "Be safe."

"You bet."

NINETY-FIVE

WE HAD TRAVELED LESS than half the way back toward the north end of the bridge before Bogan stopped.

"Is there a problem, Bogan?" I asked him.

"Yes," he said. "This doesn't feel right."

"What doesn't feel right?" RC asked.

"I shouldn't be leaving Ruby behind. I belong out there, fighting beside her."

"You belong here," I said, referring to our three Marine contingent returning for repairs.

"Yeah," RC agreed. "Your screen's burnt out. You won't survive a minute out there without an active energy field. It'd be suicide."

"I belong back there, covering Ruby," he said, obstinately.

"Bullshit!" RC said. "Do you want her to see you die? Do you want to put her through that?"

"It's better than her not coming back," Bogan said.

RC snorted. "How's that better? You might be responsible for her getting killed. With you there, unprotected, she'd want to protect you."

440

"You think so?" Bogan asked. "I think it'll be the other way around. I'll cover her. I'll keep her alive. She won't do anything foolish while I'm out there."

"I've known her longer than you have, Bogan," RC replied. "She's too aggressive to let someone make her play it safe. She'll either ignore you or kick your ass for trying to marginalize her."

"I'm not trying to margarine her," he said. "I'm trying to save her. I don't want to lose her."

"It's not your choice," RC said. "And the word is marginalize, which means to make her less important. You're not trying to butter her up."

"I know what it means," Bogan bellowed. "And I said it right!"

"Whatever you say," RC retorted.

"And it is my choice. I care for her and I don't want anything to happen to her."

"One night of sex and you think it's love," RC jeered.

"I know what love is! Just 'cause I haven't had much of it in my life doesn't make me an idiot. I love her and she loves me."

"She likes you, you mean," RC said. "But love, I don't know, but I don't think so. She slept with you. It's not the same as love. Just because it's called 'making love' doesn't mean it is love. It's just a nicer way of saying..."

Bogan leveled his plasma rifle at RC's chest. "Say it and I'll blow you to hell!"

"Enough!" I bellowed. "I don't know if she loves you or not. But if you go back out there and she watches you die, and there's a damned good chance of that happening, it'll be like you killed her. Her body might not die, not right away anyways, but it'll kill her nonetheless. Her spirit and heart will be gone. This is why we don't allow romantic relationships in the same Marine unit. So that damned stupid fools like yourself won't do something as stupid as you're trying to do right now!"

"Geez, Lion," RC said. "That was one helluva speech."

"Shut up, RC, and keep your mouth shut," I growled at him. "I've had it with you two."

"Got it," he replied.

"Let's get back to shore. Now." I made sure they both started moving toward the north shore of the river before proceeding after them.

"But I don't want to lose her," Bogan lamented.

"Stop thinking only about yourself," I growled.

"But, how?"

"Listen, if you love Ruby, then think about her feelings for a change. You're willing to sacrifice yourself for her. Don't you think she's doing the same for you right now? She's fighting to make sure you're safe. Going back out there will handicap both of you. You'll increase the chances that you'll both die by a hundred per cent. Let her do her job and you do yours. And right now, your job is to get back to shore and get your suit repaired. Got that?"

"I still don't understand," Bogan replied.

"You never will," RC said. "Because you're only thinking of yourself."

"Didn't I tell you to shut up?" I snarled at RC.

"Uh, yeah."

"Then do it."

"Got it, Lion."

"Well?" I demanded.

RC coughed. That was all.

"Listen," I said to Bogan, "my grandfather is a wise old man. And my mother is wise, too. They've both told me that if you love someone, you think about their feelings more than of your own. Ruby's feelings should come first in your thoughts and in your heart."

"Ruby does, Lion," Bogan said.

"Not from the way I hear it," I snapped at him. "All I've heard from you is your side. How you can't lose her. How you need her. For you, it's all me, me, me! What about her feelings? What about her needs? If you want to prove yourself to her, if you want your relationship to survive, then you have to leave her the room to make decisions for herself. You have to leave her the room to live. You got that, Bogan? Let go of her enough to let her love you the way she wants to, otherwise your relationship is more doomed than if she were killed today."

"But how do I do that?"

"Focus on your job. Now let's get ashore."

Bogan didn't say anything more. He headed for the northern end of the bridge. RC, quiet for a change, followed him. And I followed them.

The riverbank extended out ten meters under the bridge. A few straggly bushes grew haphazardly under the bridge, little sunlight making its way beneath to champion them. Sitting among the shrubs were five Marines. Their suits showed scars where Gorgon plasma shots had damaged them. Two of the Marines were without grav discs. I assumed their teammates had brought them in when their discs were destroyed.

"Let's go, Marines," I said. Our suits didn't carry any exterior rank insignia. However, their suits recognized my suit's identification signal, which informed them of whom I was and of what my rank was.

"You got it, sergeant," one of them said.

"Where to?" said another Marine.

"There's a battalion quartermaster unit somewhere on the other side of the bridge," I explained. "We can drop off our suits and get some hot food while we wait for them to be repaired."

"What if we don't want 'em repaired?" a third Marine said. "What if we just want to leave?"

"Where would you go?" I asked. I wanted to leave as much as they did. I wanted to get away, too. Yet, I wanted to return to the fighting. I wanted to make sure that my friends and fellow Marines survived. War is about survival and I wanted to make sure that we all survived.

I was loyal, I couldn't just run away. It was my duty to keep on fighting until the mission succeeded, even if it meant the end of my life and the lives of my teammates and friends.

So I focused on other things, such as getting these Marines, all seven of them now, to the quartermaster repair unit. And once I got them there, then I'd find something else to focus on.

"Good point," agreed the third Marine. His name was Karrelos. He was one of the Marines without a grav disc. He and the other disc-less Marine sat on the bank while the others had floated nearby. He stood up. "Let's go. It's no fun just sittin' here, with nothin' to do."

Karrelos climbed up from underneath the bridge. The other Marines followed him. And RC and Bogan followed them. Sometimes leadership is just being the first one to move.

I waited until they were all gone. Then I glanced back along the bridge's underside. I saw plasma rifle flashes in the distance, revealing the location of the fighting. I listened in and heard Chip and Mo directing the attack. I wanted to be there with them. But I wasn't. So, after a moment more of listening and wishing, I came out from beneath the bridge, into the daylight.

On the bank, just beyond the bridge's entrance, I saw a lone suited Marine, his grav disc resting on the street's pavement. It was First Sergeant Jones. I drifted over to him. My Marines and the stragglers had gone ahead.

"First Sergeant," I greeted him. "Where'd everyone go?"

"I sent them to the repair unit," he said. "It's in the city's square over there. Where that little park is."

"Got it," I said. "Where's the skipper?"

"She's out on the bridge," he said, matter-of-factly.

"Really?" I said, surprised. Colonel Grunnig forbade company commanders from leading attacks. Apparently, captains were more precious than lieutenants.

"Yep."

"Why aren't you out there?" I asked.

"Same reason you're not."

"Damaged screen?"

"Busted," he said. He sounded tired, angry, and sad.

"I understand."

"Do you now?" he replied, his voice full of sarcasm.

I kept quiet. I turned to glance down along the bridge.

"Magliano bought it," Jones stated.

"The XO? How?"

"Ambush," he said. "We went over the hump and halfway to the other side three Gorgon tanks appeared. They concentrated on the leading elements, which of course was the lieutenant and two sergeants from Support. Two good friends I've known for years. And a man I've respect more than most others. I hate those bastard wormheads. They burned Magliano and my friends away. I hate those ugly monsters more than I can say."

What could I say? I had respected Magliano in much the same way that Jones did. The hump he referred to, I knew, was where the bridge arched over the river. It was a good place for an ambush.

"A few minutes later, a pair of Sky Command fighters blew those tanks off the bridge," Jones said. "I don't know where they came from but I wish they'd come sooner."

"Got it," was all I could say.

"My suit was shot up by the uglies as they tried retaking the hump. I burned a lot of them down as they came up the bridge. I stayed until the skipper got there. Then she sent me back. And here I am."

"Got it."

"You better get to the quartermaster repair site. You might be needed out there again," Jones said.

"What about you, First Sergeant?"

"Whaddya mean?" he demanded.

"Won't you be needed out there?"

"My place is here. Skipper said so," he said. "She wants me to coordinate the Marines returning with damaged suits, see that they turn their suits in for repairs, get something to eat, and get some rest until their suits are fixed. Then she wants me to send them right back out, but not in little bits. She wants me to send them out as ad hoc fire teams and squads."

"Have you?"

"Who are you to question me?"

"Sorry, First Sergeant, I'm just curious."

There was a pause when he didn't say anything. After several long moments, I decided it was time to leave. But he decided it was time to speak again.

"I'm sorry, Biyela. You have a right to ask. Just as I have a right not to answer."

"Got it."

"I haven't sent anyone out yet. The ordnance techs are a bit overworked."

"Got it. Were you here when they brought in Lieutenant Kwung?"

"I wasn't. But I understand she's back at the aid station, back beyond where they're repairing the suits."

"Thanks, First Sergeant." I turned and scooted back to the warehouse where my team had spent the night. Just beyond there was the city square and park. And in the park was the repair station.

Landing, I dismounted and turned my suit over to an ordnance team of two robots and an unarmored human technician. The ordnance team belonged to the battalion's Ordnance Platoon, consisting of forty human techs and one hundred robots.

"How long?" I asked.

"As long as it takes," replied the Marine tech. "There are not enough of us for all the suits coming in."

"I don't understand," I said. "Chaos' Headquarters Platoon and Second Platoon are fighting on the bridge. The other two are holding the islands."

"Not anymore," the tech replied. "In the last ten minutes, Third Platoon has joined Second Platoon, while First Platoon's on the bridge, replacing the headquarters platoon. Additionally, Binary's Third Platoon is also on the bridge."

"Who's holding the islands?" I asked.

"Binary Company has taken over control of the islands," the tech said.

Almost the whole battalion was in this fight now.

"What's that ancient word describing this?" I asked.

"You mean SNAFU? Situation Normal, All Fucked Up?"

"Yeah, that's the one."

"Ain't it the truth?"

I nodded, glancing around the grassy park filling the town square. Seventy armored suits, including mine, were under repair. That meant seventy Marines who had survived combat were absent from the fighting. Seventy Marines could make a big difference in such a brutal battle.

"You wouldn't happen to know where the battalion aid station is, would you?" I asked.

"Sure." The tech pointed to one of the corners of the square. "Go down that street about half a block. You'll come to a huge hotel, covering the block. The colonel's headquarters are on the top floor. The field aid station fills the lower floors."

"Thanks."

"Anytime. You'll find few Marines there, though."

"Why not?" I asked, turning back around. I had barely taken two steps.

He spread his arms. "This is where all the survivors are. If somebody hasn't brought back a suit for repair, they're either dead or still fighting."

"Not everybody."

"Maybe not, but most."

"How long, again?" I asked.

"An hour, minimum," he said.

"See you in thirty minutes."

"Be wasting your time."

"It's mine to waste."

NINETY-SIX

THE TECH WAS RIGHT. At least, about the aid station. When I arrived, I found dozens of beds. All but three were empty.

The robot staff, there weren't any human doctors or medics present, was caring for a female Marine who seemed to be catatonic. When I asked a robot medic, it explained that she had seen too much and her mind was rebelling at what she had seen, experienced and done.

When I pointed toward the second patient the robot explained that he had fallen into the river, exactly as the lieutenant had. But though this Marine's suit had saved him, he was in shock. At the moment, he was in an induced medical coma.

Then there was the lieutenant. The robot told me that her suit had been so badly damaged by enemy fire that it had barely absorbed the impact of her fall. She had broken several vertebrae in her back and neck and had arrived in critical condition. If not for the sedatives her suit had administered to her, she would've died from all the pain. The aid station's robot doctors had put her in a suspended animation chamber awaiting transportation to the same hospital ship in orbit that I had found myself in months earlier, *The Rainbow of Heaven.*

"I'd been told her injuries weren't critical," I said.

"The original report suggested that," the robot replied. "But once she had been extricated from her armor, her true injuries were discovered."

"How bad is Lieutenant Kwung?"

"Her condition is serious, sir. Her nanites are struggling to keep her alive. The Doctor placed her in the tube to save her life. The Doctors aboard the hospital ship will perform the necessary repairs to her body. She will be out of action for some time. But she shall return."

"Thank you, nurse."

"I am a medic, sir, not a nurse," the robot stated.

"Got it. Thanks."

"Of course, sir. I have duties to which I must attend."

As the robot left, I moved over to the suspended animation tube containing the lieutenant. It had a window above the lieutenant's face. She looked asleep. I hoped that she would recuperate and return to duty. She was the best platoon leader I'd ever served under. I also hoped when she returned to duty some of the Second Platoon that she knew would still be there, still alive. There weren't many of us left.

Sighing, I started to walk away. But the robot medic had returned and blocked my way. Stopping, I stared at it.

"Sir?" the robot inquired.

"Yes?"

"You are a Marine sergeant, are you not?"

"I am. Why do you ask?"

"Why did you not challenge me for addressing you as 'sir'?"

"I suppose it's because you deserve the same respect any human medic deserves."

"Why is that, sir?" it inquired.

"You just do."

The robot stared at me. I think it did, anyways. There's always a bit of hardness to robot faces. Not flesh and blood, they always seem so solid. Yet, apparently, they have a sense of professionalism. Maybe they even have feelings of some sort.

"Thank you..." the robot hesitated. "Thank you, sergeant."

It was my turn to stare. Robots are so much more than you think they are. Made by mankind, they seem to possess the same ability to evolve that humans have. "Thank you, too," I said.

Without any more words, the robot returned to its duties.

I left the aid station.

NINETY-SEVEN

WHEN I RETURNED TO the park, I saw thirty more suits awaiting repair. Walking over to my suit, I noticed the tech leaning halfway inside it.

"Is it done?"

He climbed out. "Nope. It's going to be a lot longer now. As you can see, our work's almost doubled. But don't fret, we've taken the bridge. It's over."

I suddenly felt very tired. "How bad?"

"Don't know," he replied. "You'll have to find out for yourself. I've work to do."

"Got it. How long?"

He glanced at the sky, as did I. Thea was well across the sky. Evening wasn't far away.

"Tonight, sometime."

He re-entered my suit. I glanced around. So many suits, so much damage. How many Marines never returned?

As I started toward my team's warehouse, more suits started arriving. One landed right in front of me. I circled around it.

"Lion!" Chip exclaimed, backing out of his just-landed suit, the one in front of me. "We did it."

"I heard." So much excitement over capturing a bridge. But at what cost? How many had died to acquire it? And who had survived, besides the three in the aid station and the ones who brought their suits in for repair?

As a robot technician arrived, Chip stepped down from his suit. "You're thinking I meant the bridge," he said.

"Didn't you?" I asked, emotional exhaustion filling my voice with bitterness.

"No. I meant that you and I have survived another battle. We're still alive."

"What's one more battle in an endless stream of battles? Tell me, what difference does it make?"

"None. And everything."

"I don't see the relevance. Explain it to me."

Chip raised his hand for a pause. He turned toward the robot. "How much damage and how soon will I get it back?"

"The damage is not bad, sir," the robot said. I noticed Chip's irritation at being addressed as 'sir', but he let it slide.

"However," the robot continued, "there are many other suits to repair before yours. We will get to it sometime after midnight. It shall be finished by dawn, excepting any emergencies, of course."

"Thanks."

"You are welcome, sir."

Chip rolled his eyes in frustration. He turned back to me. "It's been a hard day for both of us."

"Why," I demanded, "because you have to deal with insolent robots?"

"No," he snarled at me. "Because I have to deal with a self-righteous friend."

"Well, we don't have to talk." I turned and walked away.

He jogged over to me. "Is this the way you want it? For our friendship to suffer because you're suffering?"

"It's as good a reason as any!"

"Is it?" Chip retorted, anger in his voice. "You haven't lost anyone today. I'm still here. Your whole team's still intact. It's the only team in the platoon where everybody survived."

I looked at him. "Ruby, Kamal, Berk—they're okay?"

"Yes, though probably hurting the same as you. Or like me."

I took a deep breath and grunted it out. "I'm sorry. I don't know what got into me. It's just that it doesn't make any sense to me anymore. We've come all the way down here by ourselves and then we engage the Gorgons for a bridge. A bridge!

"We don't need a bridge. We can zip across on our grav discs. And the Colonial Guard and Eosian Army don't need it, either. They're not limited to foot traffic. They have grav vehicles. So why sacrifice so many for something we don't need? Why the hell did we do it?"

"I don't have any answers for you. I'm not some general or admiral on a starship in orbit, figuring out strategy and issuing commands. I don't know if they had a good reason for it or not. Our job is obeying the orders given to us."

"Orders!" I spat on the ground. "We have the right to refuse unjust orders. And I'd call the death in taking a useless bridge an unjust order."

"You're right, it was a waste," Chip acknowledged. "And you're correct, too, about refusing an unjust order. But, remember, we use that right sparingly."

"This would have been a good time to use it."

"Would it?" Chip demanded. "Why not when we had to defend Belden with one battalion? Why not when you were sent to set up an ambush site with one team? Why not when we first came to Eos and lost fifty percent of our battalion in six days? Why were any of those times less unjust than today?"

I glared at him.

"The first day on Eos, as we assaulted Belden, you lost half your team," Chip reminded me. "Berk, RC, and Lipinski were replacements. And you only had Lipinski for two days. You've had more replacements for your number six slot than any other team in the platoon. You've gone through six Marines, not including Bogan, who has survived so far."

"Hunter doesn't count," I said. "He wasn't really part of my team."

"Five then," Chip agreed. "But why, now, do you want to draw the line?"

"Because I don't want to lose anyone else!" I blurted out. "I've worked hard to keep my team together. Meanwhile, I've watched people die all around me. How am I supposed to deal with that? What happens when you're gone? You're closer to me than any of my real brothers are. How will I deal when the day comes when everyone I trust and believe in are gone?"

"I don't know," Chip said. "But I've been where you are now. And not too long ago, either."

"So how did you deal with it?" I asked.

"You came back," he replied.

"That doesn't help."

"It doesn't. But remember what you said to me today about separating Ruby and Bogan?"

"Yeah," I said. "And we're going to have to do it, too. He wanted to go back out there today even though his screen was toast. He would've gotten himself, and maybe Ruby, and even some others, killed out there. I can't have those two together."

"But what did I tell you when you first mentioned it to me earlier today?"

"I don't really remember."

"I told you that life is too precious."

"I remember. So what?"

Pausing, he glanced at the ground. We stood not ten paces from his suit. Thea had set now and the sky was dimming. He looked up at me.

"You know, all the time I've known you, even from the very first day we met, you've talked a lot about your grandfather to me. Much more than about anyone else in your family."

"So?"

"So I want to tell you about my grandfather. He didn't amount to much."

"What's this got to do with anything?" I demanded. So far, I didn't understand anything Chip had said to me. I was tired, unhappy, angry. What did it matter about my grandfather or his grandfather? All I wanted was to get away from Eos before everyone I cared about died.

I didn't want to see their deaths, nor know about them. But I knew I would, even if I lived on some remote world a billion light years away. How could I not care, when I loved them all?

"Just let me talk, okay?" he said.

"Okay," I said. "Talk."

"Granddaddy never amounted to much," Chip began. "He couldn't hold a job down. He was always looking for work but always getting bored with every job he found. He was more of a social butterfly than anything else."

"What's that mean?" I glanced up at the sky. It was dark now, but full of stars. How I wished I could fly up into them, fly away from here forever.

"It's an ancient phrase," Chip explained. "It means someone whose life revolves around social events more than anything else. That was what my granddaddy was, a social butterfly. My grandmother worked instead. She took care of him. And when she was gone, my uncles and aunts and cousins took care of him. And when they were tired of taking care of him, my family took care of him." He paused and glanced at me.

"Go on," I said.

"I liked him and loved him. He was such a happy man, so full of life, so free from the cares of life. But just as I loved him, I was ashamed of him."

"How does that work?" I asked.

"It doesn't," he said.

"I don't see where this is going," I snarled. "It's getting dark out here and I'm cold and hungry. How about speeding up?"

"Just shut up and give me a chance," Chip snarled back.

I glared at him, but let him continue.

"At his funeral, I told my mother how ashamed I was of Granddaddy. He was a loser, I said. He didn't do anything, accomplish anything, or make anything. He lived off of us, used us. And my mother told me how wrong I was about him."

He paused again.

"If you're pausing for dramatic effect, you're wasting time."

"I thought Granddaddy had wasted his life. But my mother told me how he was always ready to help others. She told me how he loved people even when they didn't love him. How he loved life, and of how he lived it to its fullness. So work bored him, she said. So what? He lived by his own rules and those rules included taking care of others. He was the 'go-to' man whenever there was a tragedy or death in the family. And hundreds came to his funeral. He lived by one motto: 'Life is precious, so don't waste it.'"

"How does this story help me? So what if life is so precious? Does it relieve me of my fears? Does it save me from watching my friends die, from losing the greatest family I've ever known? How can I survive such pain and sorrow?"

"You live," Chip said.

"But, why?" I snarled back. "Why fight and die for no good reason?"

"You have a reason. We all do."

Taller than Chip, I stared down at him. "What reason?"

"We're fighting to save the people of this world, that's the reason," Chip said. "So what if we fight an endless stream of battles? We're fighting for the men and women and children of this world. We're their 'go-to Marines'.

There are hundreds of millions of people here. They need us. What are you going to do, let them die?"

I glanced at the night sky and the endless stars. "No."

"And what about your team, your platoon, your company, are you going to let us do all the fighting? We need you."

"There's no escape then?" I continued staring at the stars. I felt tears streaming down my face.

"The only escape is to live. Live each day, each moment, and fight. Fight for us. Fight for the citizens of Eos. Fight for yourself. That's what life is all about, fighting for life. Fighting to live.

"That was my granddaddy's motto: 'Life is precious. Don't waste it. Fight for it.'"

I sighed, a heavy heart-felt sigh. I looked down at Chip and wiped my face. "You're a good friend."

"So are you," Chip said. "You've lifted me up so many times. Thanks for giving me the chance to do the same for you."

I nodded. "I think my grandfather would've loved knowing your granddaddy."

"Most likely. Everybody loved him. Especially me."

"They probably would've been good friends, just as you and I are," I said.

"Most likely."

"So," I sighed, "who's left in the squad?"

"You and me, your team. Sammi Sousa and Rita Peres are all that's left of my team."

"Just nine of us?"

He nodded.

"And the platoon?" I asked.

"Mo, the lieutenant, whenever she returns..."

"Which won't be for a long time, she's badly beat up."

"So, we wait until we get another lieutenant or Kwung comes back. In the meantime, Mo is in charge. We also have three members of Gaiman's team left. That's it."

"Thirteen Marines?" I exclaimed. "And what are we supposed to do with that?"

"Hold the bridge."

"What!" I exclaimed. "Well, how bad was the company hit?"

Now he sighed. "Besides the platoon's losses, about fifty more casualties, including Magliano."

"I know about the XO. What about the skipper?"

"She's fine."

"Good. So we hold the bridge?"

"We hold the bridge," he confirmed.

"For how long?"

"Hell if I know. For as long as it takes, I guess."

I shook my head. "Well, at least it's a plan."

"A piss-poor plan, but it's all we got," he said. "Let's go get something to eat."

"You got it." We started walking toward the warehouse. "But you're buying."

"What!" Chip exclaimed. "I just saved you."

"You did. But that's just one time. While I've lifted your ass out of depression at least five more times than you've lifted mine. So, you're still buying."

"You got it, beloved."

I stopped, grabbed his shoulder and spun him around to face me. "What did you just say?" I demanded.

"That's what your name means, doesn't it? Thandiwe means Beloved. It sure as hell doesn't mean Lion."

"How long have you known?" I asked, letting go of him. We continued toward the warehouse.

He laughed. "Since I first met you."

I shook my head in disbelief. "Well, don't tell anyone."

"I won't," he promised. "Beloved."

"Keep it up and I'll back-shoot you," I retorted.

"That'll be the day," he said.

We reached the warehouse and went inside. We heard the voices of my team and the rest of the survivors making up Second Platoon. We started up the stairs.

"What kept you sorry excuses for Marines?" Mo growled down at us from the top of the stairs. "Lion, drag that old man up here with you."

"Old man?" Chip exclaimed. "I'm not old."

"That's right!" I said and laughed. It felt good to laugh. "You're the squad leader now. You're the 'Old Man'. Just as Mo is the platoon's grandpa."

"What did you say?" Mo snarled at me.

I grinned up at him.

Chip laughed. So did Mo. "Get up here, you two," he said.

"Lion and the Old Man," Chip quipped. "What a story for my grandchildren, if I ever have any."

"That'll be the day," I said.

"It sure will. Let's eat."

"You got it."

The book presents a captivating blend of science-fantasy fiction, set against military conflict, invasion, war, and advanced scientific technology. The narrative intricately details the protagonist's environment, the commanding officer, and the looming challenges that the battalion must confront, particularly their mission to advance into the heart of the city. The military setting is portrayed with grandeur, emphasizing strength, courage, and readiness to tackle various demanding situations.

The story highlights the strategic maneuvers of different armies, especially in the face of unique threats like robots poised to battle humans. The author skillfully employs descriptive language to convey the protagonist's experiences and emotions, painting a vivid picture of life at a forward base.

The writing style is engaging, striking a harmonious balance between dialogue, action, and introspection. The author utilizes a range of sentence structures to maintain the narrative's interest while the language remains clear and concise. Overall, this remarkable writing effectively immerses the reader in the protagonist's world.

— *John Burton, Independent Reviewer*